The Emancipation of Giles Corey

The Emancipation of Giles Corey

MICHAEL SORTOMME

Singing Lake Press

Rhinebeck, New York

Printed in the United States of America

Book and cover design by Joe Tantillo
Original cover painting by Michael Sortomme

Singing Lake Press in association with Epigraph Books
27 Lamoree Road
Rhinebeck, New York 12572
www.epigraphPS.com
USA 845-876-4861

ISBN 978-0-9830517-5-6
Library of Congress Control Number: 2010942697

This book is a work of fiction. References to real people, events,
establishments, organizations, locations, sacred sites, and sociomagickal traditions
are intended only to provide a sense of authenticity and are used in a fictitious
manner. All other characters, happenings, and dialogue are drawn from the
author's imagination and are not to be mistaken as real. This is not intended as a
guidebook or spiritual directive.

Author's Note: I have employed the American Indian tradition of using
capitalization to differentiate the sacred from the mundane. For example, "map
directions" is corporeal, whereas "Cardinal Directions" is sacred. Other categories
include sacred tools, Holy Days, herbs, disembodied Spirits, Gods and Goddesses,
Holy People, ceremonies, and sacred locations.

To Dr. Ian Stevenson
a genius not limited by convention
Born October 31, 1918
Died February 8, 2007

For just as the body without the spirit is dead,
so faith without works is also dead.
—*James the Just*

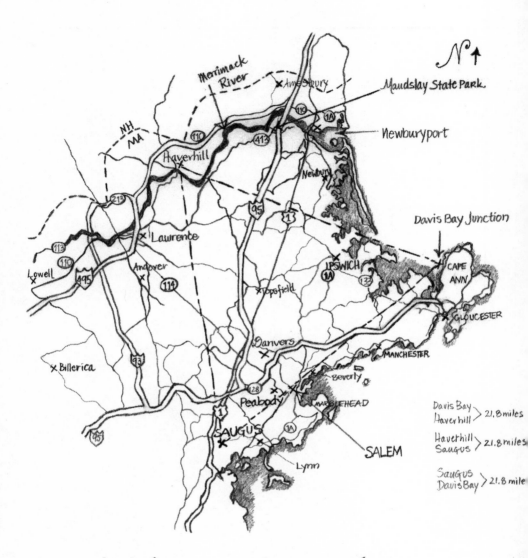

The American Camino Route

Contents

List of Illustrations and Maps | x

Acknowledgments | xi

Chapter 1. An Otherworldly Introduction | 1

Chapter 2. Life Is a Camino! | 13

Chapter 3. First Glimpse | 17

Chapter 4. Windows of Opportunities | 23

Chapter 5. Eagle Delivers the Opening Ritual | 29

Chapter 6. Charter Street Cemetery: Holder of Ancestor Medicine | 43

Chapter 7. Howard Street Cemetery: A Meeting with an Old Friend | 61

Chapter 8. Broadstreet Cemetery: A Lesson in Loyalty | 67

Chapter 9. The Nurse Burial Grounds: The Roots of Time | 71

Chapter 10. Wadsworth Cemetery: Putnam Spies Never Rest | 79

Chapter 11. Finding Mary Warren | 83

Chapter 12. The Ocean Is Calling | 91

Chapter 13. Hannah Dustin's Secrets | 111

Chapter 14. The Candy Store | 125

Chapter 15. Indian Country | 135

Chapter 16. River Road | 147

Chapter 17. The Three-Year Plan | 157

Chapter 18. The Night Reading | 165

Chapter 19. B'nai Brith Cemetery | 183

Chapter 20. The Pressing Place | 195

Chapter 21. Crystal Lake | 203

Chapter 22. Sawyer's Hill | 213

Chapter 23. Friday's Gathering | 229

Chapter 24. The Integration Walk | 245

Chapter 25. The Honoring | 269

Chapter 26. The Witch Memorial | 289

Chapter 27. The Liberation Feast | 305

Chapter 28. Sunday: Closure | 319

Chapter 29. The Anniversary | 327

Illustrations

Drawings

The Opening | xiv
Mandatory Sacrifice | 12
Grounded | 16
Manifestation | 21
Temple Pillars | 22
Eagle Speaks | 28
Rest in Peace | 42
The Sea Claddagh Sigil | 60
Loyalty | 66
Family Tree | 70
Forever Loyal and Willing | 78
Mary's Chair | 82
Family Drum | 90
Time Warp Trauma | 110
Giles's Bones | 124
Four Abenaki Directions | 134
Hannah | 146
Friendship, Family, and Immortality | 156
The Sephirot | 164
The Quaker Star | 182
Death's Tool | 194
Crystal Lake Swans | 202
Oak Offerings | 212
Saugus Anvil | 228
Giles's Light | 244
Gallows Hill Sunflower | 268
The Witch Memorial, Old Town Salem | 288
Simple Feast | 304
Flying Home | 318
The Bone Good-bye | 326

Maps

The American Camino Route | vi
Charter Street Cemetery, Salem | 45
Nurse Homestead & Burial Grounds, Danvers | 73
The Beaches, Manchester | 95
Putnam Pantry Candies, Danvers | 131
The River Indians | 139
B'nai Brith Cemetery, Salem | 185
Howard Street Cemetery Loop | 197
Corey Land, Peabody | 205
Sawyer's Hill Burial Grounds, Newburyport | 221
Saugus Iron Works National Park | 235
Salem Old Town and Integration Walk | 251
Gallows Hill, Salem | 283
The Liberation Feast, Salem | 309

Acknowledgments

Without them, this book would not have been:
Mark Stephen Freeman, my most enduring friend, partner, patron,
friend of Dragons.
Margaret Slavin Dyment, teacher and mentor. Thank you
for Graduate School.
Findla, patient editor and confessor.
Thank you for dragging me howling into the twenty-first century and
giving me confidence to go forward.
To my publishing crew: Paul Cohen and Joe Tantillo.
Thank you for your careful yet firm direction.
You made this thing called publishing *real*.
Pam Judd, fellow traveler and dreamer. Thank you for the gift of belief.
Gratitude to my spiritual parents: Master Hamid Bey,
Sri Amritanandamayi, Saint Pio.
Guardians, lantern holders, and Inspiration Keepers,
you have my devotion.
Here's to you: Sophie, Dylan, Dora, Poe, and Ali,
may you live on and on!
To love and the power it generates:
Kjærlighet er loven!

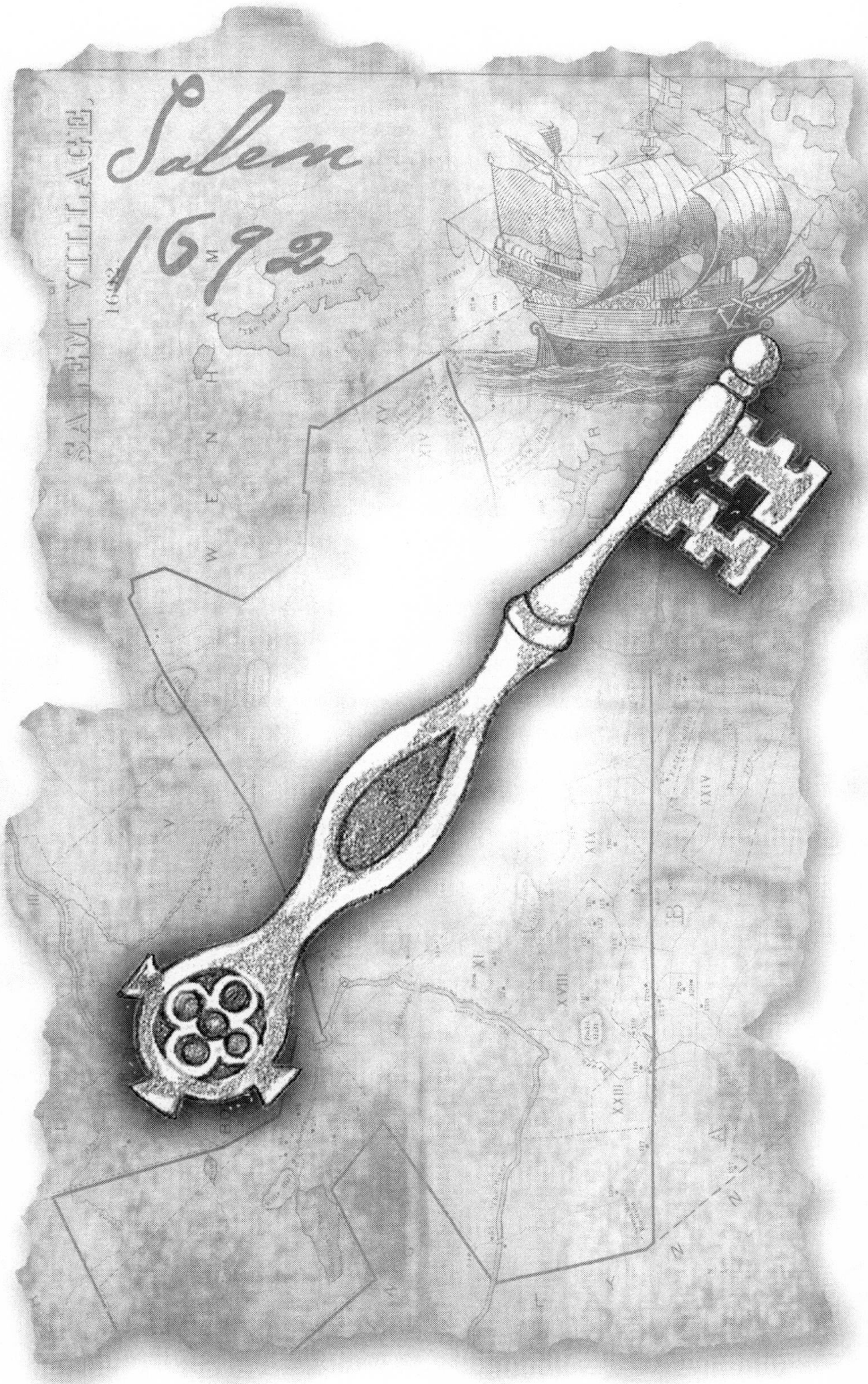

Salem
1692
SALEM VILLAGE

Chapter One

AN OTHERWORLDLY INTRODUCTION
September 22, 2009, Portland, Oregon

DETAILS OF THE DAY'S DRAMAS flashed in his mind's eye. Dawn that morning had grounded him, the rising sun bathing Mount Hood's volcanic summit in magenta-tinged light. Here in the Pacific Northwest, retired professor Dr. Mortimer Siminsky had found his place in the universe. Friends had prepared him for the glorious weather months of September and October: hot dry days, glorious cool nights, the apple and grape harvests. But, as the season progressed, he still felt amazed at the natural beauty surrounding him. Each day was a gift. A sudden cool breeze brushed his face and brought him back to the present. It was almost midnight and now, looking over the lit valley, which mirrored the bright stars above, he felt anxious.

The letter he had just finished, written on white linen paper, with a stack of hastily made photocopies, rested in his lap. He stroked the white pages tenderly, thinking of the recipient. He sighed and decided to read its contents once more before beginning his overdue bedtime routine.

M. Mortimer Siminsky, Ph.D.
3330 Overlook Drive
Portland, Oregon 97315
9-22-2009

Dr. Greta Stern
150 English Ivy Court
Charlottesville, Virginia 22007

My Dearest Greta,

I sincerely hope you are well and looking forward to the start of the school year. This represents a rebirth of sorts for you, on your own for the first time in almost forty years. Lenora's untimely death shocked us all and pulled your world down to the foundation. I am sorry I did not stay a while longer after her funeral. I so wanted to help, but I felt in your way, afraid you might stumble over me in the dark. Know that thinkers around the world miss her wit as well as her ire. I certainly do.

I am adjusting to retired life, though I miss the constant stimulation of excited first-year students discovering the importance of history. You would correct me and say *herstory*. Think of it, you in Women's Studies and me in Classical Greek History. We couldn't have been further apart in our views, and still we found common ground enough to call each other dear. I miss university life and I miss you, my first sweetheart.

There is a bright spot; his name is Reuben, my new assistant. Portland State sent him over last spring to help me clean up files and categorize my library after the big move across country. He never left after the books were sorted. I wish he would work for me full-time, but he works as a docent at the Jewish Museum in Chinatown; I have to share him. This is bringing me to the reason I am writing late on this, the first night of autumn.

Reuben told me the university had forwarded a series of personal letters addressed to me but delivered to the chair of my department by mistake. They were held up for almost a year by the time Reuben found them. They were written by a woman named Sophie St. Cloud, an interesting character who calls herself an Indigenous Shamanic Practitioner. Reuben Googled her and printed a picture of her dressed from head to toe in gold deer hide and beads, quite a sight. Surprisingly, she's as white as my legs in February before our yearly cruise. I agreed to meet with her. She insisted on this morning. She needed to be back in her hometown around three o'clock, something about an Equinox and a Liberation Feast. She lives only an hour or so from me, and so it was easy to agree.

Precisely at eleven, the bell rang. I found a striking woman, short and slightly bent, with a silver-colored men's haircut, dressed all in purple. At first glance, she reminded me of you, but soon I saw her as too loud around the edges to be compared. She asked for help unloading her presentation from her car, also purple, covered with rainbow stickers and peace signs. I felt we were back in Berkeley. Reuben was called for muscle. Immediately they embraced, but then she held him at arm's length. She made some strange movements with her hands and bent him at the waist toward her. She smoothed his curly hair flat and blew air on his head, over his yarmulke. He was overjoyed. I've never seen him so animated.

Reuben hauled in a collapsible table, an overstuffed electric-blue wheeled suitcase, and a milk crate filled with tightly packed books. Ms. St. Cloud carried a plastic container of sweets and a large thermos. It looked like she was moving in.

Few words between Reuben and the woman were said. They seemed to be in a world all their own. Within minutes, they created a full-color presentation with charts and graphs and colored files containing articles and essays outlining St. Cloud's belief structure and the dramatic happenings in her life, which are many. She had additional copies for Reuben and me. She began unpacking the milk crate one book at a time. These battered black-and-white marbled notebooks seemed to hold all her magic, all her hope.

Before I knew it, I was seated in my favorite leather chair, with a cup of hot green tea and a muffin smelling of nutmeg and apple, Reuben and the woman smiling in front of me. It all happened so fast—it's a blur. Her tone of voice was strong but oddly melodic, almost hypnotizing. She spoke of time zones, Camino Cycles, reincarnation, and conspiracies. At one point, she put her hand on top of the notebooks and patted them gently, as if the books were alive. She told me they comprised a rough draft of a novel detailing an experience she and three of her friends had in 2007, nine days of rituals to free hundreds of ghosts in the Massachusetts Bay Colony, centering in Salem. Fiction gave her leeway to tell the story her own way, she explained. Also included were several books of her preparations, concerns, and history outlining the reasons for the journey. The presentation kept skipping from one time period to another, spanning almost four hundred years. She expected me to keep up with her lengthy explanations and amazingly I did. I absorbed each and every word. It's a confusing and disturbing tale, but it captured my attention.

I explained to her my field of expertise did not include reincarnation and ghostbusting and went on to ask why she was insistent on meeting me. She explained how she came to know of me. She had found several of my articles about the Genome Project and DNA samplings from around the world. It's been a passion of mine since 2000. Retirement loomed and the Greeks had lost their luster compared with the great scientific leaps being made each day in this new century. I knew I was too old to embrace a new avenue for teaching. But for myself, my own ancestry, and edification, I had to take whatever presented itself.

I was thrust into a world of crazed genealogists, of retired scientists on quests, of possible treasures laying in wait. I was titillated. True, I kept this fascination to myself. Few friends or colleagues found my articles online or asked if I had new interests, so it never came up. I kept my new passion under wraps even from you, my oldest friend. I've had few secrets in my life, so it was a guilty pleasure. Now, it looks as if I have been discovered.

St. Cloud is a genealogy enthusiast, coming to DNA as a tool in charting her maternal and paternal lineages. Her fascination lies in possibilities—clearly my opposite. Self-branded with a title of Rememberer, a being with compact total past-life recall, she believes DNA tracing will eventually prove reincarnation and soul-clusters to be a reality. Wild, I know, but she has a persuasive way. She also believes DNA will prove the old kabbalistic saying: G-d is Science, Science is G-d.

I frankly find this woman annoying—she has strange habits of tapping her collar bone and temples. I think it's a stress-reducing technique used by alternative health care professionals, but it's disquieting. She also has lots of tics and explains them as one of many symptoms of a rare genetic disorder, waging war from within. Maybe she's obsessed with reincarnation because life is ticking too rapidly for her; she says her days are numbered. I don't know what to make of it, though it does seem to explain her sense of desperation. She mentioned that a lifetime of work would go unnoticed because she has no heir. I feel compassion for her, even in my irritation. I can see that Reuben adores her.

She has a fascinating way of talking with the royal we. I instinctively thought of Multiple Personality Disorder. As soon as the thought crossed my mind, she got a quirky look on her face, put her notebook down, bent over and grasped my hands, and said, "There are many alive inside me—seventy-five lifetimes are still in my memory banks, available information abounds, always a thunder of voices. I am we, in the real sense."

I did indeed question her, on many levels. Now, I know she knows things. She is a scholar of merit; I quizzed her on the strangest tidbits of history. She gave me an interesting first-person perspective as a priestess in Delphi, said I also lived then, one of the reasons she found me.

I admit to being agitated. She read my thoughts, got right inside me, and answered questions I had not yet thoroughly processed. She produced names, dates, and places, remarkable untold histories. For four hours, she held me in a historical trance, from Siberia to Chile to the Kivas of the Southwest. I can't sleep, Greta.

I kept asking who she was. She would respond simply, "I am a pilgrim." Looking through one of the files she left me, I noticed this piece concerning "Transforming the Karma Created in 1692 in Essex County, Massachusetts." I copied a page from the article and include it here.

Pilgrim is an ancient word meaning one who suffers. It conjures images of walking practically naked in harsh conditions, intentionally depriving the self of proper nutrition and rest for the sake of sacrifice and penitence. The American Camino differs from the Church of Rome's interpretation of suffering and sacrifice: no sin, no absolute evil, no buying salvation and redemption. I am old school; Karma is my way. True, the process has to be rushed along or put right, from time to time. This process is called Spirit Business. Shamanism is tricky, but when business is in the mix, things get downright sticky. It's all about Spirit Bargains, which are gray areas, shaped by Karmic interpretations of Cosmic Law, subject to heavy liens and fines if wrong or impetuous actions are taken, especially in the name of healing.

A responsible practitioner of the Old Ways is always subject to bargains. Successful positive deeds are earning tools. Intention counts for only 10 percent of the entire mix. Follow-through is what being a responsible practitioner is all about—in Indian Country called the Big Work. The deals you make along the way are entirely your own, even if they are predicated on survival. There are always reactions to actions; no exceptions are made on this point, ever. What is not cleaned up in this life travels with its maker into the next, then on to the next, and so on, until the cycles are broken through deeds of courage and fortitude. Sticky.

The first thing I say to a perspective student is, "If you think you want to be like me, you need therapy." My brand of Shamanism is indigenous, active, and in-your-face. Shamanism is a cliché word, presently. There are training seminars, doctoral dissertations, New Age newspapers advertising therapists with special skills. If you have the bucks, you can become a Shaman the new and improved way. Not in my world. If Spirit does not call you personally—not by telephone—and gift you directly with skills akin to a spiritual Homeland Security Force, you are not the real article. Now, another conundrum: someone receives the Call from Spirit, is gifted with special skills, can communicate to a large range of life forces including animal kingdoms—you would think the Shaman resumé complete. But, no, a true practitioner cannot call herself or himself a Shaman. Only the people you minister to can gift the moniker, or the tribal or Spiritual Elders. Shamanic Practitioner is a good stopgap. Sticky, it's usually sticky...

There's an aura of authority in this woman. When she speaks, you feel the vibration of the words. They are separate and whole unto themselves. Sitting in my office, overlooking the lights of Portland, I feel small and lost in a world not of my own making. I am punchy and sleep deprived; for an old man like me, meeting St. Cloud was an emotional powder keg. I wish you were here to make more sense of things, of her, of me, of you, and our years together and apart.

When I close my eyes, I keep seeing an image of her face, strained and pulled tight, with dark sparkling eyes. "There are no coincidences in the Universe." she chants. Do you think it a coincidence that our university maintains the official website of the Salem Witch Trials?

I know you know Dr. Ian Stevenson and see him from time to time at conferences and dinner parties. I even read his book on your recommendation, although until today it was over my head. He's retired from the university now, but, as I understand it, he's still the preeminent reincarnation scholar in the world. I want Stevenson and St. Cloud to meet. I want to hear what he has to say about her past-life memory recall and her skeletal deformations, which cause her severe seizures that she says are powerful gateways into the subconscious, not only hers, but others'. Ghosts speak to her in the waking state as well. She tells of a form of Nepalese Shamanism through which the practitioner can see many things happen from an altered, usually aerial viewpoint, seeing, hearing, feeling multidimensionally. She employs these methods daily, so she says. I have no reason to doubt her at this stage because of what she told me about myself and the way Reuben fell under her spell instantly, as soon as she touched him.

Let's make this meeting happen, between Stevenson and St. Cloud. Please let's have at least one more big adventure before we pass into the void.

Yours always,
Mortie

P.S. I am taking the liberty of including a photocopy of her first entry in her notebook titled "Prep Book 1."

Sophie St. Cloud—Yamhill County, Oregon
Book One of the Preparations for the American Camino
September 6, 2004

Two weeks exactly till Pressing Day, the nineteenth day of the ninth month of September. Tomorrow, the Court of Oyer and Terminer convenes at noon and we begin the cycle all over again, always the same, leading to the agonizing days and nights of September 19 through 22. Few people realize it took Giles until first light on the twenty-second to die. He was stubborn. My date differs from the historical record, no big surprise! Giles was there for Martha though. He had enough time to leave his body, after John Moulton bludgeoned him to death, find Martha, console her from the Ethers, and help her to the light. That was the least he could do for his dutiful wife, after he joked with the henchmen and they took it seriously.

My deformed skeleton tells the tale of Giles's pressing. People don't get it, even when I show them color photographs of people with the same kinds of problems I have, imprinted on their bodies, minds, and souls the marks of tortuous deaths, plain to see as scars, deformations, birthmarks. Thank heavens Dylan understands, at least subconsciously. Thank the Gods he is empathic, or I'd be sunk. The Gods knew what they were doing when they sent Dylan to be my partner. And the only other person who understands is my sister Ali, my Baby Girl. She knows the score but pushes the knowledge away. If she gets into Giles's story, she finds herself and shuts down. Once, she told me she hated Giles. It upset me: I never tell her I hate her. Giles is me, he's inside me. She can't have me without him.

Giles is complicated. There's three of him, depending on whom you count—Walking Giles, Haunting Giles, and Core Giles, which includes Dying Giles too—talk about warps in the time continuum! You need to factor me into the scenario too, with my entire surface past-life memory, the only one who knows all of us as one, over and above the post traumatic stress and torture. And no, this is not Dissociative Identity Disorder. It's called reincarnation under traumatic circumstances.

One thing is sure, Dora doesn't believe in reincarnation. So I told her, straight-faced, as serious as possible, "You are Mary Corey, my wife before Martha." I had given her clues for years, but I just didn't want to wait any longer. I don't know if she doubted me, herself, the work, it's still not clear; she still didn't get the connection. Time was ticking and I perceived I needed her help. She stood there not even flinching and said, "Humph." Okay, it's obvious: she is not on the same page. Although she's been to Assisi, Sienna, Chartres, the Dragon Line in England—so many of the places we have been together in previous lifetimes—she doesn't feel it. I become confused and wonder if I made a wrong choice about training her as my Shamanic Heir. It makes me feel awful when I think about abandoning our student/teacher relationship. It feels like failure. I want to try making friends with her, so I can move on and find another heir-apparent who really wants magick as a lifestyle, not as a distant second to tango or a course in obligation. I need people I choose for family to be full of passion, unafraid to speak out when there is a wrong that needs to be put to right!

I keep placating myself. Dora was only seventeen when I took her on. She was just a kid with exaggerated high hopes, good looks, and a bright future. She had lots of discipline for magick before she discovered tango. Her parents are atheists and don't believe in much other than Amazon.com and vacations abroad. Was I blind? I told her father she wouldn't want to play Indian some day.

I pray every night and still little direction is given me about Dora, how to reshape our relationship and goals. By first light of the 23 of September 2007, if she doesn't get it by then, we can part with a clean Karmic slate. That is a huge goal to pray over, to keep in perspective. Hey, Spirit, three hundred and twelve years of this torture is enough, already! Renegotiating Time: three years and counting! I'm renegotiating with the world and everyone in it, if things go as planned. At this point, there isn't a firm plan, just go and listen and feel. As I begin the work, Spirit will direct me, as they always do.

Two is a significant number in the Salem work. It's all about partnerships. Dylan was Martha; Dora was Mary. I wonder who else will travel with us by then. Three years is nothing, although right now it seems impossible. There's so much to do before we go, on all levels.

September now, the first brittle leaves falling, settling in the sidewalk cracks, crunching under people's feet. It's late, the window is open wide, the Autumn wind hot out of the East. I hear leaves being walked on, making me nervous. I feel watched. The living scare me more than the dead. The world feels like it's closing in on me. People are surfacing monthly, so many Salem connections.

Why did it take so many years for me to figure out the Caribbean connection? Giles the pirate, Sophie the waitress in the same place, in different centuries? In the Winter of 1981/82, I thought I'd die in the islands. In a very sad twist of fate, Mom's illness saved my life and brought me back to Santa Fe. Oh, what a rough island crowd I ended up with! The rum and pirates I hung with were linked directly to Giles, I know that now. I wonder if I rubbed elbows with the reincarnation of the right Reverend Samuel Parris that Winter? It wouldn't surprise me a bit. Giles was a pirate, true. It was how he got his land stake and his religion, some would think, so that he moved into Essex County, Massachusetts, with a plan to stay and get rich. Few realize the islands were swarming with Puritans in the early and mid 1600s.

Life was rough anywhere you lived then, down island, New England, South, or North. Parts of Europe were pure hell in the seventeenth century. It was harder than Giles thought it would be to give up the water, all those heady years at sea as a privateer. That's why he remained a pirate, on land most of the time, but pirate still. I can remember coming up the back sloughs, northwest of Salem Town, filled with rum. It was new to the colonies then. Giles wanted in on the action and made a pretty penny for his time and trouble.

Why do I continue to be so blind? It's all there, right in front of my eyes, all the information. Summer tourist season 1982: Work was tight in Santa Fe, and there was nothing happening after I got back from the islands to care for Mom. After she was stabilized, I needed to get back to work. I agreed to join an old friend in New Hampshire, running his restaurant close to the Canadian border. Considering family obligations, it was a gamble going far from home, I admit, and I was not thrilled about transferring buses in Boston, since I had successfully avoided the town and state thus far in my travels. It was a bad omen. I came off the bus with utter recognition of the place. Feeling instantly sick, I thanked heaven I only had five minutes to wait for the bus for the North. I was back in Santa Fe before the twenty-second of September.

Think of all the dreams: names, dates, places, even where the bodies were buried. Hindsight is the only element that has saved me all these years, finally able to piece the big mystery together, realizing many of the good guys were actually the bad guys. Remember Dad saying the best place to hide was in front of your enemy's eyes, so close they lose sight of you? The story is all there, my mind guarding secrets to this day.

Oh, more twos: Dylan and I left Santa Fe in 1990. After living in

Newport, Oregon, for two years, where Dylan was building the Oregon Coast Aquarium, we began looking for property. That was 1992. For some strange reason, I insisted we buy a house in Salem, Oregon. *Neither one of us even liked Salem, but I needed to live there for a while. I found a spiritual community around the corner from our house, the First Spiritualist Church. They had psychic fairs every Friday night; after Shabbas dinner, we headed off to church. It seemed right. I knew the work of the Spiritualist Church in Florida and New York and found it a good match. It afforded lots of opportunities for Dylan to sharpen his Oracle skills and we craved social input from like minds. All was wonderful until the beginning of September. Just like clockwork, the Salem drama started to unfold. One evening, during an informal lecture, the director of the church pointed at me and declared I was the perfect example of keeping a man through disability. He disapproved of Dylan and me as a couple and had told us so before, behind closed doors. "Why do you insist on being a family if Sophie is gay and Dylan has no benefits?" he said one evening after too much Willamette Valley wine. He couldn't accept that we loved each other and didn't want to live apart. At church he went on to explain that I had the power to heal myself. Staying unwell was my choice, he said, forcing Dylan to stay in an unhappy marriage, to be my caretaker. We were horrified and shortly thereafter moved. Our house sold in eleven days, a record for our real estate broker. It was September in Salem, what did I expect? The house sold on the twenty-second...*

Let's not forget last Spring. I met the woman of my nightmares, Corey Savage, the reincarnation of Sheriff George Corwin, all the way from Essex County. She found me and I found her like moths to a flame. How many times are we attracted to the people who hurt us the most? It's never-ending; the puzzle pieces don't stop accumulating.

In two weeks, on September 19, the three-hundred-twelfth anniversary of Giles's pressing, I begin three years of rituals—three, the number of manifestation. It's the preparation I need, building up my energy and knowledge of the area, so my steps will be utilized properly. This is the spiritual way for me to return to Salem, to integrate with Giles. The Inner Circle has bound and gagged Giles twice a year for three hundred and twelve years, in September and in April. They are good at it. Drake Putnam has taught them well. No, not an accurate statement. Lori Otto has taught them well, this generation's High Priestess. She has pulled some amazing conjuring in her years as protector of the Salem Sheriff's Department. How many people have figured out the Sheriff's Department is controlled by the Family Confedera-cy? We'll find the bodies, the ones I don't already know about, that is. We've got a lot of work to do in a very short amount of time.

The professor sensed the smell of satisfaction in the room. His heart raced as he stood up and stretched his weary muscles. The letter would be sent as written. Perhaps Greta would understand St. Cloud and her spiritual ways, her rituals, and Spirit Bargains. He would leave the matter in Greta's capable hands. If she decided St. Cloud was worthy, he would start reading the stack of black-and-white notebooks, her historical novel, resting on his office floor. All he had to do now was to sleep late and seal the envelope for the afternoon mail.

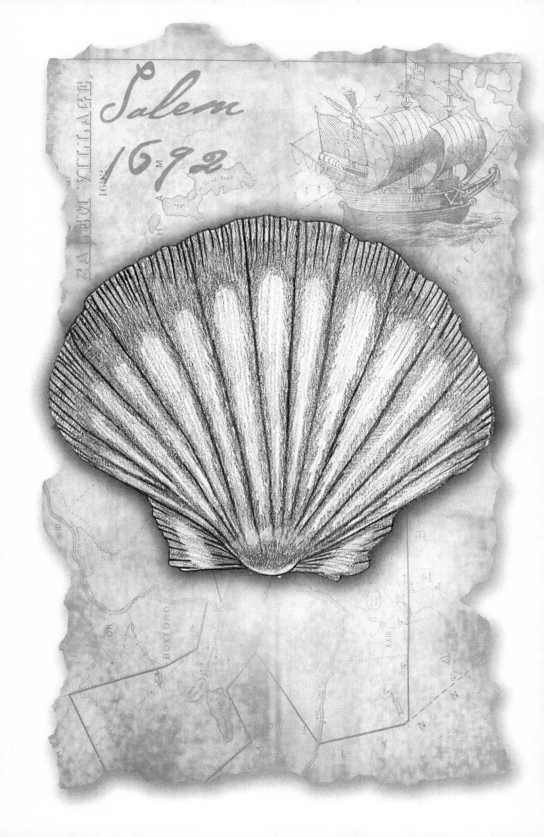

Salem
1692

SALEM VILLAGE,
1692.

Chapter Two

LIFE IS A CAMINO!

September 15, 2007, 3:00 a.m.

THREE YEARS. THE TIME HAD BEEN SERVED, the preparatory rituals completed, the itinerary set. Few obstacles lay between planning and doing, only three thousand miles, two airplanes, and legs strong enough to walk the actual steps.

Two or three hours of sleep at any one time was usual for Sophie. Her reflexes were sharp, her body toned, her mind on fire. Her stern facade and authoritative manner had not been strong enough to stop the constant wave of anxiety tormenting her through the night. Fear washed like searing waves across her hot face. Her heart felt like a blob of pumping, heated iron the size of a basketball.

"Oh my Goddess, I can't, I can't get on *that* plane!" She was having a panic attack. She did know they needed to be on the road by now. The flight took off at six. It took at least an hour and a half to get to the airport, even in the middle of the night. But none of that mattered. She had lost sight of it, caught in the swaying of her body.

She needed help from the person she trained for the job. Where was Dora? She knew better than this. "Dora is breaking my heart. Where is she?" Sophie's sobs turned into a piercing scream. "We need to be on the road now!" Her vulnerability exposed, anger found its way in and propelled her to her feet. She reached for a tissue, straightened her posture, and glared in all directions. "So Be It! Be sure to holler when Dora arrives. I'll be ready in five." Sophie made her way up the stairs, her speed increasing with each step.

She dashed into her bedroom and grabbed the burgundy tunic waiting on the bed, ran a comb through her near-bald head and blew her nose. Her strength had returned. Rational, her hurt feelings, fears, and disappointments of the past shoved aside, she breathed and reminded herself that the journey ahead was not all about her, her feelings and expectations, her betrayals, even her anxiety. This mission was for the sake of destiny, power in the now, the possibility of future. She had been asked to play a role, was made to gamble with her energy and her life. It was all a risk. But she had much to gain as long as her ego stayed in check.

Emotionally stabilized, she called out for Dora once more. Dora, usually quiet and detached, animated and ran to join Sophie.

"What is it? Why aren't you ready? Dylan said you weren't feeling well."

"I'm anxious and I'm afraid, Dora. I don't know if Drake Putnam will have his henchmen at the airport. He's warned me before. At least, the Inner Circle wants me to think he has. Maybe I can't pull this off after all. Just in case I can't make it, if I can't get on the plane, you'll have to take over. Take this envelope. Keep it close, keep it private! Follow the instructions, even if you are afraid or don't understand their meanings. Please, this time, trust me and follow through. You've got to promise me, Dora!"

There wasn't time to argue. Dora wasn't happy, it was plain to see. Her usual straight spine and haughty way she held her head, the way only seasoned tango dancer snobs do, gave her away. "Okay, okay, El General Sophie. How many times do I have to promise you? If need be, I will carry your torch all the way through the Integration Walk, I mean the Liberation Feast. I promise. Now, give me the envelope and finish getting ready, please." Clearly annoyed, Dora slipped out fast, away from Sophie's insistent grasp.

They were fifteen minutes late getting on the road by the time Sophie finished stacking bracelets on her wrists. She wore matching earrings to ward off the Evil Eye. She hung her Hamsa amulet around her throat, accompanied by her father's turquoise cross. She wanted all her bases covered on this trip. She quickly took a mental inventory of all her magickal tools: smudge and all the gifts for the dead—maple sugar, Tobacco Honor Bundles, red ribbon, shortbread cookies. She knew she would buy more gifting supplies at Putnam Pantry, the candy store in Salem. Giles's resting place had enough juice in it to levitate that flimsy jet plane they were about to ride, Sophie thought.

Thinking about Giles's strength charged her with pride. Giles had been working with her for three years on this project, teaching her to go beyond her training; she was ready and eager now!

"There you are." Sophie whispered at her three friends as she piled into the front seat. Everybody laughed, tension broken, fear abated, the Bogey Man put to rest.

As Dylan pulled the station wagon out of the driveway, Sophie pulled down the visor. Poe was seated behind her, with an open face, ready for adventure. The glossy look in Poe's powder blue eyes suggested that she had chosen to stay awake, instead of resting before the flight. Sophie sighed with satisfaction, knowing Poe was up to the challenge ahead. Poe had a Southern girl's sense of civility and generosity to match, although her hard edge shone through when reason was asked for. Sophie felt safe when Poe was around. She was a psychic diversion, pulling negative attention away from Dora. Poe understood Sophie's chronic exhaustion and sympathized with her ailing body, while Dora only wondered why Sophie couldn't do more. Poe was more than a buffer; she was a friend, a loyal and admiring equal. The four made an interesting group, all tied together, past and present.

The station wagon had windows offering a full view of the landscape. Only the green-webbed Dream Catcher diverted the eye from the two-lane road. Watching the silhouette of the Tall Ones, Oregon's ancient trees, against the cobalt and yellow haze of first light, Sophie knew she was born to do this work. She was determined to end the continuous stream of bad magick, three hundred and fifteen years old. She had to integrate, for Giles, for herself, for the future, her future. Divided time, divided loyalties had to end. The future was bright if she just could finish what she had died fighting for in 1692.

The image of Rodrigo, the big-chested Flamenco singer, filled her over-firing brain. His voice rose over the beating of her heart, as he sang out in familiar Catalonian tones.

"My life is a Camino, never-ending, always mending,
singing my despair.
My life is a Camino, walking over mountains and through valleys,
twisted and poor.
My life is a Camino, sure is my step, a pilgrim's cloak shelters me,
prayers protect my soul.
My life is a Camino, constant is my step, faith secures my progress.
All belongs to God!"

Chapter Three

FIRST GLIMPSE
September 16, 2007, 6:00 a.m., Peabody, Massachusetts

DYLAN HAD BOOKED A TWO-BEDROOM SUITE at the Peabody Marriott. The girls had their own room down the road at the Days Inn. What little space of solitude available during these remaining schedule-packed eight days demanded a sense of separation from time to time. Sophie's solitude was worth the extra hotel bill for the suite without the girls. Funny, she thought, "the girls," as if they were seven and ten, not twenty-seven and thirty.

She had her routines. Sophie began lifting the shades, one at a time, in each room. This was her protection sweep. *Always good to see your environment first thing upon waking,* her mother always said. She moved in a clockwise manner, beginning in the East

When she finally made it to the last room, she reached for the blind tentatively, feeling what was on the other side. Her heart began to beat faster. With the blind fully opened, Sophie stood motionless. Only a lone tear moved, gliding slowly down her left cheek

Bright azure blue filled the September sky, supporting fluffy white clouds, so carefully placed. A set of three gently rolling hills, dressed in dry greens and Autumn golds, one immediately following the other, filled her vision. Lines of ancient oaks and scrub hawthorns defined the farmer's field. Little had changed in three hundred and fifteen years. This was still Corey land, regardless of what the present land deed read.

Dylan said he had scored when he booked the suite online. He found the hotel on Google Earth and consulted the invaluable topo maps. He knew the hotel butted against Corey land—this was his surprise for Sophie. Sophie had made a list of prerequisites for their lodging in Peabody. As long as they were in the domain of Corey land, under the subconscious protection of the Putnams, she didn't care where they stayed. The bed had to be comfortable, and no one other than the girls would know where they were. Separating the party of four into two groups was safer for everyone involved. It made it more difficult to attack, from the outside, at least. Now she was crying grateful tears and thanking the powers that be for delivering Dylan to her as a partner, all those years ago. What a cherished gift, to be this close to Corey land with Martha.

Carefully, Sophie offered her Greeting to the Sun, marking the beginning of the second day of the big quest. Spirit had directed her to bring balance to this part of Massachusetts by *walking the steps*, not any different from a pilgrim's steps on the European Camino, climaxing in Santiago de Compostela and Finisterre, Spain. Massachusetts was Sophie's Spain. This was her spiritual gauntlet. With each step taken, the bones of the Ancestors, both red and white, would be released to join the light and move on to the big university *next door*, Spirit Speak for the other side.

She smelled the warm rich Earth of Corey land through the windows. Her senses ignited, visions popped in and out of Sophie's view, changing rapidly. They stopped and settled in one place, like a roulette wheel come to rest. Memories of her teens came into full view. She remembered her mother's preoccupation with Essex County. A schoolteacher, Sarah had been adamant that her children study colonial history. One evening, after a grueling day at school, Sarah marched into Sophie's room and threw a copy of Arthur Miller's play *The Crucible* on the desk. "This is our history, not just as Americans, but as minority people. Our family is different from the majority. We are mixed blood and do not practice the religion of our rulers." Sarah used her schoolteacher voice.

Sophie looked at her mother, cocked her head to one side, and said, "Oh, Mother, pleeeasssse…" She was sixteen and did not want another speech from anyone, especially her mom.

But she got one anyway. "Sixteen ninety-two was the defining year for our founding fathers, spiritually," her mother continued. "They knew the necessity of dividing church and state. Without a ruling theocracy, like the Puritans of New England—the seventeenth-century Mather family of Boston, for example—all peoples of this country would be ruled by one set of social laws, rather than by religious rules."

Sophie's agitation grew. She longed to yell at her mother to stop. Since her parents had discovered that she had been skipping out of the American history class all year, her choice to avoid all references to the American colonies were few.

Sarah knew her daughter hated the very mention of New England, but enough was enough. "Our founders made it possible to free all from state-defined religious fervor. Citizens were finally free from religious tyranny, at least in theory. Religious persecution was a major element inspiring immigrants to the colonies in the first place."

"Mother, please knock it off! I know all about American history. I sleep with books under my bed, as you have told me to do all my life. I showed up for all the finals in class. Since I aced the tests, I didn't fail the course, so I don't understand why you are harassing me with this information again. I don't want to hear it!" Sophie picked up the book and threw it in her mother's direction without looking. She was through.

"You are as hardheaded as I ever was and it's your downfall, young lady! We are blessed to be in this country, in the now, Sophie! Eventually, whether you like it or not, you will have to know what happened to the not-so-gentle folks of Massachusetts."

Sophie resisted completely. She refused to even crack a book on colonial history, whether novel or textbook. Even a New England Halloween story was not tolerated in her presence. She had always lived with ghosts, known their secrets—hundreds of them called her name from colonial times. Why would she tell their stories in a cavalier fashion? The mere mention of Massachusetts sent adrenaline rushing through her body, brought her tics to the surface, and flooded her eyes with bitter tears. Her visceral reactions to history didn't impress Sarah. She knew her daughter needed to go deeper, beyond the discomfort, and find the core, the causation for her phobias.

Her mother had always wanted to visit New England to see the changing leaves. Finally, the September of Sophie's final year at university, Sarah booked a holiday to Essex County. Sophie refused to join the family and opted to stay home with the cats and dogs she was so allergic to. She wanted no part of New England. The mere thought of it made her gag and her head pound. In her nightmares she already knew that place: stones, heavy stones, jeers, sneers, spitting, echoing laughter, evil, and cold. She remembered Salem whether she traveled there or not, whether she read about it or listened to old stories. The source did not matter. She knew Massachusetts, 1692—still fresh in her mind, her heart broken and betrayed.

The lay of the land was the same; it had not changed in three hundred and fifteen years, even with aggressive development, highways, and concentrated population. The hills undulated, golden light bounced off harvested fields, the smells, all the same, recognizable as home. Now in her fifties, without her mother's chiding, Sophie wanted nothing more than to be immersed in this land and its dramas. "Bring it on!" she said out loud.

So many memories flooded in, so much about her mother, her lectures and rants, her need for control. And Sophie's little sisters, Joan and Alysandra, called Ali. She reassured herself by chanting her sisters' names, bringing their energy closer, revving up for a day filled with realizations and déjà vu. Ali had wanted to be here, a part of this reclaiming. But this isn't Ali's time: she has lots of personal work to do for her to catch up with the others on this project. The gaol is still too close, too real, for her—tight confined spaces, the stench, the chaffing skin from the irons. Nothing could erase these memories, especially time. Joan had to be their strength now, and Sarah. They were already next door and knew the secrets that brought the party of four here, on this sixteenth day of September, seventy-two short hours till the Pressing Time began. Lots of work to do, always work to do.

The realization shocked Sophie into action. Quickly she finished her morning prayers and Spirit Salutes, bathed, and ate her cherished morning oatmeal, brought all the way to Peabody from Oregon, when they didn't know there was a Trader Joe's right around the corner. Sophie was still thinking 1692, not 2007. Later, they would joke that the American Camino was fueled by Bagel World and directed by Dunkin' Donuts. The party of four watched for the Dunkin' Donuts shops; they always marked their trail.

The Testimone of Mary Warren aged
or thereaboutes testifyeth and saith that
July last mr Burroughs pinched mee
me and
I
and
George Be
times torment

Mary Warren, Declared
evidence the month August

Salem
1692

SALEM VILLAGE
1692
M

All evil
can be un-
done! Say
your prayers
walk the steps
be bold, yet

respectful.
Spirit will
test you, this
is certain!
call on your
inner powers!

PRESSED
SEPT. 19, 169

Chapter Four

WINDOWS OF OPPORTUNITIES
September 16, 2007, 8:00 a.m.

IN THE CENTER OF THE NORTH WALL of the hotel suite, Sophie stood her ground and breathed with intention. Cradling her open arms, she took the Goddess stance, mirroring the crescent shape of the Moon. Before she grounded her energy into the Earth, she offered a prayer.

> *"Great Spirit, Grandmothers, Grandfathers,*
> *Earth, Air, Fire, Water, and Spirit,*
> *please hear my prayers.*
> *I stand over your Ground and under your Sky*
> *I become the link to each,*
> *endless is our bond.*
> *Bless us, protect us, love us*
> *for we are your children,*
> *many are we who sing your praises!*
> *In you, through you, and by you,*
> *we are you,*
> *Yesterday, today, and tomorrow.*
> *Blessed Be."*

The group moved in a familiar dance. They breathed deeply, standing erect in each of the Cardinal Directions. They drew energy from the Earth and directed it through their bodies, cycling it over their heads before returning it into the ground. They thanked the Fifth Element, Spirit, for protection and insight and breathed out in fiery unison for the last time. Fortified and protected, the ritual was ended.

Happiness filled the suite. The band of four was excited, amped up on bagels and tea, energized and ready to hit the road, earlier than expected. Salem was close to thirty minutes away, although it was only five miles as the crow flew, from this side of Peabody. The traffic would be treacherous, by Oregon standards. Today there would be walking, lots of it, but not traditional pilgrim walking. And driving, lots of driving because the New England roads were congested, some with few sidewalks or jogging paths, at least between towns. Ritual walking would be more of an accurate term for what they would be doing daily, driving to a specific location, creating a base of operations, walking in directional formations and patterns, leaving Spirit Tokens and gifts along the way, mainly for the dead.

There was a delicate rap on the suite's front door. Dora stopped drying dishes, looked at Sophie, and said, "Sounds like Spirit is being tentative this morning. Shall I see what the day has in store for us?" She opened the door with an exaggerated wave of the hand to find Poe waiting. No one had noticed that Poe had slipped out.

Trembling slightly, Poe looked at each member of the group, shaking her head in disbelief. "Y'all are not going to believe what I found at the front desk." She cleared her throat and began to read from a flier printed on light green paper.

"The Towne Family Association and Reunion Committee, with the cooperation and fellowship of the Colonial Reenactors Guild, are holding their yearly awards celebration and dinner at the Peabody Marriott Conference Center, September 15, 2007 at 7 p.m.. The awards banquet kicks off a week-long conference and reunion, attended by some of the most renowned historical families of New England. Tickets for the dinner and Colonial Reenactors Guild Armory Display and Tournament can be bought through Ticketmaster and at all local Marriott Hotels in the North Shore area."

Sinking into the lumpy flower-print chair, Sophie whispered, "Well, well, no big surprise. Their headquarters is a mile up the road. I should have done research on what the Family Confederacy planned the week of the last Salem hangings. I had not expected this." She felt the blood rush from her face, low-blood sugar, she thought—no—stress. Anxiety twisted in her stomach. Her right eyebrow twitched. She held onto it and squeezed in the center of the brow's severely shaped arch.

Silence surrounded them. The girls gathered up the last of the supplies for the day's travels. Dylan prepared lunch to go. Sophie processed the new information. She knew the gathering of the Family Confederacy would not have changed their travel plans, but it still gave her the creeps thinking her enemies were so close. The momentum gathered during their protection ritual had waned. Sophie's body became overwhelmed with a rush of sadness. The events planned for the day were too important to suffer emotional paralysis, she warned herself, but the harder her shell became, the farther her mind drifted.

The suffering of Essex County had already happened. There wasn't time for more. Attention to detail was critical—no errors could be made, at least ones that could not be put to right eventually. Each hour on every day was mapped out for the four. The itinerary was extreme. They could not hesitate. Her Higher Mind continued to talk her out of the stunting fear.

Balance was the commodity sought after, healing in the real sense, a practical sense. The innocent could no longer suffer under the mantle of guilt and the threat of shadowy forces beyond control.

Time was not linear. All time was now. In her worldview, the wounds of today were as real as the wounds of lifetimes past, and they all had to be dealt with in the now in order to break age-old cycles and heal.

The suffering perpetuated by the Family Confederacy of Salem Village and by the local and colonial government was felt in every cell of her body. The pain made its bloody marks on the walls of the gaol, the basement of the Old Salem jailhouse. No cleaning supplies could ever scrub the pain away. The Old Salem jailhouse sat empty, boarded up since 1991. But ghostly cries could be heard as the crows gathered next door at Howard Street Cemetery, and reverberated in her mind. She followed her mind's eye vision and found the indentation of Giles Corey's Pressing Place, evident in the adjacent parking lot, a pit sunk into the pavement. Her heart beat faster as time zones shifted. How many times had the same piece of ground been paved over, year after year? It didn't matter. The crater always came back. The lot was private parking, with a ten-foot wire fence all around it, topped with barbed wire. A part of her was held prisoner there, guarded by invisible agents. The entire block was haunted and writhing in pain. Salem's local newspaper, *The Gazette*, came into view. The words leaped off the page.

Negotiations are in process to turn Salem's Victorian Jail Complex, bordering the historical Old Salem Jailhouse and Gaol, into condominiums. The Jail Complex was purchased by the same development company, Cheever Construction, which owns the refurbished Victorian-era mental hospital project in Danvers. Many readers and Witch Trial buffs will remember the hospital was built on the ruins of Ann Putnam's house. Despite rumors of ghosts, the Danvers condo complex, located on the second tallest hill in this part of Essex County, sold out in less than two weeks. Let us all hope the same good luck repeats on Ingersoll's new project.

Who would heal those homeless ghosts, separated from the only reality they knew? She was not idealistic about healing. Sophie taught balance and moderation, with a never-ending stream of radical truth telling in between. Not all her students were happy with her ideas and teaching methods. Honesty was oppressive for many; denial was a comfortable place for most, but not for her! She was realistic and knew *healing* was a relative term. She felt a mild electrical shock, which rested in the nerve endings of her teeth.

She opened her eyes and noticed Dora was dressed in a dark fitted raincoat, although they were still inside. She pinched herself, testing her reality. Outside, the skies were blue and the temperature was close to eighty. What was Dora hiding from? This was a big day for her. The Opening Ritual was taking place in one of the busiest tourist attractions in the country, the original colonial burying ground for Salem, Charter Street Cemetery. Dora had voiced her anxieties about being so public, even while they were still preparing in Oregon for the ritual. Dora was facing herself today, with an audience. A tango dancer, she was used to an audience. You could tell she loved adoration, by the way she carried herself and the huge Jackie-O type sunglasses she wore, even inside. Incognito wasn't her style, but today she must be feeling not so sure-footed.

It was time to move. Sophie stood and shook her body gently and entreated her mind to stay in the now. The others gathered around her, a feeling of embrace. She sighed with gratitude. Dylan took a large manila envelope from the armoire that was acting as the Main Altar for the Big Work. He held it, one hand on each side, and blessed the package with his usual Sagittarian flair for drama. He finished his prayers and handed it to Sophie.

She extracted four long and tapered Parrot feathers from the envelope, the end of each shaft wrapped in red sinew and ribbon with a small golden safety pin right at the tip. Safety pins were used by the magick women of the

Pennsylvania Dutch as fasteners, links to the other side, Spirit Tools. Sophie instructed them to attach the Parrot feather on the left side of their bodies, or on their hats as she had. Parrots symbolized the Spirit Realms and carrying them in ritual opened a direct communication line to Spirit. The ritual would begin as the party of four entered Charter Street Cemetery. It would not be over until the Liberation Feast on the night of the twenty-second. This was going to be a long week.

Sophie and Dylan smiled at each other as they drove from the Marriott and headed toward Salem on U.S. Route 1. The girls were in back of the SUV. Candy wrappers started to rustle, foil crunched, and the eating of sweets commenced. No point in reminding them again that sugar blocked communication with the Spirit Realms and the use of it was counterintuitive in ritual. The futility had not stopped Sophie from thinking about it, though; she was hardwired to analyze everything. Poe was the first to sigh deeply as the party passed the other Marriott, the first of the sugar kicking in. All the sugar in the world would not block out the Spirit Realms now, not today. They had too much work to do and limited time. They had a window of opportunity and it was now.

Chapter Five

EAGLE DELIVERS THE OPENING RITUAL
New Moon, August 12, 2007, noon

SUMMER HAD SPED BY, NO TIME FOR RELAXATION or space enough to
breathe fully. It was already the New Moon in August—less than a month to
go till they greeted Massachusetts, Sophie thought. The house was a wreck,
its usual neatness overtaken by stacks of maps, notebooks, and lists of supplies yet to be gathered. She was in no mood to have to explain her reasoning
today. The others should know the details by now. The truth was simpler than
that: she was exhausted and didn't want to hear the sound of her own voice.

The smudge was lit. She watched the smoking shell in which it rested
pass from Dylan to Dora to Poe through the window. All she had been instructed to do by Spirit was to pay careful attention—Eagle had done most
of the preparations for her. She wrote every word down before time washed
away specifics. The others would be instructed to do the same, to find their
role in the dictates laid out for them. Pay attention, they had to be told over
and over again. She refreshed her water bottle, straightened her patterned
tunic and waited for the others to take their places around the huge table, the
heart of Sophie and Dylan's home. She knew she had to keep her composure
to make it through the afternoon; formality would be her method of survival.

"Blessed Be, everyone! Good to see your shining faces around this old
table. You all look ravishing." The others beamed. Sophie knew when to
flourish the compliments to garner their attention. It was human nature to
want praise, to feel desired and admired.

"Thank you for coming all the way out to the sticks, Dora. I really appreciate it. I know your dance schedule is bursting at the seams.

"Poe, thank you for being here. I can't tell you how happy I am to know the four of us will be traveling and working together. You have been my champion in so many lives, it's only right you will be in Salem this September.

"I want to thank Dylan once more for taking the lead in finding us housing and packing up all the food we'll be needing. You have worked so hard for us, especially me. Thank you. I want Dora and Poe to know you have begun dreaming finally, experiencing Martha, her faith, questions, and doubts, the real happenings of her life. This is great news: the Shamanic work we've been doing for the last three years is really paying off. I urge you all to update your dream journals and start taking better care of the information Spirit has been giving us."

"Why are you sounding so stiff today, Sophie?" Dylan looked frustrated. "I thought today was for review of the topo maps and going over each of our duties. I just want to clarify: I am driving, Dora is navigating. Poe, are you committed to being our record keeper? I'm getting nervous about Sophie doing too much; she's hitting it hard lately."

The girls nodded affirmatively in Dylan's direction. It had all been decided weeks ago, but time was moving too fast now, and everybody was struggling to get supplies and tools ready. Sophie had printed lists. They were in the blue folders she had prepared for everyone, micromanaging as usual.

Sophie continued her speech, intentionally ignoring Dylan's remarks. "We have one Moon before Salem becomes a reality. I am so relieved we have all made the grade and are able to move forward for the sake of the Work. Fortunately, I have completed the two books, making the American Camino considerably easier for us. The first book outlines the rituals, active Spirits, burial grounds, and information about Saugus. Also included are the copies of the Tarot reading that Ali and I did last January. The information is amazing, especially now with eight months of hindsight. The second book is the Camino route, including the all-important body tracings from June to the present."

"Have the marks subsided, Sophie?" Poe looked concerned.

"They haven't changed since the last set, traced from the same location on my chest, on July eleventh. I am having lots of inflammation and itching there, however, so I am concerned there might be a last minute route to add to the itinerary. We have to put it in Spirit's hands, at this point. If the marks start retracing themselves, I'll write a group email to y'all immediately."

Poe seemed satisfied with the answer and continued, "How did the last tracing change the route? Did it affect the sacred geometry patterns that were beginning to appear?"

"This is precisely what the second book is about. In it are color copies of the body tracings overlaid on the AAA road maps we got last month. They are amazing. The main route is where the majority of the remains of the colonists murdered by the Family Confederacy are located. An interesting triangle has emerged. Please turn to the first page of your folders. In red, you will find a triangle, the Southern tip being the foundry at Saugus. Exactly 21.8 miles Northeast is Davis Bay Junction, where we know Mary Warren is leading us. Another 21.8 miles to the Northwest, we find the top of the triangle at Pentucket Cemetery in Haverhill, where we know the Wampanoag Sachem Metacomet is waiting for us.

"There might be a lot of pyrotechnic action when we are dealing with Hannah Dustin. I heard an article on NPR last week about the monument we're working on in Haverhill. It sounded more like the ancient-looking, out-of-the-way statue of Hannah in New Hampshire, but I guess I could have been imagining it. Anyway, according to the report, it's the oldest statue of a woman in the United States. Her upraised arm used to hold the ten dripping scalps of the Indians she killed, until in a more genteel time, the city fathers had the scalps removed but kept the hatchet in the other. Hannah Dustin, our thirty-year relationship between ghost and Spirit Worker, has given us quite a journey. If she moves to the light, I admit I won't miss her, especially her late night visits, approaching my bed in the dark, always the dark. Hopefully we'll be able to sort out the entire relationship on our day there. We'll probably glean important information at the historical society, right next to Pentucket."

Sophie continued, "The Work of Salem has morphed and grown so many times, so different than I ever dreamed. This is my real-time now, filling in the silent spaces of possibilities with good wishes, hoping for the best.

"Binding Magick is powerful; I feel it every day of my life. Magick is magick—it is neither good nor bane. I hope I have instilled that reality into you all by now. If not, please hear me! I was explaining to Dylan the other night, as the intensity of our mission grows hourly and the Spirit activity that comes along with it stirs all feelings to the surface, the motivation for sabotage by other outside parties is understandable. The lure of so-called negative magick is intoxicating and the power raised so immediate, up to ten times as powerful as practical magick, what a rush! Everyday worship in the form of temple service and finding joy in simple mundane pursuits, elevating all action to a holy act of harmony, this is our way out of this mess. But we don't have a thousand years!

"As you know, High Magick is designed for interceding for those in need, being a link between the Spirit Realms and human and animal kingdoms. High Magick is sustained through focused service for the principle of the Highest and Greatest Good. Consistent service is enduring and *almost* impossible to change course—I'm talking about setting a negative tone and trying to divert a positive pathway, if the same spell, wish, desire, or action is repeated regularly. Remember, Shamanism is based on the action of repetition, such as chanting and toning.

"The Binding Magick used by the Family Confederacy of Salem through the Inner Circle is powerful because it is enduring. Three hundred and fifteen years of twice-a-year incantations and fraternity has created a huge energy vacuum. This is why the Salem Work affects the entire country. This conspiracy of minds and hearts has a combined energy of lust and greed, which grows in power each time it is carried out in September and April. Do the math! Six hundred and thirty times Giles has been bound magickally, representing an amazing amount of rope, tension, and pressure. So great in fact, I feel it begins on its own after Lughnasadh each year. I used to blame it on the beginning of the school year. I know better now.

"This year, as you all know, road work began on all the streets around us, encircling our block with continuous noise, blowing dirt, and strangers. This kind of outer chaos is typical and begins in August like clockwork, especially in this house. This circling process of Binding Magick is in high gear this year.

"They are circling, as we are. Look at my hair. My regular haircutter could not resist the temptation to shave my head with her clippers. Now I feel like Uncle Fester. I even tried dying the stubble a couple of days ago. Hideous! As Indians, we cut our hair when we are grieving. The Universe has sent me this reality. My sacrifice has begun and it's not even September."

Dora, sporting a new haircut, an auburn version of Cleopatra, started to laugh. "Sophie, I thought you intentionally cut your hair. I was trying to figure out its significance—nobody has died around here for a while. This is too funny. You know, you commented on my new haircut earlier? Well, I had a gig last weekend down in Eugene. Beautiful location for fire-dancing, large open garden spaces with night-blooming flowers. I was getting ready for the finale, my poi blazing, making large circles with my arms, in tune with the beat. I saw a secondary light to my top right and realized my hair was on fire. Funny, both of us, our hair messed with."

Sophie grew annoyed. "I don't find it funny at all! I have worked to train you for ten years, in part so you can earn the right to take my place in the Big Work, as a Shamanic Practitioner of my lineage."

Sophie's frustration showed in her voice and she knew it. A flush crept up Dora's cheeks.

"Secrets, map-ways, directives, processes—my life's work—cannot be handed down without the proper vocabulary to understand them fully. These methods are worthless unless they are employed as intended. After years of implementation, then methods can change and evolve. The stakes are too high to play—pure hard work is the ticket to success! The other part is more practical. Until I leave this Earth, we are meant to work in tandem on the same projects. This is the intention, although I believe you have misunderstood your role over the years, largely due to lack of questioning on your part."

Dora's face had grown a deep scarlet. Sophie could almost see the steam rush from Dora's ears. But she couldn't stop the message Spirit had implored her to deliver, regardless of the other's discomfort.

"This intense Spirit Work of the American Camino will teach us if we are connected enough to manifest discipline, respect, and success. Without this special mix, we are sunk as a team. Now, part of the deal of working in spiritual tandem is for you to open your pathways of communication to me, as I do with the Spirit Realms. Without a free flow of information, important details are always left out, creating confusion and separation. For now, if something unusual happens to you, like your hair catching fire during a performance, be sure to call me right away. Expect lots of mirroring between you and me. We could have warned each other about the hair thing, our manes, our pride and strength. I would have cancelled my hair appointment. We have to be on our game for this one, Dora, we can't miss anything! If we cannot work together positively in Salem, there will be little reason to continue as we have been."

Poe looked concerned, her brow furrowed and deep. She and Sophie had finished up the work on the Tarbell family in Salem late last Spring, the regression sessions still fresh. She was used to being the together one at work; all her therapy clients needed her to be grounded and astute. But she hadn't been centered for months, and it was starting to show. Many of her memories were tough to face, so raw, while others were stuffed down, because she did not want to see the real origins of her pain. She let her therapist's demeanor override her empathy with Dora, until remembering this too was her work.

"I feel I need a vacation from the vacation, meaning Salem. It's too heavy and it's wearing on me," Poe said. "I am concerned about recreational time outside of the Salem work for the coming month. It's Joshua's birthday month and Dora's too; lots of parties are being planned."

"Remember, Poe, we have lots of Shamanic taboos in force, until the Salem work is completed," Sophie said. "No flesh foods, no smoking Tobacco, no caffeine, only alcohol if it's being used as a clearing method or sacrament. We've got to stay tight. The Spirit Realms are really sensitive to certain odors and we can't afford to offend our greatest allies."

Dylan spoke up. "I wish you would call taboos *moratoriums* instead, Sophie. Sometimes my eyes glaze over and I miss the power of what you are saying when you use archaic terms. Taboos sounds like marrying your sister or something." It was then he caught his double entendre and smiled slyly. "Well, I never could keep a Family Confederacy secret."

The party of four broke out in a much needed round of laughter. Yes, it was all about familial ties, secrets, deeds that could not be undone, physical greed. The irony of Dylan's statements, just like the Sagittarius he is, extemporaneous and on the money. He's got a talent and doesn't even know it, Sophie thought.

Back on track, Sophie began in all earnestness once more. "I do take comfort knowing Practical and High Magick, the magick that flows through me, is evolutionary in design. The negative magick of Salem's Inner Circle—though done through rote and repetition—can be undone. The trick is for Giles to cut the bounds tied around him by Lori Otto from the inside. Let me say it again: Giles is going to cut through the magickal binding placed on him by using scissors I supply him with. It's more than a metaphor. Long story short, we can set this situation to right! Perhaps the true story will never be known outside these walls, but who would believe a story such as this anyway, with all its twists and turns, child sexual abuse, incest, servitude of women, land-grabbing, blood atonement, contract murder. Hey, it sounds more like *Big Love* and the state of Mormon polygamy."

Once again, a healthy roar of laughter.

"The Inner Circle's work is based on obsession. They have dedicated three hundred and fifteen years to it. Giles kept a rogue leg up on his privateering business because he made it his business to know other people's secrets. He wasn't pushy—he just paid attention and applied what he knew about human nature. Eighty-one years bought him lots of life experience. Yes, he was a magick man, he had that working for him too. He learned much at sea and in the many ports he visited throughout the Caribbean. He learned the gift of the shells, of seeing pictures on the clear, calm waters of the warm sea. He was shown how to hear Spirit Speak and see Spirit Vision. He learned from his captives, too, West Africans and Caribs, mostly, about magick and being stern and mean-mannered. Being mean kept unwanted attention deflected. Others couldn't see your true motivation, your angle. In time, he taught these invaluable skills to his wife Mary, and then to Martha. They were fast learners, the both of them, the reason we always tried to keep to ourselves, because Mary and Martha were so talented in Second Sight and clairaudience—they could see people's thoughts and hear their doubts and lack of faith, just at the mere sight of them. They were naturals, my mother would say.

"Giles was no saint, we all know. Martha wasn't an angel either, but they were hard working, dedicated people of nature. As long as they were left alone and respected for what they built of their land, they wanted no part in hurting anyone. It's true, Giles killed instead of being a victim. When the Inner Circle was getting really close to our core mission two Summers ago, through Rose Desmond, their historian, Rose went out of her way to shame the memory of Giles, saying that he was an Indian killer and since I was half Indian, I was paying for his Karma by being a cripple in this life. That's after she let it slip about the candy store and Giles's real burial spot. She wanted to hurt me in my soft underside, my Indian identity, my cultural and Shamanic Core Self. I was hurt but I realized it was just a tactic to get me to back off. Obviously, it didn't work!"

Golden light from the afternoon Sun was now beating in through the Western windows, bathing the stack of maps in front of her with unwanted light and heat. She stood and took pause, watching the expressions on the others' faces. Had her words made an impact on them? She couldn't tell. She walked to the blinds and wound them shut, lowering the oppressive August temperature instantly. She decided to forge on, with or without them. The dark cool would wake them up, she hoped.

"The Inner Circle bound all their bosses' incestuous, greedy secrets and bad deeds and Parris's slave-owning debacles together with Giles's pressed and bludgeoned body. They wrapped him tightly with all their poison and stoned him over, but his dark and deep grave of soil kept sinking in on itself, lower and lower into the ground. Yes, in front of the candy store, Putnam Pantry. When it was still in Putnam hands, they dug Giles's grave up, boxed him up in chains, and cemented him in an underground chamber. It took them all of one Spring to do it, before the big highway was built in front of the shop. The candy store was still small in those days, before movie stars and chocolate connoisseurs found them. They ended up securing the whole mess by paving the chamber over. It's so deep, only Earth changes would ever reveal it. All this, born out of bad behavior by old white men. They killed anybody in their way and consistently pinned the crimes on others or simply buried the bodies, deep on endless stretches of family land. When the Tarbells bought Saugus—Poe is working on her details—much of the colonial body disposal was done there, in the fires of the foundry. No need to cover up Indian dead. Scalps were taken and bounties were collected. The black dead needed deep burial and usually incineration because they were legal tender, the human element rarely taken into consideration."

She heard steps on the roof, small, bouncing hop-steps, then pecking. Maybe a blue jay or crow looking for bugs in the roofers' debris. The sounds interrupted her train of thought. She faced the direction of the pecking and waited for a sign, a reason her story had been cut short. The others shifted in their seats and faced the same direction. A loud thwack! Then another, and a waterfall of old roof tiles descended in the Southwestern corner outside the living room, where, just an hour before, the others stood smudging and praying. They no longer waited for a sign but jumped up and opened the blinds.

"Holy shit! Look at that mess! How did all those tiles get loose? The workers will sure hear from me tomorrow! What if one of us was still standing under the window or going through the gate?" In a flash, Dylan sprinted through the back door to sort out the damage.

The girls followed Dylan. The hundred-degree temperature rose off the black roofing tiles in waves, which smelled of melted tar and rot. Fortunately, nothing was damaged. Only the back gate had been blocked.

Sophie stood at the window and squinted into the bright white August light. The meaning seemed too obvious. She called everyone back inside. They filed in, grateful for the whir of the air conditioner, and grouped around the map-laden table. They were refreshed by the break, although Dylan still stared out the window with a dour look on his face. Suddenly he stood and closed the blinds, obstructing the view.

"Thank the Goddess! Block that mess! Let's get a grip on what just happened. It's a message from our Guardians in the Upper World: if the Inner Circle dares to block our passage, we will simply find a way around them. Obstacles are illusion. We cannot let our collective enemies hinder our progress." Sophie was firm and her smile indicated she was not afraid.

A round of applause rose from the others.

"Hear, hear, my darling!" Dylan roared.

Softened by Dylan's praise but as determined as ever, she continued her prepared lecture. "Drake Putnam and his entire family, the other nine families and all their henchmen and women, their Witches and accountants and sheriffs, could maintain their prestige and money, with Giles and the secrets buried deep. Ah, glorious riches. That's all Giles was trying to protect, his gold and his land. He worked hard for every coin he ever made, even if most of it came from privateering. I know the Inner Circle will spend a thousand years redeeming themselves to their Maker for every three hundred years spent conjuring; this is the tenfold law—*the powers of three times three plus one.* This is why most responsible magickal workers rest on the Dark Moon; they know of the ancient Law of Ten, Hecate's domain. Sarah always said, *'Retribution is a waste of time, Karma Man always gets her man.'* Life experience tells me Karma is never bored or without work because temptation is so great. Ten times the power! Instant power is great temptation; it's kept the Putnams in business for three hundred and fifteen years!"

Dylan was starting to get antsy. This was his only day off, and he here was listening to another one of Sophie's endless lectures about Karma. "Can you get to the point? I love your stories, but we all know this one. What's the real reason we're here today?"

"Fair enough, Dylan, I'm being long-winded again and we've got a lot of territory to cover today." Sophie speeded up her pace. "Last week, just before the Dark Moon, I was feeling overwhelmed, underqualified, and generally lacking. I turned to Trance Work for clarification and journeyed to the Higher World for direct teaching. In my trance, Eagle came to me. He flew straight for me and swooped so close, I had to move to avoid collision. Eagle called to me—circling three times—and implored me to listen carefully. He said he imprinted his message on my brain. It would sit there until I wrote down every word as spoken. I was instructed to deliver this message to you three today, without revision or abbreviation. Eagle said,

"You must begin your work at Charter Street Cemetery, early Sunday morning, before the crowds gather. Circle the burying grounds in entirety, three times, beginning in the South, counter-clockwise. You must move in this fashion to activate time-travel. Be vigilant; be careful, for you must encompass the entire property before any specific prayers are made.

"This must be done quickly with great focus and control. This action will make Spirit Speak possible. There are many prayers that keep the Spirits locked away in Essex County, unable to escape to Star Nation. This action supersedes these prayers and makes new contact possible. These locks must be broken for your prayers to be heard and acted upon!

"There is a system, a caste system, at all the burial grounds in the Massachusetts Colony. Many Spirits—thousands—have made a pact with the Divine to stay on after death and wait for the New Jerusalem to be built upon this ground. They are making ready for the rise of the Great Teacher once again.

"They will not depart from this land to join the light. They won't allow themselves to be incarnated again, not until their desires and dreams are made manifest. They are resolute to live in the new Earthly paradise!

"The Spirits are organized and well-versed in propriety and protocol. They are dressed in their finest clothes, waiting for your arrival. They are committed to assisting you in the Great Balancing, which, in turn, makes way for their combined dreams to come true. Be careful in your appearance—you will meet many important people this day! Be soft and gracious, even if you are frightened. Make a good impression, smile often in your Work. This must be a heartfelt time."

Dora fidgeted in her straight-backed chair. Eagle's words discomfited her. Sophie knew the words fear, commitment, and testing pushed Dora's buttons.

Dora's leg shaking, tapping, and irregular sighs rubbed off on Poe. Sophie saw the girls' uneasiness and walked to their side. She grabbed Poe's right hand and placed it over Dora's left and held them together.

"That's right, even if you are afraid. Fear is our friend; it is the marker that tells us to be vigilant, to pay attention. It's a sign things are getting *good!*" The girls looked at Sophie, they all smiled, and Dylan joined them with his customary Cheshire grin. She cleared her throat and continued to read Eagle's directive.

"After three revolutions of the burial ground, go to the center of the oldest part

and prepare yourself for the Headman. Lavish John Marston with shortbread cookies of the best order, his favorite. He has been waiting for this sweet treat for many years.

"You will then place red gifts, Honor Bundles, and maple sugar in all four corners of the burial ground, beginning in the East, clock-wise now. Hang bundles with ribbon; make yourselves known without words. Your gifts will speak for you.

"The burial ground will have a fence around two-thirds of the circumference of the property. It is allowable to pass on the outside of the fence for your counter-clockwise revolutions, but be sure to leave the gifts within the actual boundaries of the burial ground. Bury them, tie them, or gently place them on the ground in each corner.

"All the Spirits living here are neither good nor bane; they are just who they are, simple and dedicated to a dream, a dream of freedom, renewal, and salvation. You are here to help them, they are here to help you—you are equal players in this theater of reclaiming.

"You must bring maple sugar and red gifts to all burial grounds you travel to. This is your sign of respect for the living as well as for the dead. They are your Elders, they are your Ancestors. You must travel to many grounds on your journey, at least one ground for each town you travel to, because you will find your assistance, your power, your magick there. They are waiting, they are talking, they are praying, they want peace. They are committed to your success, through the good will of Great Spirit, the Great Redeemer.

"You will be joined by red, white, brown, and black souls. They are your friends and they no longer have sides. Their allegiance is to divinity, to greatness, to peace. Many are tired and need bodies to process and write their stories. Many need rest and reconciliation with family, friends, lovers, and neighbors.

"Your red Sisters and Brothers need your sacrifice to leave a print on the land, which will help to re-form the mountains and water, cleanse their Medicine. You must give your blood to them; leave it on their ground, in the clay. The clay of Essex County is the balm, the matter of life, so dear to all! This substance of Earth, so usable, so strong, is used by all the colors of the People. You must purchase clay pots from this place, made with this sacred Earth, this clay. Keep them with you always as a sign of life-everlasting nourishment, true endurance, and survival.

"Your Sisters and Brothers need to smoke the sacred plants of their Ancestors. You must make smoke with your Sacred Herbs, offer the Herbs to them, the sweet smoke of the lodge. This is their soothing gift, their soul balm.

"Your Sisters and Brothers crave the maple sugar as do all the colors of People

Spirits. This is their sweetness, never lost, just misplaced.

    "We are, you are, they are ONE.

    "Make it so, make it real, dream it, and it will be made manifest on all levels.

    "To all my relations, to all my Sisters and Brothers of all colors, hear me!

    "I call them now!

    "I am Eagle, your Brother, your Father, your Sun.

    "Wear the feathers of your people, be one with all the colors as you fly into your new life!

    "Blessed are the peacemakers, now and always!"

"Wow! Eagle laid it all out for us, didn't he? You read Eagle's statement to me right after he visited, but I didn't feel the charge in his words until today." Dylan stretched and drank the rest of his water.

Nodding her head, Sophie agreed. "We all want clarity. We want to know how we fit in the picture, what our strengths are. I believe we are acutely aware of our shortcomings at this point."

Dora started clearing her throat, pretending to choke. Sophie knew Dora hated feeling singled out, always paranoid about being tested. Dora had entitlement issues that vexed Sophie, who believed everyone had to earn their keep.

"Before we go any further, I would like Dylan to pull a few Tarot cards. When we gather together, energy concentrates and meanings change. The cards will help us focus and make a good comparison to solo readings done earlier." Sophie reached for her mechanical pencil and readied for notes.

Dylan brought in a wooden collapsible table from his office, complete with purple cloth and deck, shuffled and ready. Sophie sprinkled a few grains of fresh Tobacco over each person's head and on the top of the cards.

Right to left, Dylan drew five cards and turned them face up: The Sun, Chariot, Wheel of Fortune, Four of Wands, and Page of Wands. He placed two additional cards on the Page of Wands for clarification: the Three of Swords and the Ace of Swords, to specify outcomes.

Dylan squinted, letting his friends know he was concentrating. Cocking his head to one side, he began, "Spirit says this reading tells of warnings and sign posts to follow. We all know the card meanings, so I'll jump right in there and translate what I'm hearing. A great energy is watching over us and our travels. This is clear with The Sun in the first placement. It is followed by the Chariot, indicating ultimate success if you follow the omens he gives you. Look at the card and the meaning becomes obvious: we must be on the lookout for combinations of black and white. Remember the High Priestess, the Hierophant, and the Chariot. They have both black and white elements, the dual path of Earth and justice: female–male, right–wrong, good–bad. We must pay special attention to pillars, doorways, tombs, symmetrically spaced plantings or sculptures. Wheel of Fortune is next. It says to be aware of where we are walking, be careful."

"Oh! Dylan! Remember what we figured out about the Spirit Animal designations last Tuesday in our journeying?" Poe said, energized at last.

"Yes, the cards indicated to watch for slithery Earth creatures, snakes and Spirit-critters. We determined Snail was our main Spirit Animal on this trip, which fits into this category perfectly.

"Four of Wands: we'll want to party but must steer clear of premature reveling, especially publicly. This will be interpreted as daring and spiteful to our challengers. It also points to watching for air creatures, particularly birds, also all kinds of Prayer Flags, and flags in general. They should mark our path, even when we are unsure. The final outcome is a double-edged sword. It will be successful on all levels, but, with anything life-changing, it will be hard to let go of Salem, the land, the ghosts, and the past. The Ace of Wands says everything will change, quickly, overnight even. We have to stay awake or disappointment and depression, the Three of Swords, will raise its ugly head." The red heart pierced by three blades left no doubt as to the card's meaning.

"Thank you for the reading, Dylan. Would you mind telling the snails in the front garden that they are our friends and convince them not to mow down everything in their path? Their trails are easy to follow, true. It says to me, take a steady pace and don't be afraid to make a mess before moving on. Close, you think? My Totem for this journey is the Phoenix, rising from the ashes, Spirits in flight, the core intention, indeed! Birds, sounds about right!" Sophie checked the list of topics in the blue folder, a good time to take a break. The crows cawed their agreement.

Salem
1692

SALEM VILLAGE,
1692

Rest in Peace
in the
New
Jerusalem
Army
of the
Dead
2007

Chapter Six

CHARTER STREET CEMETERY:
HOLDER OF ANCESTOR MEDICINE
Sunday, September 16, 2007, 9:00 a.m.

THE TRAFFIC WAS CRAZY, SMALL ROADS, two lanes that should be four, four that should be six, whether in the country or the city. And so many cars! Was all of Massachusetts on the road this early on Sunday morning? The group crawled their way into Salem, a sense of collective anxiety growing. Sophie was barking orders silently, trying to prepare, at the same time alert to her surroundings.

The houses changed to newer paint and bright window boxes full of colorful annuals. Salem was close; the tourists were everywhere, surrounding them, actually. The party of four were not tourists—they belonged in their own category. Sophie stroked the coral nugget around her neck, which reminded her to stay strong, to stay in her body, to flow and not be afraid.

Suddenly traffic came to a standstill. Beside them, on the right-hand side of the car, appeared the larger-than-life bronze statue of Roger Conant, Salem's founding father. The street was filled with disembarking tourist buses, long lines, mad waving, and loud whistling. Memories of congested Sunday Summer afternoons in Santa Fe with Dylan filled Sophie's mind. She and Dylan looked at each other and said in unison, "Thank the Goddess we left Santa Fe."

The car was quiet and still, caught in a tourist madhouse. Dora in the back seat cleared her throat and said, "Turn left now, Dylan. I have a way out of this."

Dylan pulled out into the busy intersection. So much of the traffic slowed because their drivers were busy ogling the Witch City attractions. The buzz was concentrated. "Now what, Dora?"

"Stay on this road. Let's keep an eye out for a painted red line. That's our route to Charter Street and lots of other tourist destinations around the trials. Hey, there it is! Okay, look for a place to park. See, there it is! Look up, above the stone wall, there's Charter Street!" Dora was a good navigator. She found the way. She is buried here, Sophie thought, but kept it to herself. One by one, the others took long looks at Dora. She might not profess passion relating to this Work, might not even be a believer, but the flush on her face told a different story. She was glowing in recognition. She'd accessed her place of power—you could smell it on her. She was finally home.

Dylan found a perfect place to park under a huge hawthorn. They emerged from the silver SUV, stunned or shell-shocked, looking confused and a bit too serious for early morning.

Sophie spoke first. "Let's go across the street to the curio shop, it's already open. They'll have a tourist map. Let's get the full scope of the red line business before we begin. I don't want lots of stops and starts. When we get started, we'll build momentum and power and we'll need to keep going, regardless of audience or time of the day." She already sounded tired and the ritual had not even started. She had lots of cheat sheets for the prayers and directions and quickly passed them out.

They were greeted at the front door of the shop by a sweet-faced smile. At first, that's all you saw. "My name is Dorothy, just like in the *Wizard of Oz*," she said. "If there's anything I can do for you, please give me a call." Dorothy started moving away from the group just as Dylan spied the Chamber of Commerce maps of the Red Line Tour of Old Salem. Dorothy accidentally brushed Sophie's shoulder; she was almost a head taller than Sophie. Dorothy stopped cold. "Do I know you?" she said suspiciously to Sophie.

"I don't know. Where have you lived?"

The young woman had a regal bearing. She was tall and buxom, with dyed streaks of white and purple in her hair, which sparkled against her blue-black skin.

"I have lived all over New England, but I was born in Trinidad." Dorothy bit her lip, her agitation growing. It appeared that she had given Sophie too much information—just by the way she answered the question. Sophie knew she had been recognized by Dorothy. She suspected that Rose Desmond, the historian for the Inner Circle, had called Dorothy and told her to keep her eyes open for the group from Oregon. Had Rose circulated Sophie and Dylan's photos all over Old Town, from Roger Conant's statue to the wharf?

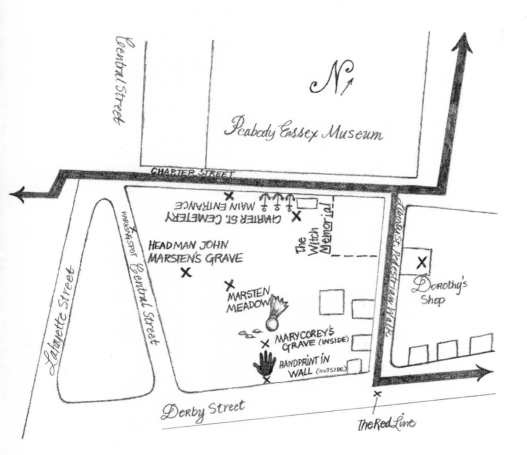

N

Peabody Essex Museum

CHARTER STREET

Central Street

Parking Spot Central Street

Lafayette Street

CHARTER ST. CEMETERY MAIN ENTRANCE

HEADMAN JOHN MARSTEN'S GRAVE

MARSTEN MEADOW

The Witch Memorial

MARY COREY'S GRAVE (INSIDE)

HANDPRINT IN WALL (OUTSIDE)

Hawthorne Pedestrian Walk

Dorothy's Shop

Derby Street

The Red Line

Charter Street Cemetery, Salem

In her mind's eye, Sophie saw a picture taken of Dylan and her at a powwow, she dressed all in lavender and he in green. She felt sure of her vision. Rose had been right about her suspicion: Sophie would end up at Charter Street early on. And Dorothy couldn't wait to shoo the party of four out of the shop so she could start calling the members of the Inner Circle, the Circle she wanted to be a part of so badly. Dorothy had to share the latest news!

Sophie read the woman accurately and directed everyone out into the street, where she shared her suspicions. Now, they knew they were being watched. They had to feed off their tormentor's energy to make this Work successful. They couldn't let themselves slip into a state of fear. They were versed in balancing chaos through using its natural kinetic energy for fuel. Sophie had learned this method of educational vampirism when she did exorcism work in her twenties. She always had a slew of customers—since Santa Fe was a sixteenth-century town with lots of ghosts and ghouls to keep her busy.

Sophie crossed the street and had her second look at Charter Street Cemetery. The fence was as it appeared in the vision when Eagle delivered the ritual in August. Yes, it was the same as Eagle showed her. She unfolded the Chamber of Commerce map and stretched the paper out in the mild breeze. Just as Eagle had said, the whole burial ground could be accessed from the outside of the fence for the entire perimeter. This is the information they needed for the required revolutions.

Sophie located South and began walking. They would begin their walk at the tall stone wall, their first glimpse of the grounds. The pace had been set. The three would begin to shadow Sophie, just a few paces behind, not wanting to anticipate her next move. They gave her space; in turn it gave them peace. They did not have to look at Sophie's focused expression.

Sophie had told Poe long stories about learning to dance in the traditional fashion, before Sophie's Coming Out in the Sacred Circle was complete. Poe had gone along to a powwow with Sophie and Dylan a couple of years ago. Poe was a quarter Cherokee, which warmed Sophie's heart, especially since her friend's family had history with Sophie's family. Poe's family was from Hendersonville, North Carolina, originally, where Rosetta Parham, Sophie's full-blooded Muscogee Great-Great-Grandmother, owned the only trading post in that part of Cherokee Country. Sophie described how dancers had to hold their spines as straight as possible, even ones with crooked spines like Sophie's. Dancers, especially coming in on Grand Entry, breathe long deep breaths, while keeping their faces unsmiling, focused on the beat. Every step is a prayer; every bead on Sophie's Regalia represented a prayer. It was serious, every step weighted. White people always look confused at the first powwow they go to. You could spot the people not coached ahead of time. So many visitors walked around the outer Ceremonial Circle saying, "Why are all the dancers so mean? I wanted to have a good time, to be surrounded by positive people, not these people on downer trips." Poe only wanted to look directly at Sophie if she had to—her face was too scary. Sophie did Giles's mean face very well.

Once everyone gathered under the center of the rock wall, they all quickly reinforced the grounding they had performed during their morning ceremony. Sophie instructed the three to look at the wall for patterns, signs, and omens. She was the first to notice a handprint in the cement patching wash that covered at least a third of the wall. Her right hand fitted perfectly in the handprint. As Sophie slowly pulled away from the stone wall, everyone else took a close look at the print. In it, you could plainly see deformed knuckles, the sign of advanced arthritis. They matched Sophie's hand exactly. The group had their beginning point.

After three deep cleansing breaths, they were ready to begin. They didn't want to be too conspicuous, if possible, so they decided to walk in pairs. They looked like a squad of soldiers marching to battle, matching one another's pace. They were transfixed and ready for anything—so they thought—willing each other to stay calm and in touch with their Core Power. Sophie said the more centered they appeared to the outside world, the more power they had and the less others could hurt them. It was Giles's down-island mean face that would do the trick, only for humans though. Sophie said it brought her enemies to tears, even in the Spirit Realms. However, they had to remember Eagle's instructions to be friendly and accommodating to the Spirits, especially in all burial grounds. Smiles and sugar were their demands.

As they turned the first of four corners, across from Dorothy's shop, Sophie instructed them all to put the mean face on. Dorothy was born in Trinidad. Her mother had worked the mean-look, guaranteed. Once they were wholly around the corner, Sophie told them all to look Dorothy in the eyes—her striking silhouette in the glass was impossible to miss. "Hold your stare," she whispered, almost a hiss. "When you reach the exact point opposite her, look straight ahead as if she doesn't exist. We'll repeat this three times, once for each revolution. By the third revolution, she'll end up being our ally, just watch and see. This is how Dorothy's mother always gets her way. It will work for us now. We need someone to cover our butts while we're in the neighborhood. Since we have so much planned, we'll be around here a lot. I'll buy something before we go for the day to seal the deal. Okay, I'm sorry, no more talking until our revolutions are completed."

They slowed their speed when they walked in front of the Witch Memorial. Sophie began to cry, not changing the expression on her face, but crying nevertheless. The memorial was constructed of loosely fitted rocks, two long lines of them, with twenty rock extensions pointing to the open grassy center. It formed a hard cornered U-shape. It was striking, mainly because of its rough appearance, mimicking the rocks on Gallows Hill, where the sheriff's men made hasty, shallow graves immediately following the hangings. Some bodies were rescued late at night by their family members. Most remains were scattered by treasure seekers and wild animals.

There were other memorials in the area, with smooth stone and bronze plaques, but this was the real deal. Each extension stood for a person who died, one pressed to death, nineteen others hanged. Since the Towne Family Association was having their big annual family reunion and colonial reenactors' gathering this weekend, the memorial had large red and white floral bouquets on Rebecca Nurse's and Mary Easty's grave extensions. Several more—George Jacob's for one, because he was buried on Nurse land—had a single rose, carefully laid. As Sophie walked by, she let the mean face go and smiled, realizing the Family Confederacy was not only close, but they were on the same wave-length. Red and white are the Muscogee colors for peace. This was a good omen!

Just past the memorial was a clapboard building, as ancient as the burial ground. It was used for storage now. Sophie, rounding the second corner, noticed a piece of rusted metal. Instantly she was rushed with recognition, passing three burnt-sienna-colored anchors, the symbol for hope, a symbol with special meaning for Giles. Three anchors and three Corey's: Giles, Martha, and Mary, another good omen.

In the center of the block was the official entrance to Charter Street, complete with a black-and-white colonial-style sign announcing its historical importance. When she saw the sign, Sophie realized she was limping, already suffering from the determined pace. Each revolution was .8 of a mile, hand imprint to hand imprint, not too far for an able-bodied person. She straightened her leaning spine, breathed deeply, and said an enthusiastic

"Blessed Be!" No one seemed to notice. She really didn't care anymore; this band had no reason to hide any longer. They would do what they came to do regardless of audience, as planned. Sophie was used to working a crowd, no worries.

Sacred trees lined the brick-paved pedestrian mall they walked at the edge of, giant oaks, hawthorns, holly, and more, their trunks woven with multicolors of ivy. How many Pagans are horticulturalists? Many. Some had secured regular employment from the towns of Salem and Danvers, obviously. Peabody had more of a hard edge to it, a rural aesthetic, pastoral land, Costco, and truck rental companies. Not much of a Pagan imprint out near Putnam Pantry, the irony of the Inner Circle and Putnam land as a whole. So, were they real Witches? No, not the Inner Circle. They were Witches, of course—that's the job description. But the question Sophie asked herself early on was about the Family Confederacy, the people responsible for ruling this piece of New England: were they Witches, Pagans even? Hardly! They just employed Witches to do their dirty work.   Thoughts rushed fast. Each person kept step with her or his partner in silence, each deep in private wanderings. Sophie speculated that Poe would be wondering about the Tarbells, what kind of people were they now, three hundred years since she had been with any of them. Poe had had several rapid incarnations in New England, back-to-back for almost one hundred and fifty years, all men. Each time she had been a doctor, and he'd been expected to be bigger and better than the rest of the local gentry. The images of Poe's past-life regression sessions filled Sophie's head. Poe fought her inner demons, never measuring up to her own impossibly high standards. Smallpox was much more deadly than the Witch Trials. It had been a constant threat. Entire Indian Nations fell to smallpox; it wasn't just a white problem. Poe had served her community and extended family. Her incarnations had been good men with integrity. But they were devastated by the high mortality rate of the pox and other diseases, always changing, morphing into new threats. They never could forgive themselves, one at a time, for not saving more people. Poe was a lonely man, three times in a row. This was Poe's reality. Sophie felt the oppression of the soil, which still held the memories of Poe's defeats. In the now, she was a therapist specializing in geriatric dementia. She had learned to flow as a caretaker, not taking each passing as a defeat any longer. But her perfectionist nature still persisted.

The party passed their parked vehicle and sighed, as if on command. On a subconscious level, they wanted to jump in and go on a holiday to the sea, just a few blocks away, eat saltwater taffy and feed the gulls popcorn. Tourist activities. Sophie suspected Dora wanted to go shopping. Poe was afraid of ghosts, although she worked with the dead and dying every day. She may not have known what she wanted. Dylan worked on hot electric panels, day in and day out, as a commercial electrician. He had been shocked across his Heart Center twice and lived to tell the tale. Now, on this Sunday morning, all any of them wanted was solace.

Their energy lagged as they turned the fourth corner. Seeing the stone wall ahead of them, they began to pick up their pace. Sophie almost sprinted, going for the handprint just at her height, imprinted on the stone face of the wall. As her hand fell into the print, everyone nodded, smiled, and were reminded what a special mission they were on.

It wasn't their job to free Spirits, not all of them, at least. Balance was Sophie's goal, creating enough calm in the center of a magickal hurricane so she could slip right in under their noses and loosen Giles's bonds enough for him to be released. Then, he could integrate with her, creating a better life for them both. Eventually, they would become one, with shared thoughts, memories, and feelings. In Sophie's next life, she would not have to be a Rememberer and carry twelve thousand years worth of lifetimes around at once. The human brain and body are not designed for that kind of Karmic stress; she wore her memory wounds for all to see, if they bothered to look at her. Few did, especially as her deformities increased with age. Now, in middle age, her life as a monk fitted well with the demands of Spirit.

Sophie had been working on coaxing the dead to the light, doing this psychopomp work for years in Essex County, long distance, safely from her home with the purple fence. Lots of red Sisters and Brothers needed to be shown the way. Because so many people died in such a short period of time, many clans had no one left to sing the Death Song and to dance the Death Dance, to light the ceremonial Tobacco, so they would not wander or get stuck. Fortunately, she had skills and could travel in the Ethers effectively, much of the time. However, when one was working on the Self, up close and personal, in the physical body was where to find the action.

She had completed fifty-five soul retrievals by Mabon 2005, mainly pieces of people's souls, lost in the bowels of the Old Salem jailhouse. Babies too. She worked on at least a half dozen of them. Sarah Good's baby, lost in the gaol, and pieces of Dorcas too went to the light, the pieces brought back to their owners so they could finally heal. So many more people had died from the deplorable conditions. Many lost their health, some confined for over a year in their own filth. So many poxes and plagues, infections and influenza, pneumonia. Tuberculosis from the damp moldy walls, fast growing because of all the cramped quarters and body heat. The conditions took so many, eventually. One hundred and seventy five were jailed at one point. They were thrown into the mess, wallowed a while, and ended up bringing the contagion home with them when they finally bribed their release. Thank the Gods for body heat, though, or they would have frozen to death; some did, anyway. So many lost their health and lived for only five or ten miserable years after their liberation. Poor Dorcas Good, manacled and thrown in the demon domain at only four years of age, was forever damaged. Dylan was starting to remember the gaol. He has always hated the cold—now he knew why.

At the next corner, they repeated their mean faces for Dorothy's benefit. She was waiting for their loop. Some of her Goth-kid spies had passed them and must have called ahead. Sophie felt them circling.

In the middle of the second revolution, Sophie saw a woman hunched in a far corner, leaning against a low wall between the burial grounds and the memorial. She was wrapped in a blanket. Even on a cloudless eighty-degree day, it was cold inside the borders of Charter Street. The woman was surrounded by shopping bags and camping supplies. She was homeless and had chosen Charter Street as her temporary home. How long had she lived there? Sophie and the woman locked eyes. They could hear each other's thoughts. A soft whisper flooded Sophie's mind, exaggerated *t*'s and *s*'s, snake sounds. The woman said to Sophie, "I bet you don't know who I am. I have been coming to you for six months and you don't know me when you finally see me. Wake up, Sophie St. Cloud, remember who I am. We're intertwined. Our destinies did not belong to us. They made me testify against you." The Spirit voice grew louder and more insistent. Then it stopped. Sophie slowed down and peered again at the woman in the corner. When their eyes locked again, Sophie said with a smile, "It's good to see you, Miss Mary. We've been waiting on you too." There were lots of Marys and Marthas in the seventeenth century. Giles was good at names and faces, thank heavens!

The oaks made wonderful shade and invited the lightest of breezes into their leaves, refreshing the walking couples. The hawthorns overhead, leaves starting to golden and fall, rustled their swooshing sound and serenaded them.

The third and final revolution began with Sophie and her handprint. No one was tired or anxious anymore. Their individual energies were large, their collective energy electric. A third time with the mean face and Dorothy came to her door in tears, crying softly. She spoke as the party ignored her. "I'm sorry, ma'am. I'm sorry what they have done to you. I'm sorry I wanted to be like them."

As Sophie neared the memorial, she slowed her pace, turned her head to waiting Dorothy, and tipped her hat, nodded, and smiled. "Everything is forgiven" was the signal. It was accepted and the entire party quietly bowed their heads for silent prayers of relief. This was a wonderful sign!

The last revolution ended where it began, at the handprint. The four, now energized and clear, began to stretch, to drink water, to prepare for the ritual itself. The offerings of loose Tobacco and Sage were doled out to each member. The herb mixture would be used to mark their trail within the bounds of the burial grounds. It would be their protection shield, left on the ground as they walked their continuous revolutions and during many of their Spirit Salutes. Maple sugar granules were next, a sweet Honor Offering for the dead. Sophie would carry the Scottish shortbread cookies herself, for the Headman of Charter Street, John Marston. He controlled the caste system of waiting Spirits not only in Old Salem, but in much of Essex County. Being an alumnus of the sheriff's department, he was privy to the business of many people, living and dead. He and Metacomet, their Red Headman, made this balancing possible.

Sophie had prepared offerings for key characters they would meet in the burial grounds. The offerings were called Spirit Bundles, often used in Native Wedding Ceremonies, taking one ear of red Ceremonial Corn and wrapping a red Honor Bundle made of Tobacco onto the corn with red twine. They were designed to balance the female and male energies, making an efficient, working, noncompetitive whole. Corn was food for the Mother, creating a base for tradition. Tobacco was for the honoring of the Father, and for ease of communication. Together, they made a powerful honoring tool for the dead. She had picked the prettiest ears and used her best red trade cloth for the Honor Bundles. She had wrapped each Spirit Bundle with a hank of red Czech beads, a trade commodity of great power, each bead representing a positive prayer in the recipient's honor.

One last time, Sophie checked her backpack, moving the grave kit to the open bag with the cookie offerings. In it was a miniature trowel, gifted to her by an old Circle member, long gone. She had blessed this trowel atop Celtic sea salt for months, blessing it each Full Moon, filling it with power since Imbolc of last year. Tiny trade cloth Honor Bundles secured the trowel, carefully placed in a red Tobacco tin, red symbolizing sacred blood, the most powerful sacrifice. Everything was red, even a small square of Pendleton fabric, in honor of her Indian Ancestors and Metacomet, which lined the tin. An ancient silver skeleton key was rolled in brain-tanned leather from Shoshone Country, resting next to a penlet blood sampler, complete with a loaded needle to draw blood. Diabetic supplies came in handy when blood sacrifices were needed. She did not relish blood sacrifice, used in only extreme circumstances, a must and direct order from the Spirit Realms for this Essex County Work. She included needle refills and alcohol swabs. She needed to be careful, with all the digging in graveyards. The necessary ingredients were checked off, one at a time; she used her imaginary list. Everyone else had cheat sheets. She felt for her miniature Athame and found it. It fitted perfectly into her right hand, as neat a fit as the stone handprint. Her magickal knife for cutting the Ethers would have to be within inches of her grasp at all times. She was ready.

The tourists were starting to trickle in to Charter Street, happily dressed families in gentle colors, with babies dressed in lace in large strollers, cameras at the ready. A few surly looking teenagers dressed all in black with royal purple accents scuffed at the already patchy ground. One was wearing red and white striped socks, another good sign.

Grass never grew well at Charter Street, at least by the ninth month of the year, one of the prices of a thriving tourist industry trampling the ground on a constant basis. In late April you could find a nice swath of fresh light green grass growing, but it quickly got smashed into the wet ground by the first of May, Beltane, the Goddess's Wedding Day, the holiday for the souls yet to be born. For a serious Witch, Beltane was equally as important as Samhain, the Festival of the Dead, beginning October thirty-first. It was about the completing of cycles, making rebirth possible. Workers of the Old Ways had to take responsibility for their actions all through the year, especially when one was both inviting and expelling, two sides of the same coin. Grave dirt was always in demand for the serious magickal worker. Sophie had a collection of dirt from all over the world, just for circumstances such as this. Charter Street has lots of juice. She would take samples and so would Dora.

One by one, they passed through the main entrance of Charter Street,

Sophie leading the way. Each of them had a pocket filled with the sacred herb mixture and were already marking their trail. The energy was electric within the boundaries of the burial ground. It was obvious that everyone else present scrutinized every move the group made—they were a striking presence, Parrot feathers gleaming and controlled gait. This was a diverse audience, Miss Mary making her presence known by nodding slowly as Sophie passed.

Eagle had instructed them to make three clockwise revolutions within the boundaries of the grounds. Miss Mary was due East; they would begin there. Slowly, single file, they made their way, trying not to step directly on the graves they passed. They followed the wall, then the fence, the backside of a small restaurant serving clam chowder and garlic bread all day—the air was full of the smell. They finally reached their old friend, the inside of the stone wall. Each one touched it and continued to make their way around the inner perimeter. The trees were ancient, some growing from the lower end of the Western side of the grounds, almost a full story below. The trees seemed to levitate the burial grounds as a whole, these ancient giants supporting the entire enclosed area, like pillars of a great temple in disguise. Many of the trees, particularly the oaks, the tree of Fire Protection and virility, had Yoni-looking openings, accessing their cores. Squirrels merrily ran in and out of the openings, traveling underground and surfacing at the bases of other trees. The entire ground was a maze of tunnels dominated by tree roots and foraging animals. Sophie decided the four Honor Bundles they were instructed to hang in each Cardinal Direction would be tied to trees like these, Journey Trees. When in serious need of power from an outside source in the future, each of them could Shamanically journey from any of these *portal* giants. The revolutions were made, carefully watching their steps and paying close attention to signs and omens.

The Spirit energy was dense, like walking in cold fog. Look high into the trees, thought Sophie. See the line where the protoplasm cloud separates, letting the sun filter to the ground below. Yes, there, the Spirits were thick. She could feel a gathering, a movement of coldish energy amassing in the center of the burial ground, known as Marston's Meadow. It was time to greet the Headman, John Marston himself. Sophie puffed up, straightened her black and white Celtic scarf and tugged her feather-laden hat to its special tilt. She moved forward to the center of the meadow. She found the shortbread cookies quickly, found North, and began to lay four whole cookies at the Cardinal Directions. In the center of the Circle, she began crumbling the cookies, making them easier to absorb into the ground as the tourists walked over them. Crows would eat the rest around dusk. Once the last cookie was crumbled, the mild breeze that had refreshed them all morning suddenly gusted, showering golden leaves throughout the burial grounds and lightening the dense energy. One could almost hear a gentle giggle and feel a reassuring hand in the Ethers.

They went in search of two graves. John Marston, the Headman, was first. His marker was low—carved from dark stone—looking different from the rest surrounding his stone. Close to the Western wall, thick with trees, John made his home. The Western Gate of the Dead was his portal to the surrounding areas that he governed, sternly yet compassionately. He had thousands to deal with, as did Metacomet. Sophie brushed clean the top of Marston's grave, using a rainbow glove she had brought for this purpose. She then sprinkled Celtic sea salt on the stone itself, spiritually cleansing it. By this time, people had noticed the staged revering of the stone set apart from the others. Slowly, the tourists, with their cameras put away, formed a large Circle around the gravestone. It was subconscious, people not realizing what they were doing. They were feeding Sophie with the energy fuel she needed to ingratiate such an important ally. They kept their distance and never got in the way of the party of four.

Sophie dug deep into the open Trader Joe's plastic shopping bag, decorated with a clipper ship superimposed on a treasure map. Giles had picked it out. On the bottom of the bag was a large package wrapped in red cotton cloth. She carefully unrolled it and exposed the eleven finely crafted Spirit Bundles resting in the center of the cloth. They gleamed with red translucent beads. Two special bundles were directly in the center, the ears of corns larger than the rest. She chose one with the brightest red beads and placed it gently in the center of the cleaned stone. Sophie rewrapped the loose package and returned it to its place.

She continued to offer gifts to the Headman, the maple sugar gathered the Winter before in Oregon for this special adventure, loose Tobacco and Sage to help with his prayer work. She reached deep into her Medicine Bag and fished out a golden heart, which she buried deep into the cleared soil. Dora reached into her raincoat pocket and brought out a handful of rainbow chocolate-covered sunflower nuts and threw them over the freshly decorated grave. Marston's honoring was complete. Still one more specific grave to visit. They each bowed, one at a time, in front of the stone. Many others in the surrounding Circle followed suit. This audience was special.

They turned toward the Southeast and followed a direct line to Mary Corey's grave. This was Dora's time. As Dora stood at Mary's grave, emotionally paralyzed, Sophie began clearing the debris from the gravestone. She continued the ceremony she performed for John Marston, having a long talk with Mary while she worked. Sophie explained about Dora. She was Mary, three hundred and fifteen years in the future. Mary was not confused and her energy and mood shifted, suddenly curious about her alter-ego. Sophie thanked Mary for the years of friendship and all the backbreaking work on the land in Peabody. Mary appreciated the praise and thanksgiving. It had been a long time since she felt appreciated. Dora seemed to straighten her spine, hearing the conversation in the time warp. This was Sophie's signal to leave Dora alone for a while, to let her feel Mary, feel the similarity, their oneness.

Sophie backed away from Mary's grave, just as Dora hit the ground on her knees, before the gravestone. She was reaching for something, finally resting her fingers lightly on the letters of the stone.

Mary Corey

Wife of Giles Corey

Aged 63 years

Died August, 1684

The others fanned out behind Dora, protecting her from tourist attention. They gave her space to feel and connect with Mary's essence. Small sniffles were heard coming from Dora's direction. Sophie was grateful, hoping Dora had been touched by the experience. Dora rose slowly and brushed loose dirt and grass clippings from her raincoat. She straightened, secured her bag over her shoulder, and began walking to the center of the cemetery.

The group of four finished the ritual given them by Eagle. Each time they hung a red bundle in a tree, four in all, the wind would pick up and cool the entire ground, showering golden leaves from the hawthorns, the Protector of Witches. They were being heard and it felt good being this close to completion of the Opening Ritual. After tying the last bundle to a Journey Tree, Sophie made a Spirit Salute, faced North, and knelt on one knee. She took the penlet from the grave kit, cocked it, and struck her right index finger. She pumped the puncture a couple of times, enticing blood to flow. Slowly, it pooled on the ground in the Northwest corner of the burying ground. She blotted the wound with a fresh tissue, bowed her head in silent prayer, and announced the ritual complete.

The others instantly went their separate ways. Pictures were taken and gravestones inspected. They left bits of Sage as they walked.

Later, as Sophie was clearing up the traces of the ritual performed, she noticed Dora was waiting in Marston's Meadow. Passing Mary's grave, Sophie noticed Dora's offerings: more rainbow sunflower nuts, M&Ms, a crust of bread, a Werther's candy, and a long wet line in the center of the stone, marking where she poured her bottle of water. Dora had come full Circle now.

It was time to go. They still had several places to reach before nightfall. They had two stops before finding the car. The first was to introduce the group to Miss Mary. As they walked in her direction, Mary stood up, stretched, and found a different place to sit, beaming from every pore in her body. She shed the blanket, straightened her clothes, and prepared to shake hands. No one claimed Miss Mary's hand. Instead, Sophie, with Dylan on her left side and the girls on her right, handed the waiting woman one of the special Spirit Bundles.

"Thank you, Giles. I needed something to help me communicate with the Spirits. It's getting cold at night and they don't like to talk to me when they could be visiting the library or the café across the grounds. They're always cold, you know, though they do lots of exercising. Their boss has his workers building things and carrying heavy loads all the time. What are they building? The boss said I had to leave them before Halloween because I would be lonely all by myself out in the cold," Miss Mary said.

"If things go as I plan, Miss Mary, you'll have a permanent home by Halloween." Sophie smiled.

"They said you would promise me something like that. I am counting on it! I don't want to have the dreams of being tied to the chair anymore. You know about the lake. I showed you two months ago." Miss Mary was gliding down to the blanket-covered ground again, sounding exhausted by the exchange.

"Don't worry, Mary, we're working on a solution to your problem. Just stay healthy and you will be fine. Is that the only blanket you have?"

"No, Giles, I have two, one for the ground, and one for me. I'll be fine till Halloween."

"We'll see you in a couple of days, Mary. Stay strong and be sure to help our friend, Mr. Marston, will you?" Sophie ended their conversation and began walking across the street. Dora reached out and hugged Miss Mary, one Mary to another.

They walked across the street, making haste for Dorothy's shop, now filled to the rafters with tourists, lined up to go on a special ghost tour. This was the place for it! Dorothy didn't see them walk in. Sophie went over to a display of Witch City shot glasses. How perfect for Giles's Memorial Toast on the nineteenth! She would get one for each Direction. She stacked five glasses into each other, making a tidy pile. Dylan had a stack of post cards and some books on local history he knew Sophie would love. The girls had their hands full of cards and trinkets too.

After they all paid for their treasures, Dorothy came over and escorted the party out. Dorothy hugged Sophie, almost picking the older woman off the ground because she was so much taller. Sophie gave the woman her private cell phone number and said if she saw anything unusual in the next couple of days, be sure to call right away. Dorothy agreed and shook Dylan's hand to finish the deal. They would cover each other's backs in a world filled with silence and subterfuge.

"Who cares for Miss Mary, the woman who lives at Charter Street?" Sophie asked Dorothy.

"Oh, is that her name? I always thought she looked like a Mary. The girls who work here with me make sure she has something hot to drink every morning. We give her the daily paper and leave sandwiches for her on occasion. She gets lots of exercise, walks all over town and talks to herself about being tied to some old chair. Nobody understands what she's trying to say, but they are kind to her, if she doesn't make a pest of herself. Most of the homeless people around here live in shelters. It's illegal to stay in the burial grounds in Massachusetts, but everybody lets her get away with it. I'll be sure to keep a closer eye on her and tell everybody her name," Dorothy reassured Sophie.

They all hugged and one by one filed into the bright September sunshine.

Salem
1692

N

W

E

Chapter Seven

HOWARD STREET CEMETERY:
A MEETING WITH AN OLD FRIEND

September 16, 2007, noon

THE SUV WAS A SIGHT FOR SORE EYES. If Sarah had been there, she would have dubbed the car Silver Streak, silver being the only color of car she would have. The sliding door came open, cooling everything off, the breeze salty and invigorating.

Dylan took the reins and put the other three in their respective seats, like a dad buckling in his princesses. Once everyone was comfortable, with fresh water cool in their hands, he began doling out lunch. The main course was salt bagels from Bagel World, receiving a genuine round of applause, closely followed by slices of brie and apple. Dessert was toffee almonds. He had had fun at Trader Joe's while Sophie was showering early this morning. That's what he did for relaxation, shopped for necessities. This would become his routine, gathering supplies and doling them out all through the trip, just as he had done for decades, gathering for Sabbats and making sure Sophie was happy with his found treasures. She was jubilant today.

Dylan often felt out of sorts when Sophie was at the helm. Not always. He was used to countless years of ceremonies and having to pitch-hit for Sophie, doing just about anything, from cleaning broken glass to being second in command. Eleven years ago, Dylan found Reiki. It had been another one of Sophie's ideas to empower Dylan, grooming him for independence. She knew, sooner rather than later, a man had to have his own thing, something he could command respect with and use as a tool for barter. Dylan took to it and soared higher than he dreamed possible, for about five years.

He had been shaky since Sophie asked for a separation. He was devastated at first but had felt the physical estrangement coming on for years.

Sophie needed to be by herself, an independent force within a family. She wanted to live like a monk and not deal with sex, suitors, girlfriends, or boy-friends—she had had it with the lot, including Dylan. Even the freedom of an open relationship didn't work anymore for Sophie. She wanted autonomy.

She was selfish to keep Dylan in a legal relationship—she knew it—she would have to pay a Karmic price for it someday. But she didn't want to let go, not all the way. He had relationships. The less she knew the better, at this stage of the game. What bothered her was to compete for time. Sundays in the garden, Sabbat meals and prayers, the feeling of belonging; she still wanted her family to be together. The truth was she loved Dylan, more today than ever. She wanted to be with him and to be separate at the same time. Now through the twenty-third, Dylan would continue to be her Martha, dutiful, brave, and amazingly strong-willed.

Sophie had been thinking of Captain Thomas Gardner for about an hour. No big surprise about the time: Giles was tried for the third time on September sixteenth, from nine a.m. to noon. The same timing was used for his execution. Thomas Gardner was Giles's close companion. They found mutual solace in rum and memories. They shared a love of poetry and Eng-lish love ballads, their tongues wagging with words for hours. The Captain walked through Sophie's mind each time she got close to Miss Mary. To honor him and find out what he was feeling, Sophie asked Dylan to drive to the opposite end of the brick mall. She had to make an unexpected stop at Howard Street Cemetery, the supposed site of Giles's haunting apparition. This was the planned location for the Integration Walk on Friday evening. But Thomas couldn't wait. He kept knocking on the inside of Sophie's head and it was getting annoying.

Rounding the Southern corner of the cemetery, driving onto Howard Street, they became aware of thousands of birds, pigeons and crows. The pi-geons moved wildly in swooping circles, above what seemed like overturned gravestones, the head markers, worn down to shards after centuries. Circle upon circle of birds made their frantic spirals, perhaps twenty lines of them in tight formation. On all the fence posts, lining the back of the boarded-up Old Salem jailhouse, the crows, glistening black in the noon sunshine, acted as security for the circling pigeons.

"I'm here, Sophie, at the center of the burial grounds, away from the first group of pigeons," whispered Thomas. Sophie knew she had to fend for herself among the thousands of birds, because Thomas expected a private audience. She followed his directions, birds fanning out on the ground, away from her, as she walked. The birds did not want to be interrupted. They had no desire to leave their repetitive dance. As Sophie approached, they simply walked away from her and began circling another grave.

In the center of the burial ground, Sophie made a Medicine Wheel with the sacred herb mixture, cleansing the area, making it possible to stand there unmolested by birds, ghosts, or humans. A fallen hawthorn, broken in half, marked Thomas's spot.

Howard Street differed greatly from Charter Street, the ground ransacked for bits and pieces of stone, relics smashed for souvenirs. Long forgotten by everyone but the freaks looking for ghouls and Giles's lit lantern, Howard Street was where you came to hear the closeness of catastrophe and taste the bitterness of betrayal.

Suddenly, the air was thick. It made a sound like a howling sea gale, the air rich with salt. Leaves, torn bits of paper and dirt swirled in tight spinning circles, like miniature tornados. The ground was electric, hot and cold at once. Sophie began a one-way dialogue with Thomas, coaxing him out, asking him questions. He found himself shy. Someone was finally responding to his demands for the first time in centuries. Giles missed Thomas. Giles was so set in his routines he was unwilling to walk a few feet to say hello to an old friend, if it hinted at interrupting the flow of his haunting. Giles was on a mission here. People had spied him sporting his bright lantern many times, but just when the Moon was full or if the Inner Circle was tampering or binding, on schedule or off. Sophie's most treasured line with her clients was, "Walk it off!" That's what Giles was doing on Howard Street, year after year, walking it off. Captain Thomas would meet him there, on Fridays. This was Giles's favorite time for walking for an audience, it was his most agitated day, always the Friday of his final trial, three days before his pressing. Giles would never be persuaded to abandon his walking, even for his oldest and dearest friend. Thomas was making Sophie wait, to even the score, his way of telling Sophie he accepted her as Giles.

She cleared her throat. She was parched because of all the dust and dirt kicked up by thousands of birds, now encircling her at a modest distance. She reached into her bag and retrieved one of the remaining special bead-wrapped bundles. She laid it carefully in the center of the herb Medicine Wheel created earlier. Immediately the air gusted around her, spinning dirt around her violently for the count of three. On three, the elms and yews on one side of the Western fence started to sway and swoosh, whispering, "Thank you, Giles. It's been a long time, my friend. I will join you this coming Friday, here, at the appointed time."

Sophie threw a small handful of maple sugar to the Cardinal Directions and said aloud, "It was nice spending time with you, Thomas. I have heard your prayers and pleading. I left you a token as an Honor Gift, thanking you for your energy and fraternity. Our friendship has endured three hundred and fifteen years. I honor you today. Until Friday, my friend." She began walking back to the silver car, not wanting to turn her back on Thomas. She never wanted to ignore her loved ones again, regardless of how needy they were, whether Thomas, Martha, Dylan, or Ali. They were all there for her then, and they were here for her now. Sophie cried gentle tears that dried before reaching the passenger door.

The birds never stopped their manic dance.

Chapter Eight

BROADSTREET CEMETERY: A LESSON IN LOYALTY
September 16, 2007, 2:00 p.m.

EMOTIONALLY, IT FELT IMPOSSIBLE, the events of the day, passing so quickly. Their bodies felt as if they had been working hard labor for days, every encounter concentrated and intense. How are the living feeling in Essex County today? Their realities have shifted whether they consciously realize it or not. The dead have been praying for this for generations; they are not surprised, although some feel a bit dispossessed, not sure what to believe. Was this the New Jerusalem or not?

Hundreds of the waiting Army of the Dead, thousands strong, have been activated today. Energy has lit Massachusetts, like Facebook on a Saturday night. But did the living feel it, other than the exhausted Oregonians? The Inner Circle was nipping at their heels, clear to see because of the drama with Dorothy. This day was one day but it was a week long in emotional pyrotechnics.

The air felt close, even in the relative cool safety of the SUV. A convenient parking spot was waiting near Broadstreet Cemetery, one of only two. Their luck was good today. They tumbled out, not carrying much. This would be a quick stop. A general meet and greet, leave a few gifts, and off they'd go for another round down the road. Today was a day of cordial introductions, of intentions made clear. No one expected anything big. They continued to be surprised but did not dare voice their feelings. It was too soon for being entirely forthright, although Sophie did not share that sentiment. Sophie wanted to know everyone's feelings and impressions, as long as they kept them to prescribed times, during breaks or meals. This was a time of corporeal quiet, so the voices of Spirit, the animal kingdoms, and the green worlds could be heard and warnings understood. The group even attempted walking quietly, hard to do for most white people.

The grounds had been brutally tortured for years. Headstones smashed, not for souvenirs, but for the sake of vandalism. The party of four felt sad. This was considered a tourist mecca, this Old Salem/Danvers area. The dead were endlessly more popular than the living, so why was there so little care given to the burial grounds outside the red line? They rounded the block, preparing for the threshold step. The giant oak marking the gateway began to tremble, a wind rushing through it at a good clip. Then it began, the squawk of Parrot. Smiles broke out on all their faces, as they said in unison, "Thank you, Spirit, we hear you!" Each of them made a Spirit Salute, signaling the direction North, a traditional call to the Great Mother. Dylan was the last to enter the burial grounds. As he did, they formed a Circle, feeling comfortable, alone here, only the squirrels as company. Parrot began squawking again. Sophie, hoping for a new feather, looked up.

Sophie would count thirteen slowly voiced *om*s. She began chanting, directing all to join in. They would continue softly, as long as they continued to be alone. On the first exhale, the wind blew through the grounds, knocking Sophie's sunhat off and sending a whirlwind of dirt flying around the group in a neat, sandy Circle. Then, the dogs: ten, twenty, maybe thirty dogs, all hounds, began barking. Obviously, the hounds were being fed, the sound of competition impossible to miss. Then the howling began—led by one dog and joined by the boisterous rest, filling the grounds—sending squirrels flying and stray cats running for shelter. The howling lasted almost two minutes, unabated.

The meaning was clear. The party's introductions had been heard. Their gifts would be accepted. Dog, the symbol of loyalty, humans' best friend: this was a treasured omen. The howling lasted two minutes, two, the number of cooperation, of shared power and intention, of Spirit Bargains. The Spirits were united in a human-Spirit endeavor. They were loyal to John Marston and his Army of the Dead and consequently were loyal and supportive to the party. This was a sign the group had been waiting for, a green light of energy: all clear to move forward!

They spied a lone tree, a giant, in the center of the ground. Elevated by several steps, now chipped and chiseled into dust, the tree dominated the only hill on the grounds. Sophie climbed the rugged steps, clinging to low branches, trying to keep her balance. In the center of the hawthorn's divided trunk, the Journey Tree displayed her Yoni portal. Sophie tied one of thirty-three prepared bundles on the closest branch to the opening. Thirty-three is the number of the healer, the transformative power of love. Each member, in turn of eldership, placed an offering in the Journey Tree. The low yew trees, the tree of death, in their closely trimmed rows, one row on each side of the giant hawthorn, rattled from the bottom of their parched lower limbs to the fuller miniature evergreen tops, covered by tiny salmon-colored berries. The yews made the distinct sound of a corn rattle, used by First Nations people coast to coast. The corn, bluer the closer one goes to New Mexico, hits its outer gourd shell and creates a sharp sheeeesh sound, electric, making the hearer feel the song in her marrow. The rattle is the Shamanic tool for Ether, the Spirit Realms. The sheeeesh-sheeeeesh-sheeeeeeesh sounds repeated, over and over, as the wind howled through the burial ground. They felt grounded and supported, prepared to take the next step.

Chapter Nine

THE NURSE BURIAL GROUNDS: THE ROOTS OF TIME
September 16, 2007, 4:00 p.m.

THEY TRAVELED IN SILENCE, digesting the events of Broadstreet, feeling acutely aware of the next stop, closer to the Inner Circle with every block traveled.

The scenery changed dramatically as they drove over the invisible line dividing Salem from Danvers, the *forgotten* Salem. The houses were smarter, more manicured, less dramatic and touristy. The people who made Danvers home didn't want to think about the Witch Trials or zealot Puritans and their greedy ways. They were undercover, every inch of this place tainted with the distrust of hundreds of years, rubbing off on its citizens daily, hiding behind beige lace curtains and colonial stars and manicured lawns sporting badminton nets and doughboy pools.

Dora was concentrating on the local driving maps, starting to chew the sides of her nails. "Dylan, you'll need to take the left turn at the crossroads, up ahead. Keep going for a quarter of a mile. That will take us to the back of the Nurse Burial Grounds."

Sophie was studying the Google Earth copies of the burial ground featuring its stone monument honoring Rebecca Nurse. "This road will take us closer to the burial grounds than the main entrance of the Nurse Homestead will. Besides, the Townes are still at it at the Big House, with reenactors offering their muskets and sound effects, just for sport, you know." Sophie was being sarcastic, but it was a cover. This stop made her nervous, the reason for all the bravado. "Okay, Dylan, let's start looking for a place to park, here on the main road. I don't want to draw any more attention to us than needed." Just as she said it, everyone noticed a no parking sign, for both sides of the street. There was a sharp right turn, which Dylan took. The road opened into what looked like an aggregate-covered cul de sac, with lots of parking places. It was not posted, so Dylan parked.

The party immediately started shifting in their seats, putting on extra Medicine and feathers as protection and for clarity. They stood in the West and looked into the East and saw all the shades of green, unbelievable this time of year. Where were the amber fields of waving grains? The colors of September were nowhere in sight. What kind of fertilizers do they use? The thought was scary. If you squinted, you could see the outline of the stone monument, in the center of the grassy thigh-high meadow—tick country. On the Western side of the burial grounds was a windbreak line of ancient oaks, probably planted in colonial times. The shadows between the Western row of trees and the monument were long, wide, and cold. They could feel the temperature dropping by the second. They rolled down their pants against deer tick attack, sprayed a coating of bug spray on the tops of their shoes, zipped their jackets, adjusted their hats and backpacks. All nodded they were ready and Sophie took the first step into the meadow.

"You can't park there! This is private property! You are trespassing on land you have no business being on," cried a woman standing on a porch overlooking the meadow.

Dylan took over. He could turn on his charm and soft voice when he needed something. He liked to think he knew what women wanted to hear. "The area is not posted. We are sorry to inconvenience you by our unwarranted intrusion." By the time *intrusion* flowed from his mouth, he was face to face with the woman, a step below her on the porch, Family Confederacy land. He continued, "We have come many miles to pay our respects to Rebecca Nurse's grave and memorial. May we ask you a huge favor and take this parking space for just half an hour? We promise not to disturb you or your family and not leave a mess behind. Is this acceptable to you?" Dylan ended with his full smile, charming down to the last tooth.

"Well, I guess it will be all right, but just for half an hour. We are expecting lots of family over after the closing ceremony ends at the homestead, scheduled soon. Since you are here in Rebecca Nurse's honor, I think it would be fine to leave your respects." She smiled broadly and winked almost imperceptibly in Dylan's direction. He was delighted.

"Let's go, ladies. After you!" Dylan ushered the women into the tall green grass.

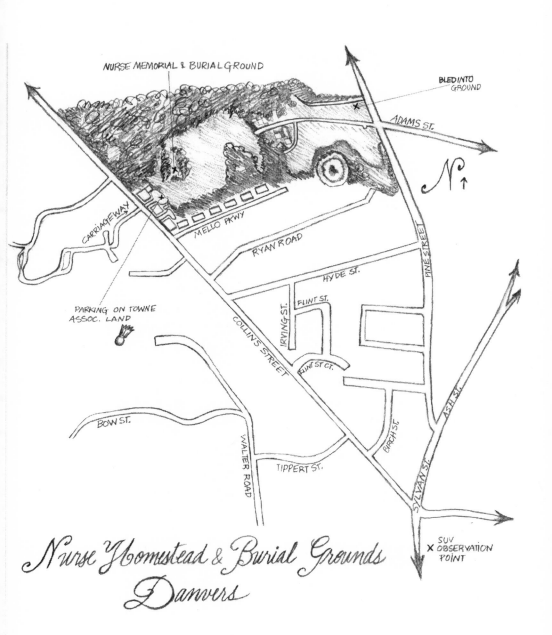

NURSE MEMORIAL & BURIAL GROUND

BLED INTO GROUND

ADAMS ST.

N ↑

CARRIAGEWAY

MELLO PKWY

RYAN ROAD

HYDE ST.

PINE STREET

PARKING ON TOWNE ASSOC. LAND

FLINT ST.

IRVING ST.

COLLINS STREET

FLINT ST CT.

BOW ST.

WALTER ROAD

BIRCH ST.

ASH ST.

SYLVAN ST.

TIPPERT ST.

SUV X OBSERVATION POINT

Nurse Homestead & Burial Grounds
Danvers

It felt like walking through deep snow, and almost as cold. They were shivering. By the time they reached the first shadow line of the tree row, diaphanous protoplasm was rising from the ground and filled the area with mist. Dylan looked back over his shoulder, looking for the woman on the porch. Did she see this? Sophie followed her gaze. In the window seat the woman was smiling and slowly nodding. In her hand, a silver glint of light—a cellphone?

"Shush. I hear something." Sophie froze. She closed her eyes and strained to hear. Telephones began ringing: one, two, and finally three. She staggered slightly and opened her eyes. "Y'all go on up ahead and stay to the Western hedgerow. I'll meet up with you in a few moments. I don't want to lose my connection. Go. Please."

She walked a few paces to the West toward the woman's house and stopped under a brush oak. Three deep breaths and the telephones rang again. She twisted her head like a wire hanger antenna. A woman with a familiar voice was telling a story.

"Remember? The family had to draw lots each Spring, figuring out which one would run the tractor in the meadow. The grass grew so fast and thick, a riding lawn mower wouldn't work. The Towne Association gardener refused to work on this end of the homestead property. Everybody could feel the ghosts and no one wanted any part of it, except for those four crazy tourists.

"Yes, yes, as I said earlier, the party has a male leader with a long sandy ponytail and blue eyes and travels with three women. Be sure to let Drake know about the visitors, will you? I'll see you tomorrow at the reunion dinner. Yes, thanks."

The telephone line went dead. Three deep breaths and her regular hum of mental static resumed. She was grateful for the information.

On a small rise the grass thinned slightly and was freshly mowed. Sophie came to a stop and unpacked her large open Trader Joe's bag. They surrounded her, giving her little breathing room, curious about what she found. "Look down and around you. Notice the tree roots. Follow them with your eyes, they make patterns."

Poe was the first to decipher the pattern. "Oh my God, it's a border that leads all the way to the monument. It's a long line of *M*s and *W*s. That's our sign—it's Mary Warren. We are in the right place!"

Sophie nodded her head in agreement while Dylan and Dora, open-mouthed, began to walk the line of letters. They discovered it wasn't a straight line to the monument—it was a T-shape. The top of the T formed the Western Gate of the Dead. The vertical trunk of the T formed an East-West line, connecting the upper property with the burial grounds. In many areas, the tree roots were visible, the roots still actively growing without the benefit of trunk and green. There were no trees growing on the East-West line to form such growths. Perhaps there had been a windbreak line here, once upon a time, although it seemed to go against the natural lay of the land.

The Death Portal was what legends are made of, talked about in Grimoires, alchemical diaries of magickal spells and recipes from the Middle Ages, illustrated with treasure maps and symbols. Sophie began lighting Cedar incense and handing the sticks to Dylan for the others to carry. She took a healthy handful of loose Cedar, the sacred herb of the West, and made the Blessing Sign as she slowly walked on the Eastern side of the root line. She spoke silent Spirit Salutations and spoke directly to Rebecca Nurse and asked her permission to be here, to do the Work on this ground. Sophie felt a deep chill run through her, the entire length of her spine, ending its journey in the pit of her stomach. This did not feel good and was not the permission for which she petitioned Rebecca. Sophie was not surprised, though. People new to the study of the Witch Trials tend to see Rebecca Nurse as a saint, a sweet old lady, infirm and put to her bed for her last days, a grandma.

Rebecca Nurse had never approved of Giles in real time. She was not shy about showing her feelings and rallied similar support from her sister, Mary Easty. She felt Giles was a hard-talking, heavy-handed, rum-drinking privateer who knew too many secrets, particularly about her fast-growing brood famous for their womanly beauty. Rebecca did not approve of Giles and hated the sight of Martha, just for sharing his bed. Sophie was not taken back by the reception.

When Sophie completed marking the Western Gate with sacred herbs, she gathered the three together and formed a close Circle in front of the monument, over Rebecca Nurse's grave. "We are not welcomed here. They are not part of John Marston's Army of the Dead. They don't like me, and they don't want us messing around in their private business. Poor George Jacobs is caught between parties, not wanting to rock the boat with the Confederacy. He was the one who wanted to go to the light, not the others."

The Western Gate of the Dead was opened enough for a steady stream of cool protoplasm to shadow and chill the group, regardless of sacred herbs used.

"I will make special arrangements to meet with George Jacobs later, if this is truly what he wants." Sophie continued. "Other than that, we need to leave this place, leave our bundles, three in all. I'll bury one, on the North side of Rebecca's monument, not too close to her grave. Then we'll tie two bundles in the line of oaks, one to the South and one to the North, delineating the Door of the Dead. Now, let's get on it. Dylan, you take this bundle and tie it as high as you can in the South. You, Poe, take this bundle and tie it high in the North. Dora, you come with me. Let's make haste and leave this place. No reason to come back, unless George wants our help. With the Honor Bundles placed strategically, George and perhaps others can find their own way to the light, if it is desired."

The woman waved as Dylan started the car. He returned her gesture, complete with a smile and finished with a salute. They were off to the main road, away from the monument and its angry cold ghosts. Before getting to the crossroads, the border point of the Nurse Homestead property, they saw a long line of cars, all with their left-hand blinkers on. Dylan pulled over on the shoulder, just South and East of the intersection, under a stand of low growing bushes. He wanted to study the cars. Sure enough, each of the cars turning took another right-hand turn into the cul de sac the party had just come from. The timing was too close for Sophie's comfort. It was an adrenaline rush for the rest.

Chapter Ten

WADSWORTH CEMETERY: PUTNAM SPIES NEVER REST
September 16, 2007, 5:00 p.m.

DYLAN WAITED FOR THE LAST CAR to turn into the cul de sac, then he turned onto the right fork of the crossroads, driving the SUV directly to the front gates of the Nurse Homestead property. This is where many tourists come, the place where the famous PBS movie about the Witch Trials was shot, sometime in the 1980s. Hollywood came in and moved treasured artifacts from other sites. They recreated the Parris house and the meetinghouse and lots of outbuildings, which doubled as craftsmen's workshops and houses.

The original Nurse Homestead had been restored, lovingly, board by board. It now was painted a brownish barn red, sharp, clean, and just re-newed for the Towne Association's yearly shindig. Sophie would have to bleed into this ground by the next Sunday. She thought she was all ready for this adventure to end, call it a success, and go on holiday for a week. If only…

A few cars from the distant lot started their engines and began driving in their direction. It was time to pull a U-ey and find Wadsworth, only a couple miles away. Dylan peeled out, sending a cloud of dust high, engulfing the oncoming cars with their dirty wake, an unfortunate and unintentional display that seemed to the other drivers like a testosterone flag to pursue.

Driving down pleasant suburban streets, weaving through congested family areas filled with bicycles and jogging strollers, the group continued their quiet countdown, for the last stop of the day. They were headed to the heart of Putnam country, where Sophie was told by Spirit there were many Spirits of like mind, ready to help. Even though they did not share direct allegiance with John Marston, they did want to join the light, eventually. They wanted peace and the return of harmony, at the very least.

There were no handy parking places, not even a friendly shoulder of the road. Dylan was bold and pulled directly onto burial ground property. The grounds were not posted, other than a large, well-kept colonial sign painted in shades of forest green and gold: ~W~ Wadsworth Cemetery. As soon as they started opening doors and making their way out of the vehicle, dogs began barking, not like the hounds at Broadstreet, but watch dogs, attack dogs. Dogs symbolize loyalty, yes, safety obviously—but protection for the Family Confederacy, not for the Oregonians. These dogs were Putnam agents of intimidation, meant to scare Sophie and her compadres, to shake them, to keep them away from their cherished secrets.

During Sophie's research about Wadsworth, she had found a record of a "Dora Smith," her Dora Smith's namesake, buried here. This seemed like a good sign at the time, but after the Nurse Burial Grounds and the instantly strange reception here, she was not sure. Sophie found it suddenly odd: Dora's last name was Smith and Poe's last name was Jones. She had never seen the pattern before—the girls had disguises of their own.

They all acted ill at ease. "Let's leave a bundle, tied to a tree, a Journey Tree, if we can find one. These trees look new to the grounds, all young; there might not be one old enough to support a bundle. We'll see. After, we'll find Dora Smith's grave and call it a day. Dora, if you would like to say the prayers and give the salutes at Dora's grave, that would be wonderful and fitting." Poe and Dylan nodded.

They formed a Circle, but they didn't have the natural shelter and privacy that Broadstreet offered. On the first exhale of the first *om*, the dogs began baying again. The sounds of doors opening and closing hard, of slamming windows, filled the grounds. When Sophie noticed one woman and two men, in their middle thirties, lined in a row, all on cell phones, she knew it was time to go. They had finally found a beautiful burial ground, a proper cemetery, with green grass, manicured graves, and lots of flowers, each inch of this ground loved and cared for for generations, for centuries on Putnam ground, and they were being forced to leave it.

Dylan walked over to the highest branch he could find and tied an Honor Bundle to it, its long red ribbons blowing in the now steady breeze. Next to the tree was a sunken area, the size of a grave. It wasn't marked, not even by a plant or a pebble. Dylan waved to Dora, instructing her to join him. She nodded and started tossing M&Ms and sunflower nuts into the sunken crater. Sophie and Poe were already in the car waiting. Sophie felt agitated and called for them to pick up the pace. Dylan made haste and pulled onto the rural suburban road, tree-lined and quiet. Half a mile up the road, two Salem Sheriff's Department vehicles passed them going the other way at a healthy clip, with lights on. Today was a narrow escape, but from what, they weren't sure. This was just the meet-and-greet portion of the trip. The lines were beginning to blur.

They made their way to their lodging in Peabody, so ready for rice and calm. Sleep was needed. Poe would write in her diary, Sophie would eat oatmeal, Dylan would look for Sci-fi on cable, and Dora would be quiet, not sharing her disappointment about not finding Dora Smith's grave.

Chapter Eleven

FINDING MARY WARREN
June 10, 2007

Back in the early Spring of this year, Sophie had not been feeling well. The truth was Sophie just wasn't well, her immune system beaten down, year after year. She remained positive, committed wholeheartedly to life, regardless of complication. Like her father before her, she wasn't taking disability lying down.

The itching of her skin had become unbearable. All the Benadryl in the world did not help and Sophie had been getting more frustrated than usual, slinging verbal arrows at whoever was available to catch them, mainly Dylan, her easy prey. This itching was different. It was constantly annoying, a precursor to something. Not wanting to go to the doctor, Sophie chose to wait. March became April, May slipped into June, and the itching persisted. She could feel something under her skin, moving, trying to make its way out into the daylight, day after day, but nothing happened.

On June 10—the anniversary of Bridget Bishop's hanging—the site of Sophie's itching became inflamed, red and hot to the touch. She applied layers of hydrocortisone cream over the affected area, from her right armpit, across the tops of both breasts, ending in her left armpit. She began her prayers…

> *"Great Goddess of Earth and Sky,*
> *travel with the Spirit of Bridget Bishop now roaming.*
> *Be with her and offer her comfort and release,*
> *remind her she has seen and experienced the light,*
> *her pain only temporary and days long.*

Great Goddess, remind her she is loved and free.
Thank you for your patience, Great Mother.
Blessed Be."

When Sophie woke at sunrise on the next day, the itching was gone, the months of suffering over. She felt the area of the previous burning and found welts, high and hard. She ran to the bathroom and turned on the light. She tore her sleep shirt off, almost falling. She stared in disbelief. Her chest looked as if it had been tattooed from armpit to armpit, mapping the veins and shoving them to the surface. She flew into her studio, finding a stack of fresh tracing paper and a black felt-tipped marker.

In front of the large bathroom mirror, Sophie traced the pattern of lines, connecting right arm with left. The pattern looked familiar. It wasn't symbolic—it felt literal. The tracing had formed a crude map, one she recognized. She made a beeline for her office and the map of Old Salem, designed by Marilynne Roach, sold at the historical society in Salem. Sophie had used this map so often that she had it laminated earlier in the year. She pulled the map off the wall, threw it to the floor, and placed the tracing over it. It was difficult for Sophie to bend, but she lowered herself slowly onto the floor. Nothing would stop her this morning, not even pain. The tracing lined up exactly over the old roads of Salem, even in the same scale. Bingo! The tracing line was Old Salem's main road, which began at the harbor. The road wound through town eventually ending at Gallows Hill, a perfect match.

Sophie felt faint. Fortunately she would not have a long distance to fall if she blacked out. In a way, she wanted blackness and sleep. Instead, she was becoming a real-life walking map of Essex County.

It was Monday, Dylan's worst day of the week. She knew it and stayed away from him on Mondays. She didn't even call him on the cell because she knew he always ran himself ragged after the long weekend. Everybody needed electrical troubleshooters on Monday, after weekend breakdowns and delays. Sophie was impatient to share her discovery, as weird and disquieting as it was. She waited, pacing in front of his study door, where he read Tarot cards every morning. She couldn't disturb his reading. It might pertain to the tracing. She had to be patient. Finally, the squeaking of the doorknob announced his reading was finished. He was jolted by her panicky reception.

"What's wrong, Sophie, are you sick? Why are you up this early?"

She struggled to find words. "The itching stopped."

Dylan looked put off by her answer. "Well, good, I guess. That's good news. It will help you get some work done today."

"You don't understand, Dylan." She began to cry. "Come with me. I'll show you."

She led Dylan upstairs to her rooms. She went into her study and found the piece of tracing paper and the map and continued on to the bathroom. "Hold these papers for me while I take off my shirt."

"Jesus Christ, what happened to you? What is that?" Dylan looked utterly confused. "Did you do that to yourself, Sophie? Are you okay?"

Sophie didn't like his tone. She was getting frustrated. "Just get on the floor and take a look at this. Place the old map in front of you, close. Then, take the tracing, ink side up, and line it up with the harbor. See, it matches perfectly. And do you see a secondary pattern in the tracing, one we have missed seeing, even though we've had this map for years? Its *M*s and *W*s—the Old Salem roads make *M*s and *W*s."

As soon as the letter sounds came out of her mouth, Sophie began to tremble. Before she was able to sit down on the bench in her bathroom, she began to feel a violent seizure come on. Dylan caught her just in time and placed her convulsing body on the bench. He rubbed her hands together, raising her temperature, bringing color back to her face. Sophie often had seizures prior to Spirit visitations or messages from *next door*.

Sophie's body relaxed into the pillows supporting her, her spine straightened, her eyes remained closed but continually fluttering, an obvious trance-state reaction beginning. With words and accents not her own, Sophie began to speak.

"The men were taking the sheriff's wagon over to Beverly to pick up a load of treasures for Goody Corwin, she being the businesswoman of the family now. George spent his free time on his new land. He loved the lake, so clear and beautiful with its fish, eager to snap on the weakest line. No wonder Giles had fought so hard for this land, it's paradise, Corwin told me.

"He had no more time for me, even though he did miss my legs wrapped around him in the dark, so different from Goody Corwin, his not-so-lovely wife. Goody Corwin liked the time when the gaol was full. She had felt powerful. That's when she started her business, buying bits and pieces off the accused before the rest of their assets were stripped and divided between the town and the Family Confederacy. She wanted her piece.

"When George Corwin told his men about the treasure trove in Beverly, he

asked them to take me with them. Goody Corwin was on the warpath and he wanted me out of town. The men did not want to be saddled with me. I knew by the way they looked at me, they gave in only because they thought one of them might get lucky and catch a poke. I was accommodating, when I needed to be. They agreed to take me along on their day-long journey.

"The treasure stop didn't turn out to be much, not by these men's standards. They had raped and plundered the treasures of Essex County all through the Witch Trials, extravagant wagon-loads of merchandise they all benefited from. This load was nothing but a few trunks of well-worn fabric scraps and old furniture, including a hand-carved rocking chair.

"When the chair was loaded, I immediately took possession of it, trying to sit on it while the wagon moved. I quickly abandoned the idea but, after spying a long roll of rope, I had another idea. 'Take me to the pond, at the top of Singing Beach. I want to do the chair!' I was manic, jubilant.

"'What are you going on about, Mary? What do you mean you want to do the chair?' John Moulton asked.

"'I want you to tie me to the chair and throw me into the pond. You've done it before, for sport, but I want you to do it for real this time. If I sink, I'm bad like people think I am, meaning I'm a Witch. But, if I float, you'll know I'm innocent and not a daughter of Satan. If I sink, all of Essex County will know where the real evil came from. It came from me!' I screamed at them.

"'We'd be done with you then, you evil bitch, Miss Mary. I reckon our sheriff would be glad to be rid of you too.' One of the men snarled.

"I settled down, feeling calmer than I had since before the last hangings. Today I would get what I deserved, what I wanted. I didn't care from whom it came. The wagon followed a dusty trail, up along the cliff side of Singing Beach, all the way to Eagle Bluff. I could hear the surf crashing on the beach below us. We turned West into the wood, close to the pond. I was anxious. I jumped from the slow-moving wagon and ran to the pond and waded right in. 'This spot will do fine,' I declared.

"The men's faces were screwed up in disbelief.

"'This cannot be happening! Corwin promised us no more violence—we have had our fill. Now, we are going to kill one of our own? No! This isn't right! We won't do this, Mary! You can't have us kill you, Witch or no. Listen, we are like your brothers, bad brothers we know, but we can't plunge you in that pond and watch you die. I have had enough killing for the rest of my days,' John yelled at me.

"I stood to my waist in water and started screaming, screaming so hard I burned from the inside. 'You will do as I say, or else I will curse you, your families, *your whores, and Corwin right along with you! You will rope me to the chair as I have asked or I will tell everyone about you, John Moulton. You killed Giles Corey with his own shovel, you did! George couldn't kill him, so you did! I will tell everyone the Witch Trials were a fake and you will all fry in hell, you leading the way!' I started to howl.*

"Just shut her up, John, I can't listen to her caterwauling anymore!' one of the men called.

"One of the other men picked up the chair, while another brought the rope. They were going to put themselves out of their own misery. I would die with their sins, put under the water where the dark reeds and snapping turtles live. All would be quiet again, no more tears for any of them. This would be the last killing. We took a silent oath.

"They tied me so tightly to the chair, I fused with it. The pond was shallow, too shallow to immerse the chair completely, except right in the center. The men stripped off their boots and breeches, each one taking a post of the chair in their hands, slowly hoisting it above their shoulders. John nodded yes and they began wading slowly, the chair bobbing up and down, as if it were a queen's litter on the way to a ball. I smiled and stared at the diffused light streaming through the trees. The men could not see my silent tears.

"One lost his footing, then a second. The other two, instead of falling, threw their weight up. The chair seemed to have its own way of flying. It levitated above their heads for one split second and then, a loud splash! Down, down, the chair and I went. At first, John made a move to pull the chair to the surface before reeds caught it. Then, he stepped back. The water turned cloudy. Bubbles rose, first a few, then hundreds.

"I felt numb after struggling, after opening my mouth wide, letting the pond rush into me. After some minutes, the water calmed. Then, a strange creaking sound began, as the chair began to rise. I felt a floating sensation and thought of the flight of Witches, testimonies from the trials. I saw my honey hair bobbing free, close to the surface. I was now separate from my body, floating, watching from above the men's heads.

"My body was still tied to the chair, my face contorted in agony, discolored and bloated, as if I had been hanged. I could not feel pain. John was the first to paddle out to the center of the pond. He was astonished that the chair floated, he told his men. It was heavy oak, and the combined weight of the rope and my body was too much to float. 'See, Mary, you are no more a Witch than I am!' he yelled, tears streaming down his already wet face.

"The other three swam to the center of the pond and helped John pull the chair to shore. They cut my body loose. One of them was relieved at having retrieved the chair. 'Goody Corwin would have gotten me good, if she didn't get her chair today.' He didn't even see my corpse, just the chair. He took his breeches and started rubbing the chair dry with the pant legs. He walked it back to the wagon, feeling accomplished, losing sight of the fact he had just killed someone. They were used to it. I did not fault them.

"The men took my body deep into the woods and dug a grave so animals would not claim me. I was quiet and still, hovering in a holding pattern, watching the men's faces change in the afternoon light. John Moulton said the Lord's Prayer over my crude unmarked grave. He told his men it was the least he could do considering the circumstances.

"I stayed by my grave for some time, until the weather changed and leaves covered the dirt covering. I had not expected to feel so lost. In my heart of hearts, I thought I would go to heaven once I died, be released from my private torture. But that is not what happened. The surf drew me to the beach. I loved the feeling of wind on my face and through my unruly hair. It was the closest to being free I had ever felt. But my isolation did not resolve my pain and walking became my nature."

Sophie sat up rigidly, her eyes opening with a start. She would never become used to this kind of spontaneous journeywork—it sapped her energy, sometimes for days afterward, regardless of her spiritual training and feeding methods. She felt oddly energized, however. A steady spark of enthusiasm was growing within her.

Dylan looked queasy and concerned, not sure what to expect next. He knew he had to get on the road soon. Commuting any later than six a.m. was insane this side of Portland. He looked at his watch, as he felt Sophie's head for fever and hands for tremors. She seemed fine, despite the red welts across her bare chest.

Sophie finally spoke as herself, her timbre steady and growing in volume. "That's it, Dylan! The *M*s and the *W*s stand for Mary Warren. She's leading us to additional places. This is the answer to my pleading! I have been praying to Spirit for months for a clear route for our steps, that's when the itching began, when I started the Spirit Petitions. I hadn't put it together before—we are onto something here! Obviously, Mary will lead us to the routes we are meant to walk. This explains so much about the other Spirits who have been haunting me, every single night for months, for years. It's all starting to make sense. We have three full months before we leave for Salem to do the Big Work, to piece the puzzle together. The final walking routes have not been drawn in ink yet. We need to stay more flexible. Additional information will surface, the more planning and research I do. This is hopeful."

Dylan yawned and realized this was the meaning of the Seven of Swords he could not decipher earlier in his reading. It's obvious, he thought. Mary Warren is from the enemy camp, remembering her rallying cry for the arrest of old Giles. Now, she's on our side and will make it possible for us to steal the weapons from our adversaries in broad daylight. Just as pictured in the card itself, she will lead us. He stood up and kissed Sophie on the top of her head. "Take it easy today. Take the day off and go back to bed. Don't give me that *look*, Sophie, just do as I say for a change. I have a busy day and can't afford to worry about you getting sick and not being able to phone out. Be good, I'll call you later, keep your cell close."

Sophie nodded compliance, put her soft pink robe on and walked down the stairs. She followed Dylan to the back door as he finished getting ready for work. Her mind was already racing, studying the maps from memory. She found a Tylenol and swallowed it with a large gulp of water. She knew it was going to be a wild day of realizations and research. She wouldn't waste time by going back to bed. She reached into the freezer for a fig tartlet made the day before and gently placed the sweet treasure into Dylan's lunch bag. "Cuz you're my special sweet guy, the food of Venus, for inspiration. Be safe, please." She smiled and sent him an air kiss as he hesitated at the door.

She quietly moved through the house, the Altar lights guiding her way to the stairwell. She heard Dylan locking up after himself, first the back door, then the back gate. This gave her permission to get started, but she'd wait till he was a block out of sight before she'd turn the lights on.

Chapter Twelve

THE OCEAN IS CALLING
Monday, September 17, 2007, 7:00 a.m.

THE BREAKING OF DAWN FILLED THE HOTEL SUITE with an orange glow, energizing Sophie into action. Rising to a world already expectant—waiting for input—was a joy for her. Today belonged to Mary Warren. She had waited patiently for Sophie to discover the importance of her imprint on the Witch Trials. It was Sophie who would play catch up as she gave her morning Greeting to the Sun.

After saluting the directions, offering sacred herbs to the dawn's light for purification, she thought of the relationship forged with Mary Warren since the Spirit visitation last June. Mary felt like a dear friend now; they confided in each other often since Sophie's violent spontaneous journey. Fortunately, Mary was close. Little effort had to be made to contact her for help. No Trance Work or Oracles were needed. Mary was always there, although she was careful not to get in Sophie's way. She was quiet and respectful of the living. She learned her lessons well over the last three hundred and fourteen years as a Walking Spirit, caught between three realities. In psychology-speak, Mary had dissociated into three separate personalities at the time of her tragic drowning death. The first personality was living as a haunt, walking endless days on the beaches of Essex County. The second personality was the damaged Miss Mary of Charter Street Cemetery, caught in a compromised body without the skills to understand why she heard so many voices, which were her own in different dimensions. The third personality, her "control" alter or the boss, was Mary Warren the active, rational, Walking Spirit. She, like Sophie and Giles, was ready for peace and integration.

Mary Warren had a small window of opportunity to integrate, to walk with herself, Walking Mary and Haunting Mary blended into one. Sophie would bring both parties together this morning, if all went as planned. Sophie and Mary would work together, creating enough energy so Haunting Mary would see them and be jarred out of her repetitive behavior. If Haunting Mary and Walking Mary could join forces, they have the real chance of changing Miss Mary's life for the better before she dies in the elements of Charter Street Cemetery. All three, if Miss Mary is healthy and clear, can become one. This is the goal—this is Soul Retrieval of the highest order. In return, Walking Mary will lead Sophie where she needs to go, as she has already done, through vision, journey, and simple Spirit Speak.

Obscuring the orange sky, a frosty mist rolled in from the sea. Finally, it felt like Autumn. Sophie could smell distant fires and hear the sound of heaters blasting on throughout the adjoining motel. The hot shower felt good against her chilled skin. Her mind grappled with the possibilities of today's ceremonies and planned integration. Haunting Mary was a wild card.

Haunting Spirits were difficult. It was hard to make contact with a haunt, for she was stuck in a never-ending cycle of physical activity, which had a life force, independent from its source. This was the reason Mary Warren was so desperate to join forces with Sophie. She knew Sophie was good and went where few had the courage to go. She owed Giles in a big way, so there was no hesitation on Mary's part to make the connection. Sophie had made a career of joining the bits and pieces of broken hearts, minds, and psyches together, creating whole people. It was like cleaning auras, though. If the client did not stay on top of her own inabilities and weaknesses after integration, a separate life force could be created, generating the same condition, more soul loss.

Time was progressing nicely. Dylan had left to gather their favorite morning fare at Bagel World and pick up the girls. Only minutes were left to sort through the details of the day ahead. Shit! Ghost dramas had so many variables, Sophie thought, knowing she could never figure out all the angles.

It was sticky work, all of it, with a big psychic price if wrong steps were taken in any direction. Karma and reincarnation were often complicated and were not just a series of one-way lifetimes to deal with. All time was circular, one time zone connected to another, on and on forever, all able to communicate with one another; the living were haunted by missing pieces of themselves all the time in the form of disease: emotional, physical, psychic, or the combination of all three.

Sophie's thoughts became overwhelming. The possibilities of healing, of setting the story straight was almost too much to hope for. She left the din of her thoughts, inspired by the joyful sounds of her friends' return.

Sophie tapped out the traditional Heart Beat Drum on her mug of hot tea. Poe broke Sophie's rush of anxiety, saying, "I'm still not sure I understand how the Spirits of Mary Warren, the Spirits caught between the worlds from Casco, the Spirits of the ten Indians Hannah Dustin killed, and Rebecca Eames all figure in the schedule for today. I know Mary died above Singing Beach, but why are we dealing with Hannah's ten and Rebecca Eames too? I'm confused; you have seen and dealt with so many Spirits recently."

Sophie was glad to focus her energy out of her head into the real itinerary facing the party today. They needed to finish grounding and going over the astrological information for the day. The explanation would help. "Mary Warren first had Soul Loss in Casco, Maine, during the big Indian attack that killed her entire family and, some estimate, about one hundred and fifty others. The one hundred and fifty are connected to Mary Warren through their mutual pain and loss—they eat from her energy. Since Mary is divided into three sentient personalities, she is a powerful source of fuel. They have had an uneasy relationship for over three hundred years. If we are successful in integrating Haunting Mary with Walking Mary, the one hundred and fifty's fuel supply is ended, forcing them to the light and rebirth."

Dylan and Dora quit washing the breakfast dishes and joined Sophie's morning explanation. "That makes perfect sense, Sophie," said Poe, finally seeing Walking Mary in her true power role. "But why are we dancing for the Indians Hannah killed on the Singing Beach?"

"Because they came to me shortly after the spontaneous journey with Mary Warren; they are linked. Mary Warren's family and friends were killed by Indians; the ten Indians from Haverhill were killed by whites. Again, the Great Balancing at work. The ten said they were sad no one was left to sing their Death Song or dance their Death Dance when Hannah killed them. King Philip's War had taken so many of them, and smallpox took even more. They were alone, caught between the worlds without anyone to remember them and their deeds of skill and bravery. Two were tiny children, forever crying for their mothers. They need to be remembered. Their Ancestors spoke of ancient fishing parties on Singing Beach, with Eagle Bluff above. This would be their Power Place. Perhaps they would travel to the light if they were remembered. Regardless, they were waiting and hoping to greet us on Singing Beach. They would witness our Work and pray for our success.

"Rebecca Eames has been visiting every night for the past week. She is lonely and misunderstood where she is now. She is old and well off, but restless and disconnected. She is still nervous and overvigilant and has not been able to rest long enough to be reborn into a new body. She requests to eat with us today. She is hungry to be with people who can actually feel her. She never told me why today was her special day for contact. Rebecca was from Gloucester, which is on the way to Cape Ann and the site of the original Puritan landing. It works well with our schedule today. Just this morning, I was double-checking today's date, the seventeenth of September, in the Witch Trial Chronology by Roache and found Rebecca Eames noted. She was sentenced to hang for Witchcraft on the seventeenth of September. She narrowly escaped being hanged on the twenty-second, although she rotted in the gaol till March of 1693. It makes sense. Any other questions?"

Dora looked a little distracted when she spoke up softly. "Why are we going to Graves Beach? What's there for us?"

"Dennis Graves is an old friend and Spirit Guide of mine. He came to me when Dylan and I were first married and living in Gainesville, Florida, where, incidentally, Poe went to college before graduate school. When I noticed Graves Beach on the map, just North of Singing Beach, I knew we had to go there. Dennis made a brief appearance shortly after my realization. He tipped his black bowler hat in my direction and said, "*I will show you secrets at the place carrying my name. It's always a pleasure to assist you.*" In other words, we won't know until we get there. One more point. Remember my email of last week? Spirit instructed us to remain vigilant, reminding us to look for black and white pillars. I have noticed lots of Dunkin' Donuts shops in Peabody, Salem, and Danvers, so let's keep our eyes open for them as well.

"We are looking for the Saltonstall residence on our way to Graves Beach. We need to leave an Honor Bundle there. He was the only judge to stand in protest of the Witch Trials, calling them dangerous and speculative. He suggested a possible family conspiracy at the time, speaking against the Putnams by name. He moved to Haverhill. We will honor him more formally at Pentucket when we meet Metacomet tomorrow. By the time we get to Haverhill, we'll know the status of the ten Indians. Lots to keep track of today." Sophie finished the explanations, put on her shoes, and walked through the door. Dylan had already loaded the car. He had caught Sophie's eye earlier, beseeching her to get on track. The party was off to the ocean.

Route 62E to Route127 would lead to Cape Ann, where Sophie had to bleed into the ground again. Sophie wondered if her DNA would come close to matching Giles's in a comparative test. Blood is the way to give back, to offer sacrifice. One's own blood is sacred, the most personal tribute possible.

Dylan's travel plan was fairly easy today, their path veering away from Salem and all the tourist traps. Lots of congestion and Summer homes around Cape Ann, but it was manageable in September. Route 127 went through Beverly, leading gently to Manchester and Singing Beach. Today would be more action than talk. Sophie was ready.

They would find the Saltonstall residence first, following black and white pillars and Dunkin' Donuts at every turn, just as Spirit had directed. The area was packed with Summer people, the wealthy of Boston and beyond, congregating at every bend of the road. Congestion was thick and the Saltonstalls unfortunately were at home. Sophie instructed Dylan to pull over and park next to the stately winding drive, which was complete with security fence and squawk box. As if to signal hello, the branches of an ancient hawthorn blew in Sophie's direction, as soon as she slipped from the passenger seat, out into the Fall air. With the lightest of touches, she caught the substantial branch and tied the red cotton bundle to it. With her other hand, she offered up a pinch of maple sugar and threw it towards the closed electric fence, sweets for the dead. She said an audible "Thank you!" and let go of the branch, sending the attached Honor Bundle flying in the hazy blue sky.

They drove to Singing Beach and parked in the municipal lot. They were surprised to see an open beach—accessible from two directions, far from private—not the expected place to sing and dance for the prayer benefit of the dead. The weather turned from hazy baby blue to gray and blowing, in seconds. By the time the party of four reached sand, the beach was deserted. Waves began to rise. An unexpected storm was headed directly for them. This was the opportunity they needed for their Work, Sophie's Work. They tromped onto the beach, forming their usual queue. Sophie walked to the Southern point of the beach, bordered by a row of huge boulders, delineating the property of the local yacht club. Sophie offered up a solitary red bundle to the directions and nodded a silent prayer before throwing the bundle into the cracks of the boulders.

On cue, an Eagle flew from atop Eagle Bluff and soared over the beach—North to South—heading directly for their heads. Sophie held up both hands and greeted the regal giant, its golden head gleaming. Eagle called out an acceptance of respect and turned and flew back where he came from. This was the sign to begin. She instructed Dora to follow directly behind her, carrying the Trader Joe's magickal bag. Poe would follow Dora, and Dylan would protect the rear. Sophie would begin the dance, one slow step at a time, while she cried out the Death Song requested from the ten Indians from Haverhill. Just as she began her first note, two men dressed all in dark gray, the color of disturbance and depression, walked right up to Sophie, who was obviously in prayer. One of them made an attempt to shake Sophie's hand. Both wore expectant smiles.

"Why have you come to this beach to pray?" the taller of the two asked.

"I was instructed to perform ritual here by my Ancestors and Elders. Why do you bother me in my Work? What is your motivation?" Sophie hissed at him.

"We've needed help for years. Few have seen us; we are alone in our misery. There was talk that you could see and hear us and now here you are, talking. We are weary of disguises and need to be released from our bad deeds. Mary has to stop her wandering— she frightens us. We have no peace!"

"You have kept Mary here through your fear. If you desire real change, you will leave me to my Work." Sophie snarled at the men.

The wind rushed off the ocean, sending a chill over the entire beach. The water lapped the rocks, long enough to drench Sophie's ugly white sneakers, the ones she depended on. The two in gray looked startled, their faces shimmering with the movement of the wind. They turned in slow motion and began walking away and faded into the rock bluff before them.

Sophie began her Spirit Salutes again. She offered new prayers, the old charm broken by the interruption. She glanced back at the other three over her shoulder and saw them with their mouths half-open in disbelief.

Dylan cleared his throat. "You need anything, Sophie?"

"Yes," she replied. "Let's form a small Circle and do our chanting, regardless of audience. We need to refocus. As the men implied, we have no time for disguises. We must be brave and not be intimidated by this sandy stage."

They began chanting in their usual fashion, Sophie counting and directing the breaths taken. By the second of thirteen *om*s, several people appeared and sat about nine feet away. They were human, their fashion and demeanor matched with the now; they were smiling and expectant, yet respectful and quiet. This felt like the Prayer Circle formed around the party at Charter

Street Cemetery when they were honoring John Marston. Soon, another couple joined the Circle to the North.

Sophie knew Water Salutes were called for. The energy needed to be concentrated for the song-filled dance. In Shamanic fashion, she took long draughts of water and spit out controlled sprays, one for each Cardinal Direction, the last, coming directly down on her head. After the Spirit visitation, she needed to be cleansed. Her head was now as wet as her feet. Balanced and focused, she prayed…

"Great Spirit of the spheres,
old and new, always growing,
hear my prayers!
Great Mother of Earth and Sky,
shelter us from your directional fury,
bless our work with a Mother's love."

The wind whipped violently off the ocean, sending long lines of sand into the air. The wind was coming from the East, a good sign. The prayers made would be heard.

"Sisters and Brothers, red and white,
hear our songs in your honor.
Feel our dance in your marrow;
hear us sing:
We remember you!"

The wind calmed and sunlight broke through the cloud cover. The small audience gathered to experience the drama looked amazed. They remained hushed. Slowly, one at a time, they picked up their beach bags, lowered their heads, and began moving toward the municipal lot.

Sophie became aware of the presence of many Spirits, diaphanous and white, like a gentle sea mist. The shapes made a semi-circle in the center of the ridge line, dividing hard sand from soft, as if they were lining up around a huge Family Drum. The shapes began to bob up and down, an orchestrated Honor Dance to feed the party, just as promised. Everyone felt the beat, first in their hearts, then in the ground under their dancing feet, emanating from the invisible drum.

Sophie pointed, instead of speaking, concentrating her focus on the dance. Fortunately, the sun and wind dried Sophie's head and face quickly. The same fate was not true for her white sneakers, sloshing with every step. Three deep cleansing breaths were taken. The three others followed Sophie's lead, as they were taught. Then a Cobra Breath, Sophie's face now wide open and red. Silent salutes asking the Spirit Realms for protection and Second Sight were made.

Sophie started to hum. Dora chanted behind her, carrying the tone sweetly. Sophie began her familiar quick in-and-out Shamanic breath, promising deliverance of the Trance state. Dora followed the sounds of Sophie's breaths with her own, the different sounds creating Invitation Songs for the Elementals. In and out, in a rapid one-two beat, the breaths came and went, growing in power and volume. Dora could tell the difference of timbre when Sophie finally relaxed into the Trance and began to sing a long note, followed by another and more broken breaths. Sophie sang the Death Song as she danced a careful toe-heel-right, then toe-heel-left, the traditional step of Native women dancers. The others followed her across the long beach, their steps landing directly on top of Sophie's, each step a prayer multiplied by four. Each Cardinal Direction had a dancer. Sophie was North, Earth Tradition. Poe was East, Inspirational Air. Dylan was South, Fire Passion. Dora was West, Dream Water.

The length of the beach was covered in good order, a slow pace, but solid and fluid. The dance did not stop until the rock shelf of Eagle Butte ended the beach at the far North end. Each began to salute the Directions and spitting into the air, their way of ending their prayers. Dora began throwing M&Ms onto the wet sand, creating a small Circle. Like a choreographed dance, Poe followed by arranging the special fizzy water and shortbread cookies for the Sacrament, ending the ritual dance. Dylan cast a Circle of Tobacco. Sophie walked to the center of the candy Circle and sang a long, mournful song with no words, making almost hiccupping sounds, mimicking the sounds of weeping. She whispered, "You are remembered." The rest joined in, the volume growing with every exhale, "You are remembered!" The Circle was enveloped with a sweet-smelling mist, not lifting until the last sip of water was offered to the Mother and the last bite of cookie was offered to the Father.

The group quietly packed up their tools and offerings, wet shoes, and sandy jackets and walked back to the SUV. The sun was blinding, bouncing off the ocean, warming the air rapidly. It was close to eighty, a bright New England day. Offshore, glistening white sails skimmed the narrow strip between sea and sky. Dylan passed around another dose of sunscreen and didn't move on to the next person until she actually used it. He was in his glory now, feeling accomplished and surprisingly unshaken by the Spirits he had seen this morning. No one talked about the two visitors in gray or the protoplasmic clouds until the trip back to Peabody, arriving home past dusk. They had all seen the apparitions and had heard every word of Sophie's harsh words to the gray visitors. Sophie had to be strong. She was the only one of the group who was unafraid to be curt or rude when needed. It was in the job description and necessary when dealing with some forms of Spirits, particularly the Walking and Haunting varieties, not to mention living human beings. You must hold your power securely and demand respect, or chaos ensues. The Spirit Realms were not far away from the realities of corporate life: always a ladder, always rules and behavior codes.

Poe wrote frantically in her soft green journal. She only looked up when the car began pulling out. "Wow, how is everybody? Okay?" The others breathed out in unison and nodded fine, still silent, still feeling the sand under their moving feet.

Before finding Graves Beach, the party circled Eagle Bluff looking for Mary's pond. Google Earth showed it plainly, sending shivers up Sophie's spine. It was there, but held in private hands, a part of a huge estate covering most of the bluff and all of the woods surrounding the pond. They never saw the entire pond but were able to glimpse a sliver of it, between a thick swath of evergreens and an ornate black iron fence. All they could see was a solitary Adirondack chair, painted green, resting beside high growing reeds and wild iris. Green was Mary's favorite color.

Graves Beach was the next stretch of sand after Eagle Bluff's enormous boulders and sheer cliff. Pavement turned to hard-packed dirt. Before they caught a glimpse of the beach, through the haze of dust appeared a middle-aged man as sun-beaten as a raisin, sitting in a white resin chair reading a book. Dylan slammed on the brakes, intensifying the dust cloud, coming to an abrupt stop. The reading man never moved, engrossed in his fiction. Sophie knew Dylan could have used a shot of vodka after the near miss.

"Yeah, Graves Beach all right! Spooky…" Dylan said, blinking the grit from his eyes. He felt the sting of sudden awareness and snapped, "Okay, everybody! There's so much here, we don't dare miss a thing."

They all looked at Sophie, not wanting to state the obvious. "Walking Mary wasn't on Singing Beach. Neither was Haunting Mary," Sophie said. "There was a dark-haired woman with porcelain skin, about twenty-five, dressed in a see-through white shift, very classic ghost fashion, which is rare. She made brief contact but wasn't interested in what we were doing. She was just waiting to have her beach back. Obviously, she is the ghost that the two men were talking about, although she looked nothing like Mary Warren and they should have known better. But they are easily frightened now. Imagine phobic ghosts! Now you've heard everything!"

They all laughed, but at what they weren't sure. It just felt good to let off some steam. Sophie lightened up and sank back into the comfortable passenger seat, sighing deeply. "If we're successful with Mary's integration, it will happen here. It's a small, private place, sheltered on all sides, perfect for our work. Now, I have an idea. We need to break up and move individually. Dennis Graves said there were secrets here. Where there are secrets, there are Spirit Tokens, hidden treasures, symbols, and omens."

They looked out across the beach, scanning from side to side, noticing all the rocks. This would not be easy ground to navigate, especially for Sophie, sure-footed only on level ground.

Sophie started pointing her orders, using sign language wherever she could. Regardless if they could understand it or not, the Spirit Realms did. They cleaned their auras, centered their energy, and grounded in quick Shamanic fashion. They all silently prayed for protection, while leaving themselves sensitive and open to Spirit contact. The thought of disembodied Spirits usually terrified Poe, but not today. Sophie noticed Poe looked like a knight, armored and ready for action. She knew Poe would figure prominently here. It was decided they would work in their individual directions, covering all four areas of the crescent-shaped beach. There they would search for clues and tokens.

Standing still, Sophie closed her eyes and breathed the gritty warm air. She waited for each of her friends to find their bearings and places to search. Opening her eyes, she saw that Poe looked like a clam digger, walking the far Eastern edge of the wet sand, head down, looking for clues. Poe called out that she had found a treasure: a Captain Morgan rum miniature bottle with a gold metal cap.

Dylan climbed the high boulders wedged against the edge of Eagle Bluff, a miner looking for treasures in brown rock. His silhouette black against the bright sky, he offered Tobacco to Eagle and Sweetgrass to the Spirits in his usual fashion, asking them to talk with him. He always wanted actual sound, words, clear communication.

Dora walked the crescent edge of the beach, more on dirt than sand, on the road, looking ahead and behind, eventually leaving the beach all together, moving toward Crow Island. She was far away, dividing from the group on a core level. Sophie was sure that Dora wasn't feeling it, didn't understand the mission today, would rather be in Salem, in town, by herself.

Dora began looking away when Sophie spoke to avoid any sign of disapproval. The sight of the way Sophie's eyebrow arched when she didn't approve of something made Dora shiver. Sophie was used to her. Dora wanted her freedom as a student. She wanted dance, not Shamanism. She had told Sophie this over and over again, for the good part of a decade, but Sophie had not given signs that she was listening. She still hoped that Dora would follow her. It was becoming increasingly clear that Dora wanted out of the heir-bargain with Sophie. The main reason she came on this trip had been to let the older woman down when she was in a great place around dear friends, tasting spiritual and emotional success. Dora was ready for freedom. She wanted to tell her teacher at the end of the Liberation Feast at the Lyceum; she had pictured it for months. She believed Sophie had no idea of any of this.

Sophie's eyes caught a flash of hot pink. She followed the blowing trail and found a pink satin sash, embroidered with sequins. It was staked in place by two plump round rocks and looked like an arrow pointing North. She followed it and saw Poe, smiling and squatting low, having a private conversation with the sand. She could feel the Spirits gathering. This work was about love, the symbol she read in the sash, young innocent love. They had to slow down, be lighter, more inviting. The wind picked up and the sky filled with birds. First gulls, then crows, and then, from the farmer's fields West of the beach, red-tailed hawks began flying in patterns over the beach, Spirit Speak for *Yes!*

Sophie felt excited, tingly even. Bright golden light created patterns on the water as she walked North, in Poe's direction. Poe noticed Sophie, motioning her over. In turn, Sophie waved to Dylan. All three moved in slow motion. The trees on the shore of Crow Island began to dance. Thrashing against each other, the branches began rustling and making the sounds of playing children: splashing, giggling, gently tinkling sounds tapping time in the busy branches. The sounds of children playing blended with the golden light shimmering off the surface of the shallow water close to the shore. Shapes formed: small silhouettes of girls in muslin shifts, black and gold against the bright reflected light. Haunting Mary was there, but not as a full-grown woman. Her personality was created as a side effect of the massacre of her family in Casco, when she was still a girl, not quite in puberty. Haunting Mary brought all the disembodied girls from Casco here to play with her on Graves Beach.

The realization hit Sophie in a split second, no time to explain. They all had to flow with the magick of which they were a part. Poe was playing with the little girls, giggling and scampering in the water, looking for shells and squealing quiet delight, barely audible. The innocent joy on Poe's face created a light whirlwind of energy, flowing and twisting like a small tornado on a mission.

Walking Mary initiated a mind-to-mind conversation with Sophie. Neither one of them wanted to break the enchantment. They decided to walk together, Sophie on the West, Walking Mary on the East, with Poe in the center. When Walking Mary and Sophie reached Poe, Sophie signaled Poe to walk on her right, directly into the shimmering shallows. Sophie motioned Dylan to stop and cover their backs. She spoke to him in sign, telling him to witness what was about to happen.

Poe stood, transfixed between two worlds, in slow motion. As she turned to the East, Sophie and Walking Mary noticed Haunting Mary's attention was captured. Haunting Mary recognized herself in the slim young woman's reflection of Walking Mary. For a split second, Haunting Mary knew what was to come as she picked up speed and flew into Walking Mary's Spirit Body. Motion stopped, the breath knocked out of everyone on the beach, Dylan's lungs filling up the loudest, letting Sophie know he was in the thick of Spirit activity.

The Spirit numbers grew and grew, shimmering in the golden light of the shallows. The birds, once there and gone, returned, all cawing the strangest sounds, catching the protoplasmic bubble in their talons and flying into the Eastern sky, the giggling and crystal tinkling sounds traveling with them. Poe, Sophie, and Dylan began to jump up and down, tears streaming down their faces, triumphant! The birds escorted the tiny playing children with sun-bleached hair, their parents greedily holding onto to them, their tears becoming wails of joy.

Walking Mary united with Haunting Mary. She stood at the Northern edge of the beach and watched her childhood playmates move on to waiting bodies and families full of love to share. Mary looked proud and strong, but profoundly lonely. Sophie wiggled free of the group hug with Dylan and Poe and walked up to Mary. She gently embraced her, then wiped her tears. They both nodded a warm smile to each other, knowing success was theirs. The rest would sort itself out or not…

Dora found them hugging and crying on the North end of the beach. She had missed the show, the integrating, the movement of Spirits, one hundred and fifty strong. Sophie smiled a sad smile, feeling both successful and a failure, knowing Dora would be leaving soon to build a new life without Earth Magick, without the Shamanism Sophie had taught her. It was too late for Sophie now to find another heir. She didn't have ten years of hard training left in her; she was too tired and had her own Work to complete. If she was lucky, Sophie would last another decade, but with many modifications only Dylan knew about. She was sad to have Dora go, but relieved not to feel burdened by the responsibility to protect her at all costs for the rest of her life. Dora was too much work now. The magickal moments on this beach were so organic, unforced, profound, that only a subtle nudge in the right direction was needed. Sophie's sadness wouldn't last.

The group slowly and quietly walked up the gravel road to the iron gates of Crow Island, the bird symbolizing sacred ritual and ceremonial death. The wrought iron was decorated with crows in profile. At the bottom of the massive gate, a long row of *M*s and *W*s were scrolled into the metalwork. A Golden Labrador casually walked over to the sitting party still studying the intricate scrollwork. The dog visited each member, nuzzling, kissing, and jumping up on Sophie, then running in the other direction. Sophie kept yelling, "It's all about loyalty and love!" The dog stopped pestering the group long enough for Sophie to get away without her allergies kicking up. She caught her breath. "We must know the difference between love and loyalty and not confuse it like Haunting Mary did, out of fear and loneliness. To be successful in Spirit Work, we must be unafraid to combine the inherent strengths of love and loyalty, as we did on Graves Beach!"

Nothing else was said. Sophie's companions were finally realizing the scope of this Work. What she laid out and planned for was actually happening, succeeding. Not everything had gone as expected. Singing Beach, for example, ended up being surreally profound, ghosts actually manifesting, testing faith and perseverance. Graves Beach would live on in stories forever, sweet and tender.

The three of them looked at Sophie; she had seen the look before. They were piecing together how each fitted into the big picture. She could feel their collective anxiety, could hear their questions echo inside her head. What would happen to them after the American Camino? Would she move on to new people to facilitate another Spirit adventure, Spain the next stop? Would they feel held apart from Sophie if they found their individual paths were different from hers? They had come as support, granting an aging woman a wish, perhaps her last. Now they knew it was much more than that. Had they not been paying attention for the last three years? Why had they not seen the real power behind this Journey before today? They heard words, but hadn't really thought much would happen. Memories were more than shadows now, still out of reach but closer. They held many secrets. What would happen next? They all shook with tremors of cold on the warm beach. Sophie reacted with a series of tics, which ended in an abrupt pointing motion.

Sophie took off her favorite brown sunhat, the collapsible one she had worn throughout Europe. She wetted a kerchief and washed her face of sticky salty sand and reapplied generous amounts of sunscreen.

Reflected light surrounded them, shining off every surface: ocean, sand, sky, road, trees. Particles of Prana, spiritual fuel, filled the sky, causing eye-rubbing and eyeglass cleaning. Their psychic energy was accelerating; their vision displayed a rise in consciousness. The eyeglass cleaner was passed around, and still not a word was said.

Sophie checked her grave tool kit for fresh needles and alcohol wipes. All was in order: bundles, sugar, digging tools, water from Oregon, West meets East. Small gentle capes flowed one into another, against azure skies. The rugged coastline was behind them. Scenic sailing routes and, later in the day, marshland would be their muses.

Cape Ann State Park, the site of the 1623 landing headed by Roger Conant, rose higher than the other small capes. It sat above a natural port, suspended by huge boulders looming over the rich Atlantic. Leaving a noticeable trail, Sophie walked due East, toward the boulder point. Before dirt ended, she knelt and dug a trench three inches deep and six inches long: three times six equals eighteen, the Romani number for good luck and completion. She lined the furrow with Tobacco and maple sugar. She motioned Dylan to stand guard and protect the trench while the Spirit Salutes were done.

Sophie walked dangerously close to the edge of the boulder, close enough to touch the Sky Gods of Old Europe. She washed her face and hands, first in Celtic salt, then with spring water, and made her Salutes, quickly, with liquid moves befitting a medieval wizard. She turned from the ocean and grabbed Poe by the arm, escorting her to the edge of the great brown rock. She sprayed water over Poe's head, cleaning her aura and alerting her Guardian Spirits. Poe's ancestors had landed on this spot in 1623, one of the original Dorchester Adventurers. Poe had to reclaim her ancestral link now, energizing the lessons of her past, before the team could progress Northwest to Indian Country.

Silently Sophie called the Elementals, using sign instead of words, a token of respect. The ocean presented a constant, suspended inviolate, glittering gold and turquoise, breathing with gentle tugs of tide. Spirit offered quiet knowing in response, pointing to balance, piety, humility, silent courage, all spare communion. Each person received direction to spit on the rock, binding them to this place of promise. The three formed a triangle around the now kneeling Sophie. She cocked her penlet and released it on freshly cleaned skin, sending a steady stream of blood straight into the air. Controlling the stream, she pumped her finger, creating a continuous line of blood directed into the trench, from West to East, symbolizing the dead feeding the living. Binding the puncture wound tightly with one hand, she placed an Honor Bundle in the center with the other and began filling in the line, burying the DNA treasures. She tapped its top, blending it softly into the well-worn path.

Rebecca Eames awaited the party at Halibut Point in Gloucester, fish and beer being a fitting feast for three hungry assistants, the flesh moratorium now lifted. Sophie brought her own oatmeal and asked for hot water. When the oatmeal swelled to fill the bowl, she deposited one teaspoon of it and a healthy pour of cold ale into a window box of red geraniums, the closest dirt she could find. The ritual was complete. "Blessed Be!" they all sighed: tired, scared, elated.

Their last official stop of the day, Davis Bay Junction—an absolute requisite stop according to Mary Warren—proved difficult to find. Topo maps were studied; road maps were turned in bizarre configurations. Minutes turned to an hour. A road that had been clearly marked on the topo map was blocked by the construction of two new houses. Dylan took the gamble that no one was at home at either property and drove across their back sand lots in four-wheel drive. On the other side of the far property stood an old road sign crafted from beach wood, obscured by an overgrown thorny hedgerow.

"Once we leave our tokens and Honor Bundles here, we must travel through the woods behind us," Sophie said. "Mary insisted that in order to bind the Work of today and to insure future success, we had to travel down a road with no end after we left Davis Bay. That road is the road she spoke of; I found it on the map."

The map was passed around, the route acknowledged.

"It connects to a paved road and ends here, on sand. See, a road with no end! It is only a couple of miles long, a small area with lots of switchbacks, between building lots is my guess. This whole area is under construction." She was satisfied with her explanation.

Dylan studied the map again and concurred with Sophie's observations before moving out into the late afternoon air.

Expecting a breeze, they were greeted by dead calm. Only the spirals of hundreds of tiny gnats moved. The Sun was hot, but the air was cold, icy in some spots. Sophie moved her hand over the Earth and it groaned beneath her, responding to her touch. A disturbance began from deep within the wood. Sophie could not see a change, but she could feel it, could hear it. The others could too—she could tell by the looks on their faces. Blowing, the wind whistled and roared through the dense pines. "Let's tie our bundle to the sign post and be done with this place. We need to get through those woods, sooner rather than later. See? See all those shadows, dancing on the grove line? Something is brewing in there and we just need to get through it. Let's move out!" Sophie did a Spirit Salute and jumped into the front seat. Dylan had the engine started before the doors were shut.

The sheer force of the wind whipped the front windows of the SUV with tree branches as soon as Dylan pulled into the woods. Sophie could hear the girls gasp. She turned to look and found horror in their faces. She followed their line of vision and found what was frightening them. The densely planted pines appeared to be people. The Spirits were hysterical, lashing out, screaming cries of anguish, now audible through closed windows. They were surrounded by angry Spirits who were unwilling to listen, desiring to do harm to those who recognized them. They had dealt with hundreds of Spirits today and had never been in danger. Now, threats were real. The only way to deal with it was to move through it.

Sweetgrass for the Spirits, Sage for purification, Cedar and Rosemary for protection. Sophie opened her window a crack and told Dylan to put his foot into it. The herbs flowed from her hand. Many times she refilled its contents. Many times the wind married the herbs with the Spirit's torment. They took no time to see if their acknowledgment soothed, they simply moved. When they finally met blacktop, Dylan came to an abrupt stop. They unleashed their seat belts and turned to look at the wood behind them. The Sun, low in the sky, offered no light. The wood was dark and still and offered no secrets. Silently, they buckled up and left the wood behind, making their way back to Peabody.

The first thing Sophie had to do, once they were back at the hotel, before unpacking the day's provisions and tools, was to lay out the large pristine AAA road map on the dining table. There were two road maps, one virginal, one marked with the final trail of the itinerary. Out came her red marking pen, touching the map at Davis Bay Junction.

She declared to no one in particular, "We have visited our first stop in the 21.8 mile triangle of this journey. Two more stops to go: Pentucket tomorrow and Saugus on Friday. We have begun in earnest. Yesterday was our hello, today was our intention, tomorrow we'll take real action, striking a Spirit Bargain with Metacomet and wrestling with Hannah Dustin.

"We kept our cool all day, through the ceremonies and ritual dancing at the beaches. Cape Ann was touching—I found it profound. After our feast, we got sleepy and lazy—we let down our guard, even though we knew Davis Bay Junction was ahead of us. Mary Warren warned us about the importance of the land around Davis Bay, but we were too busy being overwhelmed to notice the danger we faced. We entered the dark woods, knowing it was haunted, knowing we had to keep our focus. Instead, we became afraid and let it show. We barreled our way through the woods, ghouls gnawing at our backs. We saw and felt the real consequences of using a location as a favorite killing field. The woods were fluid with anger and grief, the SUV's wheels slid like it was on a spit of melting sand and mud. The unbridled, willful killing done in the name of the Confederacy created a negative army and put it into action, haunting the woods and charging it with negative energy, the opposite of what we found at Charter Street. We are unscathed because we weren't paralyzed in our fear; we didn't have time to get stuck. We crashed our way through, clumsily. Unfortunately, we did not create any closure or peace with our presence in the killing field and perhaps we exacerbated the wood's negative charge. We were lucky we didn't bring any of the haunts home with us today. It was a good reminder to be more focused and display fearlessness tomorrow. Courage means survival on all levels. We'll always remember the woods at Davis Bay Junction, another Family Confederacy hot spot, filled with red, black, and white bodies, all confused and angry."

Sophie shook her head, yawned, said no to supper, and said, "Sleep well, my friends." Her bed awaited her aching body.

Chapter Thirteen

HANNAH DUSTIN'S SECRETS
March 15, 1977, 3:00 a.m.

SANTA FE IN MARCH IS USUALLY HARSH. The year of Sophie's divorce from Stephan proved to be one of its coldest and windiest. Sophie hated the wind. It made her feel beat up and mournful. It was a hard night, tossing and turning, the blankets too heavy on her feet. She felt strangled, overly hot, but plagued by a constant icy breeze through the old adobe walls. Sophie was alone for the first night in years. She had grown weary of her marriage to Stephan by the end of their first year together. They were on year three now, but Sophie decided she had her fill. Relationships didn't have to be like her parents, fighting or fornicating, the passion confused and furious. She had been only eighteen when she married Stephan, the first Karmic stop on her path to independence. Her mother, Sarah, had met Stephan's mother, Eugenia, when Sarah was pregnant with Sophie. Both women felt their meeting was kismet.

When Sophie decided she knew best and wanted a taste of the world, her mother had called Stephan, who was newly divorced and lonely. She asked him to pick Sophie up at the airport, knowing her daughter would feel the connection and latch on, if Stephan was interested. Sarah knew he was.

The Spring before, Sarah had gone to Southern California on a numerology tour of spiritually oriented churches. Stephan had been her in-state manager and had done a wonderful job organizing the tour. After a packed house at a Spiritual Frontiers convention, they shared a meal of room service around the dining table in Sarah's hotel room. Feeling sentimental as well as tired, she decided to share a fresh batch of family photographs with Stephan, including one of Sophie. Stephan's mouth hung open and he asked in an astounded fashion if the picture was really Sophie. "Oh yes, Stephan, Sophie has grown into a beautiful girl. I think you would like her. You know, she's doing well at university but feels the need for adventure from time to time."

Stephan cocked a crooked smile and said, "I bet she does."

The lights of the Los Angeles basin shone for Sophie as the plane landed—she was excited and flushed with adrenaline. She thought she was having her first adventure without interference from her parents; how wrong she was! Stephan was waiting, prepared for her visit, complete with a bouquet of daisies, her favorite flowers. It was love at first sight for him. She would catch up after her first orgasm. The tempestuous couple married six weeks after her arrival in Los Angeles, having being begged out of a Tijuana elopement on day four of their dance as supposed Soul Mates. Three years later, here she was in a bad bed, alone, with only a leaky wall to keep her company.

She dozed off, finally bored with the endless recitation of past mistakes. Seconds, perhaps minutes later, she opened her eyes and knew she was not alone. She reached under her bed and grabbed the heavy oak bat a friend had carved for her to carry during her late night prowls. All her friends worried about Sophie, her part-time job as an exorcist. She had too much bravado for her own good. Wild dogs and Cholos didn't frighten her. At twenty-one, Sophie was naïve. They had problems in this neighborhood—one block from the Agua Frio barrio—with break-ins and rapes.

The people on Park Avenue lived as an extended family, separated only by the compound's walls. People drifted in and out in all seasons of the year. Everybody trusted everybody else and kept their doors and windows carelessly unlocked. The police always said, "Those hippies invite criminals to live with them, what do they expect?" The police were no help at all. The Park Avenue residents were forced to protect themselves, especially the women. Fortunately, other than a frustrated suitor stealing her fiesta outfit the year before—he was upset she was married and unavailable to marry him—Sophie had slid through unscathed. She was prepared for her life to change tonight; she felt it piercing the back of her skull, migraines being one result of Second Sight.

The bat was wet and slippery in her grip, as she held it close and tight in anticipation of having to use it. The small apartment filled with a heavy, sweet smell she gradually realized to be blood. Fear surged through Sophie's body, but she couldn't move. She was paralyzed in Stephan's sagging bed.

The floorboards creaked at the bedroom's entrance. The light of the alley's street lamp filtered through the curtains, just enough to reveal a protoplasmic shape, crouched low. Sophie began to stir, realizing a Spirit was approaching her, not a living human. The danger had not passed, but it had changed. She always came prepared for physical battles with Spirit entities when cleaning a space. Her ears filled with a sound like rushing water, from rapidly rising blood pressure. Time was nonexistent: Sophie and the Spirit stalker were caught in a time warp.

The Spirit took on a defined female shape, dressed in a strange collection of filthy clothes, a white woman wearing moccasins, her face smeared with charcoal to disguise her from the light. She carried a hatchet in her right hand and a dripping bundle in her left.

"I know you are here. I see you. Stop! Come no closer!" Sophie began to lift the heavy covers, feeling too vulnerable lying down.

"No, no, Miss, don't move. I only want to talk with you. You know my relation, she lives across the street and speaks of you often. She doesn't know I'm there when she talks with her friends, although she shivers fiercely when I'm with her. She doesn't believe what she can't see—she comes from New Hampshire, where they are a practical folk."

Sophie sat up with a flash of realization. "Oh, you are talking about Spruce. We work together at the Hilton."

"I know her as Lydia, Lydia Dustin," the specter offered. *"Through Lydia, I found you, a Seer who can hear as well."*

"Can you please lay down the hatchet? If you insist on being here, lay your weapon down and compose yourself!" Sophie was wet with sweat. She was in her exorcism mode now, talking tough, scared to the bone. Why do these Spirits always seek her out? She had to pee, the adrenaline rushing through her body working overtime.

The Spirit nodded in understanding, bowing her head, knowing it was time to change her walking ways. She was so used to carrying the ominous hatchet and bundle of bloody scalps. The specter looked in Sophie's direction and motioned her over.

With bat in hand, Sophie slowly moved to the ghost's side and looked at the bundle being opened and presented to her with pride. She did not believe what she saw, her eyes playing tricks on her in the dark, only a sliver of street lamp and reflection of the night light over the Main Altar to depend on. Sophie didn't want to play games. "Why do you pester me with your gross offerings? Who are you and what do you want with me?" Sophie exhaled a long, acid-tasting breath in the Spirit's direction.

The Spirit took a rag from her apron and rubbed her face clean of the soot disguising her. She rearranged her filthy clothing and shook her apron down for loose debris.

She began in a formal manner.

"Hannah Dustin is my name. I am a settler near the New Hampshire border, close to a fort town called Haverhill, in the Northern top of the Massachusetts Colony. The English have an outpost here, standing guard for the growing number of settlers, protecting the Crown's claim against the French. The French are few in numbers, so they had a scheme to hire mercenaries, many small bands and families of Indians from many disconnected clans, mainly Abenaki. Thousands of Indians were dying of the pox. Many had no loved ones left. The French gave them a new name, Croix Rouge. They are powerful but have few friends among other red people. They live in a world of their own making.

"Some said there was talk of starvation among the Croix Rouge, the French refusing them rations when the game animals left last Fall. The ones who survived the Winter were angry at any white people and went in search of food and weapons among the settlers. If they were lucky, they would capture sturdy young women to sell to the French brothels in the North. Because of hunger, the raiding parties of men brought their women and children with them. Their food booty could be divided as soon as it was gathered so their charges would not die. The men would leave their families just out of range from their battles, close enough to run with, if something went wrong.

"It was a night like this, clear and cold, the ice making a creaking sound, the river rushing hard, filled from the early Spring thaw. The wind was frigid and had a relentless howl. I rose from the bed, away from snoring Thomas, holding the new babe in my arms. I couldn't sleep because of a state of panic growing inside me since the birth of the babe, six days before. Goody Neff, the midwife, said the panic would pass, the baby would stop fussing and begin to suckle properly, and she would finally stop crying.

"I wanted to please Thomas. He wanted a tribe of children for himself, a human legacy to work the homestead and grow fat from its yield. I lost four children who came to term: the baby twins, my dear Mary when she was fifteen, and John when he was a lad of four. I stopped counting the miscarriages and stillbirths. Twelve live births was enough, one too many, I hate to admit. Thomas loved babies. He named the new one Marthia. Screamer is what I called her. After losing

the twins three years before, I lost patience for babes. Fortunately, Thomas was a willing and able father.

"I heard rustling in the trees. No animals ventured this close in the night, other than a rat looking for Spring seed. This noise came at a man's height. I nudged Thomas awake and handed him his rifle with my free hand. Goody Neff was still in the house helping me, because of sickbed fever. I was feeling better, stronger than the previous days, but not well enough to care for the other children. She crept up behind me and took the babe from my arms. Marthia was wrapped up in Goody Neff's shawl, kept in place by her husband's heavy leather belt. She placed the babe close to her chest, under the security of her wrap. She went out the back trap door, through the woods to safety. That was the plan. Thomas instructed the children to stay silent, crouch low, and to follow him into the root cellar. I would stay upstairs, by the door, available to supply a diversion to keep the children safe.

"From the front window, I could see a man carrying a torch, illuminating the patch of wood on the East side of the house. I saw Goody Neff held tight by another man. She kicked and clawed, but still he restrained her. Marthia began to cry, not a gentle baby cry, but a desperate fearful howl. The other man pulled the babe from Goody Neff's middle, held her up by her feet, and swung her hard, her little head smashing against a tree.

"I screamed and fell into a pile on the floor. I hadn't wanted another babe, yet another mouth to feed and life to fret over. But she was my flesh and blood and when I saw her in parts, my heart shattered into a thousand pieces. My shrieks brought my captives directly to me. One wrenched me from the floor and tied me tightly with hide, while the other man searched the house. He missed the hatch to the root cellar; the rest of my brood was safe and had Thomas to care for them. The searching man became frustrated and began upturning baskets and bowls looking for food and trade items. At long last, he found the small cache of withered potatoes, late carrots, and smoked bits of pork and turkey I had brought up from the cellar earlier in the evening for soup. The man also found a bag of cornmeal, left under a bucket to protect it from mice. The men seemed happy about the paltry find; the rumors about starving Croix Rouge must have been true.

"Goody Neff and I were tied together and forced deep into the woods by the river's landing. Canoes waited and were being pushed into the water by several children about the same size as my middle ones. I counted six in all, including our two captors.

"They paddled quickly and before long we arrived at a small island in the middle of the river. It was first light now. The rising yellow gave a golden glow to the fresh campfires on the horizon. Seven people waited close to the main fire, three women, two suckling babes, a toddler, and a young white man, lean and loosely tied with hide. They were a large family of two brothers, one with a young bride and two babes, the other brother with two wives with five children between them, all under ten years. The family had captured the young farmer during the Summer grain harvest, half a year ago. He looked dispossessed and lethargic, half-starved.

"The women tore into the bags of looted food and gnawed on bits of the smoked meat as they began to prepare a soup with the potatoes and carrots. I looked over at the young man, the skinny captive in rags, and asked him how long he had been a prisoner. He wouldn't answer. He bowed his head as the other man came and nodded well done, as if he were a pet dog. Goody Neff and I were forced to sit down in front of the fire and keep silent. One of the men, the young bride's mate, started to recite his exploits of the night of plunder. He started to act out the killing of my babe. I couldn't help but understand his movements. I bent at the waist and started crying. The young bride rose and started to hit her mate over his neck and back and screamed a tirade, obviously angry at the murder of Marthia. The allegiance had no effect on me that night. I wanted them all dead, all Indians dead.

"By midday, we were floating down the river, swiftly. The men and younger boys paddled. Two weeks went by and I reckon a hundred and fifty miles of river and trail we traveled, up the Merrimack, all the way to the mouth of the Contoocook near Penacook, New Hampshire.

"I confess to liking the life, leaving one campfire for another. If one area was too hard, then another was secured by the next day. It didn't feel like we were running, which in fact we were, from the English and the French. I had no chores. I felt semi-free, the best I have ever felt, which made me feel terribly guilty with so many mouths to feed at home. It made me all the angrier with my captors. How dare they live better than we! There were the two babes to remind me about the loss of Marthia. The young bride, who had stood up to her mate over my babe, then kept her distance from him. They were not happy after I came to live there in the wild. She gave me extra rations and liked to comb my hair, thinner and finer than hers.

"Samuel, the skinny boyish man, a quick learner and smart enough to survive his ordeal, had a working knowledge of our captors' language. He had caught enough talk to know Goody Neff and I were in trouble. We were too old for the brothels, so we would have to be sold as slaves to other richer Indians. It didn't promise a good life. If we didn't sell quickly in the villages, we would be killed and left for the wolves. We would find the first village by tomorrow's eventide. I had to make a plan and be willing to follow through with it that night.

"I was allowed to prepare roots and fish meals with the other women, as well as a kind of porridge made of corn, plundered from my kitchen. The bride made an easy life for me, preferring my company over her husband's. This worked in the burgeoning plan. The family had their routines and lived around the waning and waxing day. By the time dark was upon us, the children demanded sleep and the adults followed suit soon thereafter. I assumed it would be different for them if they had a permanent home, instead of preparing shelter each night, the traveling group's constant diversion. Food was not plentiful and there was just so much energy to go around. Sleep and quiet were desired treasures. Able to move around more freely, now trust had been earned, I moved slowly away from our captors and quietly woke Samuel. While Samuel loosened Goody Neff's bonds, I secured three large sharp rocks, one for each of us. Amazingly, no one woke as we split up, Samuel taking leave for the other man's side. I would kill the bride's husband, the murderer in my dreams.

"The bride tried to stop me, once she realized what I was doing. I pointed to the infant at her breast and the wood. Although silent, I demanded she go. She faded into the dark on silent command. Samuel bludgeoned the other man and began the same on his woman. Samuel screamed, realizing the impact of his deeds. He dropped his rock and ran in the direction of the river, covered in blood. Goody Neff had bashed a few of the children silly and they were still. I finished the rest. God help me, I killed the wee ones too. Once I killed the man, nothing stopped me from picking the rest off, one by one. Goody Neff hurled her supper, miserable and inconsolable at what she did, at what I did. I yelled at her to grab a bag and fill it with whatever food was left, including the fresh game caught earlier in the day.

"I heard the canoes, first one gliding, then another hitting the rocks and breaking up. We ran with the goods as fast as our legs would travel. We could see the bride gliding down the river, directed by current only. I saw Samuel, scuttling the canoes. I yelled for him to stop. We needed an escape. One was left, thank the Good Lord. We crawled into the boat, placed the goods in the center and began to paddle, catching the swift currents.

"Instant grief hit me, all the murders and nothing to show for it. Spring seed was still lacking, fabric was needed for clothes for all the children, the children would be hungry. I stopped my furious paddling and yelled for the two to stop, we had to go back. There was a ransom of scalps waiting. I would burn in hell for killing small children, why not do it with a full stomach? I don't know if it was hate, or panic, or hysteria motivating me to go back, but there I was, searching for retribution, my only salvation.

"Samuel had seen scalping done before. I had done my share of rendering meat and birthed all the babes. I was used to blood and I knew Goody Neff was too. My thoughts lasted split seconds. I barked out orders and had a blanket brought to me for making a bundle. Samuel was hysterical again. "Just come here and show me what to do and then I'll leave you be. We will share in the bounty, we have all earned it!"

"Samuel showed me where to hit the skull for a clean break of the top notch, all that was needed for the bounty fee. I did the rest, and in a minute's time it was done. I was covered with blood, sticky and thick. It was first light. I could see the carnage wrought. It didn't belong to me, it was abstract and removed. But the pictures of human destruction will never leave my mind!

"Paddling into the landing point at Haverhill, I couldn't believe what had happened. How one minute I was happy, relieved, and uncomplicated, the next I was a savage child murderer. I thought of my sister Elizabeth killing her own beloved twins in 1693, four years ago already, the fever taking her to dark places. She hanged for it, and it haunted me how my own sister could kill her own flesh and blood, two beautiful children. Now, I will burn like my sister. I took all their scalps and am responsible for all their deaths, since I ordered Samuel and Goody Neff to help me with the bodies in quick order, getting the larger ones first. The babes just cried and waited their turn.

"I could never go home again, could never look into the faces of my children and love them as innocent beings. I am too corrupted and will always be so. We didn't go home, none of us. We were in the state of shock and didn't know whether to cry or shake or run. We walked instead. As a group, with shared footsteps, we dragged ourselves to the Garrison House. They would know how to handle the reward and get us to our respective families.

"It came to pass, just as I said. After several testimonies to various men in charge, a reward was paid out, a bounty split three ways. I never saw Samuel again, even as a Walking Spirit. He must have gone to the light. I saw Goody Neff, though. Shared sadness was our bond. We rarely talked but would reach out to each other and hold hands and sometimes cry. She helped me with my last babe, the following year in October while the trees blazed in hot colors. Her name was Lydia, a handsome, well-fed girl with lungs on her strong enough to wake the whole river basin.

"I could never get over the loss of Marthia. I vowed if I were to make it to heaven, I would find her and never let her go. The guilt of not wanting her to begin with was too much to bear. I thought Lydia could fill in the missing place in my heart, but it never worked, I only ached for Marthia. I could not look at innocent faces the same way ever again.

"I was never a churchgoer, even when the Puritans got their dander up and demanded the meetinghouse be filled. After the reunion with Thomas and the children, I began going to meetings regularly and seeking counsel, my grief being so great. The Reverend Cotton Mather himself told my family he could cure me of melancholy and teach me to regard myself as a woman hero of the colonies. I found him dull and touchy, he wanting to caress my hands, arms, and knees. He said it would ease my fears and allow myself to surrender to the will of God. His touch felt intrusive. Even Thomas's touch would burn me sometimes. It was no use. Reverend Mather said he would cure me, save my soul, and make me a hero of the New Jerusalem. I let people think what they wanted: me, a brave lioness, evening the score for her lost cub. It didn't help me, the saving of my soul. I began living in hell every night, my dreams filled with the bloody deeds. Time doesn't heal; don't believe people who tell you that! Time makes the wounds deeper, they fester and do not heal and eventually poison your soul with grief.

"This is my story of neverending nights, pursued, hungry, lost. I was not brave. I was deliriously grieving and in a state of constant unforgiving guilt. It drove me mad. I was a murderer of children for profit.

"I decided to stay as I am after I left my mortal body. Perhaps my decision was based on my fear of hell. I could always hear Marthia, I knew she was there, her Spirit so strong. I could watch the ripple of her cries on the river where I walked, her energy strong, unlike her frail baby's body. I prayed to God for her suffering to end, for her to go to heaven and wait for me there. My prayers were not answered, making me feel distrust for God, not sure he really existed in my heart. I still heard her outside the front door, upstairs in the sleeping rooms, high in the rafters of the barn. Her cries haunted my days and nights. She only rested in the deep night, too exhausted to rally her ghostly sounds. I swore to her I would find her. One day I would leave my body. I would die and join her. I would find her and bond to her as I was unable to do when she was a squirming bundle in my arms. I would cradle her until she cooed, I would feed her until she found sleep in easy milky excess. I would save her from her haunting and she would save me from my guilt. I swore to her I would do this.

"When I left my body, before it was buried, before others had stopped their human tears, I found her in pieces under the big tree where I heard her last scream. I knelt above her, not knowing what to do, not knowing how to put her together again. I felt a gentle breeze on my cheek, like a reassuring brush of an angel's *wings. It inspired a breeze of my own. I began blowing and humming a mother's lullaby, rocking on bended knee, crying waterless tears. I picked up each piece of her, still warm and wet, and fitted them together, easing the ragged seams with my breathy humming. Slowly, Marthia mended before my eyes, first her head, then her arms. She became whole and rose her expectant arms up toward me. I reached for my baby daughter and felt her impatient fidgeting and placed her on my breast until I felt a familiar feeding tug. I found her, she found me, we are whole, impaired but together.*

"She lives with me, between the worlds. She is still a babe and does not grow like normal children. She hardly cries or makes a fuss. She is in the blissful suckling stage of a brand new baby. She is not a bother, does not cry or ball her fists in the air, growing red with anger and frustration. She coos and suckles and sleeps. See, she is with me now, under my clothes, near my heart, my warmest part. While I am here, neither one of us can journey to the light and find new bodies. This is my choice. Separation from my precious girl is not possible. She is so young she never speaks. Even in her mind, she is all innocence, captured forever in our special time."

Sophie felt confused, rubbing the last of sleep from her eyes. "Why do you come to me, when you are in the place you desire to be, with your baby? Isn't that what you wanted, to be reunited with her? All your needs are met where you are now and it doesn't sound like you want to leave."

"You are right, I do not want to leave. But I would like to give Marthia a choice. This is the reason I sought you out; my conscience needs mending. I must know what Marthia desires. I have disquieting thoughts and do not find pleasure walking the late night hours as I once did. Once, all I needed was to be in the deep night, quiet still times, the snores of the living my only music. But it no longer completely satisfies."

Without farewell or notice of any kind, Hannah began dissolving into the street lamp's sliver of light. Sophie glanced at the clock—it was 4:15 a.m.—a full hour and a quarter spent with a ghost, too long a visit for Sophie to handle easily. Spirits are usually thrifty with time, provoked to talk with the living only when an important agenda was pending. Spirits shared split seconds of information, perhaps a lone misty finger pointing in the dark, maybe a whisper, a hint of why they came, that's it. Hannah was decidedly different; she was cordial, not in the least aloof, she wanted to talk. She was a whole person, as solid as any corporeal being. She wanted input, a relationship.

Sophie sensed Hannah's need to share, to have human-to-human communion. On some level, Hannah wanted a body again, wanted a life not so routine, wanted fate to affect her survival once again. The life as a Walking Spirit was too predictable. A friendship with Sophie would serve to placate her simple wants for the time being, until she knew the most intelligent course of action.

Hannah would visit in March, on the fifteenth or sixteenth, sometimes the twenty-second, depending on what aspect of her ordeal bothered her most on a particular night. She began manifesting at three a.m., a desired hour for Spirits with agendas or Spirits using fear and anger as their tools of communication, the *deep night* Spirits talk of. She was volatile at times and always bloody, even when in a cordial mood. She was used to her terrifying demeanor and used it whenever possible, not unlike Giles's down-island mean face. Hannah was stuck and wanted a friend to understand her motivations, bored with the life she created. She did not know what she wanted but could not imagine her life any other way.

Hannah's visits persisted. Sophie grew accustomed to Hannah's bloody apron and her sneaking ways and didn't feel guilty for turning her back from time to time, when sleep was more important than psychotherapy. Phobic ghosts, would they ever find a new counselor?

April 1, 2007, 3:00 a.m.

THIRTY YEARS LATER, SOPHIE PREFERRED SLEEPING on the reclining sofa in the living room to her bed. She was never in the mood to be at the mercy of Walking Spirits in need of grounding. Spirits loved Sophie's bedroom even more than she did. The Crown Chakra colors sang even in the dark. She had been dealing with a constant flow of disembodied Spirits from Massachusetts, from three to four a.m., every night for months. She had tried going to bed at five in the morning, staying awake through the common haunting hours, usually abating visitations or at least putting them off until the next night. But it proved to be an impossible hour because Dylan got up for work every morning at five and she could never fall asleep after hearing the final latch of the gate. She was weary of the steady stream of petitioners, most still in their death gear, smeared with dirt, the human grease of fear and blood.

She had to take the gamble and try to sleep in her own bed tonight; she needed to get flat and really rest. She was keyed up after an intense metaphysical conversation with Poe and needed soft comfort and familiar surroundings to relax. Sophie completed her nightly devotions, turned off the pinkish nightlight, and wiggled into her soft foam mattress. As soon as she closed her eyes, inviting sleep with relish and controlled breathing, someone turned on the lights. Not the overhead lights of the ceiling fan, but an eerie green glow, surrounded by a protoplasmic cloud shimmering like Mylar, like bouncing rainbows. This was precisely why she had been downstairs for two weeks, where the Walking Spirits rarely bothered her.

Sophie rose from her warm bed and followed the acid-green mist into her office. She found the source of the protoplasmic cloud, the silver Dell. Out of the two dim green lights on the computer tower were lines of mist, dry-ice streams cooling all of her isolated second-story rooms. She finally grasped the importance of resting your computer and turned off the machine. She knew the computer and the telephone were direct energy links to different consciousnesses, one reason why psychic counseling and channeling via the phone or internet can be a powerful tool for radical truth-telling. These electrical devices supersede bodies and expressions. They are not stopped by the body's barriers to confrontation. The truth flows right out, uncensored and concentrated. The best psychics use the telephone for intuitive readings; Tarot readings flow well too. Sophie had a high-speed computer connection, because so much of her counseling work was done via the internet—and emergency energy-work too. Dealing with the dead and dying comes at unorthodox hours. She always kept her computer on and her phone plugged in. She smiled and swore she would turn off the computer and unplug the telephone landline every night from now on.

Maybe she could sleep after the mist lifted, perhaps. It was then, sitting at her desk in her oversized office chair, that she felt a gentle tapping on her left shoulder, a familiar signal from her main Spirit Teacher and Protector, Padre Pio. Sophie could not contain a broad smile and felt a flush of warmth in the frigid room. She turned her swiveling chair clockwise, wanting an embrace from her Spiritual Father. Instead, she found Hannah Dustin, standing tall, freshly cleaned, faintly smelling of lavender and clove.

"I have asked you to listen to my stories, feel my pain, and counsel right actions. This time I need more. I know you are preparing for a ritual journey to the Massachusetts Colony, Essex County, then North to Newburyport and Sawyer's Hill. I implore you to travel a bit further and visit me in Haverhill. I keep to myself there, not walking much anymore, staying close with Marthia. But I am bothered of late by the presence of my husband, Thomas. He wants me to come to the light now, to let Marthia come too. He's found us all a place, a mother expecting triplets,

a womb big enough for the three of us, so he says. I don't want to go, but you know I have been feeling guilty about Marthia, still so small and dependent, year after year. Thomas is pushing me. I need help dealing with him and his expectations. I must act soon, because the triplets are due in December of this year. You are travel-ing in September—the timing could not be better! Please come and visit with me, come persuade me if you must. I need peace, peace from Thomas, peace from guilt. Come to the rock in Haverhill, I'll be waiting; all three of us will be there, the Good Lord willing."

"I will come and parlay with you, Hannah. I will be there for Marthia and Thomas as well, if they choose to speak." Sophie used a firm voice. "We must intuit the right action for Marthia. She has been in the infant state, six days old, for three hundred and ten years. She will need big energy and lots of persuading to join us conversationally, if she is able—it's iffy. I will work on you, the three of you, from now till we meet in September. But you must agree to stay away from me, give me space, and do not visit me, especially in the deep night. If you need to be close to me, stay out of sight and guard this energy portal and help keep the Spirit activity to a minimum. The more rest I have, the more prepared I am to do battle in the Spirit Realms and the more successful I will be. If I am depleted, I am no use to anyone, including you. So, what say you, Hannah Dustin, do you agree?" Sophie sighed.

"Agreed!" Hannah whispered, as she disintegrated into the Ethers.

Sophie turned around, made sure the computer was off, no green lights showing, no more pyrotechnics tonight. She walked into her dark, snug bed-room and removed the pink comforter and her favorite pillow. She did not wait till the mist cleared; she was too tired and wanted her life to be her own, not shared in some communal otherworldly think-tank. But she knew better than to ask Spirit to go away, because they did, with absolutely no fanfare, just gone. Sophie could not survive without her link to Spirit; it was her salvation regardless of how impossible it made her life. She walked down the stairs and found her familiar sofa and prayed for the release of sleep.

Chapter Fourteen

THE CANDY STORE

Tuesday, September 18, 2007, 6:00 a.m.,
Putnam Pantry, Danvers

ENERGY SURGED FORWARD, forcing Sophie out of bed. The bed was torn apart from constant tossing and turning. She was excited, maybe afraid even, and definitely tense about going to the candy shop. The shop didn't open till nine, so how would she stay calm and cool for three more hours? She held her expectations to a minimum—at least on the surface, keeping up a cool front for the others—thinking about visiting Giles's true burial spot. She hoped to delay any possible anxiety or paranoia, hers or the group's, but it wasn't working.

Putnam Pantry is the core of Putnam country, held in their hands for centuries. In the latter half of the twentieth century, Drake's father had sold the candy store and rights to use the adjacent field—some of it already black-topped, perfect for a parking lot—to an old friend. Of course, the new owner was a distant member of the Family Confederacy.

The Family Confederacy was comprised of one source family, the Putnams. Over the span of three short generations, the Putnams, rich in ambition, lust, and loose connections, married and became one extended family with ten surnames by the time of the Witch Trials. Some names would shock a veteran genealogist, the real reason for secrecy. Now, in the twenty-first century, there were hundreds of names, with origins from many states and countries, who claimed Essex County as their birthright. Who were these original people, easily organized and galvanized in their greed? The answer was simple: all you had to do was look at the arrest warrants issued from Sheriff George Corwin's office. They were on display at the Peabody Essex Museum. The same names arose, time after time: innkeepers, farmers, soldiers, linked and bedded with judges. The scholar only had to compare the arrest warrants with marriage records from Rev. Samuel Parris's Meeting-house, the First Church of Salem; the secrets were in full view.

Judge Saltonstall had figured out the conspiracy for riches and land in 1692, the reason he removed himself from the bench of the Court of Oyer and Terminer. He suspected that incest was a secondary issue galvanizing the families into a solid fretful front. He wrote a report about his findings and sent it to several people well placed in Essex County, hoping for their assistance and support, which he never received. Some families didn't try to hide their greed and lascivious ways, so steeped in ego the Confederacy was. Saltonstall would be no party to it. He complained to everyone—his power of persuasion fiery—including Governor Phipps and the Reverends Mather, father and son, of Boston. No one would listen. Accusations of Witchcraft could not be ignored by the government for any reason; they had to be acted on, swiftly and with force. There were many people paid off with promises of rich booty from the pickings of Essex County's accused. The bribed would realize at the dissolution of the trials that the Confederacy and their favorite agent, George Corwin, had already feasted on the treasures, leaving them nothing but scraps. Then, the property lines were redrawn, and new Con-federacy tenants filed their rights of ownership and were speedily granted occupation and safety rights on rich new parcels.

It was Sophie's dream to lodge in Peabody, close to Corey land—bor-dered on all sides by Moulton and Confederacy land. Dylan made it hap-pen. Corwin had eventually lost his deed to Giles's land. Upon his death, it reverted to the Moultons. The Moulton family had several brothers, one as different as another. One brother, John, married Giles's daughter Eliza-beth. John was surly and easily brought to anger, unafraid to use his large girth when bullying the weak. Another brother, Robert, married yet another claimed daughter from Giles's first wife. In contrast to John, Robert was even-tempered, hardworking, and loyal to a fault. Giles favored Robert from the beginning, and John hated him for it.

John was no farmer. Years of failed crops followed his naturally lazy ways. He received regular dressing-downs from Giles, claiming he was an even poorer pirate than farmer when, in desperation, Giles took him into the family business of rum-smuggling. John forced himself out, unable to cope with Giles's demanding ways, and found regular employment as Sheriff George Corwin's labor foreman. Giles felt betrayed by John's new employment with one of his archrivals, choosing the nefarious ways of Corwin and the Confederacy over his own family's enterprise. Giles swore John Moulton would never see a farthing of his money from that point forward. John bit his lip and under his breath he swore he would be an agent of Giles's undoing. He would plunder Giles's fortune, using whatever method was offered him by Corwin. He wanted Giles Corey's blood.

Sophie was afraid to be stranded alone in Salem or Danvers, in the open, recognizable in hostile territory. She thought she had overcome the fear of public display at Charter Street on Sunday and at the ocean yesterday. But, deep inside, she still feared the same shapeless Bogey Man. She knew she needed to be vulnerable in her Work with the Spirit Realms. Soul Retrieval and integration work demanded a base of empathy. Without it, trust was never established between parties, human and Spirit. The mission stalled before it began. She wanted to be close to the Putnams, wanted to feel surrounded by their energy, able to smell them, coming and going. If she was able to move with them, in harmonious tandem, they would be less of a threat. She would become one of them, so she could anticipate their reactions to the magick she was weaving. The Inner Circle had no idea that their binding of Giles would be rendered useless when Giles integrated into Sophie, haunting and walking parts united equally with Giles's Core Self. Sophie and Giles would make an irrepressible force.

Sophie wondered how many more years the Inner Circle would gather in September and April to bind Giles with no chance of success. Would they feel their failure? Lori Otto would figure it out; she had a sound understanding of the binding and loosening, the tug and pull of kabbalistic path-working systems. She would follow the pathways to their final length and discover all bonds cut and dangling in space. Would she share her ultimate failure with Rose, with Drake, ending three hundred and fifteen years of organized bad magick? Would Confederacy property holdings lose value, would tourists stop coming to Essex County if they knew the Witch Trials were fake, based on lies, innocent people put to death to cover up their schemes, murders, and rapes? Essex County was divided into the haves and the have-nots in 1692, the Putnams growing rich by land-grabbing and brash enough to use bragging rights.

Would Lori Otto continue to compete for followers with Laurie Cabot, or would she retire to her not-so-secret holdings in Puerto Rico with her flighty devotees and dozens of shedding cats?

Sophie didn't care what happened to the illegal spoils gathered by the Confederacy. She understood she could not go back to her land and claim it as Giles. She would not want to be in Massachusetts after integration. She wanted a new and improved base of operations, separate from the sting of betrayal and torture received here.

The Inner Circle had regular informal lunches at Putnam Pantry, gathering over Giles's bones before the twice-a-year bindings began. Mainly middle-aged women, with dyed blonde and red hair, wearing easygoing capris and walking shoes, comprised the Inner Circle. They fit in with the rest of suburbia and the rural money folk of Essex County, mothers, wives, and spinster caretakers of invalid parents. The Circle Sisters wore shades of pastel, finding the black of the rest of Salem's magickal workers too stale and predictable and a little too Puritan for their tastes. They liked spicy food, mainly Thai, daring each other on with the hottest red peppers this side of the Orient. Chocolate motivated the sisters of the Inner Circle, always an endless supply over Giles's bones. The Circle Sisters could not gather without being recognized in Salem and Danvers, but Peabody and Beverly offered them protection of anonymity.

Sophie loved dark chocolate as much as love itself, as much as the Circle Sisters of the Inner Circle; they had many things in common. They knew eating chocolate over the bones of Giles Corey would give them power, fortitude and courage. The lure of the candy shop was irresistible and they abandoned reason over sweet seduction every time.

In the early 1990s, Lori Otto accepted the post as High Priestess for the Inner Circle, a well-paying position most manipulative Witches itched for, if they actually knew of its existence. In most Salem Circles, populated by transplants from San Francisco to Nova Scotia, the Inner Circle was a myth, a rumor with no basis in reality. Natives of the Commonwealth knew better, and for people in the know, there was no greater choice to be had than Priestess Otto. She was born in Massachusetts, spoke in a thick local accent, and was plainly a scrapper. She could talk with legislators as well as garbage collectors; she was a skilled chameleon. Lori proudly claimed a strong Strega lineage, a magickal tradition of Italy, particularly popular in the Renaissance. She seemed irreproachable and perfect for the job.

Lori had always been in a combative, competitive relationship with the Official Witch of Salem, Laurie Cabot. Lori desired justice; she wanted the public Salem post for herself, knowing she was more gifted than the cartoon façade of Laurie Cabot. Once Drake paid the first installment of her twice-yearly paycheck, Lori called a public news conference, a popular ploy to attract the tourist dollars around Halloween each year. All the public Witches were encouraged to draw public crowds in October, the Chamber of Commerce preferring taking the heat off September, the twenty-second being the date of the last hangings of the trials. Lori called Drake's secretary, an old Circle Sister from the sixties. She extended Drake an invitation to stand at the podium with her during the conference. Lori knew if she talked to the secretary first, she would enlist her friend's calculating prowess, making Drake's appearance a sure thing.

Drake did not return Lori's phone call. He was enraged, anonymity being the major requisite for the job of High Priestess. So what if Lori knew Barney Frank and had visitations with the pope in Rome? Drake would fire her promptly, as soon as the media dust settled.

Salem was all abuzz, preparing for the Halloween Crush, a month ten times more lucrative than Christmas in Witch City. The town—wrapped in purple, black, and orange—sang out its Halloween hymns from the last weekend of September through sunrise on November first. Each year, Salem prepared itself for an onslaught of international travelers, sporting Pentacles and black velvet, supposedly preserving ancient magickal traditions through public ritual at the site of one of the most provocative Witch Trial hysterias the world has known. The varied traditions spoken of in Salem during Halloween Crush were inventions of the twentieth century—Gardnerian, Alexandrian, Celtic Wicca, Neo-Pagan Hedonism—they had little to do with the magickal practices of the seventeenth century, either in Europe or the Americas. Witch City tried to be inclusive and welcomed these darkly clad visitors with open arms and cash registers.

In the center of the pedestrian walk, next to the giant gray stone fountain, the city built a covered stage of black plywood. At noon sharp, a favorite time of executioners worldwide, on October third, the day the Court of Oyer and Terminer was ordered to stop its trial judgments, the Salem High School Band began playing "That Old Black Magic." The mayor ascended the stage, followed by Salem's Official Witch in Residence, Laurie Cabot, in her black-and-white clerical robes, several Chamber of Commerce officials, the president of the local chapter of Rotarians, the head of the Massachusetts Shriners, and finally, Lori Otto. No Drake. Stunned but not daunted, this would not hold Lori back.

The day before, she had dyed her hair with an auburn rinse, pressed her favorite purple gown, and did the final edit on one of the longest speeches she had ever written. Her bitter words revealed an unrequited desire for power. She cut the original to almost nothing and began afresh, barely a paragraph finished before she left home, ten miles South. Lori was the shortest one on stage and the roundest. She was grateful they had not placed her next to Cabot, almost a head taller than she. She closed her eyes, took a deep breath, and began, "Welcome, magickal sisters and brothers of Salem. I have called you here today to share some exciting news. I have just accepted a position as Magickal Liaison and Protectrix Witch of the Salem Sheriff's Department. This post is separate from Ms. Cabot's. She, as Official Witch, continues to serve this city to the best of her abilities and I would like you all to join me in thanking her for many years of service. Please, give a hand for Ms. Cabot's efforts on our behalf. Wonderful, thank you!

"We have recently suffered the premature loss of our beloved sheriff to heart disease, the same disease taking the twenty sheriffs before him. This is a tragedy few of us wanted and even fewer expected, although it is written in our history in the form of Giles Corey's Curse. Corey cursed all of Salem, especially our protectors, the Sheriff's Department. The curse has plagued us for three hundred years with death, fires, floods, and drought. This curse will be ended with my tenure; I commit my magickal energies to the nullification of the Corey Curse, once and for all!

"With the three-hundredth anniversary of the Witch Trials behind us, we are able to look ahead and decide how we want the rest of the world to view our special community, celebrating the world's oldest religion and encouraging the equality of all religions, as long as they do no harm. Please join me in recreating a new Salem, by protecting the continuation of our great American legacy of fighting for the justice of all! Blessed Be and thank you, citizens of Salem!"

For Sophie and her group, finding the candy store was easy, just off Route 1 North, not far from the Peabody Marriott. The site, with its blacktop parking lot and red painted, barn-look "shoppe," took Sophie's breath away. Fifty feet from the main entrance, wedged between two parking places, was a sinkhole about six feet in diameter. This was Giles's burial place. He would leave his mark on this lot just as he did on the lot next to the Old Salem jailhouse—it was Giles's graffiti.

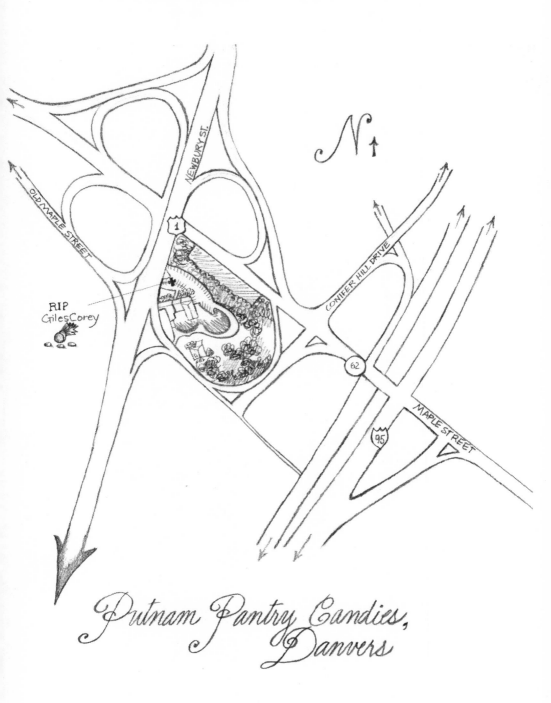

Putnam Pantry Candies, Danvers

On September 19, 1692, Giles Corey was pressed here.
On September 22, 1692, Giles Corey died here,
smashed over the head with his own shovel until he closed his eyes
forever.
On September 22, 1692, Giles Corey was buried here.

Sinkholes were his signature upon the land of Essex County.

The four slid out of their seats and made their way for the sinkhole. They reached out for each other, all with tears in their eyes. Times like these made them shake the doubt from their heads, clear the blinders from their eyes. They could feel Giles here, smiling, joining them for a casual stroll into the shop. Walking Giles—inspired by their camaraderie—joined Sophie directly to her left. Dylan hopped out of the way, as if he had just been stung by a hot wire. "Shit, what was that? Did you feel it?"

Sophie smiled and told everyone they had a visitor. Walking Giles would not miss this visit for the world! Dora smiled broadly and hooked Sophie's right arm into hers. The group moved fluidly through the parking lot, up the ramp, and to the front door of the shop. Dylan opened the door, the group now single file. Directly in front of them, impossible to misinterpret, a purple painted sign with a flying green Witch greeted them, proclaiming *"Pressing done here!"* It was Sophie's turn to jump.

The party was greeted by a salesgirl, snickering, seeing the group's reaction to their new Halloween sign. Sophie asked the grinning girl if the sign was for sale. "Oh no, ma'am, it was a gift to the owner, delivered last Sunday. It's gotten lots of attention in the last couple of days."

Dora let out a squeal, so clear, so pure, the sound of a four-year-old discovering puppies for the first time. Hanging above the pressing sign was a flying Witch, dressed in purplish black, painted with a broad smile. "See, I told you I had plans!" Dora reached into her pocket and produced a shopping list. The first entry was "flying Witch for new house," written in purple ink. Dora asked the salesclerk to pack up the Witch in bubble wrap, without even seeing the price.

Sophie began calculating how many different kinds of candy she would need. She planned a Putnam Pantry treat for each Sabbat for the year following the American Camino. This was the recipe to keep Walking and Haunting Giles contained within Sophie. Complete integration would take a full year, if the healing process was grounded in the now on a regular basis, through ritual if possible. Nutmeg was Giles's favorite flavor, in custard preferably. He also had a taste for coconut. Sophie could feel the electric chill in the air as she thought of coconut, Giles's way of putting in his two cents. Martha loved honey, in the comb.

Not a word had to be said to Dylan. He delivered Sophie a handbasket for her growing list. They ended up tag-teaming it, Dylan holding the basket and Sophie filling it up. Coconut cashew clusters for Giles, chocolate-dipped honeycomb for Martha, chocolate brownie chews for Dylan, chocolate-dipped almond macaroons for Poe, chocolate mint squares for Dora, coconut haystacks and chocolate maple sugar drops for Sophie. Everybody would love the Sabbatical Sacraments for the coming year. Sophie's favorite was a set of four chocolate flying witches on lollipop sticks for Samhain, and Ali would get a long honey straw for her mint tea.

Dylan set the filled candy basket near the cash register so the clerk could begin wrapping up the goodies for the flight home. Maple sugar shaped into leaves would be kept unpacked for the Liberation Feast, and Sophie found a Chief Head molded maple sugar coin, perfect for Metacomet. She'd get two, one for the Anniversary Feast in 2008. Sophie chatted with the girls, giggling over Dora's Witch and new supply of chocolate-covered sunflower nuts, colored yellow, green, and orange. No one knew what kind of candy Poe bought. She kept it close while it lasted, no more than a day or two. When the box was filled and secured with ribbon, Dylan appeared with a brown-and-white stuffed horse, the size of a Beanie Baby. He presented it to the clerk and said, "For Sophie. Your Power Animal should come from Putnam Pantry."

Sophie kissed him lightly on the cheek and said, "Thank you, Martha, I'll always treasure her." The clerk looked confused but shrugged it off in favor of cash.

They filed out of the shop, mouths full of maple sugar samples, free hands fumbling with cellophane packaging, lots of sighs. Sophie was the last one out the door. At the beginning of the ramp, Sophie bent down with an Honor Bundle in her hand. Without a word, she passed the bundle to Dylan and he placed it under the yew tree, the Death Tree, in the back, so it would not be discovered.

Dora separated herself from the group and walked over to the sinkhole. She gave a simple Spirit Salute and quickly tossed a small handful of colored sunflower nuts in the hole. When she finished her silent prayer, she looked up and saw the clerk in the main front window on a cell phone, a sign that it was going to be a long day.

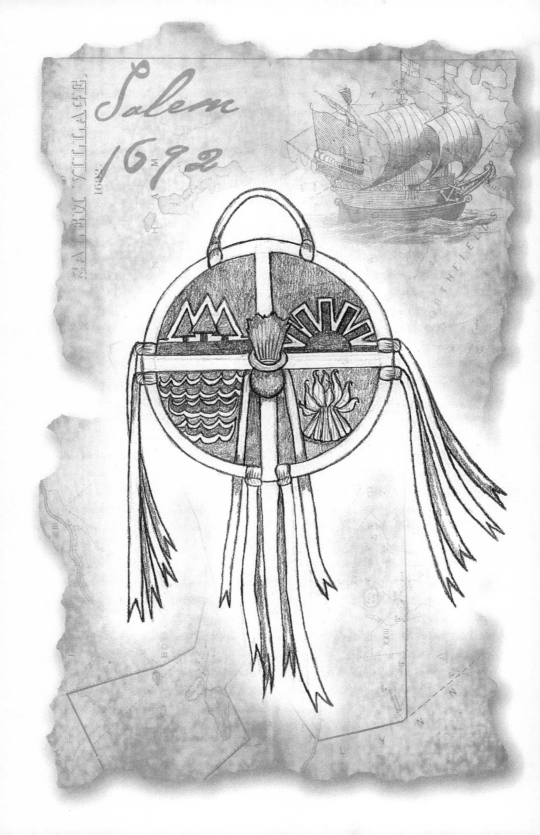

Chapter Fifteen

INDIAN COUNTRY
September 18, 2007, noon

THE ENERGY WAS TENSE. No one but Sophie understood the relevance of the Work this afternoon. After the sugar gorge and ghost-walking at Putnam Pantry, three of the four could have called it a day. They persevered, listening to Sophie's stories politely en route to Haverhill, but they felt little connection. Poe had been vested in the smallpox work on Thursday, but she was lost today. Who was Hannah Dustin to them? They only knew her as a spook that bothered Sophie for thirty years, an Ancestor of Lydia the apron maker from Santa Fe. Who was Metacomet to them, John Marston's red counterpart, the boss of Indian Country? Today was obtuse for everyone but Sophie; they were not keeping their displeasure to themselves. Shortly after leaving Essex County, lulled by the rhythm of the moving SUV, Dora fell into a deep sleep, infuriating her mentor.

"Wake up, Dora! This is no time for sleep! You need to be paying attention to the countryside, to everything: signs, signals, omens, Dunkin' Donuts, black and white columns! C'mon, what is your problem today? We need to be united in our energy and enthusiasm. If you are not sure how you fit in the Work today, start asking questions!" The vehicle occupants were silent. Only the dance of car and highway making a dull thudding sound every couple of seconds was heard.

This was the first time Sophie had been bitchy to the group as a whole. She was frustrated by their reactions to today's journey, the longest day of the itinerary. The energy had to stay high to commune with the Spirits directing the group's progress. Each day had to build upon the previous until the climax of the Liberation Feast. Much was at stake—the trip couldn't afford being sidelined or diminished, regardless of reason.

Sophie continued her lecture. "West of Essex County, on the river systems in this part of the state, red people lived for thousands of years. Only the natural competition for resources served to drive them to violence, as it does to all people, hunger being a tough taskmaster. European soldiers and settlers brought disease to Native people, wiping out millions along the Eastern seaboard, the results of de Soto's march of 1540, ninety years before Boston was founded. By the time the Puritans landed, Indian numbers had been decimated. The remaining Natives were disillusioned and hungry, suffering day in and day out. Their lands were closing in around them, closer and closer. They were crammed together, inched out by foreign concerns, the French to the North, the English all around them, their territory's resources seriously diminished.

"Remember, this Big Work deals with the very soul of this country, the collective soul of us all: red, white, black, brown, and yellow. It is important for you to realize that the people displaced by the trials had displaced many before the trials. The early settlers portray the Indians of New England as bloodthirsty savages who killed for the glory of the battle and blood itself. The Puritans saw them as devils and believed the fix for the Native problem was simple: extermination, no different from Hitler's 'final solution.'

"Dora, you protest against the present government because of its genocidal imperialism in the Middle East. I am proud of you for taking to the streets as I did in the 1960s and '70s, for peace and equality. I wish more of your generation would rise up against injustice. I ask you now to localize your fury, concentrate it on Massachusetts. The dramas and tragedies here represent the human condition, a New England microcosm of betrayal and oppression. If anyone rises against the injustices of the government entrusted to serve the people, the dissenter has the responsibility to keep standing in the new power place of free speech, and work and fight with all possible might, creating justice. The pain of our Ancestors is our pain. If we truly want to save the world, we must start taking responsibility for our collective past. It is a shared problem and no one is exempt, especially those of us who know what we are up against. Maybe I should rephrase my last statement. I hope you trust me enough to follow my lead, stay plugged in, and react instantly when action is demanded!

"And if this subject bores you, Goddess help us all! Know this was the mind-set of the New Jerusalem: kill before you are killed, build a God-centered government ruled through dominance and threat of everlasting hell.

Does this sound familiar, the Christian West and the Islamic East? Killing was the way then, and it still is today. Iraq or Massachusetts, are they any different? Only the carnage belonging to their prospective centuries hold the issues apart, one from the other."

Sophie breathed out in frustration. She was not sure if she had ever really been heard or taken seriously, not just today but ever. Has the group been leading her on, pretending they were interested in doing their part in saving a healthy chunk of this planet? Sophie doubted her mission again and, like her traveling companions, doubted she knew what was actually needed in Haverhill. The three weren't sure what Sophie expected of them, thinking all Sophie wanted was a small army of robots carrying out her bidding. If there was a time of near mutiny on the American Camino, it was here and now. Sophie's frustration was contagious.

"I am pulling over at the Dunkin' Donuts at the next exit. Everybody stretch and get their shit together. I hate this negative vibe—it needs to end now! Get out and get your heads together!" Dylan looked Sophie square in the face, grinding his teeth and sweating. She knew he wasn't happy. It was mutual.

Dylan parked, snapping the SUV sharply into a space and applying the brakes with a harsh step. Poe and Dora exited quickly, rats jumping off a sinking ship. Sophie sat still until she was alone in the car. When the time was right and no one was looking, she slipped out of the car, reached into the back for her backpack, stuck her water bottle and cell phone in it, and walked to the main drag, the road for Lawrence and Haverhill. She had to walk it off, the tension, her drive and passion becoming a toxic overload. The party would find her quickly; she wasn't deviating from the planned route.

Sophie couldn't help but think about her autocratic father and his miniature tribe of Kundalini yoga–practicing, biracial, metaphysical super children. Sophie had hated his rants; now they sounded like hers. When had she grown into her father? The faster her pace, the more frustrated she became. She had always judged her father too harshly until this moment. She wanted to reach for him, for comfort and help, but decided against it, since Richard was hard to shake once he made an appearance.

The red chair—Richard's place of residence when he visited from the Spirit Realms—burned in her head. She had tried giving the chair away many times. Her father must have blocked her attempts, because the chair remained in the living room, next to Sophie's arm of the sofa. He sat in all his ghostly glory, sporting a straight spine, relaxed in his bearing, patient to a fault, barely moving, never even blinking. He came whenever Sophie was caught in a precarious situation or seriously ill. His favorite time to visit was the month of Samhain—two weeks before Halloween, two weeks after—during the Festival of the Dead, always the King of Drama.

She had figured out years ago that her mother and father did not live together in the Spirit World. Their relationship was strained for a decade before her mother died. When Sarah tasted the freedom of life *next door*, she decided to remain unencumbered until she chose a permanent body for incarnation. Sarah was in no rush to join the mortal coil; she wanted to remain free for as long as possible, a thousand or maybe two thousand years. Richard was different; he had little patience for the contemplative nature of Spirit life. He craved friction, drama, and sex, at least in theory. He never gave himself an opportunity to divest from life; he had to guard himself daily against the lure of a Walking Spirit's life, filled with the emotions of the living without all of the burdens, at least financial. Richard's dreaded downfall was money paired with obligation; he had no emotional reference for it, the reason it haunted him in many dimensions. He sat in the red chair for a month each year, contemplating his life and all of its twists and blind intersections and dead ends.

Why were Sarah and Richard so miserable, intimately and with the world? Sophie knew her parents' problems were based on their knowledge of prophecy; they knew enough for other people to fear them, a primal, self-serving, paralytic kind of fear. Sophie and Ali carried on their parents' traits of self-enforced isolation, preferring the stimulation of literature and music to human company. They both knew too much, and it would always haunt them. Their brother Erick lived on his own planet. The only son, beloved for his gender and not judged on his deeds regardless of how careless he was, Erick took to nothing but acquisition, his way of bolstering his lack of belief in himself. Ali and Sophie were close, although they lived thousands of miles apart and rarely saw each other face to face.

Dylan opened the locked car and found it empty. Dora double-checked the bathrooms and counter area; they knew she wouldn't eat anything in the store. Poe told Dylan to expect Sophie on the main road. "She's just walking it off!" Dylan smiled and told Poe he appreciated her sanity. They weren't surprised when Dora came back to the car alone.

Dylan turned the SUV right onto Route 495N. About a mile up the road, the group spotted Sophie walking briskly on a bike path that

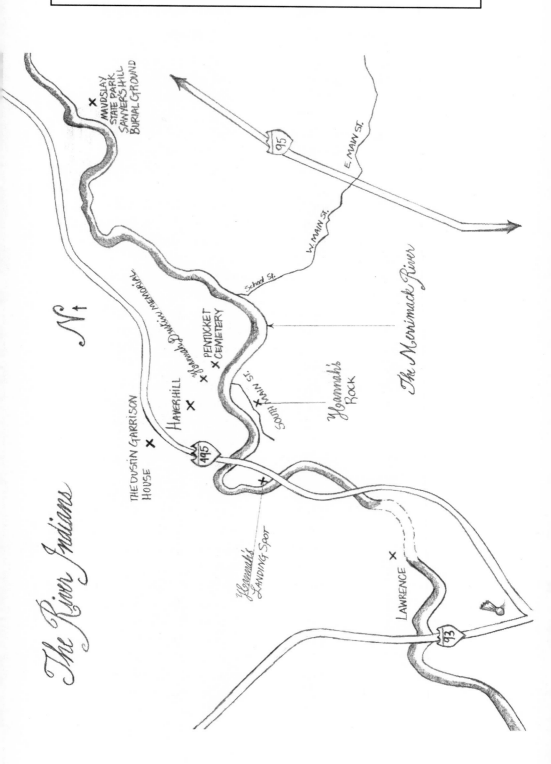

The River Indians

N

MAUDSLAY STATE PARK
SAWYER'S HILL BURIAL GROUND

95
E. MAIN ST.
W. MAIN ST.

School St.

THE DUSTIN GARRISON HOUSE

HAVERHILL

Hannah Dustin Memorial

PENTUCKET CEMETERY

SOUTH MAIN ST.

495

The Merrimack River

Woannah's Rock

Woannah's Landing Spot

LAWRENCE

93

connected two small hamlets of shabby houses. She smiled and directed Dylan to pull into the small cul de sac and park by the large bronze sculpture in the center of the roundabout. He parked and the three tentatively disembarked, obviously not sure what mood they would find her in. Would she eat them alive or ignore them the Indian way?

"So, you thought you were rid of me, aye?" Sophie smiled and handed each one an Honor Bundle. "Look around, we're in Indian Country. Look at the houses and mail boxes, what's growing in their gardens. See any Prayer Flags?"

"It looks like Grande Ronde in Polk County on the way to the old pow-wow grounds," Poe said. "I see Sage blooming and house signs cut out of wood to look like feathers. Yes, I see what you mean. Who is this statue supposed to be? I thought we wouldn't meet Metacomet until we hit Pentucket."

The bronze was a stately piece, out of place, partly shaded by scrub trees, right off the main highway, no markers or signs. A bold young man stood on a rock bluff, overlooking a valley or scouting a person or game. He was surrounded by animal shapes and faces embedded in imaginary rock. Perhaps it depicted a Vision Quest or a Warrior's Rite of Passage.

"His name is Passaconaway. He is depicted as a man at his height of virility here. It's an unusual take on him because some say he lived almost a hundred years. You usually see him as an old man. Passaconaway is a lesson in Saturn Cycles." Sophie stopped her explanation when she saw Dora and Dylan rolling their eyes in unison.

Sophie looked unfazed. "Dylan, would you like to share something? Perhaps you have insight on the subject?"

"I have to be honest, Sophie, I've never heard of the man before today. I didn't even read anything specific about Metacomet. I'm getting frustrated with you because you always blame everything on Saturn Cycles. Dora is facing her first Saturn Cycle and I am hitting my second in a little over a year. We are fed up with hearing this explanation."

Poe spoke up. "I don't think this tension has anything to do with Passaconaway. Sophie, I don't know about him either. Nor do I think blaming discord on astrology is altogether beneficial at this juncture, although I admit being curious how Saturn Cycles figure in this situation." Poe continued, "I think we're all nervous about Hannah Dustin's ghost. I know I am. None of us have talked about her and her violent tendencies—she scares me —she's just plain creepy. We've heard her story and sympathize with her plight as a mother trying to hold onto a baby she thought lost forever. We get it, at least I do. From my perspective, the other element today has to do with how *you* are feeling about us. Why are we here exactly? What do you want from us? We had no idea every day would be packed with issues we have little to do with, personally."

Sophie felt like taking off again, wanting to commune with the Spirits she had come across the country to help. She had no idea what all this battling was over. She didn't get it at all.

Dora struggled to let her in. "I'm angry with you, Sophie, for thinking so little of us. I am fed up with taking orders from you! There was a woman we both know who said in Circle in the '90s that all you wanted were bodies for your continuous human experiments. She's right. I feel like I am nothing but meat to you, just something to push around to benefit your personal agenda." Dora's eyes filled with tears, a sign of her frustration; she could no longer contain her percolating rage.

Sophie attempted to communicate her truest thoughts to the group, as patiently as she could. "I believe we are all reacting to each other's inadequacies, me included. This isn't a fantasy, people. I thought I made myself clear at the beginning. The three of you only see Spirits on occasion, mainly in dream-form or during Shamanic Journeywork. My perspective is far different from yours. You think I am an agenda-driven robot—well, obsessive perhaps and driven yes—a robot no! Everywhere we go, we are greeted by the Spirits, some a surprise, like this beautiful statue symbolizing Passaconaway's presence. I had no idea this was here, even though my research has been extensive. The bottom line: whether or not you realize your importance, or see yourself in a specific drama, I assure you, you are all important to the success of the American Camino. You all have vested interests in its success. You are all driven on all levels to be here. Even if it frightens you, you are meant to be here! Your souls and Guardian Spirits have demanded your awareness, your connection." She looked around at the group, willing them to listen.

"You all have agendas, not just me. For example, Dylan desires the ending of secrets with Martha. When Martha and Dylan come face to face on Saturday, Dylan has an opportunity to feel his true self worth, evaluate how his true talents will manifest in the future. With elevated self-esteem, he may give himself permission to be as sensitive a Seer as Martha was. He has been successful at psychic faires and metaphysical events thus far, but he has stopped himself from Oracle Mastery and a personal following because of the fear of persecution. He's afraid that if he becomes as good in public as he is alone at divining and Oracle Work, he will be misunderstood, isolated, and tortured as Martha was. His desire to be the best person he can be is what has propelled him here, to do his Big Work and free himself from mediocrity."

"Of course you've calculated our personal reasons for being here. I should have known." Dora started to scuff the toe of her leather clog, distracting herself from her own vindictive tone.

"If I hadn't figured how each person fit in to the puzzle, I wouldn't have been doing my job, Dora. You are no selfless saint in this past-life scenario. The missing piece of Mary was broken from her before Giles's time, when you were originally sold as an indentured servant to pay for passage and room and board. You owed the ship owner and his financier six years of hard labor. Although the sentence saved you from the debtor's gaol in England, living as an indentured servant was living as a slave, with no rights and little say in anything. Giles bought you; he owned you and felt justified ordering you around for six years, the time of your contract. You worked like a dog, but a free dog. He never held you against your will. Giles married you as soon as he struck a bargain with the agent and paid for Mary's hide, before you even saw Corey land. You would be free of the label of indentured servant; *wife* was a term of respect and made it possible for Mary to move freely about the countryside without feeling like a criminal. After six years, Giles gave Mary a choice: stay as his wife, grow to like him and earn a piece of the homestead, or be set free, able to move on as she chose, with a modest stake of gold and a new set of clothes. Giles never bedded you, despite being legally married to you; he didn't force women to love him. You had a bargain to strike of your own and told Giles you would live with him as his legal wife for as long as Mary lived, share a stake in the land, and be included in the rum work and revenue instead of plowing. In exchange, Mary would never turn Giles over to the authorities for his pirating ways. You blackmailed him, and he was grateful you stayed regardless. In fact, an adept blackmailer himself, he considered you a fine student in the privateering trade, one who could deceive with a smile. Mary was a good worker and a born pirate, as irascible as any mean man dared to be. Mary and Giles became devoted friends; she died eight years before his pressing.

"Dora, my point is that your soul has chosen to rise above being bought and sold as a woman, regardless of reason, in this incarnation. It is up to you to make hard decisions and transcend the natural sexual push-and-pull of ownership in relationships. This is the lifetime you must rise to your true power and do your share of the Big Work. This is a time of service and giving back, learning to dissolve Karmic entanglements. You don't even know what it means yet, to serve. You have demanded people do for you all your life. You have much to learn about returning owed energy."

Poe interjected, changing the direction of the energy from Dora to herself instantly. "Since you are playing the role of therapist, Sophie, I want to control my own analysis. I was a Putnam as Jonathan Tarbell, the heir of Saugus Mill Works, where many of the murder victims of the Family Confederacy were disposed of. The foundry was out of my personal control for the majority of its horrendous use. I was a gentle and thoughtful man, a healer of sorts, but I felt guilt and shame because the ghosts of those burned there visited regularly. This is why I am still afraid of seeing ghosts. Working with death and dying has helped me considerably with many issues this time, but not the guilt. I continued on as a Putnam, marrying into the family when I was Richard Dexter. I was a doctor, isolated, afraid, over my head in the deadly diseases of the day. I lived life in a constant state of guilt, feeling a sham, unable to save many from smallpox when it was raging through entire sections of Essex County. The pox covered whole valley areas with contagion. I was still guilty when the pox came knocking at Sawyer's Hill in 1759, in my next life after Richard as a doctor. I was weak and allowed an entire area on Sawyer's Hill to be quarantined, forty people in all. I didn't travel to the spot for a full year after the lodge holding the contagion, bodies, and possessions was burned. In the preceding time, I learned the people quarantined there were sealed from the world, without water or medical supplies. Whatever took them first—starvation, thirst, or smallpox—they all died slow agonizing deaths, with no hope of help or escape. I'm still afraid to see these people, the same visitors plaguing you all Winter, Sophie, the eight Spirits from Maudslay State Park.

"I am giving you the facts without the feelings, I'm afraid. I'm not so good at analyzing myself. But it is time for me to shed guilt, compounded for many lifetimes. The guilt goes back to the first landing in Cape Ann, where we were yesterday, my Ancestors' landing place. The same family supported the Putnams and Tarbells in the Witch Trails, sixty years later. When I shed this guilt, back into the soil where it came from, my perfectionist nature will take a back seat. I also hope my fear of ghosts will diminish, so I can go deeper into my investigations of altered states of consciousness."

"I know we are afraid to change. We all are. Is that what you are saying?" Dylan liked to cut to the chase. "Is that why we are all acting terribly to one another today?"

"*Acting* is a good word for it, Dylan. I don't think we are being intentionally nasty to one another. This is subconscious. I believe our Core Selves are afraid of confrontation and failure. We're all vested in the success of this trip; we just get in our own way. Freedom is a scary proposition—relationships change, old patterns lose their powers of persuasion, people either bond at deep levels or grow apart. It's about change and we feel victimized by it, far too often." Sophie was unusually calm.

Dylan looked sheepish and made a move to say something, but before he was able to get the words out, Poe said, "So please, Sophie, let us in on why Passaconaway is a lesson in Saturn Cycles?"

Dora added, "Yes, please, tell us about good old Saturn. He is the reason I am so miserable lately."

"Passaconaway was born around 1580. He grew to be a powerful Seer, mystic poet, and Medicine Person of his people, the Pennacook."

Poe interrupted. "Pennacook, New Hampshire, the location of Hannah Dustin's captors' deaths."

"Right you are, Poe. Passaconaway was a dedicated Peace Chief of his tribe. Wars and skirmishes came and went, but he convinced his people to stay on the path of peace, of balance. Close to his fifty-sixth birthday, the time of his second Saturn Cycle, give or take a year or two—you all know it takes full three years, beginning to end—Metacomet was born. He would grow into a powerful Sachem, or War Chief, of his people, the Wampanoag. Passaconaway preached peace, Metacomet preached war; both controlled their people, one loosely through love, one with a ruthless and sometimes bloody hand.

"Seduced by the fashion and adornment of the English invaders, Metacomet dressed in the best English clothes of the day and took the name Philip as his own. He added the word King in front of Philip, King being synonymous for Chief. Disillusioned by treachery, he was shot in the heart in 1676, after waging an unsuccessful, bloody war against the English for a year. Many horrific deeds are matched with his name, some real, others not—he was committed to the survival of his beloved family and tribe, his bottom line."

Poe's nose was dripping, which happened when allergies met stress. "I think I get it. *The Soul of a Nation*: it is our choice to wage war or peace, to live or die, to go to the light or stay to haunt. Today is the make-or-break day, just as you said. Okay, and Hannah is how women figure in the scenario. A mother's behavior is acceptable as long as it involves the protection or memory of her precious children, even if her acts are bloody and deplorable. You always say, Sophie, it's all about choice. That's what today is for!"

"Yes! We are all important. We are all apart of this dance on every level. It involves all of us, over three hundred million of us, the entire country, its survival as leader out of chaos, unlike the present administration, which specializes in *into chaos*." Sophie pulled out her charm, the red Honor Bundle with hanging ribbon. She motioned for each of them to offer it up, while doing Spirit Salutes. She brought attention to the eight bushes that had been planted around the statue, signifying the Equinoxes, Solstices, and cross-quarter days of the Natural Year, the foundational number of the Warrior, of Grandmother Spider. Sophie tied her bundle to the Northern scrub and motioned the three to follow suit with their specific directions, clockwise. Sophie walked to the Southern point of the sculpture and raised her hands in the Goddess position,

"Great Spirit of Earth and Sky,
Mother and Father of Star Nation,
Hear my prayers!
We enter the country of the Red Fathers Passaconaway and Metacomet,
two sides of the same coin,
one old and wise, one young and brash,
both lovers of their people.
We, people of many bloods,
followers of the Gray River of Balance,
ask humbly for your free passage in this wild and sometimes dangerous land.
Show us what we need to see, tell us the stories we need to hear,
sing us the songs of future dream waters.
Please give us the tools for change,
blow the Four Healing Winds our way.
Let us grow the wings of Eagle, the paws of Bear,
let us be witnesses to wounds closing."

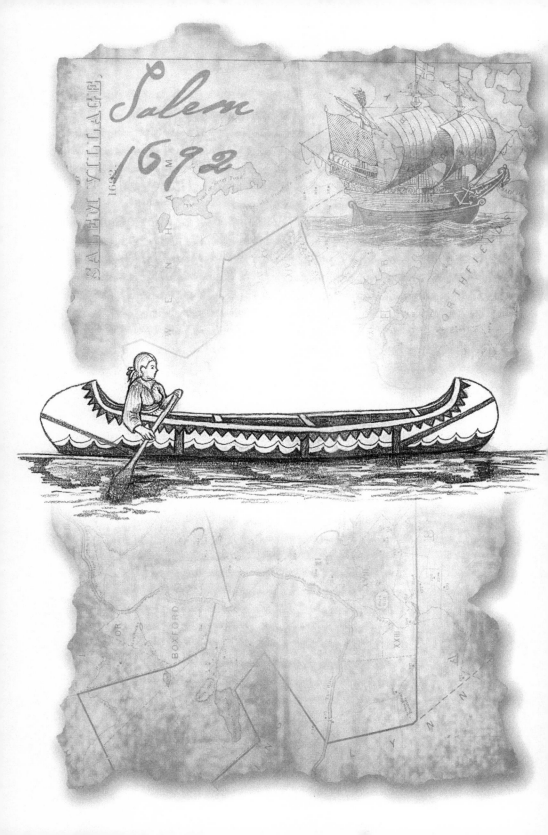

Chapter Sixteen

RIVER ROAD
September 18, 2007, 1:00 p.m., Haverhill

RIVER ROAD RAN NORTH AND WEST from the statue of Passaconaway, following the Merrimack River. A gently rolling landscape made way for the occasional outcropping and granite hill. River access was possible, coming and going. The sky had a deep Autumn hue, accented with gold; the trees, grass, and rows of orange marigolds shimmered in the warm light. The river began to widen, trees became sparse, and brick buildings rose on wooden river pylons, casting long dark shadows. "*Welcome to Lawrence, Shoe Capital of the World!*" announced a carved wooden sign with painted lettering secured to the railing of a painted steel bridge.

Lawrence had become the destination location for many immigrants in the middle and late 1800s. Large families would divide their children among the factory district shops, tanneries, and mills, brick monsters crammed together tightly the length of the entire town, stacked on both sides of the river. A family of ten, with all members over the age of six, would have ten incomes. Pooled together, after several years of hard toiling, the workers had seed money enough to buy several small houses in a row, ensuring roofs for several generations. By the beginning of the twentieth century, Lawrence became a battlefield for the labor rights movement, trying to change child labor laws, freeing a small nation of workers for toiling with books over brawn. Every European language was heard in Lawrence in 1890: Russian, Yiddish, German, Polish, Irish, Spanish, Italian, and English.

The mournful sounds of the whispers of thousands of small children enveloped the group as they cruised the main drag. Poe, with fresh thoughts of happily playing children in the shallows on Graves Beach, felt the shared pain of exploitation of children too weak to use the voice of rebellion. Her

147

nose began to run and her eyes filled with tears of defeat. "I want to make an offering at the river, for crying children. I feel them and it's oppressing me, it physically hurts—my knees, arms, and hips."

"I like the idea of sending prayers to Great Spirit for the children. The pain in your joints is probably caused by the stress of sixteen-hour work days on small skeletal frames. It is amazing more children didn't die while working in the open, instead of slowing melting into their beds at home, from exhaustion and deprivation. Dylan, there's a park sign turn-off at the next right, let's take it. We'll have lunch while we're here."

The city had built a long boardwalk the length of the factory row on the river's Eastern bank. From the first creaking board, the wooden planks made crying sounds when walked over, woeful and hurt. The party noticed struggling vegetation, parched and dried by the season's warm wind, ignored and undervalued, mirroring the working children's lives.

Each member carried a bag, something for the prayer-picnic. Poe shared custody of the Trader Joe's Medicine Bag with Sophie. Deep in thought, finding the right words for the children's prayers, they made their way down the long squeaking boardwalk to a gazebo, where they found Dora checking out the menu for lunch. Dylan walked ahead of the gazebo, looking for easier access to the river for Poe's offering.

Together, without direction, they formed a Circle and began breathing in, to the count of eight, holding for the count for four and releasing to the count of eight. Intentional Breath carried them to different levels of consciousness, heightening their senses. A steady breeze from the East brought feelings of purpose, an open channel to receive thoughts and wishes. Poe moved to the center of the Circle, took a deep breath and faced North.

"Goddess and God, hear me please.
I hear the whispers of working children,
old before their time, in pain,
walking without destination.
These voices tell me their sorrows and stories of abandonment.
I am lost, not knowing what to do for them,
my voice feels too small to help.
Mother and Father, assist me as much as the children,
come to our aid and set us free from our senseless suffering.
Blessed Be!"

Poe dug in her pocket and brought forth a small handful of sacred herbs and offered it up to the heavens. The wind, peaked and gusting, whipped the herbs from her hand as soon as she opened her fist over her head. Vanished, each speck of herb, not a grain of Tobacco on the boardwalk, nothing. The prayer was ended, the wind shifted, and the group moved on to lunch.

Driving out from Lawrence, they felt the congestion and urban closeness lift at its city limits. The vista opened. Trees began to appear in tight, old rows. Traveling Northeast, the river began winding, eventually making a rounded M shape. Each power place on this journey formed a letter M or W, sometimes both, combined or separate, shaped with hard points or with rounded humps. The Spirits repeated their visits, making sure they had been heard and insuring Sophie's allegiance and compliance, while maintaining her power. Spirit's map direction designs would naturally repeat the same symbols, enhancing their point. Shamanic people learn the power of repetitive behavior from the Spirits, spiritually induced OCD.

The landscape began to roll, insinuating mountains ahead and the joining of other river systems. It was wilder here near Haverhill. Dense conifer woodland separated the highway from the river, the trees still a dozen shades of green this far North, not like the shedding golden hawthorns of Salem.

Pentucket Cemetery butted up against the Haverhill Historical Society property. Only a long line of ancient trees separated them. The historical society boasted a large collection of weaponry from King Philip's War and an impressive array of Hannah Dustin memorabilia. Sophie loved the way Spirit put things together. This small museum housed prized collections of Metacomet and Hannah Dustin artifacts, honoring both energies, even though they were far apart physically in time and place. Not so in this space. Both existed simultaneously, as they do in the Spirit Realms, not separated by human time but joined because of it. The party would visit the museum first, gather as much new information as possible, and get a feel for Metacomet's energy, and for Hannah's.

The docent was a charming young woman in her late twenties, tall and slender, with chestnut hair and blue eyes, like an English doll from the 1950s, alabaster skin and rosebud lips. She greeted the party warmly and asked what brought them to their sleeping house of collections. Dylan, beguiled, took the floor and told of their attraction to the unusual—and some would say creepy—collections.

The docent made a sweeping motion toward a closed door, marked by a red sign. "Yes, we have been accused of entertaining the macabre. But most of history is bloody, conquered land over conquered land, building time upon time, church built on ancient temple. Without it, we would have no archeology."

"Quite right, my dear!" Sophie enthusiastically cheered their animated guide on.

"Take our Hannah Dustin collection, for example. Some tourists come to see the bloody hatchet, while others come to see Hannah's image carved into a whiskey bottle. Same person, same story, different perspectives—both important. Would you like to see the collection? We keep it behind doors so we can control the temperature. This close to the cemetery, the weather is freezing most of the year, with no buildings to stop the wind. It howls through here. We are challenged in the winter when snow sometimes drifts over the windows. The park administration keeps us well dug out, though, thank heavens! Come this way. I would love to show the collection to you."

Sophie stood at the outside of the door, waiting for the congenial guide to have her fill of shoveling information and leave the party on their own. Sophie gravitated to the Metacomet collection: hatchets, tomahawks, knives, silver buttons, etched bone, flint work, and arrowheads. How she wanted to open the cases and hold the items, divine their owners, get a feel for the Red Headman! The guide ended her spiel and left the room to greet other guests. Sophie slipped into the room after her. Poe and Dora were standing fairly close together, staring at the bloody hatchet in disbelief, their mouths slightly open, their eyes focused and red. Poe sniffed her runny nose clear and said, "I can feel Hannah. She's close." Sophie agreed. Dora was nervous. Dylan had moved on to Metacomet.

Sophie parted the girls and placed her hands on the glass, over Hannah's hatchet. An arc of electricity flowed from Sophie's index finger to the metal of the hatchet below. In a split second, the magick had connected and left. Clearly, it was time to move to the next display, greet Metacomet, and get on to the real work with Hannah. Sophie had her walking orders.

Sophie made several small purchases: three amber-colored glass bottles with the image of George Washington pressed into them, a Garrison House refrigerator magnet for Lydia Dustin, several images of the green monument in New Hampshire, and a series of postcards of the bronze memorial here in Haverhill. Dylan bought old English and colonial money replicas, Poe bought a series of photographs of child workers of Lawrence, and Dora bought a maple sugar drop. The group was ready for Pentucket.

Sophie pointed out the row of ancient hawthorn Journey Trees, the center one, bigger than the rest, with a huge Yoni-shaped opening large enough to fit a small person. This was their destination, the meeting place with Metacomet. They circled the outside of the perimeter and entered the cemetery by way of the main entrance in the front. The wind picked up, out of the East again. Eagle was there and ready for the meet-and-greet. The group would meet Judge Saltonstall and honor him properly here too.

The grounds were not kept well. Many stones had been vandalized, leaves needed raking, and excess debris cluttered pathways and staircases, making walking slow, the pace deliberate. They found the Saltonstall area as a group, in the North central quadrant. Sophie took out her grave kit and rainbow glove and got to work, clearing small patches of rubble and leaves from the bottom of the judge's marker. With the large chunks dealt with, she made haste with her rainbow glove, cleaning the top of the marker and the words on its face. After clearing and cleaning, she dug a small hole and lined it with sacred herbs, finally placing one of the special bead-wrapped Medicine Bundles in it, saying "Thank you!" as she compacted the dirt over it. She covered the area with the same debris she removed, fooling everyone but the squirrels and not leaving a trace of their presence, until Dora showered the entire gravestone area with multicolored chocolate sunflower nuts. They had nothing to hide here, the bundle safe and appreciated.

The air was fresh, the wind steady since the prayers in Lawrence. There were no Parrots here, no protoplasmic clouds or singing Spirits. There was calm, a new sensation for the group. They had finally found a place of peace. True, it was a bit dilapidated, but the longer Sophie spent within the grounds, the more she realized it wasn't vandalism taking the larger stones, it was time, weather, the freezing Winter temperatures. This ground was free of animosity. No wonder Saltonstall insisted on making his family burial plot here.

They were getting ready to move on, when out of the woods a baseball landed at Sophie's feet. She called out, lightly at first, then louder on the second call, "Anyone lose a baseball?" Silence. Then, pretending to bark at a dog, Sophie called, "Here boy, come here, dog, fetch!" Nothing. Dora had stood next to Sophie as the ball landed. She was the perfect person to claim the ball as hers. Maybe it would break the awkward tension between them, the ball and a piece of chocolate, perhaps?

The group had not been greeted like this in Massachusetts—here there were no cold temperatures, howling winds, spinning dirt devils, or psycho birds caught in a ritual dance. They were met with quiet here, no Walking Spirits, no squawking Parrot. Sophie realized why they had had to travel here—they had to greet Metacomet, the great Sachem, in neutral territory. They would have to gain his trust on peaceful grounds, so he would know they were sincere. Metacomet had to know accepting the offer as Red Headman wasn't a spiritual trap, as it was when he was ambushed and shot through the heart.

Sophie covered her heart and said a special silent prayer, thanking Spirit for the insight she would later share. The wind shifted and the Journey Trees, hawthorns similar to the giants elevating Charter Street Cemetery, began to rustle, their leaves sounding like rain sticks, freshly turned, hearing sand fall like cascading waterfalls. Metacomet was here. Sophie's hair was standing at attention, on her arms, her legs, the back of her neck. He was ready for the meet. She reached into the Trader Joe's bag and pulled two loose bundles from it. She unwrapped the smaller of the two, revealing a maple sugar candy formed in the shape of an Indian Chief in full headdress. She placed the piece of fabric in the center of the Yoni opening of the tree and secured the cloth with the sugar medallion. She knelt in front of the giant tree, directly below its opening, and began digging a hole for the Medicine Bundle. She placed sacred herbs in and around the hole, finally burying the corn bundle with its transparent shiny red beads. Four ribboned Honor Bundles were hung in the tree, one for each of them, for the Cardinal Directions, for grounding, to seal the deal.

The other three left offerings under and in Metacomet's tree. When the last M&Ms and sunflower nuts were thrown and the last bit of Sage scattered, Sophie remembered Spirit had asked them to let the Red People smell their sacred herbs. Making a Spirit Salute in thanksgiving, she reached deep to the bottom of the Trader Joe's bag and pulled out her Smudge Bag. Out came a long braid of Sweetgrass. Lighting it straight away, she sprinkled bits of Rabbit Sage onto the burning Sweetgrass, filling the burial grounds with its powerful sweet odor. The wind responded to the smoking herbs, making long and high hooooooo-hooooooo-hooooooo sounds through the trees. The deed was done.

When the group was all buckled in and ready to take off for Hannah's boulder, Dora straightened, cleared her throat, and said, "For a while, I thought we were in the wrong place. Then the owl started to hoot and I felt relieved. I had the feeling Metacomet joined forces with Passaconaway right then, symbolizing wisdom gained through magick."

"Thank you, Dora. Insightful and, I am hoping, spot-on!" Sophie smiled and braced herself for Hannah. Anything could happen. She felt it in her bones. Portending success or failure was anyone's guess. At least Hannah had cleaned herself up a bit. If she did come out and greet the others, she wouldn't be so scary.

"When this is all over, when everyone is in their destined locations and we can finally let down our guard and have some fun, whatever that means, I am quitting." Sophie said it as if she meant it.

Dylan laughed, which turned into a sharp cough. "Oh, here we go again, Sophie. How many times do I have to hear the same thing? Whenever you are pissed or overwhelmed, you pull the same stale card. What exactly are you going to quit—art, writing, teaching, Shamanic Work? You always dream up another reason to go at it, the same dream, reinvented in a different image. I want to quit too! I could live the rest of my life and never fit another electrical fixture or bend another piece of pipe. *'Dream on, bud,'* I hear whispered in my ear every morning. Because of this economy, I'm stuck working for another eleven years. I want to be sympathetic, Sophie, but I'm having a hard time listening to this." Dylan adjusted the rearview mirror and asked Dora to double-check the turn-off for Hannah's boulder.

"Stay on this road for another couple of miles. When we get close, I'll tell you. We're looking for a major fork in the road; we'll be turning onto the left fork," Dora instructed.

It was hard for Sophie to hear that Dylan didn't understand what she was trying to say. She realized she had been vague when she retired from community and took full-time Eldership. Simply stopping the duties of being an everyday Priestess, ministering to broken hearts and emotional breakdowns, was what she retired from. That, and from being a confessor for anyone who happened to stumble upon her services.

"I never wanted to retire from life, Dylan. I think people got confused when I stated it was time for me to leave and take a different, more independent path. I want to live; I might have a chance once integration happens," Sophie responded.

"Have you always felt confined as a Priestess, as well as a teacher, Sophie?" Poe asked.

"Yes, I did feel cramped as a Priestess and do now as a teacher. I need more freedom from others' needs, both human and Spirit. I want enough time to create again, to do my art projects regularly, not crammed in between clients or students. It's time to get shows again. Get a manager who cares.

Make art, not sell art." Sophie's eyes filled with tears. She crossed her arms over her heart and leaned back.

"Don't hold back, tell us how you feel," Dora snapped.

"Okay! I want to quit teaching, quit bossing everyone around, as you say, to do my bidding. You're right, of course. I've have always expected the people I've trained to follow in my footsteps and give back through helping facilitate my Work, the price of a free education. It's happening now, the three of you devoted to this Work, or at least humoring me well past convenience." Sophie sighed again, feeling unheard. She wanted quiet now, even from her constant thoughts.

"Is it possible for you to make friends, to have people to socialize with, not an audience to preach to?" Dora wanted answers. The others knew Dora was beyond annoyance by the way she tapped the side of her water bottle with her lapis ring.

"That's a good question, but difficult to answer because I always have lived according to the whim of others and have been brought to action by their emergencies, not my own. Rent-a-Slave, I used to call it, but stopped because I don't get paid. Other than Dylan, I have never had a friend my own age who consistently cared about my personal wellbeing, I'm sad to say." Sophie felt forlorn and related this conversation to Hannah Dustin's travails, her search for Self against the odds, in a world of extreme isolation.

She continued, "One thing is clear: in order for the dynamics of our relationships to change, everyone has to make their own decisions and follow through on them, despite peer and Elder pressure. And, believe it or not, I am thinking about a reinvention, one requiring a great deal of normalcy and calm, a lifestyle demanding vacations and shopping sprees. How absurd, right? Sophie St. Cloud passing time in a strip mall, buying new lawn chairs or a fresh lipstick. Don't laugh, it could happen!"

Dora piped up. "I'm going to dance in a Milonga for a solid week without stopping. I'll wear my highest heels and brightest necklace and make the women hate me even more than they already do. And I want to make the boys cry. Ooooh, that sounds so Argentine!" Dora drooled at the prospect of tango for an unbroken week. "And I'll eat ice cream at every meal and smoke clove cigarettes and not feel guilty once!" Everyone knew Dora would do exactly as her fantasy dictated, as soon as they were back in civilization, back in Portland, Tango Country. Maybe she would never utter the word *metaphysics* again. It would be an interesting resolve.

Instead of taking the left fork, Dylan turned right into a Dunkin' Donuts parking lot. "So, I want to know what you are planning on doing when we get home, Poe. What are you up to?"

"I want to go to Vietnam, start in Ho Chin Minh City and travel to Saigon. Fly to Japan and pick up my old BFF Eve, take a week on an isolated beach in Thailand before Vietnam. I have always wanted to go there, remembering my father's stories of the war, in the Naval Communications Corps. I have always felt that I lived during the Vietnam War, close to the DMZ. I would rush with adrenaline when one of Dad's Navy cronies talked war details, seeing his words come to life in front of my eyes. I *have* to go there. I want to be brave enough to face myself in other dimensions, in other lifetimes, so I can do my Karmic work and understand my authentic self. I don't want to be afraid anymore. So, Dylan, what is your fantasy?"

"I'm going on a singles cruise to Alaska. My new motto is *Irresistible!* Celibacy is not working for me anymore. I want more for myself. I love you three, especially Sophie, but I need something and someone just for me. I don't know what it feels like to be spontaneous, to be scared down to my toes and not want it to end. I need stimulation of the human variety. I want all of what Sophie mentioned earlier, in regard to Martha and not being an emotional flat-liner, escaping from my fears and doubts. After I get back from the cruise, I will win the Lotto and retire to a beautiful parcel of land in the Willamette Valley and grow food for the rest of my life and drink lots of Pinot Noir." Satisfied at everyone's response, Dylan circled the donut shop and turned onto the left fork of the road, drove two blocks, and turned into a large nursing home parking lot.

Sophie doubled-checked the address. Dylan was right—this was the place. Somewhere on this very public facility's grounds was Hannah's boulder, the original monument erected in her honor. Some said it also marked her original homestead, but the historical record pointed to the site of the Garrison House for Hannah and Thomas's land. All Sophie knew was that this was the place Hannah had insisted they come; this is where she lived with Marthia, where Thomas more recently had been bothering her. Sophie squinted her eyes and scanned the property from South to North. Under a huge Western Cedar, a transplant from the Pacific Northwest, hidden to prying eyes from three sides, was Hannah's boulder, the bronze plaque's corner catching a bit of late afternoon sun and reflecting its location.

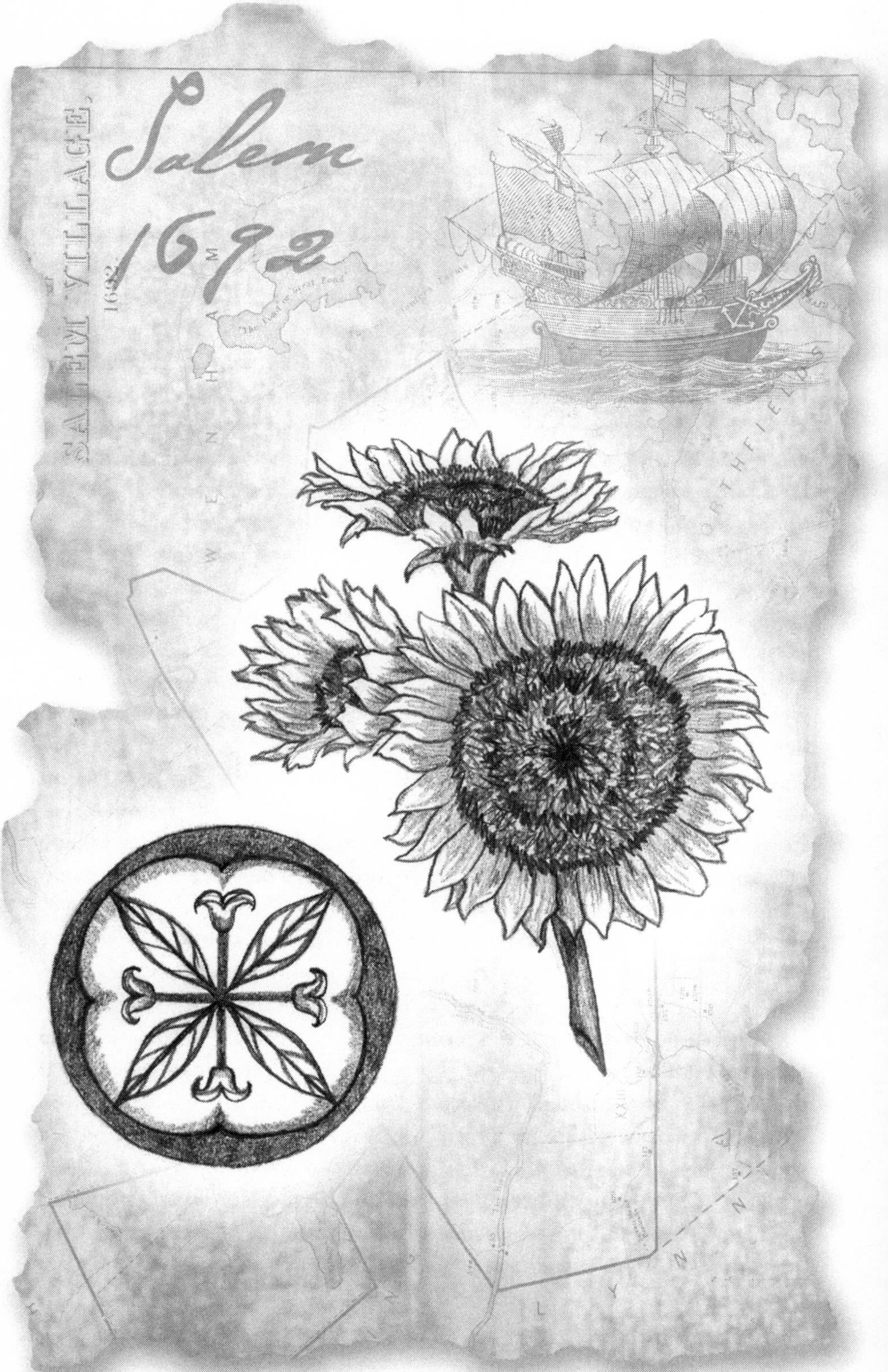
Salem
1692
SALEM VILLAGE

Chapter Seventeen

THE THREE-YEAR PLAN
September 18, 2007, 4:00 p.m.

SOPHIE, BRIEFLY OVERCOME WITH ANXIETY, closed her eyes and held her head with both hands, rocking gently. She regained enough composure to tell everyone to clear, center and ground their energy, and raise a Power Cone for protection. They would all meditate and practice Intentional Breath for five minutes.

Once a panic attack took hold, Sophie knew she needed to let it run its course; she had no choice but to relax into the moment and breathe into the energy block. Five minutes of calm restored her usual pulse rate. She was now ready to deal with her companions, both corporeal and otherworldly.

"The symbolism of being flanked on two sides by parking lots is amazing," she began. "Hannah Dustin living between the worlds, holding her child as emotional hostage in limbo; her husband, Thomas, ready to incarnate, using the parking lot only temporarily. The ghostly traffic in this spot is palpable—it is an otherworldly crossroads and common meeting place. Look at the grounds all around us. See the shimmer? We all know this phenomenon—Spirits so active their combined energy creates wave patterns of heat, illuminating the natural Prana, psychic food, already there. Squint, as I was doing several minutes ago. Focus on the areas of shimmering patterns and let your eyes relax, until you can see auras around all forms. Remember: everything is alive.

"Once the auras appear, follow the patterns for as long as they extend, organically, across the horizon line. Keep your focus on close range; don't stretch it with your conscious mind. Now, tell me what you see, Dora."

"I can see long shadows creating lines along the grass. The longer I stare, the more they look like trails or walkways."

"Excellent, Dora! Right, these are pathways, Haunting and Walking Spirits using the same paths over and over again, for three hundred years. Where do the paths end, Dora?"

"At the boulder, under the tree," Dora said, sure in what she saw.

Everyone nodded in agreement, all sharing the same impressions and visuals.

"We need lots of space for this ritual. We have limited space under the Cedar, but it is private. People will be unable to see what we're doing, even if they were straining to see. The traffic will disguise our noises. If we need to chant or pray loudly, we'll be able to do so privately, without calling the attention of a mortal crowd as we did at Charter Street and Singing Beach. I won't be able to stop what I am doing to tend to your fears, doubts, or questions. You will have to hold yourself together, regardless of what happens. Whether threatened or not, you must hold your ground and stay out of my way. I use my body for leverage, in tugs-of-war or hitting matches. I never know what to expect. We have been invited here, so things should be civil. Only time will tell. Is everyone agreed to stay out of my way, keep quiet, and not freak out, at least on the surface, be as calm as you can?"

Again, the group nodded slowly.

"I want to make myself clear before we go any further. Regardless of the final outcome of the American Camino—success always being relative—you have earned your freedom. My time as your spiritual guide and mentor will end after the Liberation Feast. You each make your own best teacher; substitutes are only rungs of a ladder leading to your eventual enlightenment. Hold this reality close, store it in your heart for future reference, and despite obstacles: be brave!" Sophie took a deep cleansing breath and let it out in one fluid, directed breath, sounding like a whistling bomb ready to land.

Sophie made the Blessing Sign over each friend's head, bonding with each one afresh. She was relieved the group had calmed down and accepted the responsibility for their psychic work. They were motivated by the carrot of freedom, each one interpreting a personal meaning, all different, one from the other. Sophie had felt too full for too long. This was another way for her to gain more flexibility, to claim some of her lost years.

Sophie checked her bag, her tools waiting for her useful fingers. Nodding her approval, she unlatched the passenger door. They all flowed from the car, almost floating, relaxed and present, experiencing Middle World travel.

The group found a rain-tight room under the giant tree, about nine feet square, with a smooth floor of root and dirt, floor to ceiling green branch drapery, and at the base of the huge light-gray boulder, the best discovery of the day—a flat ledge about six inches wide and twelve inches long, perfect for an altar, part of its updated cement base. No need to crouch, the group had plenty of room to stretch and ground properly, standing in their power, solid and strong, with straight spines and activated Chakras.

Sophie cleared the cement ledge of leaves and grass clippings that had been propelled through the tree curtain by the force of an industrial lawn-mower. Pieces of the fine old Cedar were lovingly collected, dry twigs separated for a small smudge fire. A white votive candle was lit, an Athame placed beside it. A charcoal briquette spit and sputtered awake. Sacred herbs were offered to Great Spirit, the Great Mother and her children: Sweetgrass for Spirit Speak and recognition, Tobacco symbolizing honor between human and Spirit Realms, Sage for cleansing, Cedar for right thinking and bravery in Dream Waters. People walking by or leaving their nursing home shifts would think a visitor was smoking pot under the tree, a favorite hang-out when patients were critical. A fresh penlet was cocked; alcohol and tissues and several bottles of water flanked the altar. The scene was set.

She stood in the center of the clearing with eyes closed tightly, silent prayers murmuring through moving lips. Rocking began, to and fro. Holding her face in the palms of her opened hands, she began reciting prayers softly, in Hebrew, Latin, Aramaic, the origin alluding, the tones transfixing, the movement hypnotizing. Sophie opened her ancient book of records, holding it under her heart, the Akashic Records, the Book of the Ancestors, names and prayer petitions flowing from it, as it does at the Western Wall in Jerusalem. Clearly in trance, Sophie found her rainbow glove and began rubbing it over the surface of the stone, followed by a poured line of bottled spring water from the rock's top to its mica-rich center. She blew long streams of hot air over the rock's surface, polishing it with her palm after her breath was spent. The rock reached up and grabbed her, as if it grew arms, and embraced her forcefully. Sophie responded by throwing the whole of her body over the rock's middle. Her head moved from side to side—eyes closed tightly, twitching and fluttering under duress—she was listening for something. Suddenly she grabbed her heart with her left hand and cupped her face with her right, shielding her view. She was wet with tears and sweat. Her legs held their ground, placed exactly a shoulder's length a part. "Thomas, I know your argument. I have heard it many times. I know about your birthing place and I realize you have a time limit. However, Thomas, you must grow composure and listen to me plainly: stand down and step back, your girth does not intimidate me!"

Reaching up with both arms, stretching several feet, on tiptoes, Sophie grabbed something, a leg, or an arm, or a neck, something round, pulling on it with all her strength. Pierced by an ear-splitting siren, Sophie could hear Hannah's primal screams, *"No, no, no, you mustn't take her, that was no deal of ours! I wanted Thomas gone, not Marthia! No!!!"*

Sophie hung to the rock, hearing Hannah's screams, feeling her trying to split her skull in half—this time there was no bounty. A baby's screams filled the space—Marthia, confused and panicked, feeling her father pulling her from one end and her mother pulling from the other. She couldn't last much longer, meaning yet another fetus would be lost prematurely.

"You have asked me here to arbitrate, to hear both sides, making way for an easy peace among you three. But Hannah, you are fighting and blocking the process. This must stop or I will leave with no closure for any of us. I will close the Spirit Door to you, blocking any further communication." Sophie spoke with force. "Now, Thomas, you are no angel here. You have had your agenda from the beginning, playing your hand with three available bodies. But hear me now: these bodies are no longer viable. There are no more triplets, only twins, and soon there will only be you. You are partly to blame for this situation. You have caused undue stress to the mother and fetuses through your constant struggle with Hannah; it has waged its war and has damaged two possible lives."

Thomas pulled away, not wanting Sophie or Hannah to see his tear-soaked face. *"I feared this stress would lose our place. I am too tired to blame Hannah as I normally would do. It is my responsibility. I am heartsick, so sad to have Hannah deny me again. What shall I do in this family all alone, without my wife and darling daughter? Why am I trapped in this curse against familial love?"*

"Spirit has a solution, Thomas. Marthia has awakened. You heard her screams, her fear. Those were her first sounds other than gentle coos for three hundred years. Her time is coming—she has grown and changed. Your new blood family, although compromised by genetic factors, will create another baby space in three years. If Marthia agrees now to this placement, her space will be reserved. Thomas, you will keep this family focused and together until Marthia can be born full-term. Do you agree to the contract?"

"Yes, Sophie, I agree!" Thomas stepped forward and shook on the deal.

Sophie bent down, grabbed the penlet, and stuck her left middle finger, Saturn's finger, Karmic Fate, causing a large crimson spot of blood
to ooze from the small puncture wound. "This is how the deal works,
Thomas. Focus, Hannah, you must listen too! When I bleed onto the rock,
Thomas, your birth will begin. You will be born in minutes, grossly premature at twenty-five weeks. The last baby was stillborn, too weak to support
Marthia for long; she chose to pass to make a firm place for you. You must
go and trust, praise your daughter's and now your sister's courage and sacrifice! The mother will feel my blood, it will become hers, and Marthia's
place will be secured. Life will not be easy for you for three years, but
you will survive and learn to thrive. Go now, feel your birth, remember
the Spirit Bargain. Travel well, Thomas!" Sophie pumped a gentle stream
of fresh blood and made a vertical line, then crossed it with a horizontal
streak. Thomas was born!

Sophie—still standing and bound to the rock—dropped her arms from
exhaustion and sobbed softly. She must regain her composure. Her Work
was incomplete. She reached up and grabbed a round object and began to
pull, this time accentuating her movements with low long grunts of hot air.
"I cannot force you, Hannah; you must surrender and meet me halfway."
Sophie pulled again, almost falling backward from the physical effort. Hannah stopped struggling, slowed her movements, and met Sophie face to face.
Sophie opened her eyes and gazed into Hannah's endless gray eyes, watching
specks on a circular horizon. Without words, Sophie explained to Hannah
a transformation had happened. Marthia had grown. No longer a suckling
infant, she was now a demanding toddler, who would tax Hannah of all her
remaining strength. The energy making her life between the worlds possible
would now be spent caring for the quickly maturing Marthia. She had three
years and seven days to continue to raise her child. Marthia could no longer
be manipulated or stunted to fit Hannah's escapist agenda.

Marthia was preparing for her future incarnation. After her fortuitous
and easy birth, she would grow tall and lean, loving nature in all its shades
and seasons, although Winter always would be her favorite. She would attend the finest universities and become a doctor of skill and merit. Eventually, she would return to her home on the reservation on the Canadian
border and administer Medicine of all sorts to her people, always sensitive
to the Old Ways. She would have a special place that only she knew about,
the old, worn Hannah Dustin green stone memorial off a dirt track outside

of Pennacook, New Hampshire. This was her people's country. She loved her Ancestors and knew she loved this place. Even though it had a bad reputation of being haunted, the Spirits would never frighten her.

Sophie, finding words, continued with Hannah. "This is Marthia's future as a First Nations person. The rage, death, and blood cycle is now over. It is a time of healing and rejuvenation. You have three years to learn to let go, Hannah, three years to realize there is no hell. We make our own hell here on Earth, and we stew in our own poison. No outside force can oppress a human forever—only the Self can do such an efficient and enduring job of torture. You have three years to learn to be free."

Hannah wiped the tears from her face and thanked Sophie for the years of friendship. She would learn to be on her own, a busy mother of a toddler, living under the ancient sacred tree.

Sophie began a seizure, gently shaking at first, her body quickly surrendering to shudders and violent tics. Dylan saw her releasing her grip and took two swift steps forward, catching her under her armpits. Feeling his strong grip on her shoulders and back, Sophie straightened herself and stood upright. The shaking ended. Time had been suspended. Confused, she asked the time. "Five-fifteen," Dora said.

Sophie wiped the snot from her face and the tears from her glasses and took a long look at her three compadres. They had been crying, frazzled and green around the gills. They looked as if they had been chased by a ghost, headless and menacing. "You'll have to share your observations of Hannah with me, later. Know she is fine, better than she's been in a long while. The rest I'll tell you over dinner."

"We'll put our two cents' worth in then, too, count on it. Until then, we've got two quick stops to make before leaving town. We have sundown in forty-five minutes." Dylan picked up Sophie's bag, now full because Dora and Poe had wrapped the altar tools and herbs and placed them carefully where they belonged. Dylan extended his left arm in Sophie's direction, urging her to take it, letting him lead her to the car. Sophie relaxed into Dylan's hold and quietly complied with a sigh of relief.

Sophie's explanation would never come. No questions were asked; realizations and impressions were never shared. Her friends took her seriously concerning their new freedom and, on some level, they all released Sophie when Thomas traveled to his new body. Only time would explain why, hindsight being the gift for a special few.

Dora directed Dylan to the Garrison House, the supposed site of the Dustin homestead. The party circled the property, each of them opening a door or window, promptly shut behind them by the wind. A welcomed entry was impossible. Smiling, Dylan tied an Honor Bundle to the closest tree next to the front door and herded the tired women to the SUV.

Dora's directions to Hannah's river landing place, recently reopened by the parks service, would take them directly in front of the large bronze statue of Hannah, so famous for its bloody scalps. Dora prepared Dylan for its location a block in advance. He quickly responded by circling the park where the monument was planted. Sophie counted ten homeless people sitting around the worn foundation of the bronze. Ten people, men and women, Indian, black, and red-headed Irish. All ten had missing pieces grafted on, successfully placed during the Death Dance and Song at Singing Beach. Sophie had no way of knowing whether these ten people would heal, ten people with new lives awaiting sound choices. If they were not successful in this life, perhaps they would be in the next—it was out of Sophie's hands. She wished them well: the ten, Thomas, Hannah, Marthia, hoping she'd never have to meet them again.

The horizon was yellow by the time they reached the river landing, just enough light to get a group picture for their travel book and skip a few stones. Sophie slid down the bank on her butt, her arms and legs too weak to carry her down the treacherous embankment. Sophie didn't mind being entertainment, all of them wanting to laugh at her antics, watching the older woman acting a fool. Sophie stood upright at the bottom of the landing and was the first one to laugh out loud, the others being too shy to let loose initially at Sophie's weaknesses.

The crickets sounded sunset, the sky slowly turning cobalt blue. They would offer the fish maple sugar granules and shortbread cookie crumbs, after their own greedy bites of Sacrament. They were happy now, released from a ghostly burden too great to face without fear. Dylan tied an Honor Bundle to the tallest branch he could reach. He reached for Sophie, hugging her hard. She reached for Dora, and Poe united the four in a group hug, needed and deserved. "Blessed Be!" Sophie cheered and they all jumped up and down on the deserted beach, tasting the sweetness of success.

Salem
1692

Kether

Binah   Chokmah

Daath

Geburah   Chesed

Tiphareth

Hod   Netzach

Yesod

Malkuth

Chapter Eighteen

THE NIGHT READING
January 25, 2007, 9:00 p.m.

WHEN SOPHIE WAS A GIRL, her parents moved the family a lot: California, Arizona, Michigan, Tennessee, New Mexico, one foot ahead of the bill collector, night rides zigzagging the country. When Joan was diagnosed with cancer, two weeks before turning two, Sarah and Richard decided to settle in the Midwest, close to family so they could build a support network to help them with the relentless demands of a dying child. They had three other mouths to feed; they were in a state of hopelessness, oppressed by their prospects. They gave up their ranch in Arizona and quit their jobs as teachers in a two-room schoolhouse in Mormon country, metaphysicians marooned a hundred miles from the nearest city. They moved away from their dream in order to survive the Reaper. They were defeated and destitute before they even began.

Joan died a week after her fifth birthday, her only wish to go to school. Wish granted: a half-day in a crowded kindergarten class was her heaven, her life complete. Crushed by debt and emotional paralysis, Sarah and Richard knew what little they had would never sustain them, their other children, or any kind of future. They hustled and jived and talked their way into buying a dilapidated three-story turn-of-the-century box, in a marginal neighborhood, flanked by a fire department depot, a tavern catering to veterans of foreign wars, and a Catholic rectory a block over. The houses in between were clean, a far cry from their four-thousand-square-foot fixer-owner contract. And the dogs, Sarah's pride and joy, collies, the closest creatures to lions, her familiar, her passion. The constant barking, competing for the most noise made against the brigade of fire engines.

The house was a wreck, huge and falling down around them. They took solace in the fact it was theirs—they wouldn't be moving until all the kids graduated high school, ten years they reckoned. It was 1969, a heady time, riots, war, and love-ins, a continuation of lifestyle for the bohemian family originally from California.

Friday was family night, the only night Sarah insisted the family be together for the whole evening. When children protested, she assured them it was their familial duty to stay, to pray, to eat, to be together. Sophie would cook. Fried chicken was the favorite for family night, or burritos. In leaner times, only the spices changed in the beans and rice.

Sarah would set the dining table with a white linen cloth belonging to her grandmother. Slowly and somberly, the reduced family would sit down in their respective places, put the cloth napkins in their laps, and sit patiently as Sarah lit the two white candles in the special silver candlesticks, once belonging to her mother. Richard would say a Blessing Prayer over the food and the heads of his remaining children. Sophie served. This was the closest to civilized they would ever get. Once the prayers were said, the wine toasted, and the food eaten, the decibel level rose and lively conversation flooded the curtain-less dining room, with its carved oak columns and peeling plaster.

Richard was in charge of dishing up the ice cream for dessert, exclaiming in his hoarse breathy voice, "A bowl about the size of your head?" They howled, all of them, every Friday night, loving the ice cream, the connection, the tradition.

Immediately following dessert, the ritual began. This was Sarah's job. She took this ritual more seriously than any of her other duties.

Sarah took them through aura cleansing, centering in the now through Intentional Breath, and grounding their energy deep into Mother Earth. They formed a Circle, with a TV tray in the center doubling as an altar table, with a solitary white candle burning. After chanting oms and toning their out-of-tune voices, Sarah led them in the Money Chant, three times repeated. It was a long and ancient Voudon chant, passed on to her years before while traveling through the South on a family vacation. Sarah had connections everywhere.

The chanting was sealed with a communal hug, the family huddle. Richard and the two small children were encouraged to read or go to bed early. It was Sarah and Sophie's special time to study the Tarot, numerology, and astrology, each adept in one and needing advice on two. Ali would wait in her room at the top of the stairs for the house to quiet, Erick finding refuge in his basement room, Richard turning in early, his only solitary night. The gentle murmur of women's voices kept low filtered through the old house. Ali waited like this every Friday night.

Ali would fool them all. By the time she was sixteen, Ali was a talented Seer, a clairvoyant with her own symbol system, attracted to kabbalistic Tarot perspective and Santería ritual. Alysandra Sarah St. Cloud would become the Cartomancer for the Stars and would set up shop in Malibu. Several years later, she moved home to Santa Fe, creating a comfortable niche for herself as a psychic counselor, specializing in private phone readings, money finding its way into her bank account via Western Union and Visa.

Sophie had not seen Ali in five years. This didn't bother the sisters; they talked on the phone almost daily. The highlight of their coming together was a January night, a single night for them only, no students, groupies, or psychic vampires wanting free readings and instant healings. Ali and Sophie had the big house, a clean animal-free Oregon version of their parents' Michigan home, to themselves. They ate a light supper—the first bit of peace they felt since the weekend—before retiring to the large dining table for probing talk, Oracle Work, and distant viewing.

Sophie's attention could not be diverted from the Salem work. Like Giles, Sophie could not be sidetracked by others' agendas, regardless of importance. She didn't want to know if she was going to meet the woman of her dreams or sell the historical novel she had put on the back burner until the Salem work was completed. She wanted details about specific people involved in the American Camino. Ali wanted an in-depth personal reading from Sophie—it had been over a decade since Sophie had read her cards with Sarah's ancient Tarot deck—but she knew Sophie only wanted information pertaining to Salem. Ali didn't mind; it was her way of being involved, on the front lines without having to do the dirty work.

Ali had the tendency to relate to the abuser or perpetrator psychically. She worked on missing-people cases, sexual abuse charges, abduction, murder for hire, brought in by the police or other psychics hired by vested parties. She saw from predatory eyes, felt their feelings, from revulsion to titillation. Sophie had no patience for perps; she needed to stand on the outside, watch the Big Picture, unravel mysteries, catch the bad guys, set the story straight. Salem involved ghosts, murdered people, unsolved disappearances, open cases still cold, most so obscure nobody realized their significance. Ali knew she'd go right there, into the murderer's head. She didn't like to do this kind of work, but she was good at it and if she could offer Sophie some sound Oracle advice, all of them, their lovers, husbands, and extended families, would be better off. She was up for it.

Sophie cleared the dining table, smudged it, sprinkled kosher salt on the wood, and laid a royal purple cloth thirty-three inches square on top of the protective salt. This would be their psychic ground, their link with Spirits with information. Purple is the color of power, extreme thought and behavior, transcendental and zealot consciousness. Paired with cobalt blue, the color of otherworldly communication, a magickal combination was born, known to levitate objects, gifting the Seer with secret portals to chambers containing sensitive information or missing objects or people.

Sophie decided she would not touch the cards; she wanted the most objective reading possible, although she realized it was difficult, working with Ali. It was a natural response for people well acquainted with each other, similar to a surgeon operating on a family member. Ali and Sophie were a fantastic team though, microcosm and macrocosm, covered to the last detail. Sometimes, when Ali had the cards, Sophie would do distant viewing based on the information Ali was supplying. Ali didn't need the cards. As long as there were no distractions, the information flowed. But Sophie preferred the cards, just-the-facts-ma'am-attitude, a focus, information from an outside source, more objective. Sophie needed a paper trail for documentation down the road, for edification now. Ali was more patient than Sophie; she was used to waiting for people to catch up. Paradoxically, Ali made decisions on a dime, preferring to move rather than to paint a wall. Sophie painted murals on walls, her self-driven schedule never allowing for boredom.

Sophie lit a lone white candle in their mother Sarah's silver candleholder and allowed smoke from Cedar incense to cover the tabletop and cards. They wouldn't eat a crumb when reading the cards. It was considered disrespectful behavior. They drank lots of water, though, bottles of cold spring water, flowing as much as their words. Ali sat in the West by the Door of the Dead; Sophie sat in the East by the Door of the Living, St. Michael's protection portal. Only invited guests were permitted through the openings.

Spirit Salutes were done in Sophie's traditional manner. Ali's personal rituals differed from Sophie's, more relaxed, eclectic. Sophie prayed to her main Spirit Guide for his protection and deliverance from doubt and worry, the Kabbalah meets the Red Road. Sophie prayed to Sarah and Joan, asking their perspective on the Salem work; they were intimate with the gaol of Old Salem. Ali wanted to call forth their father, Richard, but Sophie talked her out of it: one month a year was enough for Sophie.

Ali held the cards with her eyes closed, head slightly raised, a broad smile. Then she began: hands moving quickly, snapping cards, shuffling, cutting, stacking and restacking, all business. Three stacks cut toward her and set aside, she was ready to lay the cards.

"I want the lay of the land, to know who our supporters and enemies are. The spies' identity is a good beginning point, although I already have suspects, three in all. I just need verification." Sophie took a long chug from her water bottle. Anxious, she was sweating despite January temperatures. Anxiety creates hot flashes, especially at night. The later the hour, the more violent the sweating.

Ali stopped shuffling and looked away from Sophie, concentrating on an abstract point. "I'm using the Kabbalah Spread. The Tree of Life, the Sephirot, tells a story ten chapters long, think G-d plus one, meaning eleven cards. From time to time, I will read additional cards, either because they fall out of the deck or they're placed for clarity. A reading such as this, using the proper placements of the Tree, leads to endless path-working systems. Tonight, I am reading the Sephirot in the opposite order. I usually read the Tree from the top, Kether the Crown, to the bottom, Malkuth the Root. Since you believe the Old Ways come from Inner Earth, I will honor your worldview by reading Malkuth first and work my way up the Tree, ending with Kether. I have a feeling it will yield more information. Let's see…

"In the first placement of Malkuth, the Sephirot tells a story of realization. The divine plan—with you center stage—is recognized and given its true power to inspire. Malkuth reminds us of our limitlessness and on the physical level indicates the importance of personal accomplishment. We find the Ace of Wands here. Obviously, personal success is all important on this journey, not a surprise. The Ace of Wands tells of the ultimate union of human and Spirit, in communication, indicating a clear channel already in place. I would expect nothing less—this is a green light! The Five of Cups fell out, the pessimist in you, seeing failure and half-measures, before the journey gets started. This tells you to trust Spirit and shut off the rat-mind tapes of low self-esteem you put in place to intentionally hold yourself back. The Page of Pentacles fell out as well, indicating concerns about money: he says you cannot afford to subsidize or sponsor anyone other than Dylan and yourself on the American Camino. This is your culling tool. Whoever refuses to pay, doesn't go. Right off the bat, we have symbolically: a beekeeper, a slave with knowledge and victory in binding and unbinding, a wonderful start!

"We move on to Netzach, symbolizing our energy valve, the Solar Plexus of the reading, right-brain in orientation. We have the Knight of Pentacles; he is riding slowly, his speed imperceptible to others. This gives him a great advantage in warfare; he is undervalued, so much so that he is ignored. Undaunted, he gathers his lucky charms and glides into enemy territory and takes over, bloodlessly. This is your warning, Sophie: stay slow, keep your movements deliberate, and you will be able to produce enough energy to succeed. You must reserve and ration your energy from this point forward, till you return from Salem. It will take that amount of time to prepare properly, for you to weed through the muck and find the deserving places to spend your valuable energy. I'm not worried; I know you can pull it off. But you must not feed pearls to swine; you must keep your treasures to yourself and not give your power away!

"Yesod is our next step. Remember, I'm simplifying the pathways and using unorthodox placements. Bear with me, it will make sense. Yesod is our foundation, the Pillars of the Temple. This represents your spiritual tool chest, your natural talents and basis of your power. We have the King of Swords here. He is sad, chronically depressed, and his lament is contagious. I think this represents Poe and her past-life connections, the depressed doctors who are caught in a cycle of loss and regret and lots of guilt. It also points to Dylan and his lack of love success recently. He is sending mixed messages to the Universe, that's why he's still single. You know him—it's romance and commitment. He has to walk on the wild side for a while, shock himself into another reality.

"Hod represents our left brain and is the flowing visual of our subconscious mind. It's your past-life memory, Sophie, propelling this journey forward. You are bonded to take these steps for the sake of your own sanity, for the sake of destiny. We have the Eight of Swords here, indicating a fear of imprisonment, a public death. You fear persecution. Don't make it a persecution complex, however. There's already enough danger present without manufacturing more. This is Giles not wanting to repeat the same pain over again. Who could blame him? You have to visualize success, Sophie. You cannot drag this event down because of your petty fears. Yes, you might think you are important, but not so much in the grand scheme of things.

We'll come back here for clarification later. This does indicate having a hard time finding someone to chronicle this experience for you. I have been nagging you to get a film student or documentarist involved in this project. Wow, what a movie it would make! Anyway, just relax and know your brain is the best movie camera, better than money could ever buy. Besides, you and the Elders and all your protocol, you'll be using Eagle and Parrot feathers. They wouldn't approve you filming during those times, which will be constant while you are doing your thing, you Shaman-woman, you!"

"Knock it off, Ali. I know we need levity, but…" Sophie stopped, cleared her throat and resettled into the reading. She knew her hypervigilance was silly sometimes, but she couldn't help herself, especially with her little sister.

"Okay, the next one isn't any better, though, so take a deep breath and think of your favorite color, ground yourself. Let's get revved up here.

"We're going to jump over the Sephirot, excuse me, all the way to Chesed, now. Chesed is how we give, what importance we put on gratitude and the ability to give credit where credit is due. It's Mitzvah. It also rules the power of intention. Considering the timing—this close to achieving our goal, I mean your goal—we need to pay special attention here. In this placement, we have the Nine of Swords. There is an interesting pattern beginning to emerge. Here's the Five of Pentacles for clarity. I believe this relates to the disembodied Spirits coming to you in the night. I can see lots of people here, dirty, disheveled, sounds like twin Hannah Dustins; they refuse to let you sleep. They don't have homes any longer, they wander; that's why they don't give great importance for your private space and rest. They are connected to you, big time! Also the people with smallpox, the ones quarantined and sealed to die, they're mentioned. In addition, four others— two groups of two are represented here—are trying to get through to you."

"You are absolutely right, Ali. I was going to bring this subject up later, but no time like the present. Since I announced on Mabon of 2006 that Dylan and I were going to Salem, four Spirits, unknown to me previously, began visiting. Ali, I tell you, it's like a line for a hockey game every night. They are all banged-up, dirty, and bloody. The two groups of two in question show up separately, but at the same time. For instance, if the meeting is in my bedroom, one group stands on the right side of the bed, while the other group stands on the left. They are from different times, one colonial, the others victims of a serial killer during the years 1978 to 1992 in the North Shore area of Boston. They explained they were killed in other locations and brought to this place to be buried; all four have this in common. They've described the place to me. The land is shaped like a human profile. If you turned it on end, it would look like a scrolled *M* or *W*, you know, a big curly bracket. Anyway, one group is buried close together on the bottom half of the profile; the other group is buried on the top half of the profile. We have topo maps of Massachusetts on order. I hope I'll be able to pinpoint the location when I study them. Both groups are buried halfway from the edge of the riverbank, to the top level of green, in the center of a strip, perhaps fifty feet wide. The younger group points to a large bridge and at least one busy highway, perhaps to their Southwest.

"I haven't psychically located the serial killer. I just won't go there, too creepy. I can't deal in cases like that anymore. The other group was killed most likely by the Family Confederacy, probably Corwin's men, meaning the site is relatively close to Salem or Danvers. I don't know if John Moulton was working for Corwin when they were murdered, although it wouldn't surprise me. After all, John Moulton, now reincarnated as Lynda Waters—that's right, you met her here yesterday for Circle—has declared she is planning to go to Boston at the same time we will be in Salem. It wasn't a friendly announcement either. There are no coincidences in the Universe. She's staying with my old friends the Steeles, but, hey, this is getting into another subject I want to deal with separately.

"The bottom line: these Spirits are miserable; both groups have been unable to go to the light. The landscape is radically changed from the time they were buried. So much building has been done since the early 1990s, they are unable to tell me how to find them, their bones at least. They were either dead or unconscious when brought to this place, so they have few reference points. I'd know it if I saw it, clearly! These bodies are close to Salem, or they would have chosen another time to appear to me. Salem wanted to be spiffed up for the three-hundredth anniversary of the Witch Trials in 1992, the year I moved to Salem, Oregon. Strange, huh? Anyway, crazy building went on, mushrooming into a decade of changes. I understand they are at it again, particularly after the tunnel collapse in Boston. I need to find these people. They want to move to the light and I am willing to help them, so I can get them out of my house at night. Okay, let's be honest about motivation. What did you say about intention a couple of minutes ago? Any insight on these people would be appreciated."

Ali looked at her sister and then returned to the spread of cards. "Okay,

I will stay sensitive to them. The information is good to know. If I don't pick up anything further on the subject tonight, I'll stay open to contact with them later. I don't want to do predator work if I don't have to, but I will for you. But for now, let's move on. I feel the creepiness too.

"This is when it always gets interesting in the Kabbalah spread, the center or the heart of the Sephirot, Tiphareth. This is how we see beauty, what effect it has on us, what inspires the human heart to create. Tiphareth is an important placement for you, since you are an artist. It is emotion, solitary and shared; it's the human heart's capacity to love. We have the King of Wands here, representing an assertive energy who demands an audience, a Leo temperament personality, the center of attention doling out gems to his eager entourage. This card configuration has many meanings. On a personal level, you must speak clearly, move with purpose and consistency, adopt a chameleon sensibility. Too much grandstanding is not a good idea. It will be hard to resist, more than once. There is a warning to rise above thrill-seeking and self-aggrandizement. For the group dynamic, Dylan will demand a certain amount of time in the limelight—he'll be eager to prove himself, and if he's in a social situation with beautiful women, he might make himself available for falling in love. Heads-up, so to speak. This placement is also where it gets juicy in regards to betrayal, crimes of passion, and lying.

"This would be a good time to deal with your questions concerning spies and negative attempts to derail this project. I know you have been having a hard time with Rebecca and Frank Steele from Boston. How in the world did Lynda Waters become involved with them? Did you connect them?"

Sophie sighed. "Well, stop me if I get repetitive. Yes, I put Lynda together with the Steeles. I'm my own worst enemy, most of the time. It was before I realized who Rebecca really was. I always thought she was the reincarnation of Rebecca Nurse—she's a nurse and her name is Rebecca. It was a good guess, because past lives work that way—names, dates, talents, professions, and features repeat. I really thought it was a no-brainer, especially since she is married to Frank, the reincarnation of Francis Nurse. This is where it gets amazing. This is how I finally put the puzzle piece of Frank's identity in place. Frank, from the time he was a small boy growing up as a townie in Boston, was fascinated by the roads of Essex County. The first time he visited the Nurse Homestead was on a field trip in junior high school, part of his civics class section on colonial history. He stood transfixed in front of the red board building, knowing every inch of the house before stepping over its threshold. The homestead clung to him, like Summer clothes slick with sweat. He made at least a once-a-year pilgrimage to Danvers. He just spent Samhain there, a few months ago. This is the point where I caught on: Francis Nurse worked for Thomas Putnam, considered the Old Man to know in Essex County, the patriarch extraordinaire. Francis Nurse's job description was road builder. Subconsciously, Frank knows I know. Just last month, he emailed me a photo of his newest painting, a couple strolling down a country road, dressed in black with white collars, surrounded by changing leaves. He calls it, 'A Stroll to the Meetinghouse.' I kept it in my file—remind me and I'll show it to you tomorrow.

"So, knowing Frank was Francis, it made sense that Rebecca was Rebecca, until Rebecca told me the story of her nursing school experience. In the sixties, it was mandatory to live on the grounds, usually a wing of a hospital. In Rebecca's case, her place of residence and work was the Massachusetts State Hospital at Danvers, built on the ruins of Ann Putnam's original house. It has been converted to condos now, can you imagine? Most of the young nurses hated living and working at the hospital. They felt it was haunted and of course it was—is, I should say. There was one person who loved it there, felt more at home there than anywhere she had ever lived. The young nurse with a love affair for the state hospital was Rebecca. She once told me a story of a levitating bed and a gray smoky mass she was able to calm and reason with. Her colleagues were terrified, but Rebecca wasn't scared at all. She talked to the apparitions and floating bed as if they were old family friends. It was at the climax of Rebecca's story that I realized she was not Rebecca Nurse, but Ann Putnam herself. The irony is perfection. The Nurses married into the Confederacy and Francis worked for them: a double-whammy.

"The Family Confederacy wanted to kill five people: Tituba, Sarah Good, Bridget Bishop, and Giles and Martha Corey. They were all visible or powerful in the community, hard to get rid of, not like indentured servants or half-breed Indians. The Confederacy had to concoct a scheme to rid themselves of five dangerous people, people not above blackmail. Tituba was targeted because she knew all of Reverend Samuel Parris's dirty slaving secrets from Trinidad. Sarah Good was hated by the Putnams because she knew everyone's secrets, including what beds they shared. She was such a skilled beggar that she never used a front stoop for her handouts—she would linger at back doors, under woodsheds, in dark alleyways, near outhouses, always an eye peeled for expensive information. Bridget Bishop had gone rogue, buying much of her tavern supplies from Giles—rum and Carib Tobacco—shunning convention and the meetinghouse at once. She tasted profit through ingenuity, and it stuck. She was a woman fond of color and spirits; she had to go, as you should know. We know Giles and Martha's story, Goddess bless us!

"You know this part, at least most of it. The Family Confederacy had to cover their tracks and make it appear there was another reason the five had to die. With Samuel Parris's help, they concocted a story of Witchcraft, inspired by the exploits of Tituba. Perfect—she would be easy prey. Tituba would be front and center, blamed and gotten rid of right away, along with Parris's past lascivious exploits and embezzled funds. By the time of Bridget Bishop's hanging, the Confederacy was over their heads, their scheme out of control. To cover their double-dealing and to point guilt elsewhere, the men of the clan decided to draw lots among the ten main families and decide who of their own would be sacrificed to the hysteria. Francis pulled the short straw; he had to sacrifice one of his own, in order to protect everyone. Old Man Putnam had threatened Francis's property in the past; this sealed the deal based on Francis's greatest fears, even after many years. He went to Rebecca, now ailing and in bed till her passing. He confessed his dilemma to her and asked her advice. The solution would be to sacrifice her. She wouldn't hear arguments; her life was ending anyway, and it was a good solution.

"Rebecca called her sisters together and told them the deal, which was already enforced. Mary Easty, her favorite sister, fell apart and insisted this was too high of a ransom for the Townes to pay. She threatened to blow the whole deal, to go to the authorities in Boston and spill the truth. Mary's threats ended her in the gaol, too, giving her life to this intrigue, as did her older sister.

"When you think about it, it's fitting Francis married Ann Putnam in this life. Rebecca probably wouldn't have him back, is my guess. Ann felt personally responsible for Rebecca's death and suffered from years of guilt over her own relative being hung because of her fantasies, what her father and uncles put her and the other girls up to until the girls started to enjoy their power. Their fathers decided to use the girls' fervor and get rid of any further opposition, and the whole mess became tragic quickly.

"Bottom line: I do not trust the Steeles, regardless of our decade-long friendship, not anymore, not since they teamed up with Lynda. Rebecca has been showing her true colors lately, being confrontational and abusive. She even wrote this awful poem about being pressed to death and sent it along with a video of a pride of lions attacking a wildebeest. And this is a friend, supposedly! Talk about passive-aggressive! She's the one who calls me a control freak. I'm trying to get more information out of her, stringing her along, but it's not going well.

"I have an idea. Let's make a separate row of cards for all the people I have questions about, all dealing with the Tiphareth placement. I'll say a name, then you draw a card. We'll read them all in conjunction with the King of Wands." Sophie was getting amped now.

"Fantastic idea, Sophie! Okay, we'll begin with Rebecca. You call her name and I'll draw the card. Good. Wow, the Devil. Okay, let's pull one more for Rebecca and read it with Chesed, her intention. Okay, it's Death. I really like this form; we'll use it for all questions pertaining to spies, friends, and enemies. Understanding another's intention is major information, exposing much more than their heart alone.

"Right off the bat, I see Rebecca has lots of personal problems she likes to stash—hides, in fact. She doesn't share her weaknesses with people other than Frank, pretty typical of the generation. She's a real fan of herself and it is clear she does not respect you."

Sophie nodded her agreement. "Rebecca told me once that Shamanism is dead. She said it didn't help the Native peoples against the whites and it wouldn't help me now, because I was hopelessly out of touch with modernity."

Ali continued, "This combination of cards suggests Rebecca is in a lot of pain and is taking too many drugs. She is apparently hooked, making her appear hostile and depressed. She's strong-willed and will eventually kick it, but she's got a good year's struggle ahead of her."

"I think you are right, Ali. She has been suffering from a back injury and had a bout of Lyme disease last year. I understand it's quite painful, bless her heart, poor thing."

"Obviously on target, good feed-back! Okay, another name. Good, Lynda. Ah, King of Cups in Chesed. Intention: Two of Cups in Tiphareth. Lynda is a case in contradiction. She has the best of intention, at least on one level, and truly believes she is working for the benefit of others. She, however, aims to undermine your authority and present a different scenario for the Witch Trials, one which is not so hard on John Moulton. You paint him as the murderer and scoundrel he was, and Lynda is not happy about it. I believe she wants to write a book about Salem before you do, doing her part in setting the story straight, so to speak. Very interesting. Don't trust her. Try to separate from her for good, as soon as you can maneuver it. My Spirit Guide is whispering a message about Lynda; he says Lynda served under Alexander the Great. This is where she learned to keep going despite opposition. This is the reason she wants to compete with you for the most powerful seat, instead of getting out of the way and letting you work. She hates the spotlight being off of her; it drives her a little nuts. She wants to offer all participants the real Holy Grail of Immortality in Salem. What that is, who knows... Next? Frank, good timing, we have all three now.

"We have Five of Pentacles on Chesed, Four of Cups on Tiphareth. This brings home what you told me about Francis's terrible mission and the reason he bent to Putnam pressure—it was the threat to his land and estate he had worked so hard to build. Five of Pentacles represents homelessness, being unable to fight, and thrown away without honor or worth. Frank has no self-esteem and probably does whatever Rebecca demands from him. Sad, really. He's probably a nice guy. Spineless, though. Okay, Four of Cups indicates he is overwhelmed. He believes you; so much, in fact, that it has caused him to doubt his life as a whole. When we cut to it, he'll side with Rebecca to keep his uncomfortable home intact. He loves her and she would be lost without him. I'd say to go Indian on them, simply ignore them. Then send them a Christmas card next year, when you are successful and feeling strong. Let them know you made it. Rebecca will leak the information to the Inner Circle."

"I think they are covered, Ali. We know what they are up to, and they simply are unimportant from this moment forward. I'll let them know a few secrets, a burial spot, conversations no one would have been privy to. Something juicy, but not too revealing. They'll get word back to the Inner Circle. They'll figure out we know who the leaks are. Lynda is manipulated by them, she's acting out of ego. She's gone, of no concern any longer. What's going on in Geburah?"

"Geburah is our determination or, as you call it, follow-through. Geburah exposes our weaknesses and makes us vulnerable on deep subconscious levels. The Hangman is here, telling a story of two possibilities. On one hand, you see defeat before the battle and have decided to surrender to greater powers than you, again the pessimist at work. The other hand tells a different story, of surrendering to the truth and, as we said in the 70s, let it set us free! Obviously, it is your choice; you have a battle with your own self before you begin. You must give yourself a big talking-to, surrender to your truth, and work it! This is your lottery on all levels if you just let it be, Sophie! It's more than just healing, balancing, and creating peace. It's about lasting success and right over might, although you've got might working for you too. You know you are powerful. Screw others if you scare them, they'll get used to it or burned by it—it's their choice. You've got to be true to yourself! You told me of the Circle Sister who left last month. Her reason for leaving was that your anger terrified her. What a load of bull. You can't let people like her shape the rest of your life—you know better—you're braver than that!

"Just four more. We'll get through them quickly. I'm getting other pictures now and it's becoming difficult to concentrate. Chokmah is wisdom, Pistis Sophia, the All-seeing Eye, the door to the subconscious world of dreams and memory, the Akashic Records. Here we have the High Priestess. She is Sophia, proud, holding the secret of black and white, controlling the door of higher illusion. She is the ultimate God-Knowing, or the villain of lies; she is the temptress of fate and hates to lose a sparring wager. This speaks directly to you, as an Elder and teacher. Don't get caught up in traps of the ego. It's another ego warning—you know all the answers, but they are yours to keep. Beware of those from whom you seek counsel! You learned this the hard way through dealing with Lynda Waters. As Lydia Dustin says, know your audience—don't confide in a Pisces again! This speaks of the Inner Circle too. They are a powerful lot. Lori Otto knows what she's doing and her underlings are disciplined. I wish your people had the same kind of background and determination, but that's another story, isn't it? You have to know your battles. Pick them wisely, only when you can win. Be careful! Now you have your answers about spies and enemies, you'll be able to cover your ass much more easily now. Spirit is whispering a warning: be careful of a man, age forty to fifty, very dynamic, with a long ponytail. Dylan's opposite, dark instead of light, lean instead of stocky. I hear he is bent, but his back looks straight to me. I think it is a metaphor, meaning: this guy is bent. Yes, that's it! Beware of this man!"

"It sounds like Drake Putnam, the ultimate boss of the Inner Circle."

"Yes, he fits. Thanks. Now, let's jump to Daath. Daath portends the next great adventure, the next rung of evolution. It is a realm of fantasy, as well as future promise, with its successes and failures. Some say it doesn't belong to the Sephirot, that it is separate, a fortune-telling tool. I believe it's our window on possibility. It represents a level of focus and concentration, in which you have the power of dreaming your own reality, a different reality, depending upon your mindset and skill-base. Look at it as a form of divining or creative visualization. In this placement we have the Ten of Swords, not the greatest card to find here. This tells me of your opponents, how they are working to defeat the American Camino, to scare you off before you begin. They must know you have refundable tickets."

The sisters laughed, shaking the house with their late night revelries. "We're getting punchy—let's be patient and get through this." Sophie was getting tired—or overwhelmed.

"We will, my sistah! This talks of enemies from within and enemies without. It says you are your own worst enemy, your worry and anxiety. You have to learn to relax in your power and go forward, regardless of who is trying to block your way. You've got the power, Sophie, we all know it! Obviously, forces from the outside want you to fail. Here's an interesting warning. Look at the Swords, they follow the Kundalini, suggesting someone from within is talking about you behind your back and planning a departure from your good graces by manipulating the situation, making you look like the bad guy. This person is close to you physically, not close emotionally, although he or she probably was at one time. This could also point to the fact that several people might leave your presence. I've seen this configuration during a divorce or when a Circle is breaking up. Just put it down as something to keep an eye out for. Other than giving yourself a good talking to and working on raising your confidence level, you just have to flow with it.

"Binah represents the mother and child, the accomplishment of birthing. It is manifestation of a nurturing spirit; it speaks of future successes and evolution. In other words, will this mission be a success? Since we have the Strength Card here, I would say, yes, there is success, stamina, inspiration, courage, heart, all waiting for you to manifest them. You are the only one holding you back, Sophie. All the ghosts, goblins, and spies have no chance of beating you at your own game! Keep focused, stay on stage, but keep your ego in check. Be the center of your Universe.

"Now, for the last one: Kether, the Crown Chakra of the Sephirot. This is God-Head, destiny, the All. Ultimately, this reveals your true reason for undertaking this mission of integration and healing. Six of Cups is here, the card of responsibility. This is you, Sophie, the taller child serving the smaller child. I was your smaller charge, Erick and Joan too. All Spirits who seek you out—you feel compassion for them, you feel responsible for their happiness and success. Of course, it is your choice to serve, but this is what you were raised to do, to care for others, to minister to their wounds. This is your lot in life. This is how you will earn your eventual rest. You have an opportunity to rise above your compulsion to incarnate constantly. You need to stop; this is your way to do it! The only warning here is to not get bogged down with perceived success or failure. It is your selflessness commanding you to do the American Camino. When you walk the steps, you are walking for all of us, for the country. It doesn't matter who knows it—it's your mission regardless. We will all benefit from your steps. It's the choice of these Spirits whether they move to the light or if they stay haunting. You cannot be responsible for their choices." Ali sighed. "I've had it! Let's smoke a joint under the tournament tent, breathe some cold night air, and end our night with one of your luscious desserts. Lynda Waters did say she was disappointed when she discovered organic cookies still had calories. I told her they usually had more, yum!"

"Sounds perfect, Ali! I'm rolling; let's have ice cream in bowls about the size of my head!"

The sisters broke out in laughter, long before they smoked or cleared away the cards. Just the thought of Richard was enough to inspire ice cream on a cold January night.

The testimonie of Mary Warren aged

or thereabouts testifyeth and saith that

July last mr Burroughs pinched mee

me   I said and

I   all com to

and goe   witnes

Mary Warren Declared upon her oath: to yo

evidence   month August

Chapter Nineteen

B'NAI BRITH CEMETERY
August 27, 2007, 10:00 a.m.

IT WAS A HOT SULTRY DAY IN OREGON WINE COUNTRY, the sun bleaching leaves white before Autumn gold took over, two weeks before Sophie left for Essex County. She stood unmoving, lost, in her front room, feeling disconnected from all time zones, even the one she breathed in. In front of her, the ten-foot-long dining table, its top covered with maps of many descriptions, was piled high with books and folders of research. The neon-colored pen tops lured her in. She was a crow, fascinated with shiny colorful treasures. She stood silent, waiting for a sign. The laminated Old Salem map was positioned in the center. Charms, pens, rulers, and shells full of sacred herbs held it flat, keeping it from rolling away. She had not slept for two days, the itching and burning on her chest acute. A new set of body tracings had surfaced at dusk the night before.

She knew she was looking at a secret, the fresh new tracing on gleaming white paper, stacked on top of the other tracings, five in all. She absentmindedly rubbed the raised veins on her chest, looking for a directive secret. Over and over she rubbed a small section; it felt like a curly bracket mark. Finally it hit her; it was the shape she had been searching for: the human profile symbol. Could it be directions to the two groups of two, still haunting her nightly?

Hannah made sure the Spirits did not enter Sophie's bedroom, but they lurked in the hallway, their energy strong and constant. Dozens of them gathered on their nightly vigils, quiet now, thanks to Sophie's new Spirit bodyguard. They sent Sophie pictures that ran day and night, landmarks to look for, omens to be heeded. She willed sight, clarity, cried for it, aching for realization. Then she saw it, plain as day! She doubted what she saw at first, her eyes full of wasted tears; she thought it was wishful thinking. There it was, in the center of the new tracing, a profile. She scanned the Old Salem map and found it in the same scale as the tracing, as the Spirits said, as Sophie saw and Ali recounted, the two sides of the property, sloped and flat both, located on the Endicott River. The Endicott Cow House's location was carefully printed on the map, exactly in the center of the profile, where the nose is located. It was obvious: two bodies to the North, two bodies to the South, the cow house in the center. A wave of relief rushed over Sophie, almost knocking her over.

Hurriedly she rummaged through the stack of topo maps. On the bottom of the pile, she found the map of Salem Harbor. She followed the landmarks North and West and found Endicott Road. There, South of Interchange 24, on the banks of what is now called the Waters River, was the site of the Endicott Cow House, the site of the four elusive bodies desperate to join their families waiting next door. Success, finally!

She laid her left hand over the mark on her chest, close to her heart, and waited for another sign. A minute, then two, went by. Nothing. She laid her right hand over her left and breathed in a deep cleansing breath. The hair on the nape of her neck rose. Sophie opened her eyes and found the two groups of two, swirling around her clock-wise, spinning a Circle of what looked like silver spun sugar. They were whispering among themselves, all parties now a united group of four. They stopped their spinning and faced her. The eldest spoke.

"I am Ann Jayne and this is my son, John. The two of us are from a Quaker group. All of us but John came to Massachusetts looking for a better life. We follow the words of our teacher George Fox, a hearty man in love with brewing and bringing souls to his way of thinking. We are persecuted in England, because we are a freedom-loving people. The government prefers absolute power over thought and imagination, impossible for us to bear. We believe humans should not be persecuted because of their state of poverty, imprisoned because of debt. Nor do we believe in the bondage of women through marriage. No person is greater than another, regardless of color, gender, or age. True, some of our people are in the slaving trade, God save them! We do not share their livelihood.

"My son came to me through civil disobedience, a trait most say unbecoming. We were a group walking the Massachusetts Bay Colony, looking for a hospitable place to build a community. On a bright Summer day, buzzing with bees and hum-

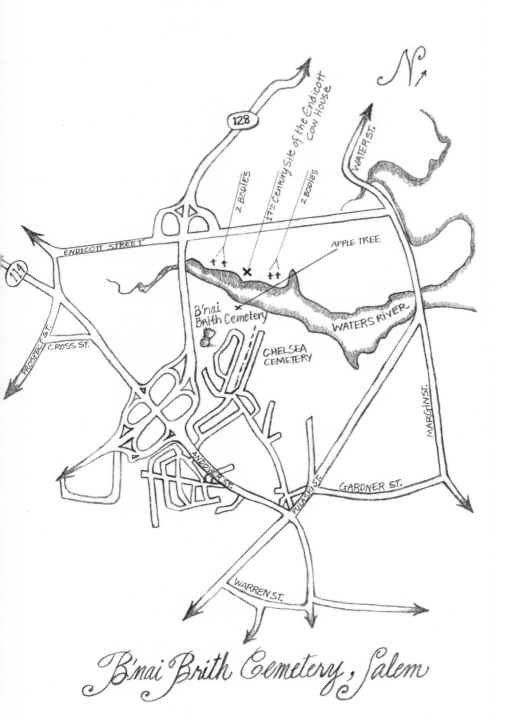

B'nai Brith Cemetery, Salem

ming with green, we passed a meadow filled with flowers and high grass. We could hear crying but could not find its source. Many of us became distraught; a mother knows the sounds of pain. I spotted a dark lump, curled in a ball, under scrub oak. Near it, a spike with chain connected. I was almost over the lump when I realized it was a child, with bushy hair and skin the color of aged boot leather, naked against the sun, swollen with hunger, lips dry and splitting from thirst. The child was no more than five or six, or older maybe, stunted from hunger. I knelt and took sight of his wrist, wet with blood and rust. I asked him if he could speak, if he understood. He nodded yes and began to whimper anew. I asked one of the few men traveling with us if he had tools. He replied he did and proceeded to set the boy free. The blows on his little wrist made him scream out in pain, although all the women pleaded with him to stay silent. None of us wanted to be caught setting a slave free: we would surely hang—it was thievery of a high order. But it stopped none of us. He bellowed out despite our pleadings; his pain dictated his actions. On the last blow, the wrist guard broke in half, freeing his small arm. Luck was on his side, or perhaps the Light of God. His arm was not broken, although he held it as if it was shattered.

"I asked him how old he was and he said seven, but he had been without a mother since he was four. He volunteered his name. 'My mother called me John, the same name as my father. After she died, he found no pleasure in me and sold me to a man up the road. My owner has done this to me. He finds me of no value, too much trouble to train, he said, too much trouble to feed and provide for. He has left me here for some days now; he said he wasn't coming back again. I was glad, but that was days ago. I have been afraid I would die here and the wild dogs would eat me. They sniff me at night.'

"I asked him if he wanted a new mother. He said he was too old for a mother; he had been on his own a long time. But, when I reached for his prickly thin body, he embraced me with the fondness of a loved one, long lost, awaiting a lavish welcome meal. We'll love each other for a long time, I promised. Edith, our beloved Grandmother, could not keep from little John's side. She picked his frail body out of my arms and carried him down the road to the river bank and slowly waded his bleeding, half-starved body into the moving water. She held him lightly, letting the gentle current of the shallow river wash over him, renewing his soul and soothing his wounds. Edith's daughter went from person to person, looking for clothes for the lad. Soon, she had a full set. Edith laid John on the soft tall grass, giving him time and space to dry in the sun. He was ours now. We would share his love. Edith bound his weeping wrist with an herb poultice and clean rags. I gave him some bread and a cup of wine. He took them both so fast, he retched them up.

We all laughed softly, feeling pity. He rested a bit before taking a few small sips of water, he then repeated bread and wine, the sacrament of his new life. This time he chewed slowly, and drank drops, until the wine washed away his pain and gentle sleep replaced his fear.

"I knew I broke the law, freeing the lad. We all shared the guilt, but it was mine to carry. We became fugitives, though no one outside our group knew who took the boy. While we traveled, we kept him hidden in the only hand wagon we had. He didn't like the tight air, but he soon became fat on Edith's fine bread and he loved the mellow feeling wine bestowed.

"Before the leaves began to fall, the boy and I were discovered far off the road, picking late berries. A lone white woman, wearing the clothes of Quakers, with a small black child, was all the proof they needed, two for the price of one. We hardly struggled. We are defiant people, but useless fighting did not fit our demeanor. They took us, two of them did. Tied us, arms and legs, and threw us bound into the back of a two-wheeled wagon. Every rut the wagon hit, bounced us hard against the boards, tightening our bonds. Escape was impossible.

"John Endicott—the good governor and ruler of these parts—hated Quakers. When we landed in Massachusetts, he had vowed to kill us all. He, like many other Puritans, believed we were full of sin because we see God in nature, in ourselves. We call God 'Light.' The Light Within tells the story of our faith: the Light of God shines within us all! In the good governor's eyes, Quakers should be driven all the way to hell, the sooner the better! The Puritans believe it's a sin to think we have God inside ourselves. How poor and lowly and undeserving they feel humans are. We are sad for them.

"The men took us to John's present owner. Without a word, the owner motioned he knew the boy and pointed at me with disdain. Without word, trial, or fight, we were taken to the tallest oak tree on the man's property and hanged. We left our bodies and hovered, watching our old selves hang, surprised by our end, caught off-guard. Our family and friends had no way of finding us; we were lost in our shock. At dusk, the men took us to a spot by a river, the spot you now know. John's owner was given permission to bury the bodies on Endicott's land, removing him from future detection or imprisonment for unjust murder, although who would bother over a Quaker and a useless slave boy, too scrawny to work? Nothing would happen, especially if the claim of missing person or runaway slave did not exist. If discovered, Endicott would put in a good word. We were lost to history, John and I.

"The other two, killed three hundred years after we were, are quiet, still shy

and in disguise, even from us. They are fearful of their murderer, his family still alive and living in Essex County. They are not cowards, just young and lost, even though they feel stronger now, with your discovery.

"The four of us are singing jovial songs; we are prepared and willing to fly into the light, God's Light. Our communication skills are not honed enough to guide you. Although we hold vigil for our bones still, we wait for you to set us free."

The swirling Spirit display vanished with Ann's last word. Alone, Sophie stood over the familiar maps, wondering which to tackle first, the topo of Interchange 24 or Google Earth—in that order, she decided. Quickly, she determined the Endicott side of the river was impossible to access because of construction chaos. The only point of entry would be across the river, on the edge of B'nai Brith Cemetery. Chances were, on a Wednesday morning, she would be left alone to do her Work, with only the sound of creaking cranes and jackhammers to serenade her prayers.

September 19, 2007, 4:00 a.m.

AT HOME IN OREGON SOPHIE RARELY SLEPT; she catnapped in front of the big-screen TV Dylan had waited in line for the day after Thanksgiving at Costco. It was the greatest relaxant Sophie had ever known. The pulsing light of the screen, against the dark of the rest of the first-story rooms, lulled her to sleep. She preferred sleeping to the Home and Garden Channel rather than the History Channel or PBS. Unwanted historical detail found its way into Sophie's head. Sleeping in front of the TV was dangerous in this regard. When she began feeling drowsy, usually reading a book in front of a muted screen, she would turn the channel to Home and Garden, turn up the sound, and prepare for a nap.

She had put herself in training for a solid year before the start of the American Camino. Regardless of how she was feeling, day to day, she forced herself to walk with a full daypack three miles each morning. Rain, shine, snow, or ice, she forced herself into the cold or the steamy hot of Summer to build up her strength. She had always eaten well, lots of salad and soy instead of dairy. When she found out she was allergic to soy and couldn't digest greens any longer, she switched to white, soft foods—oatmeal, yogurt, pasta, with toast for crunch. She surrendered to it and learned to thrive when others might have given up. The deep night was the hardest, especially the haunting hours of two to four. She pulled herself from the ugly, overpadded sofa and dragged herself to bed. She lay there for a minimum of six hours, giving her body space and time to heal from the rigors of the day before, to energize for the next. Those six hours drove her to some interesting mental exercises. Her prayer petitions went on for hours when the night was particularly spooky. She coped and grew to be the strongest she ever would be, then or again.

In her bed at the Marriott, she tossed and turned, and her head still battled with her body, fighting the surrender of sleep. First light wouldn't come till 5:30—an hour and a half to put her life in order and solve the problems of the world, although the world outside of Essex County didn't exist for Sophie, not today, Giles's Pressing Day.

Why had it taken so long to put the puzzle pieces together? She had had the Old Salem map of both Town and Village for years, the topo maps since late Spring, the body tracings in June. She knew what to look for, the shape of a human profile, plain and to the point. She knew her body tracings lined up with the Old Salem map, but still, she didn't see it, not until August. Typical, Spirit keeping her just an inch off balance, keeping her alert and on her toes. Only she could regulate her moves. No one else would dare try.

Sophie moved to the center of the memory foam bed, the softest bed she had ever felt, and began to breathe with intention. Soon, her body relaxed, feeling supported. Weightlessly and slowly, without jerking or hesitation, she entered the warm black world of dreamless rest. She intentionally overslept; the Spirits would have to wait for a few more minutes for their release.

September 19, 2007, 9:00 a.m.

TOURISTS RARELY SAW THIS SIDE OF SALEM, with its mid-century bungalows sheathed in asbestos siding, the occasional ranch style, amid well-placed roads complete with sidewalks without handicap access and a conspicuous lack of bike trails. The real Salem lived on the South side of Waters River, the property tax–payers and city council members. Pastel houses with striped awnings lined both sides of the street leading to B'nai Brith Cemetery, seafoam green the favorite by far. Where were the trees? Block after block without natural green, grass the only marginal exception. The neighborhood felt like a sturdy Winterized version of South Florida, minus the palms.

The burial ground was different from any seen by the group: three separate areas of monuments, laid side by side, divided by shiny new chain-link fences and connected by gates with locks. Sophie had never seen a cemetery with a locked entrance. Dylan drove slowly, giving her plenty of time and space to find an area to do psychopomp work for the two groups of two. There were no trees or bushes in the first two sections of the burial grounds. Sophie sighed and muttered they should have done a drive-by yesterday morning before going to Haverhill, to scout the location. It had never occurred to her to have a run-through for today; they had experienced such great luck with ritual locations thus far. This spot had to work. It was the only place close enough to all four bodies. The only better location would have been a boat—this also had never occurred to the fearless leader and map reader.

Dylan came to a stop at the end of the paved road, even though the fence continued halfway down a gently sloping embankment. Marking the end of the fence, suspended on a thick pressure-treated pole, placed chest high, was a wooden box filled with light gray pebbles. A small handwritten sign read: "*Memorial Stones.*"

Sophie wondered why the keepers of the grounds would even bother with fencing, when it was open and fully accessible, even by car or truck. It might have involved a lawn mower. There were graves in precise rows, some a hundred years old, some recent, no grass planted or monuments yet. Why this area was open when the others were closed escaped her. Maybe this was the wayward bunch. It made no difference—the spot was perfect—unseen from the road above, thick woods on three sides, absolute privacy, as long as no humans visited. The property faced due North. Just a stone's throw over the river was the site of the old cow house, the view totally obstructed by a thick bush growth of scrub oak and apple, obviously an orchard at one time. Grateful for the tree block, the four stood, feeling close enough to touch the building cranes and cement dump trucks, the machines responsible for the group being on this side of the river. The constant backing-up beep of the trucks created a consistent beat, similar to the drum Sophie journeyed to.

Sophie signaled the others to bring the supplies, then reached into the pebble box and removed a small handful. She walked to the front row of gravestones, pristinely clean, surrounded by freshly cut grass and not a leaf, twig, or acorn to offer distraction. Each person buried here bore a Star of David on the stone, and most were topped by pebbles—one, sometimes as many as three or four. She laid one for one. These people were visited, missed by the living.

She cleared her throat and spoke to the assembled stones, with their hidden quarry of bones and memories. She spoke softly, addressing the first row by name, telling her story of the lost dead and the hope of reuniting them with loved ones already passed on. Their permission was needed to Work on this ground, far away from the domain of John Marston and his Army of the Dead and Metacomet and his Medicine Ways. Were these Spirits, some still walking the grounds, willing to lend them support? Sophie heard no reply. Temporarily feeling off-center by the lack of communication, she reached into her bag and brought out the maple sugar granules. She spread the granules in sharp, long strokes, landing in front of three or four stones at a time, a form of Shamanic clearing. Four long whooshes of sugar and the row was marked, the Spirits fed their sugar fix. West of the tight rows of monuments, the line of oak scrub and apple rustled loudly. But animal it was not—the entire hedge began to sway, in a North-South motion. Oddly, no other wind was felt, not a stir. The clouds and morning haze began to lift and, at the exact moment the Sun pierced through the last hazy sheath, all the trees, in all three directions sheltering the grounds, shook violently, sounding like the largest gourd rattle of all time. Permission granted!

The Sun was hot, burning the back of her neck as she carefully rummaged through her bag of tools, looking for the sandalwood drumming sticks and Honor Bundles. She offered smoking Sweetgrass up to the directions, enforcing the Power Cone put in place this morning for protection. Suddenly, she was surrounded by the hum of insects, some buzzing bees, others mosquitoes, moths flapping wings. Sophie swatted and swatted and they kept coming. She straightened to find the others with odd expressions; they couldn't see the bugs, hundreds of them. Sophie felt covered now. Not even mosquito netting could save her. Swat, swat, slap, she circled in her distress, the bugs relentless.

The tallest apple tree, in the center of the Northern hedge bordering the river, began to shake. Nothing else moved in the forest strip. Sophie swatted her way to the tree, stopped, and asked the tree for direction. The tree slowed its movements, the last of its apples stopped falling, the bugs' pesky sounds replaced by sharp whispers, easily mistaken for the hum of bees. "*Just, just, just, sing now, sing now, sing now, pray, pray, pray, for us, for us, for us, just, just, just, sing now, sing now, sing now, pray!*" The tree ceased its whispered song and stopped moving.

Sophie walked back to the Western line of trees, where the others stood in line, waiting for instructions. She explained that friction and speed were important to this ritual. Words would be silent; prayers should be for one thing: release. A murder of crows flew over their heads, circled the grounds, and, one by one, lined up on the top of the Northern tree hedge, overlooking the river.

"The Spirits are ready. The three of you stand in place until you breathe together. When your rhythm synchronizes, begin bobbing up and down, as if you were Honoring the Drum. Now, stay together in your movements and imagine carrying an enormous ear of Dancing Corn in each hand. Stay together and move your arms up and down, shaking the tops of the corn at the end of each downward stroke. Good, they are your rattles, now add sound: shooooosh, shooooosh, shooooosh. Keep it up! Your movement, the friction you are creating, is making my fuel. This dance will be challenging—you'll have to keep up your motion and sounds for at least ten minutes, maybe more, until I stop. It's exhausting, but you must stay at the speed hit now, regulate yourselves, and stay together. I am going to dance quickly across the grounds, West to East, the dead leading the living to the bones of the two groups of two. One, perhaps two, maybe three turns should do the trick. I'll be drumming for myself, using the sticks, pounding the upbeat between the truck beeps for my dance. I plan on using no words for this ritual, we'll see…"

The three's dancing, the even beat, the shooooshing sounds of the corn rattles focused Sophie's intent. She tied a lavender bandanna around her neck, protecting the space between shirt and skin, already red and burning. She put on her hat and cocked its brim, giving the Crow and Parrot feathers pinned to it room to move. She lifted the drumming sticks and timed her first beat to follow the truck's beep. She began the dance. When she arrived at the once-talking apple tree, the point of the nose of the profile across the river, she turned and faced North, not missing a beat. She began a pulling dance, rising power from deep in the Earth, squatting and lifting, over and over again, pulling the energy up from the Mother into her body. Her Solar Plexus fully filled; she reached over her head, making the sign of the Cobra, opening her Crown Chakra. Fully opened, she turned and continued her dance to the Eastern edge of the tree line. She completed three dancing lines, Bear to Eagle, Eagle to Bear, Bear to Eagle. The third line complete, she stopped her drumming and ran to the front of the apple and collapsed on the now warm Earth. She began to dig madly at the grass, down to the dirt, then to rock. When her hands could take no more, she rose abruptly, placed her hands over her belly and pulled with all her might, letting out a deep groan as she pulled. Sophie excised bugs from her abdomen, bugs belonging to the two groups of two, their mortar holding them in place for years, decades, centuries. Hundreds of bugs, the size of fists, flowed from her gut. She threw four large bundles into the river, splash!

The crows grew agitated but did not take flight; they stewed instead, talking riotously amongst themselves. With the final hurl into the river, Sophie turned and ran toward the rise; she needed higher ground to watch the birds' movements. As soon as she turned to face the apple tree once more, four white lights, seen plainly, backlit by aqua sky, took their place, hovering just above the crows' heads. Sophie raised her arms above her head, closed her Crown with one smoothing move, then clapped three times, loudly. The crows cawed in unison and began flapping their wings, now playing with the white orbs of energy, which looked more like stunted contrails of jets. Three more loud claps and the white forms and crows took flight, flying North. Like a balloon lost, higher and higher they flew. A soft golden eclipse-like light settled over the grounds, the construction site silent. It was 10:10, break time.

Chapter Twenty

The Pressing Place
September 19, 2007, noon

Sophie felt alone, unaffected by the people who shared the SUV. The familial bond had ended with Thomas's birth in Haverhill, the enchantment broken. This was the fear discussed between Mary Warren and Sophie on Graves Beach. It had happened. There was love, although it felt changed, no longer the product of obligation. The others would have to catch up. Sophie no longer felt compelled to drag them kicking and screaming. Those days were over! The important relationships pivotal for the success of the American Camino were now between the Spirit Realms and Sophie. She empathized with her friends. Who knew what they expected when signing on for this Shamanic whirlwind? People want to be entertained and courted spiritually. They want the Journey to be soft as billowy Summer clouds and as inspirational as *Jonathan Livingston Seagull*. The truth was something far more confrontational—physical acts bending wills until at last surrender is called. Most want miracles. They are given, seen sometimes, hardly ever felt—and as to the effort, they had no clue. Energy spent on ego-props. It was no use pretending any more, for any reason. People who charged for Shamanizing deserved the miracle-trap. Sophie was almost free of it; it had taken only twelve thousand years to get it right.

She was blood and guts, too intense for anyone to handle over a long span of time, the reason why she kept her private visits short, under three hours usually. People can handle almost anything, even ghouls, for about three hours, the length of a meaty film or novella. A minute past the three-hour mark, even with gourmet food and fine wine, confusion and fear set in—the true gravity of Sophie's beliefs sinking in—too real for most. She tried to be looser and more detached socially. It was hard: no Spirit Speak, channeling, or readings. Trying to stay quiet drove her nuts when solutions to simple problems abounded. Why were people so blind? Sophie's reputation preceded her. People spent most of their interaction time with Sophie trying to calm and quiet their own thoughts, out of fear of detection, or bad behavior uncovered. Two-way conversations were rare—that was Ali's domain and Dylan's too. The reality is: people wear their compulsions, wounds, and illusions, as real as clothes, some hardened to armor. No need for mind-reading, just body-reading. All the information is right in front of you!

Would they ever share their experiences with Sophie, what they saw or felt? She was pretty certain they wouldn't, all fearing being judged if they didn't see the expected image. Nothing is ever as one expects, regardless of the level of planning; they didn't get it, or maybe they did, but who would know? She was feeling like a pity party, deserved in her estimation.

Sophie's mood changed instantly when Dylan turned off Route 114, rounding the corner of Howard Street Cemetery. "Be Here Now!" she demanded silently, everyone fidgeting, feeling her order, not knowing how to prepare. Almost noon, a block away from the target, Dylan found a place to park on St. Peter's Street, under a sign saying: *"Bingo! Every Friday Night at 6:00."* They all understood its meaning, a reminder of what was to come: Giles's Integration Walk began at six on Friday evening.

"Should we laugh at this irony, or take it as a sign of success to come?" Sophie chuckled, hoping to break the ice, barely a word spoken since B'nai Brith. All red-faced from the early sun, they checked each other's expressions and, once satisfied with their restraint, broke into a round of laughter; they were energized, they would talk until the jailhouse.

"The yew trees are all bearing fruit, the orange a month early for Salem's taste. I wonder if the town horticulturalist is working on this problem." Sophie was on a roll. Only Earth-based people would get the reference to the Death Tree and Halloween. At least Pagans shared their green knowledge, or in this case orange.

Sophie came to a sudden stop, as did Dylan; he raised his hand and made the sign to listen. Sophie took a sharp right, leading to the back entrance of the Old Salem jailhouse. There, inside a ten-foot-tall, barbed-wire–topped, chainlink fence, separated from the jailhouse property itself, was Giles's land signature: a sinkhole, about the same diameter as the one in front of the Putnam Pantry candy store. "This is the spot!" Sophie exclaimed, taking a

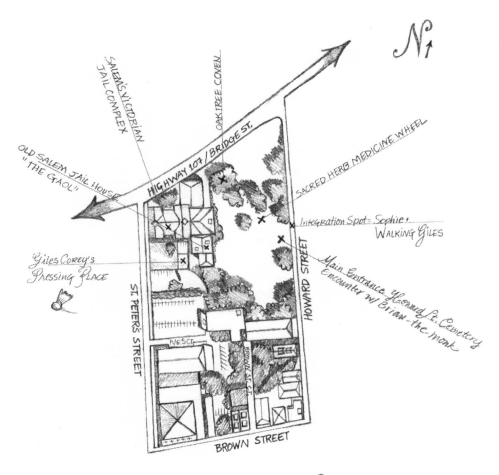

Howard Street Cemetery Loop

long swig on her water bottle and turning in a quick clockwise Circle. She stopped—her back turned to the sinkhole—and spit a spray of water to the West, the Door of the Dead, inviting Walking and Haunting Giles's attention. She noticed the Morency Office Complex directly across the street. Morency, the name of the hotel where Dylan and she had stayed at the base of the ancient La Citi entrance in Carcassonne, France, the scene of a very demanding but successful Soul Retrieval. This was an excellent sign! She took a deep swallow and repeated her spray to the East, facing the sinkhole.

They noticed the private lot was entirely enclosed by chainlink fence, the fourth wall detached and unlocked during business hours only. All the parking spaces had painted names on them, familiar names. Sophie knew this was Confederacy land, still locked up—contained for three hundred and fifteen years—by six p.m. each day, the beginning of Giles's favorite haunting hour.

The jailyard sinkhole was different from Putnam Pantry in one respect, its color. The Salem hole looked like a puddle of fresh blood, feathering to an outer ring of darkness, creating a sharp edge on the surrounding pavement. Putnam Pantry's hole was solid black, probably freshly paved each Spring. Church bells rang out fiercely, twelve chimes declaring high noon. Sophie's sunglasses were not dark enough suddenly, like the movie about a virus creating blindness, its victims seeing a field of bright white instead of the blackness of a dark sea. Beginning to focus, she saw them, a crowd: yelling, spitting, huffing, lifting, stacking, busy laborers and their cheering assistants.

They had never pressed a man to death; they had no way of knowing the tricks. Corwin had been given an old book of drawings outlining the building of an apparatus specializing in pressing, but it was complicated, with pulleys and weights, ropes and iron hardware—impossible, they would not even try. Corwin was so full of bile and ego on the Monday in question, he was determined to practice on his prisoner, develop a torture technique all his own, instilling fear in others. No one would question his power again!

John Moulton was conspicuously absent that day, standing down with his wife Elizabeth, Giles's legal daughter, although Giles felt he had no true child to call his own. Elizabeth would not miss her stepmother, Martha, but she would think fondly of her father always, the reason she chose to stay away from her father's execution.

Corwin's first order was his downfall. He told his laborers to dig a shallow pit, about eighteen inches deep and seven feet long. He had ordered his men to gather the necessary wood needed the day before, after the meetinghouse adjourned its fire-and-brimstone sermon and display of God-fearing allegiance. Two long planks of thick oak, destined to be doors, were secured in the back of Corwin's wagon and brought to the rear entrance of the jail-house. Rumors abounded in the bowels of the gaol when the wood was delivered. A whisper from the darkness hissed, "And on our Lord's Day..." Captain Thomas Gardner pleaded with Giles for days, explaining what to expect, begging him to speak and change the plea.

Precisely at noon, or as close as possible, Corwin gave the order for Giles Corey to be brought front and center. He was half-standing in the shade of the building, chained, roped, and guarded, not put back into the deep straw-covered filth, after the final trial pronouncement of death. He was free to breathe deeply the air of Salem he loved so much. Giles endured a long line of Confederacy oglers as Corwin's men dug the shallow hole, climaxing with Reverend Parris himself, softly reaffirming that the right-hand man of Satan was about to join the Horned God in hell. Some of the family girls yelled and spit from the corner of the jailyard. Corwin ordered all to leave except his men and helpers; he needed concentration for the torture ahead. The governor sent a witness and Essex County insisted its clerk write a detailed report of all goings-on and visitors. They would stay until the end of day one.

The blacksmith, new to Corwin's employ, brought his own hammer and stone to pound off Giles's chains. Why lose a pound's worth of iron to a moldering grave? Corwin would need those irons and would be unable to collect his fee if they were not usable. The blacksmith, nervous and not used to an audience, came down on Giles's left wrist with his hammer, crushing it. Corwin laughed and relit his pipe, his eyes twinkling with excitement. The small crowd of workers and selected witnesses grew hushed at Corwin's bold chuckles. Giles lost consciousness and crumpled on the ground, under-neath the blacksmith's boot. He looked his eighty-one years, fallen and gray, blood seeping into the ground, flowing from the fracture in his wrist. One of Corwin's men kicked Giles awake; he was too thin and broken to kick back, although he would have loved nothing better.

He was dragged to the shallow hole, not quite six feet long, shorter than Corwin had asked for. They kicked Giles in face-first, Corwin's men quickly righting him. The wound in his wrist clotted, the dirt serving to close it. He would not bleed to death today. They placed the two long planks over Giles's body, shoving them close enough to support the large stones gathered from the base of Gallows Hill. What Corwin didn't know was that by putting

Giles in a shallow pit, instead of flat against the ground, Corwin would only wound Giles, not kill him. Corwin's men followed his orders and tried to find just the right position to squeeze the air out of Giles, once and for all. It was of no use, broken ribs, smashed pelvis, a lung collapsed, but far from fatal. The fluid loss was the hardest on Giles, even though he was used to deprivation after five months in the gaol, so little left to begin with. Why didn't he die? Late in the night, unable to stay awake, despite the fire and talk, Corwin took to his bed and left his men to carry on the pressing. As soon as Corwin was out of sight, they brought out their bottles of ale and suppers of bread and fresh cheese. They let Giles sleep, shattered and weak. He fell and would never be able to stand again, even in his dreams.

Three days and two nights passed and Giles would not die. Corwin would not blame himself or his faulty plan. He made his men swear the pressing was over to all outsiders, their cover. They guarded the site carefully, letting only wives and mothers deliver food, ale, and blankets. On the third night Corwin, now past frantic, ordered his men to reach into the excrement- and blood-filled pit and pull Giles from it. They were ordered to deliver him to John Moulton; he would finish the job—John's fee for staying away all week.

Sophie felt Giles's presence but not all his pain, not today. He wanted her to stand there and see what he had gone through. Giles needed Sophie to witness the carnage, hear his cries, not from within but from the outside, experience how barbaric an ending—dragged out for the torturous three days—he had endured. She went in and out of time zones, feeling sick, then tired, then angry, then frustrated, ending with surrender. She had a job to complete, to end this misery for Giles and for Martha still sitting in the wet mildewed straw, listening to Giles's incessant torture. Sophie would stop Drake Putnam and Lori Otto, would end this insanity. The reason for this Spirit show was to build energy that was pure enough, hot enough, to burn through the years of binding and put the Inner Circle out of business. It had to be done; they could no longer torture Giles to preserve their riches!

Spirit kept whispering in Sophie's ear: "*You must gather Essex County clay, it holds your power!*" Sophie walked to the chainlink fence and began to comb the outside of the brick jailhouse, looking for brick shards. Dylan figured out what she was doing and started climbing the fence, clearing the low row of wire without causing damage. He walked over to the Southern corner of the old building and removed the brick cornerstone, effortlessly. It slid into his hands. He reached through the fence and handed the crumbling brick to Sophie. She gave him Honor Bundles in return, one for the jail, one for the shed holding the garden tools for Howard Street Cemetery, and one for Giles, buried under the one small window opening for the lower level of the gaol. Dylan found a back wall about four feet tall, plenty low enough for him to shimmy over. He walked on the outside of the fence into the adjoining parking lot, followed it to its end, and made his way to the sinkhole where Sophie and the girls stood, holding hands.

Sophie hurt everywhere; her chest was on fire, heavy, the feeling of brewing pneumonia. Her hips felt unable to support her torso. She had to rest, had to think, to compose the best she could.

"Thank you, Giles. I'll see you Friday at six. Be ready for a long walk." Sophie swung her hands. The others followed suit, like little girls do when standing together in Circles. Dylan loosened his grip on Sophie's hand, took a ribbon-wrapped Honor Bundle from the Trader Joe's bag, and climbed up the chain-link fence. He tied the bundle to the metal close to the barbed wire with one hand and quickly scrambled to the pavement below, only to notice people watching, from the sidewalk, from the neighboring lots, from the Morency complex.

"Ladies, it's time for lunch. A lovely woman told me this morning at Bagel World to try Red's, famous for the mac 'n' cheese, Sophie's favorite." Without a second's hesitation, the group picked up their bags and walked away, leaving a trail of sacred herbs behind them.

Chapter Twenty-One

CRYSTAL LAKE
September 19, 2007, 3:00 p.m.

DURING THE FESTIVITIES OF THE THREE-HUNDREDTH ANNIVERSARY of the Witch Trial Hysteria in September 1992, out of the way of tourists, a local dedication of two memorial gravestones had been held. A photographer from the local paper took shots of children inspecting the newly planted mums atop the two mock graves. It was an event many missed.

The children of Kiley Brothers School in Peabody, kindergarten to grade six, were horrified that no one remembered the Coreys, their memory abandoned all but for Longfellow's fiction. They felt it was their responsibility to enshrine the memory of the Coreys, since their beloved school, one of the best in the county, had been built close to the original homestead on Corey land. The ancient apple trees bordering the modern, one-story school were once part of Giles's orchards. Ask the children escaping to the woods around Halloween if they hear anything unusual in the woods and they'll tell you stories of old Giles walking the rows of trees. What the kids don't know is that Walking Giles is testing for taste and hardness—one of his passions, apples. How he loved fresh warm cider and rum, sweetened with a touch of blackberry honey, the libation of the Gods. He had wonderful memories of sitting under the stars, feeling the first bite of Autumn, sharing a mug of hard warm cider with Martha, tasting the spice of nutmeg caught in his whiskers.

About a mile up the road from Kiley Brothers School is a vegetable stand specializing in local produce: apples, corn, pumpkin, squash, sunflowers, with jars of last Spring's maple syrup take and fresh apple-blossom honey. How perfect for offerings, vegetables and fruit raised on old Corey land! Corey land was once more than three hundred acres, one solid piece of the richest farmland in Essex County, with views, lakes, and creeks, enough game to fill your belly year round. How many would lust over this land? A whole town called Peabody. Now it was reduced to a farming strip on a main highway.

Sophie decided they would buy two full bags of heirloom apples for the Witch Memorial Ritual on Saturday; they would need twenty apples, plus several for commemorative spots on Gallows Hill and still more to eat. She dickered with the woman farmer over fresh-cut sunflowers for early Saturday morning pick-up. For now, they bought miniature pumpkins, fresh ears of corn for their supper, memorial and eating apples, and two sunflowers, a perfect pairing with Cruzan rum bought in Giles's honor.

The SUV filled with the fragrance of freshly picked apples, sending shivers of joy through Sophie; she could feel both Walking Giles and Haunting Giles lusting for more than smell. Barely a half-mile up the road, Dylan took a sharp right turn, marked by a small green park sign: *Crystal Lake*. Their eyes had to adjust to the deeply shaded lane, trees towering. Evergreens and conifer woods with trees hundreds of years old surrounded them. A short distance up the road it widened, generous shoulders on both sides—it felt like a welcoming. Dylan pulled into an open area on the left-hand side of the road, next to the red and white sign declaring this a protected area under rezoning. Crystal Lake, Giles's lake, was being reclaimed by conservationists and fishermen for the good of Peabody. The lake provided a rich habitat, the sign explained, for endangered wildlife: frogs, turtles, and birds, although the fish were planted by humans. Bass fishermen loved this piece of Essex County. The fauna was equally endangered, indigenous species still not entirely crowded out by cultivated varieties of choking vine.

The four sat suspended, watching the lake, still in the close SUV, with the air conditioner turned off. Another beautiful eighty-degree day—the golden afternoon sun catching the white barks of alders and bouncing off yellow water reeds—the sun inspirational to the Oregonians, their eyes eager for light. Early Autumn at Crystal Lake or, as Giles called it, Singing Lake. At dusk, the birds sung a mournful song, which bounced off the surface of the lake, signaling the end of sunshine. Time for supper. Giles would know that Martha's fresh biscuits and root vegetable stew, his favorite, awaited, the birdsong sending him home.

The cemented curb of the lake's shore supported a long line of fishermen with hooks baited and coolers full. They sat smiling, staring at the party

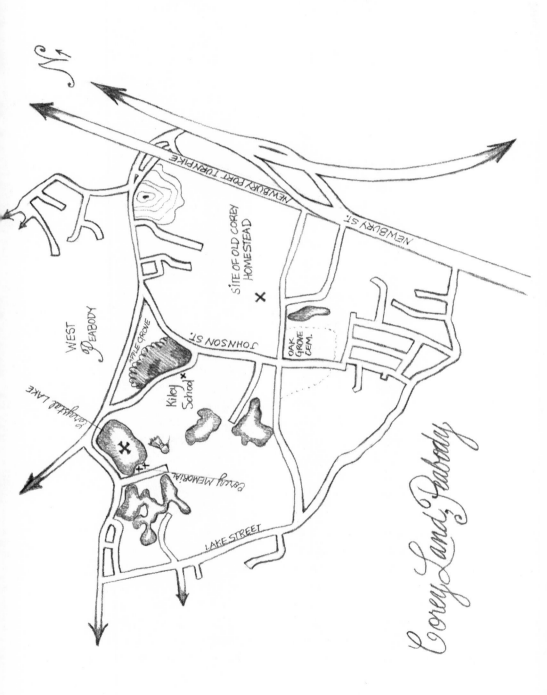

Corey Land, Peabody

of four as much as at the lake before them. Sophie could see Giles sitting among them, line in the water, pipe in his mouth, enraptured by the paradise surrounding him.

Sophie was the first to get out of the SUV. She wanted to get on solid ground, feel Corey land beneath her feet. The modern care of the fishermen and schoolchildren brought tears to Sophie's eyes, so touched and grateful was she for positive energy. She was used to being despised for various reasons. It was touching to feel simple love, an emotion she could get used to. Sophie brought out a clean white towel, opened it, and slung it over her left shoulder.

Before Sophie was able to remove all her tools and special offerings from the back of the SUV, a man caught her with both hands occupied. He enthusiastically stuck out his right hand, wanting to shake despite her full hands. Just as Sophie opened her mouth, Dylan came to her rescue and grabbed the man's extended hand and began to shake it with purpose, not the gentle solid down-stroke of Indian handshakes, called wimpy by white people. "My name is Don and this is my daughter Angela." Neither Dylan nor Sophie had seen Angela, hiding behind her father seamlessly. She was small in height and wide in feature, with a sweet smile filled by an overly large tongue: Angela had Down syndrome. Angela moved forward and approached Dylan first, with an extended hand, just like her father's. Dylan grabbed it, displaying a broad smile; Angela appeared impressed by Dylan's vigor and presence. Angela moved to Sophie, now standing beside full bags, and threw her arms around her with a deeply satisfied sigh. Poe appeared and Angela repeated her hugging. Finally Dora received her share. The party of four looked kindly on these strangers, trying to fit them into the happenings of the day. Sophie and Dylan both wondered who they had been in 1692, still bound and living near precious Corey land.

Don explained he was the self-appointed steward of Crystal Lake. He was a disabled vet who stayed at home to care for his daughter. He loved the out-of-doors, as did Angela, so Don had deserted housework years before in favor of hanging out with his bass fishermen friends and Angela at Crystal Lake. Between May and October, they spent the daylight hours here, seven days a week. His wife didn't mind and would sometimes join the jovial two on the weekends. She worked to support the family during the week and cooked and cleaned on the weekends. The house stayed much cleaner in the summertime because of Don and Angela's conspicuous absence.

Dylan couldn't help but think about all the hundreds of strangers over the years to come up to him, in all parts of the world, and proceed to tell elaborate, highly personal life stories. In these instances, he could never quite figure out if he was simply a passive witness to people's stories or an active therapist needing to deal with their problems.

Dylan told Don the party had traveled across the country to honor Giles Corey on this spot, today, his Pressing Day. They were distant half-Indian family members, come here to perform a ceremony for Giles and Martha. Don's eyes filled with tears as Dylan wove his tale, Angela holding tight to the corner of Don's loose polo shirt.

"I have waited almost twenty years for someone to love the Coreys as much as I do. You are a blessing. God bless you all, and on his Pressing Day. I'll pray with you, but I'll get out of your way and watch from a distance. I have seen lots of programs on the Discovery Channel about Indians and their need for space and privacy during rituals. Bless you all!" Don reached for Angela's waiting hand. They walked away slowly, not stopping until they reached the end of the line of sitting fishermen. All banter stopped by the lake. Only the soft sounds of the swan movements were heard. Dylan looked over his shoulder and saw Don crying like a baby in the arms of one of his friends, who wore a black POW hat. Angela smiled and waved at Dylan.

The four were overcome by the beauty of this place. Chartreuse lily pads atop sap-green water, black swans and white swans and too many kinds of trees to count. Not more than ten feet from the lakeside were the memorial gravestones bought and paid for by schoolchildren, with the funds from car washes and bake sales. Silver-gray stones, planted deep, side by side, with a permanent bed of Cedar bark outlining the form of graves in front.

Sophie took the white towel off her shoulder and buried her face deep, shedding tears, snot, and spittle—her DNA—into the cloth. She was overwhelmed with gratitude and love for people she didn't know. Ali had once told her, "You love strangers more than your own blood family." Sophie had accused her sister of being melodramatic, wrong in her opinion, but now she saw the truth in these words, and she said a quick hello to her sister, one of only two people who ever got her. The other was Dylan.

Sophie laid a large red cloth on the ground and began setting out her tools and offerings; it looked like a Give-Away blanket, filled and ready to end mourning. She didn't feel like she was grandstanding, despite an audience of men, many of whom had stopped their fishing and were standing with their hats in their hands, taking a veteran's stance. The men, with little Angela at their sides, loved this place as much as Sophie did, perhaps more. They had a stake in its survival and guarded it like hawks, all through the year. Teenagers rarely bothered the place, knowing that the men who cared for it, most of them disabled vets or retired military, would have a piece of their hide if they even thought about defacing the lake or the property surrounding it. They knew better than to mess with the gravestones, creepy to most, day or night.

She decided to work on Martha's grave first. She began as she always did, removing leaf debris from the stone's base and gradually cleaning the stone with water, air, and her rainbow glove. Often she stopped her cleaning and cried, deeply, woefully, into the white towel, now brown around its edges.

> *Salem Witchcraft Martyr*
> *Pious, Outspoken, Steadfast*
> *Martha Corey*
> *Hanged September 22, 1692*
> *"I am an innocent person.*
> *I never had to do with witchcraft since I was born.*
> *I am a Gospel woman."*

She continued her cleaning-weeping-cleaning cycle. She dried her eyes, finally, and began burying treasures in the bark in front of the stones: corn bundles, beads, Sacred Herbs, Honor Bundles, cookie crumbs. After smoothing the bark, Sophie placed a small pumpkin, an apple, rose petals, topped with a huge sunflower grown on this side of the lake. Martha loved sunflowers, finding magick in the seed geometry, inspiring visions for hours, especially on late harvest nights. Dylan knelt beside Martha's stone, filled with food, offerings, and memories. He gently reached for Sophie's hand and placed a small Honor Bundle into her palm with a squeeze: "Thank you, Giles."

"You are welcome, Martha," Sophie replied.

Sophie made her usual Spirit Salutes and bowed in front of Martha's stone. Tears falling once more, she whispered, *"Blessed Be!"* and moved on to Giles.

She repeated the cleaning-weeping-cleaning cycle she had performed on Martha's side and moved on to burying Medicine objects and food in the bark in front of the stone. The others expected her to top Giles's mock grave with the other sunflower and move on to the Sacrament, but she surprised them. Her eyes, now red and swollen from crying—as were Don's across the grass from her—gazed downward and saw her target. She took the wet, brownish-beige, once white towel, and buffed the surface of the stone with her DNA. She was now grounded here, not nailed in place but connected with a silver thread, as thin as a single strand of hair. This was Giles's place of honor, at last, her place of peace. She rubbed the towel into each letter...

Salem Witchcraft Martyr
Irascible, Unyielding
Giles Corey
Dies under the torture
of stone weights
September 19, 1692
Would not
put himself on trial
rather he chose to
undergo what death they
would put him to.

Sophie laid the sunflower on the filled bark topping the grave, feeling grateful and light. She realized she was smiling, no longer crying, touched more than ever, happy to have come this far. One last thing to do—she placed four pebbles on the tops of each gravestone.

As Sophie straightened, a line of cars began driving down the road, away from the lake, the fishermen, the veterans, going home after the ritual. None of them shouted out hello or goodbye; they were in veteran mode still, quiet and respectful. All saluted, hands tugging the brims of their hats, two of their own honored, Martha and Giles. Don and Angela, the only ones left of the line of fishermen, walked over to the gravestones. With Angela still hanging on to the corner of his shapeless shirt, Don thanked the group for the honoring he had not known how to perform, although he had craved doing so for years. The group formed an Honor Line, one at a time, standing in front of him, shaking his hand in Indian fashion, then placing an Honor Bundle in the center of his open palm before moving on. Angela wanted hugs. They would all comply. They waved, Don pulling over his car before leaving,

"Remember us in your prayers. We'll light candles for you."

Sophie had a Sacrament spread ready, including chocolate-covered honeycomb for Martha and dark chocolate coconut squares for Giles, directly from Putnam Pantry. There was loose nutmeg, Giles's favorite spice, more shortbread—the favorite food of pirates and John Marston—Cruzan dark rum, and sparkling water. The Witch City shot glasses were brought out, all five, one for each of the group and one for Spirit, set between both stones. Sophie poured the glasses full and ended with a prayer.

"In perfect love
and in perfect trust,
We drink you, Great Mother!"

She handed out the candies and cookies, sealing their sacramental food with …

"In perfect love
and in perfect trust,
We eat you, Great Father!"

Sophie did not drink alcohol; she had been sober for twenty-five years. She took her full glass of rum and the nearly full bottle and faced the gravestones. She poured half her glass on the top of Martha's stone and the other half in the center of Giles's, the liquid streaming down the front, filling and dissolving into the gray stone. A big splash of rum was showered on top of the bark ground covering; it would keep the Spirits high for a bit, Sophie thought—she couldn't help but smile. She found the dirty towel on top of the red altar cloth. She breathed in its smell, making it her own. She loved this place; she remembered it before its cement-reinforced banks and wooden signs. There were fewer evergreens three hundred and fifteen years earlier, fewer vines too, but its golden glowing reflections were unmistakably Singing Lake, the calm water for which Giles had traded sailing the wild seas.

Dora walked to the center of the bank, sat down, and stretched out her long legs. She began humming a Celtic lullaby. Soon there were words for her songs, Irish songs sung in English, Mary Black and Loreena McKennitt songs, favorite sailing songs, woolly stories and laments, haunting and sweet. Soon the swans, once evenly spaced across the surface of the dark olive-green water, followed the melodies, brushing the edges of the bank, trying to make body contact with Dora, the Mistress of Swan Song. Poe slowly moved in, cooing to the swans, between the notes of Dora's songs. She had a bag of goodies for them, bits of cookie from the Sacrament and a couple of bagels, torn in pieces. The swans didn't spook, tame and trusting. They took their turns, first floating in front of Dora, soaking in her songs, then on to Poe, for edible treats.

The four each took dozens of pictures, of the lake, the memorials, the swans, each other, lily pads, the trees, giant and small. There was sweetness to the afternoon—different from the other days on this Journey—hard to describe, but yes, it was Martha's chocolate-dipped honeycomb.

Half an hour before dark, the group slid into their respective seats. They had just enough time for a group picture in front of the shack sitting over the original Corey homestead, just down the lane. The mailbox read "The Moultons" in cherry red letters. The winding road led to a fine colonial house on the hilltop, surrounded by alder and hawthorn, yellowing in the late sun. A quick click of the automated flash, an Honor Bundle tied to a low tree, almost undetectable till mid-Winter, a flick of maple sugar granules, and the party was off for a light supper of leftover mac 'n' cheese and fresh corn on the cob from Corey land.

Sophie let out a deep sigh of exhausted gratitude, causing the SUV to fill with the smell of cider and nutmeg. "Hey, y'all, let's go to the lovely little French bakery in Peabody and buy an apple pie for our supper tonight. Giles wants an apple dessert and so do I. Agreed?"

"Agreed!" they sang out happily. What an end to a near-perfect afternoon, they all thought.

Chapter Twenty-Two

SAWYER'S HILL
September 20, 2007, 9:00 a.m.

THEY CAME REGULARLY, HERDED BY HANNAH, Sophie's otherworldly bodyguard, eight Spirits ordered to wait their turn in the office painted like the inside of a tree. Usually, they preferred queuing in the hall with the other dirty ghost stragglers with heavy petitions; Hannah had little patience for them.

Sophie was used to the regulars, several coming to her for years, names unknown, faces kept in the shadows. She knew they were from Massachusetts—all the information Sophie had. She had not pressed the point. The others had started visiting less than two years earlier, clearly from the same group. They came with Poe when she walked into Sophie's life. Poe was looking for a new way to believe. More accurately, she desired embracing—with others of like mind—what she had always known to be true: Karma, reincarnation, the Law of Attraction, Soul Mates, all concepts making sense outside of hard-line Christian belief and practice. Poe's people—descendants of the Dorchester Six, the first landing on Cape Ann—were Congregationalists, at one time wearing the title of Puritan. They judged others harshly and were not comfortable with any belief structures outside their own self-limited worldview.

Poe told Sophie that she had always believed in reincarnation. From early childhood, she had dreamed of Africa, being stalked by lions, abandoned by aggressors, and adopted by peacekeepers. She dreamed of the rich forests of Southeast Asia and the pre-Revolutionary French elite, she danced the Flamenco under the stars of Northern Spain, and as a knight roamed the lonely heather-covered mountains of Scotland. She remembered, but under the safe guise of dreamtime. The lifetimes defining her in the now were conveniently set aside by her subconscious, forgotten details lost to trauma, the ever-changing face of tragedy, the misery of chronic soul-loss. Poe's disconnection came from chronic depression and guilt, drowning in her own despair as the doctors of Essex County. Earth-bound Spirits sense Karmic anxiety. It is food for them. They claimed Poe in 1760.

Memories of the bad times dig deeper holes in the mind; they hide tethered to the dark, unlike pleasurable lifetimes that dwell on the surface in the forms of likes, desires, and wanderlust. The body always shows the real picture, storing the tragedies and leaving their imprints, impossible to ignore. Watch people in a crowded airport. Pick out the ones with poor posture, not from laziness but from carrying heavy burdens for decades. It's easy to see the difference between mental and physical disability. Burden is a magnet for the needy—they smell it—giving them permission to latch on, true for corporeal humans and Spirits alike.

Poe carried the weight of eight Spirits on her back, visible when she was tired or not well. Her posture bent and crumpled, although she was in excellent health and fit enough to work out each morning at the local gym. Once a gymnast, Poe danced and loved yoga. She was painfully thin till Christmastime each year, until the chocolate came out in earnest. Still she carried too much weight. Poe was unable to release the burden of Sawyer's Hill, although she had paid the debt a hundredfold by dedicating her time to the mental problems of others. She specialized in guilt transference because she knew it well; there were many reasons why the Haunting Spirits of Sawyer's Hill shifted their persistent attentions to Sophie.

The historical record of the tragedy differed greatly, depending on the source, which is true anywhere. No one knew the exact number of people who died during the Newburyport smallpox scourge of 1759–60. Just under a hundred people became ill with the pox, including a doctor, maybe one of the two from Boston who quarantined the area. They fenced off Sawyer's Hill, not allowing anyone or anything in or out, from December to March. The sealed remains were burned after the Spring thaw. Some say twenty-four died, while others claim thirty-six. Sophie knows the number to be forty—clusters of extended families of Sawyers and Merrills—sealed off from the world, with few provisions, many in one long cabin, nuclear families refusing to be separated. It was an awful way to die, one by one; the men dying first, leaving the women to feed, clean, and carry. Near the end, no one cared that the supplies had run out; all prayed for quick release. The young adults were the hardest hit in 1760.

Sophie thought again of obligation to the Spirit Realms, her Chosen Family, the ones she loved best. Sixty-eight years after the Salem Witch Hysteria, almost thirty miles away from Salem, forty people died a miserable death and eight were lost between the worlds, unable to free themselves from the imprisonment of haunting. How they knew Poe was destined to come into Sophie's life, she didn't know. Sophie had no idea why they found her to begin with, the case with Ann Jayne and her son John, and Hannah Dustin too, although Lydia did set a straight track for Hannah to find Sophie. All it took was time and opportunity and it happened. The whys became less important when there was work to do. It always had to do with Karmic debt, perceived or owed. They were all connected at one point. Sophie's job was to help Spirits go away for good; psychopomp meant a literal "moving of the mind," a radical shift in perspective, enabling Spirits to disconnect from negative bonds and fly free. The Spirits had choices: they went to the light, opted to reincarnate or rest, went for long journeys as Walking Spirits. After separation from their traps of paralysis or vengeance, they decided.

Sophie thought how ironic mystical work was. Humans complained she discarded them hastily, perceiving ill-crossed boundaries, betrayals of slander, and thievery of ideas. Part of her job as a Shamanic Practitioner was to cut to the quick, to excise problems with sharp, precise tools. It made no difference what realm they were in. It was relative. Humans were lazy and it pissed Sophie off—it made too much work for her. In her introductory lectures, after the bit about *"if you think you want to be like me, you need therapy,"* she claimed Shamans were no more glorified than spiritual garbage collectors. People were easier for Sophie to shake than Spirits. At least she could reason with Spirits.

The group had the whole day to leisurely make their way up Route 1A, a perfect example of a scrolling *M* with humps, rather than points. Each road the party of four traveled was a part of the network of body tracings, each mile on the trail a prayer for balance and release.

The marshlands between Plum Island and Newburyport, filled with birds and bugs, rare grasses and wild onion, had a unique quiet beauty. Willows grew thickly near estuary waters, their branches swaying the mosquitoes away. Beehive boxes sat on long thin strips of land between reed and water. The first farmers lived here. You could see their short stocky horses if you squinted toward the water.

They had three burial grounds to visit on the way to Sawyer's Hill, quick stops, enough time to tie, place, or bury a bundle, throw handfuls of maple sugar, bow and salute, Trader Joe's bag in hand. Old North Burying Ground in Ipswich was loaded with Equal-Armed Crosses, ancient Pagan symbols for Earth Magick, adopted as a pictorial symbol for the Four Gospels of the New Testament by Pauline Christians, still the Sun Cross for millions of indigenous people and Pagans. The Burial Ground of the First Settlers, the oldest of its type in this part of the Bay Colony, was located behind a strange house, with blackout curtains made of trash bags, rusted axes and knives hanging in clusters as wind chimes, the garden filled with rusted cars from the 1950s. The burying ground was on public land, but it felt possessed by the house, even sharing a fence with it. The four marched in single file, respectful and quiet, with treats and prayers. Before they could bring out a thing or make a move, they were engulfed by an angry swarm of mosquitoes and black flies, bugs of New England legend. They tied an Honor Bundle on the fence post behind the blackened house and sprinted for the SUV. Their third stop was considered one of the most haunted places in Massachusetts, Oak Hill Cemetery in Newburyport, with its enormous crypts, rolling rhododendron-covered hills, and scenic vistas of the marshlands and the ocean beyond. Frog Pond, yes, where howling Spirits flew from its center each night; Oak Hill Cemetery had to be visited and respected, although they were careful not to pick up any protoplasmic travelers.

Sophie had to visit the harbor. Giles knew it and had worked it many times. He worked the tunnels in the early days. He liked it there. It was a town of men, wild and loud, colorful. A man could buy almost anything. There were grand houses planned, some already taking shape; it was up and coming, a town of privateers, pirates, and merchant men. The ground under Newburyport was not solid. A maze of tunnels traveled the length and breadth of town, used by smugglers of people and trade goods from the Indies, escaping taxes of the crown. They would get rich here.

The day had turned from bright and hot to gently hazy and warm, the smell of salt in the air refreshing their auras. They would have been content lazing away the day, sipping iced tea, watching the boats sail by. Sophie knew, despite the draw to lounge, she had a job to finish in Sawyer's Hill. She also knew it was more fun for the others to hang out and eat seafood and drink beer, salute their realizations and commit to travel fantasies. "I have a deal for you three. Support me with as much pure energy as possible, free of opinion and challenge, and I will agree to leave this place immediately following our mutual success and head straight for Ipswich and the most famous clams in the states. Yes, they have beer too. Is it a deal?"

Sophie looked into the most innocent, fragile faces she had seen in years, her friends. They were exhausted to the point that simple pleasures, or the promise of them, bloomed fresh enthusiasm and naïve compliance. Whatever worked, Sophie thought.

"Of course, Sophie. Hadn't we already agreed to this arrangement yesterday?" Dylan quickly responded.

"I am up for it! Me too!" Poe and Dora replied. It was easily decided, the course charted for a direct confrontation at Sawyer's Hill.

Dylan turned inland from the harbor, into farmland, some hilly, crops harvested and fields resting. Swaths of woodland appeared, some dense, still dark green, pretending to be August. They were North and East of Haverhill, on the Merrimack River once more. Sawyer's Hill was outside of the 21.8 miles triangle, connecting the Family Confederacy to Indian Country. The group of eight Spirits haunting Sophie belonged to a different set of problems than the Salem Work, more personal and private here. She would benefit by the Spirits' hopeful departure, but the work belonged to Poe and had little to do with Sophie, or so she had convinced herself. She had told Poe the main reasons why Sawyer's Hill was important, she had found two dozen ways to tell her—but Poe still didn't get the connection. Perhaps Poe would feel released from her torment of perfectionism and fear. Perhaps she would be free of her guilt complexes. Only time would witness her changes.

Maudslay State Park neighbored the burial grounds, famous for diverse landscape and frequented by equestrians and softball players. It wasn't easy to find the grounds. Sophie had the Google Earth map, Dylan had the local topo map, but still they circled and circled the same bit of affluent, newly built New England neighborhood. All they saw were two-car garages and carriage houses in back of two-story Cape Cods and colonials.

Sophie saw movement from outside her peripheral vision. "Stop the car, please, Dylan. I see a small lane between two houses. It's not posted. There's movement and a different light source in the woods where the lane leads. Look at it. I'm sure we've found it."

Parking was easy, both sides of the street open and commuters not home yet. They assumed woods protocol, rolling down their pants, wearing protective shirts and bug spray. Sophie was confident with the location, but Dylan hesitated. "I am not putting poison on if I don't have to, Sophie."

"Okay, I'll scout it out. Poe, you want to tag along?" Sophie and Poe crossed the suburban street and walked onto the footpath between houses, feeling as if they were invading the neighborhood. Poe looked awkward, fearful—she didn't want to annoy anyone with her actions. Sophie wanted to get the job done. The tree line was dense near the path's ending. Squinting and crouched, Sophie peered through the oak woods and saw gravestones. Dylan and Dora leaned against the side of the SUV, looking in her direction, waiting for her signal. Sophie waved them over. Sophie turned her back on Dylan and Dora, the kids forced to put on bug spray. She felt too old for this kind of tug-of-war. Neither Sophie nor Poe wanted to go into the freezing wood, too dense for much sunlight to penetrate, hidden completely from the people living on three sides.

"Whatcha doing, up the path?" A young woman in yellow shorts with a thick blonde top-notch of hair, a toddler clinging to her leg, called from her back deck to Dylan.

"We're investigating an old burial ground, located in the woods. This is public property, the path, I mean, isn't it?" Dylan replied.

"Of course it is, feel free. I didn't know there was a graveyard in the woods. Is it old?"

"Middle eighteenth-century. Have a good day." Dylan waved and caught up with Dora on the path. He didn't want the woman coming to investigate, although this place wasn't what you called inviting. He could smell Cedar incense and hear the sprinkling of something heavy on leaves. Sophie was already at work.

Sophie found the boundaries of the burial grounds, careful of where she stepped. She knew there was potentially more than one mass grave here and a few dozen single marked graves, from times since 1760, familiar names, Moulton among them. She did a series of Spirit Salutes and asked to be forgiven by the Walking and Haunting Spirits for disturbing their rest. The light through the trees had an otherworldly feel to it, similar to the golden eclipse-looking light they had seen before and after impressive Spirit displays. The grounds were located atop a hill, its top leveled, as one would do in preparing a building site. Yes, this was the spot, the long cabin. Sophie walked its footprint, awakening the Spirits still living in the sealed building.

Three Circles of the cabin, three revolutions of the grounds, leaving a steady trail of Sage and Tobacco behind her, Sophie walked and greeted the Spirits. The eight began to animate, more solid in the shadows, three couples, two middle-aged and one young, a single older woman, and a small boy of about five, her regulars. Sophie greeted them, the Merrill family, John Sawyer and his wife. The boy was nameless, for now. They walked, heads down, blankets over their shoulders, all rail-thin and hollow-faced. Ann Merrill was the strongest, the tallest, and she was stubborn by nature. Her husband John had brought the contagion to the hill, contaminating many families who were supported by the mill, felling timber or shaping it for building houses and ships. The pox ripped through the community. Some said the pox didn't jump the river but flowed down it, right to the ocean. No area of the valley was spared.

Sophie wondered what overall significance Sawyer's Hill held in the grand scheme of things, over and above Poe's guilt. She saw the answer, watching the forlorn ghosts, skin hanging off bone, lost between the worlds. There was a mirroring happening, a hidden message in the slow movements of the haunts. "*This is how able-bodied people in the West view people with disabilities*" were the words that kept running through her head, until she stopped, slowed her heart, and began to listen in earnest. "*Separate and almost equal*" was the answer she slowed for. Sophie added, "*If their slow-moving vehicles followed instead of led.*" She knew the surface cruelty that people showed toward the disabled; she had experienced it first-hand. Of course, Sawyer's Hill defined how the world handled disease and contagion—from a fear-base, leaving the rational behind. Everyone had seen it and had been affected by it: plague, smallpox, tuberculosis, influenza, cancer, polio, AIDS, super-bugs, pandemics. The ill were already suffering, regardless of what medicines were given and taken or what prayers were said. It was the human way to wage war with Karma, single lives burning away the debt of ten. The ill were misunderstood, held apart, shunned, ignored. They were made second-class citizens, regardless of their place of origin, race, age, or demeanor. Sure, "the special ones." Sophie remembered her third-grade teacher explaining how Hitler had disposed of handicapped children, gassing them in the back of school buses and travel vans, "the special ones." The explanation of the tragedies of the Massachusetts Colony mirroring and manifesting the Karma of the entire country rang true again. The women and men hanged symbolized the country's intolerance of differing belief structures and Gods. Giles's death represented how the aged were regarded and easily abused. Hannah illustrated the perils of women. Ann Jayne and John represented the exploitation of the weak for monetary gain. The Spirits of Sawyer's Hill symbolized how the disabled were treated: warehoused, neglected, undervalued on all levels, regardless of malady.

Energized and inspired by the realizations, another piece to the puzzle placed, she called for her friends' attention. She now knew this work of Sawyer's Hill hit home—hit her heart and weakening body. The three milled around Sophie, feeling chilled and disconnected. They waited for her directives.

Pressing the need for concentrated energy, she began, "You manufactured enough energy for me to work independently from y'all at B'nai Brith. If a Shamanic Practitioner has to generate the energy needed for ritual releasing and free a soul from negative cycles at the same time, she is lucky to succeed, or stands to lose as much ground as gained. You gave me enough juice to free up the bonds of the two groups of two, sending four souls to the light—that's the possibility of manufactured channeled energy. You three filled a large funnel and directed the energy to me. You freed my hands and heart to work the bonds loose for the four. Amazing! Today, we face not four souls hungry for the light, but eight. Eight weathered, drained people, who deserve a long rest. It will take luck as well as a masterful generation of power. Remember how high you got at B'nai Brith? Afterward it took almost ten minutes of dancing with you, bringing you down, guiding you to corporeal reality. Your generated power blew your minds, rightfully so. However, you must double the amount of energy you created yesterday, for our needs today.

"I have spoken to your Spirits and they are prepared to help you, as much as they dare. The lion's share, no offense, Poe, is on your shoulders. The three of you have a focus: me. I will be doing much of the work with my eyes closed, some Spirits demanding to be seen in this manner, rather than with the human eye. It will take both approaches before I am through. As always, I am prepared for battle, but I have been petitioned long and hard for this and they are already waiting, so the battling will probably be with me, the hardest kind."

Sophie scouted a perfect place for the ritual. On the Western side of the cabin footprint, two narrow strips of land with no bodies buried, crossed, forming the sign of St. Peter's Cross, or seen from a slightly different angle, Thor's Hammer. The cross's long top faced North, its bottom faced South

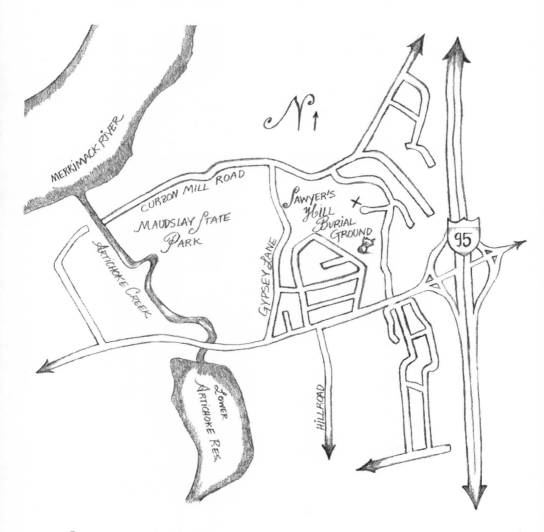

Sawyer's Hill Burial Grounds, Newburyport

and ended at the base of a lone pine. Sophie would use the tree as a launching pad; with the force of her body—supported by the muscles of her thighs and calves—she would pick up the Spirits, one at a time, bounce them off her flexed thigh and shoot them up the tree directly into the Higher World. There they would be directed to the light and their journey to a new life would be almost completed.

Sophie faced North, stood, walked, circled and danced in the South. The three faced her. The awakened Divine Feminine would inspire action; the spark of the Divine Masculine would create a powerful electrical current, traveling unhindered from North to South, Sophie controlling the flow of energy-fuel at the cross's Southern tip. She was manhandling them now, lining them up, on the vertical line of the cross, Poe in the East, Dora in the West, Dylan in the center. They breathed in their cleansing and then grounding, moving from one to the other effortlessly, flowing like Tai Chi Masters.

Sophie studied them. Eagle stood on Poe's shoulders, controlling the flow of information, directing the energy of prayer and incantation. Lion sat at her feet—her Guardian Spirit—semi-resting, directing positive masculine healing energy from the Sun. Squirrel sat in Dora's hair, eating a fresh acorn, its smell sharp and distinct. Squirrel was in charge of storing and dispersing energy. Snake crawled down Dora's legs and into the ground where she stood, directing the power of the Earth into the North-South axis line, Sophie's energy wave. Dylan stood between the women; Owl perched atop his head giving Medicines and soul-balms to the souls caught between the worlds, preparing them for journey. Crow sat on his left shoulder, directing energy flow into the ritual itself, charging the happening, binding success in the Spirit Realms. Elk stood in front of Dylan, directing energy toward human protection and survival. Sophie's compadres were ready for the Big Work, making it possible.

She directed the group to stay focused, synchronize their movements and, above all else, not stop the dance once begun; they must stay moving for the entire time Sophie is moving. If the flow of energy stopped, so did the ritual, regardless of its progress. They would stand a shoulder's length apart and squat, opening their energy channels. They would draw energy from deep in the Earth and pull it into their open body channels, energy growing in mass and strength with each bend and release. Sophie had performed this Shamanic Dance energizing her Earth Chakra at B'nai Brith, essential for revitalization of Core Energy. Any extra fuel was kept in the Storage Chakras, located behind the knees. A practitioner would tire but would not die, doing this Dance. Sophie had heard of Mongolian Fire Dances lasting four and five days, constantly moving. The same stamina was used at Sun Dance on the American Plains, lasting a full four days. Once their movements were in step, they would breathe in unison, deep, sharp breaths, in and out quickly, like hyperventilating into a paper bag, but with puckered lips, precise inhales, forcing the lungs open with electricity, forcing the participants into trance, then directed into trance-dancing.

Soon, the energy wavelength was alight with power, brightening the grounds, eating shadows with its waste, like a flowing river of iridescent lava. Sophie stood in its path, soaking in its static charge, learning to navigate its frequency.

"Come friends,
come families caught between times old and new,
come to the pine tree,
come to me."

Sophie whispered her pleas, over and over.

The eight Spirits lined up, images now sharp, in order of height, the first time the couples had ever been separated since their deaths. The small boy was the last to queue, closest to Sophie, he at her pant leg, pulling and wiggling and poking. He kept saying *"Why, why are we here: why, why, why."* Sophie wanted to shake him softly and send him to his mother for caretaking, when she realized his mother had gone on long before. This little guy was on his own. She bent down to him and asked his name. He had never been so full of energy in Oregon; he was different here, excited! *"Jamie is my name. That's what my maw calls me."* Sophie replied it was a fine name—if it was good enough for his mother, it would do well for her. She outlined what to expect to the Spirits.

The Spirit's first instructions were to open their hands and point them toward Owl, sitting on Dylan's head. At first, they were not sure if they could commune with the animals, feeling blasphemous, Witch-like. Sophie soothed their fears and begged them to concentrate; it would take all their combined energy to succeed, in psychopomp terms. They had to focus, even little Jamie.

Sophie tried to be patient. Jamie had never had the courage to talk before. He was acting like a well-adjusted, curious boy, not depressed, defeated, and dead. She had to be there for the tyke, on several levels. "Jamie, I want you to travel first, you can fly higher than a bird. I want you to jump up on my right thigh, the one balanced on the tree, and jump with all your might. If you are strong and brave enough, your mother will find you. Listen, Jamie, can you hear her?"

"*Are we going to heaven, is that why we have to fly into the tree?*" Jamie sniveled. She knew she needed to act now. The others were fidgeting, getting nervous and fearful. Would they end up in hell, they thought?

"You must trust me, all eight of you. You were the ones to seek me out, five of you for two solid years, not giving me one night of peace. You must know this hell, this lonely life on Sawyer's Hill, will end only if you are brave enough to act for yourself. You must step on my thigh and jump—it's easy— move quickly, don't hesitate and hop. C'mon, Jamie, try it!" Sophie bent slightly, took Jamie's left hand in her right, and urged him to step up, shift his weight toward her. She gently but quickly lifted him up and bounced him on her right thigh, like a rubber ball. Feather light, he rose without effort. Jamie was gone to the Upper World with a "*Wheeeeeeee!*"

Old Margaret was next—bent, she was afraid to be broken. Sophie reminded Margaret she was broken here and now. If she trusted, she would no longer be bent. She sighed agreement and took one step and jumped and was gone. They followed, six more, no longer apprehensive, proudly leaping to their new fate. Sophie glanced once at Poe and saw her eyes filled with tears. She knew Poe felt their release. How could she not?

On the eighth hop on Sophie's aching right thigh, the burial ground filled with the demanding cries of an infant, wet, hungry, and impatient for her mother's care. The baby was lost. Sophie thought of poor Marthia and her three hundred and ten years of limbo. Sophie called out to the baby, cooed in her direction. Like a lost dog hearing the voice of its owner, the baby floated to Sophie. Happy, bubbling gurgles filled her arms. This Spirit had so much light, was so loved, had a newer fresher energy—she came from one of the new houses. With Sophie's realization, the baby grew in length and girth and started to kick wildly and happily. This Spirit had an irresistible vibration; Sophie would have loved to keep her, if she were corporeal. She was ready for the Grandma stage. She balanced the rapidly growing baby on her thigh and began to bob up and down. The baby responded with howls of ecstatic laughter. Trusting, Sophie bounced the infant one last time and threw her with all her might into the tree. The grounds filled with the sounds of joy, pure, sweet, ecstatic joy. They were all in the Upper World, one more than expected, nine Spirits, and success was theirs!

Sophie faced the three—sweat pouring from their faces—all red from constant movement. The Sun was much lower; the ritual had taken much longer than expected. Sophie joined them in their movements and gently guided them to change their beats, slow down to hers, ease their breathing, the three looking like they would either explode or faint if another trance breath was taken. Slowly, she brought them down and out of the trance state, into the Middle World of Sawyer's Hill Burial Ground, back to the dense oak wood, now quiet and peaceful.

Sophie staggered, face wet with tears, exhausted from the physical energy expended. The ritual stopped, as Sophie had said it would, as soon as they stopped moving. Dylan was the first to break the dance, taking several long strides, catching Sophie inches from the ground. The sound of crickets was thick, far too early, not evening yet, Sophie thought as Dylan grabbed her.

Dylan forced Sophie to stand straight. He reached into his jean pocket and brought out a purple bandana and began wiping the sweat and tears from her face. Poe grabbed a cool water bottle from one of the bags of supplies and gave it to Dylan, who proceeded to open the bottle and start rubbing Sophie's face and hands with cool water, lowering her temperature and blood pressure. This was his routine when Sophie was out of juice. She had sworn to him she would not let this happen on the American Camino. He opened his mouth and formed the beginning words of a lecture. Sophie gently placed her hand over his mouth and nodded, a knowing look. She grabbed what was left of the water bottle and chugged its contents.

It was then a wind began, not through the grounds but surrounding it, shaking all the tress on the perimeter, the sounds of acorns dropping, their skins splitting. A light grew with the sound, a sound of tinkling glassware in a busy kitchen, morphing into the gentle giggles of little girls playing alone. Skipping, swirling stars and whistles, a cartoon fairyland, outside of the grounds. Then, the skipping stopped and a last giggle filtered through the dark trees, whispering, *"Thank you."* The baby girl had grown, and she had come briefly to say goodbye to her mother, goodbye to her old pink room painted with multicolored butterflies and life-sized robins showing their Spring blush. She loved her room and had spent three years there as a tiny brand new baby, before hearing Sophie's cajoling of the other Spirits this afternoon. The baby was stillborn, dead only minutes before the birth, strangled by the umbilical cord, proving birth was still a dangerous process, even in the twenty-first century. "You are most welcome, sweet soul," Sophie whispered. The giggles faded to the tops of the trees and the Spirit was free to find a new mother and try the dance of life again. She would keep her next life close by. She could hear the faint prayers of a would-be mother from Newburyport. She was finally free to choose.

The Ipswich fried clams lived up to their reputation, recommended by locals and the Food Network. The place was full, a line circling the rural parking lot, in the middle of farm and marshland, far away from stoplights and intersections. News traveled far and wide—foodies loved their traveling treats. The three toasted the nine freed Spirits with frozen mugs of frothy beer. Sophie wanted to toast, but her paper cup full of vanilla ice cream didn't make a clicking sound. She loved watching her friends drink tap beer and eat mountains of clams. They left a few French fries for Sophie; she was courageous and tried the potatoes, surprisingly tasty with ice cream.

The twentieth of September—three more days and they would be home again tucked safely in their beds, free from haunts, Sophie hoped. Three more days to honor the process of death and rebirth, tie loose ends, honor the lost at Saugus. Three more days to create peaceful closure for Giles, Martha, Mary, for Tarbell and Dexter. Success was already theirs, although Sophie was too insecure to admit it. They would drive the long way back to Peabody, travel to the site of Richard Dexter's house, let Poe feel the place. Perhaps she would resonate and remember. Sophie would insist on leaving offerings, reinforcing Poe's positive ties to Dexter's land, at Poe's disposal when the need arose, when she was ready.

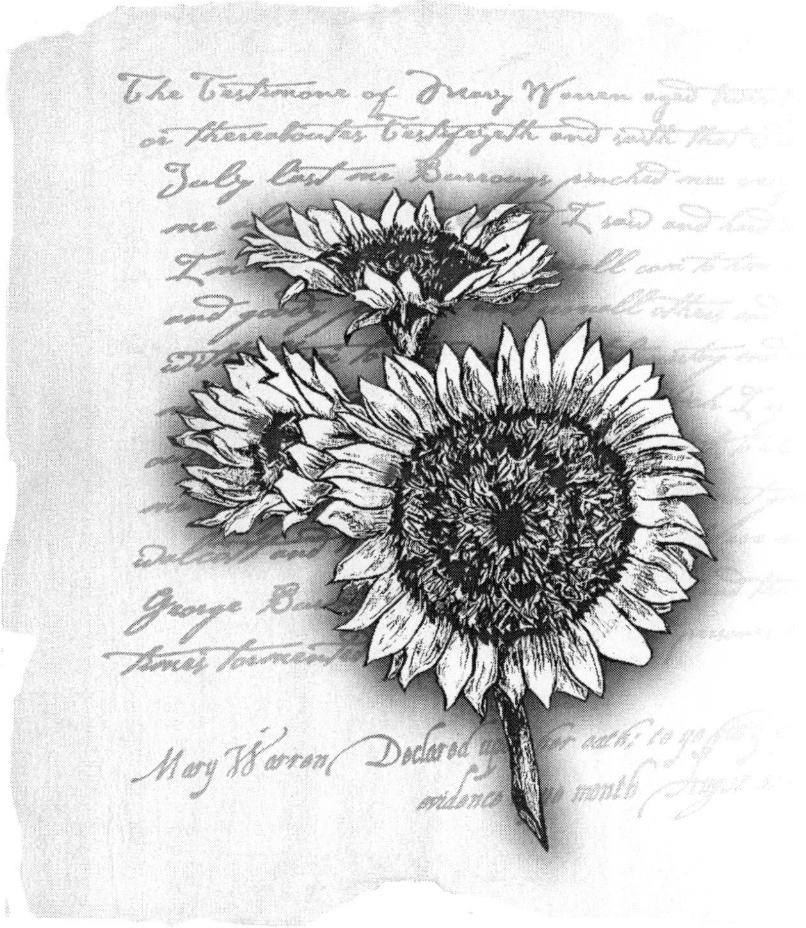

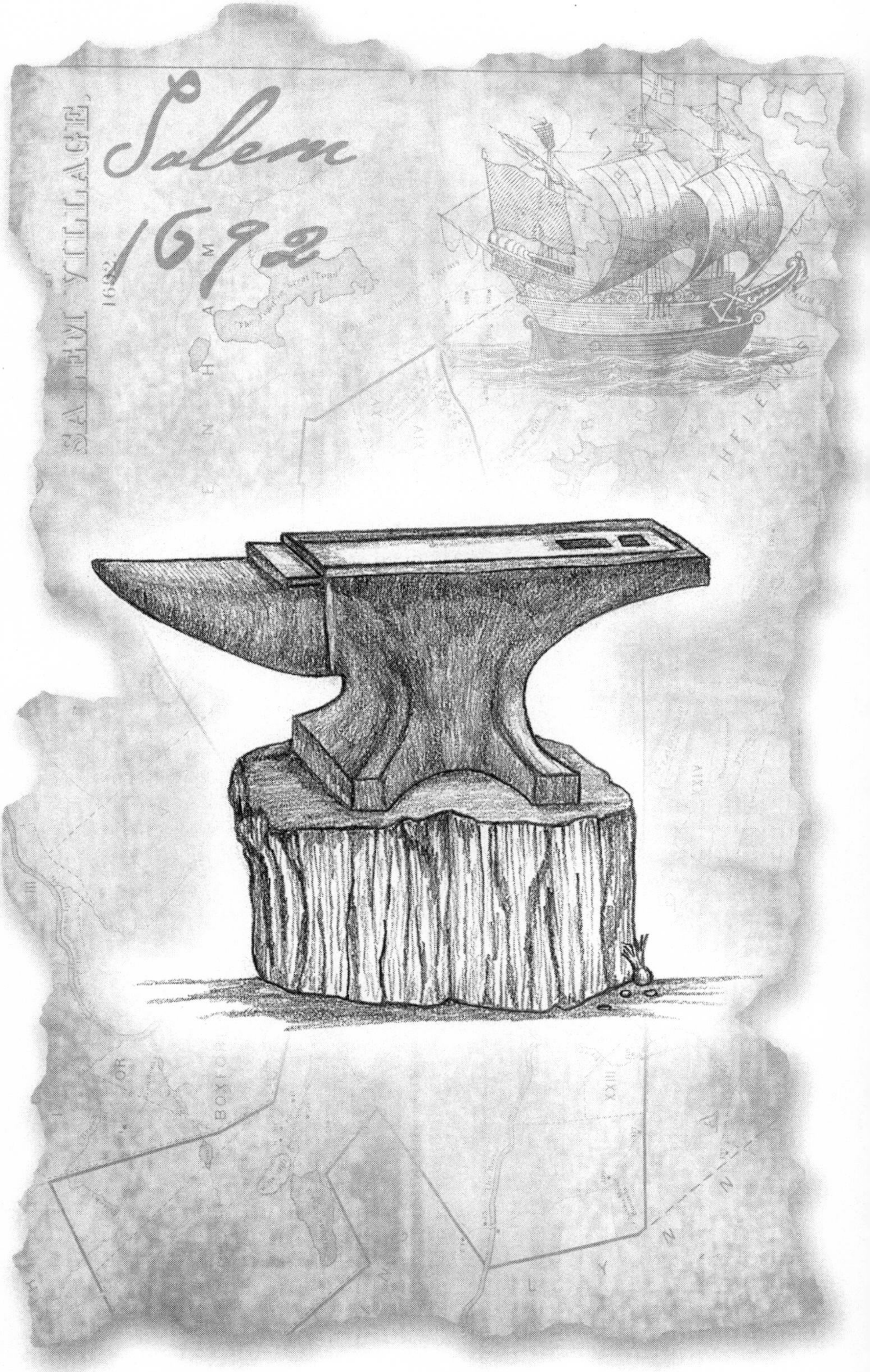
Salem
1692
SALEM VILLAGE

Chapter Twenty-Three

FRIDAY'S GATHERING
September 21, 2007, 6:00 a.m.

SHE WATCHED THE SUNRISE FROM HER BED, the window opened wide, catching reflections of pinks and orange. The room filled with light, the hour a key to mysterious color and motion. Fridays are ruled by Venus, the mother of art and beauty. Vain and able to use her sexuality as a tool for domination, Venus teaches humans to risk for the sake of love, to express one's heights of passion, inspiring others to lusty action. Sophie wore pink on Fridays, her tribute to Venus, Aphrodite, to love and always passion. It was also Padre Pio's favorite color; one of his only demands on Sophie was to wear more pink. Today, she did not hesitate to wear her softest and freshest shade, in her mind ensuring Padre's presence and, she hoped, his protection.

She lay in the soft bed—her butt sunk deep into the center of the mattress—and made mental lists of all the items to gather for the Honoring Ceremonies planned. More rum, spiced this time, and Challah bread for the Witch Memorial at Charter Street. Pick up the four cut sunflowers at the Corey Vegetable Stand in Peabody, one for Gallows Hill, one for Mary Corey, two for the Witch Memorial. Also another small pumpkin from Corey land should go on the Liberation Feast Altar on Saturday night, tomorrow night, so soon. It would all be contingent on success tonight. The Integration Walk was already challenging her: five miles, maybe more. She felt too tired to keep going, but she would. At least three dozen small white teacup roses and more red satin ribbon had to be purchased, commemorating people *in the know* and power places in Salem. Nice stationery for invitations to the Liberation Feast: they had a list of forty-five people and Spirits to invite. A fleece blanket for Miss Mary, lightweight and easy to wash. They would see her on Sunday, perhaps at the ritual at the memorial on Saturday. Sophie had no idea how large the audience would be in the middle of the day on Saturday—big, she assumed, and remembered the continual warning not to grandstand or show off. They needed a special trinket from Saugus for the Feast Altar. Who could forget a miniature tea set for the Spirits, for the legions of helpers on this journey, almost complete?

Her mind was on fire, too much information to process. Would she write another book? Would it be necessary? Could she live through these experiences once more and drag out the memories for months while the book was being written? She had failures in the past, literarily; most people didn't even know her struggles. Her first book, penned at eleven when her sister Joan was at the height of her battle with cancer, was about death and dying, the grief of children left behind after the Reaper finally visits. It was about the rebirth of a family, all based on anticipation of Joan's demise, trying for a positive spin. The front cover she painted herself: dark purple, a white dove, with red lettering, the colors of Hecate, even then. She shared it with older family members and never saw it again. She guised her grief by saying: *it was a gift...*

Her second was written for her undergraduate degree in literature, illustrated prose, the story of her complicated life, involving magick, genealogy, sex, and not-belonging. It was stolen by her faculty advisor and lesbian mentor; this theft put Sophie back in the closet for five more years, afraid to trust anyone promising sexual liberation and freedom.

Sophie's third book, another illustrated collection of poetry and prose, was sent to her half-brother for possible publication. He knew people, so he claimed. Richard and Sarah were excited at the prospect of their daughter being a published author at twenty-two. Her brother phoned a week after the manuscript arrived, only to say he was embarrassed by the stories, implications of gender disorders and confused loyalties. He said it was far too autobiographical. She never saw the manuscript again, the original and only copy, with its rich line drawings and haunting prose, lost. She would never trust her half-siblings, from Richard's numerous wives, again.

Then, there was her Big Book. For years, people had tormented her to write her beliefs on paper, write directions, recipes, and how-tos in detailed form. She had relented in the late 1990s, producing a 776-page manuscript, which completely boggled the minds of publishers. *Shaman* was a cliché word that few understood, not yet a household term used every day in New

Age Circles; that would come in the middle of the next decade. She began the book: "Witch, Shaman, Priest—makes no difference—the beginning opening is the same, one is Called by the Spirits." It launched half a dozen careers, inspired by materials never returned. It was never published, pulled at the last minute; no one could wrap their heads around the concept of an author who was a Pagan Jewish Catholic Indigenous Shamanic Practitioner, a half-breed Indian with an attitude.

Just last year she wrote two books outlining the American Camino: names, dates, and places; she would keep them to herself. Would she bother trying to write about this amazing experience, from a first person, non-fiction perspective? She didn't think so—she couldn't picture it coming to pass. Where would she find the energy? It all seemed to be draining away; regardless of the safeguards in place, her Core Energy had been weakened by the psychopomp work done. Her right thigh was severely bruised, deep purple from the inside of the thigh to the outside, six inches wide, wounded from being a launching pad yesterday for the flight of nine Spirits. Others do not realize that Spirits are heavy—the bigger they are, the harder they fall. Some babies, although small and harmless-looking, weigh as much as gold because of the hope and promise put into them; it's too hard for parents to lose children waited and planned for. Dylan took several pictures of the bruise, for her files and medical records. Perhaps someday she would find a lucky fit with a student and give her precious files to her, even though she vowed to give up teaching once and for all when she returned to Oregon. She had thought Dora was the woman, her search complete, but it was not to be. Where would the typed files, recipes, prescriptions, pictures, charms, and liturgies end up?

The few who knew that Sophie kept detailed records of her cases felt it was dangerous, proving she was practicing Medicine without a license. Sophie would have to remind them this was the reason she had gone through a proper, above-board ministerial program, supported by other Shamanic Practitioners who were academics, not indigenous like Sophie. She was an ordained reverend, not the internet-style *"for ten dollars you too can be a minister, even if you do not believe in God."* That was not Sophie's style; plus she needed real protection. It was illegal to practice hands-on healing in Oregon, unless one is a licensed doctor or minister.

For a liberal state, Oregon was one of the toughest on would-be cult behavior involving money and possible scams. The powers that be had learned the hard way through dealing with the Rajneeshees in Antelope, on the Eastern side. They had had a scandal: four attempted murders, thirty-five Rolls Royces, and lots of devotees paying three hundred and fifty bucks a head to attend the Chosen One's birthday party. Oregon had no time for cults, nor did Sophie, remembering Lydia's six years as a Moonie, brainwashed forever, never the same, one individual out of twenty-five thousand couples married in a single ceremony in Shay Stadium. Was this the price of being related to Hannah Dustin? There weren't many towns in Oregon that had neon signs on main drags advertising *"Palms Read Here,"* not in Oregon. If the authorities decided to crack down on spiritual practitioners, without her connections and licenses Sophie and Dylan both would be in a lot of trouble. Neither one of them had the time or energy for nonsense, impossible battles, fighting with the government; they had learned this lesson in Salem in 1692. They kept their heads low, particularly with George W. Bush in office, paid their taxes, not more than was required but the full amount, always early. They were hardwired to stay out of the way of the government. They both expected services and highways for their dollars, but no interference; they shied away from local politics and did not like having their pictures in the paper. They tried hard to maintain their cool demeanors.

Sophie groaned when she saw the clock read seven, time to prepare for the day. At least her head would tone down its wanderings. She feared failure. It no longer fit with her plan to make a mark, set the story straight, find some peace. She had no idea if her story would remain silent. She knew she was stubborn and believed in her work. She wanted recognition, had waited for it, was overdue, but it was out of her hands. The Spirit Realms would decide what her course of action would be. She had to trust—she hurt too much not to. It was Friday: Saugus, shopping, and Integration.

September 21, 2007, 9:00 a.m.

SOPHIE'S FATIGUE WAS SHORTENING HER TEMPER. Her agitation surfaced when she noticed Dora was wearing a new pair of red high heels. The shoes set off her rust-colored skirt, true. But so what! Had she forgotten the deal was for the three to shadow Sophie, half a block away, for protection and as witnesses? How could Dora do that in heels?

"I certainly hope you packed another pair of shoes for the Integration

Walk! You can't walk five miles over cobbles and bricks, in those tools of torture." Sophie sounded her disapproval.

"You're being paranoid, Sophie, seeing potential injury and distraction on the walk, just because of the shoes I chose to wear. You forget: I'm young, strong, and a seasoned athlete. I am a dancer, with feet of iron. I can do anything in high heels!" Dora beamed, looking like an illustrated picture of little French Madeline, her hands firmly placed on her hips, defiant and daring.

"I am not paranoid, young lady! I am a seasoned planner." Sophie had raised her voice—it was beyond her control. "I have made up my mind: no one will divert my energy from the prize of Integration! All else is secondary, despite guilt, tantrums, or red shoes!" She motioned for Dora to get out of her way and closed the back door of the SUV with a slam. It was out of her system now, and she felt better for it.

Route 114 passed the candy store; they would have one more time to shop there, tomorrow, when the roses were delivered. Inspired by their path, sounds of opening cellophane wrappers were heard, the girls hoarding their chocolate treasures, even from each other. Dora's signature chocolate-covered sunflower nuts were for graves only. Route 107 headed South and became the Old Boston Road. It had been called dozens of names, but the path was the same as it had been for over three hundred years, matching the body tracings exactly. The land began to change. Congestion increased, even on broader highways, three lanes in each direction in some stretches. Dylan claimed Massachusetts drivers could merge but were insane, none deserving licenses. "See! Jesus, they think they own the road! I haven't seen this kind of aggressive driving since New York City." Dylan's blood pressure rose with the temperature, hitting ninety degrees in the shade today, the sky hazy, the air clammy hot.

The town of Saugus had a dingy look to it, its main street deserted except for the overflowing tavern, the doors tightly closed and the air conditioner cranked high. The memory of Bridget Bishop flooded Sophie. How she would have loved air conditioning and Monday Night Football! She saw a vision of Bridget with a bright purple swath of lace brushing her amble bosom, her black skirt lazily laced, loose enough to breathe. She suffered for no one but herself, plenty to keep up with. She loved her rum. Giles had given her his recipe for Initiation Brew, his favorite nutmeg hard cider—she adopted it as her own—boasting its healing properties when the hives were heavy with honey. Bridget could strut, although she preferred singing to dance.

They followed MapQuest directions, printed out before leaving Oregon. They passed a lavish strip mall, lined with carefully trimmed trees, the most affluent site thus far in Saugus. Directly across the street, Sophie spotted marshland and the contours of a river, swaying with reeds as tall as men and as green as Irish moss. "We're close, Poe, we're almost there. Look for markers. Wait, I see the main mill foreman's house, fenced on the East side of the road." Dylan saw what Sophie had, moved into the turning lane, into mill property, now controlled by the U.S. Park Service.

The house, a large two-story, dressed in black clapboard, loomed eerily. The party of four was enthusiastically greeted by a Park Ranger in full green-and-gray uniform, although in Summer short sleeves. Fortunately, half of the old foreman's house was air conditioned, for the benefit of its archives and artifacts, not for the comfort of the rangers. They were asked to join the assembled group for a film history of the mill. All but Sophie quickly found seats. Sophie walked up to the ranger and asked, "Does the film include the history of the mill during the time of Tarbell ownership?"

"And where did you say you were from?" the rotund man asked.

Sophie asked him why her residence mattered. She noticed he had a personal phone book, small enough to fit in his chest pocket. It was open and he was starting to look flustered, but he was having a hard time covering up his discomfort. "Because I have never, in nineteen years as ranger here, been asked about the Tarbells in connection with this place, not once."

"I'm surprised; I would think many historians would find the information useful," Sophie replied with a crooked smile. She wasn't hiding anymore. She was curious about the allegiance of this place. Were there people still trying to cover the tracks of the Family Confederacy? Did this ranger know of the bodies incinerated here?

Out of frustration, now sweating profusely, he laid his book down and sighed. "You must be part of the Towne's Association shindig this week, in the area for the festivities, for the reenactment this weekend." Sophie stopped smiling, thinking of the blood she still had to leave on the grounds of the Nurse Homestead.

"We have been to the Nurse Homestead this week, all of us, yes," Sophie said, almost whispering.

"I thought so. You even look familiar. Do I know you?" Sophie didn't respond, but instead she turned and asked about the small metal black anvil in the curio case. She expressed her interest, so he switched his attention

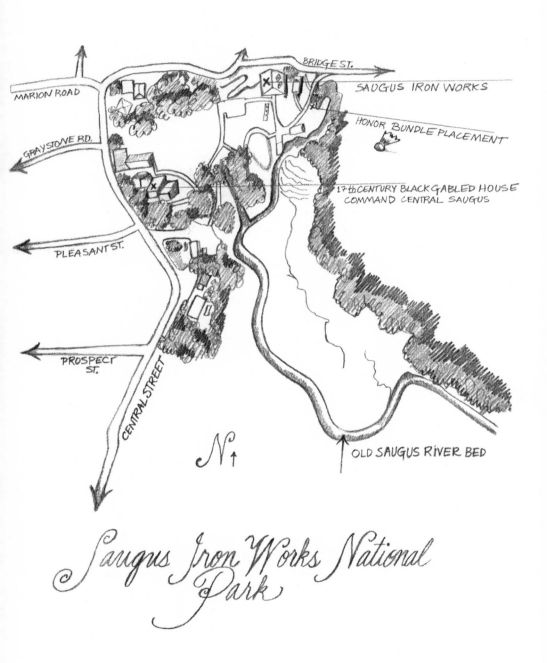

MARION ROAD

BRIDGE ST.

SAUGUS IRON WORKS

GRAYSTONE RD.

HONOR BUNDLE PLACEMENT

17th CENTURY BLACK GABLED HOUSE
COMMAND CENTRAL SAUGUS

PLEASANT ST.

PROSPECT ST.

CENTRAL STREET

N ↑

OLD SAUGUS RIVER BED

Saugus Iron Works National Park

and brought out the replica piece for her inspection. "Perfect, I'll take it, just what I need!" Sophie exclaimed, knowing it was the perfect Saugus piece for the Liberation Feast Altar. "Just make me a pile; I'm sure I'll buy lots more before we're done. I'm interested in watching the movie. But before we get started, perhaps you could help me with some information. I'm looking for clay pieces, especially made from Essex County clay, for my collection. Do you have any ideas where I might find some?"

"I only know of one person—she's a historian, trained in Boston, now a full-time potter. Most of her pieces are pre-purchased. She is widely collected, especially among a few dedicated collectors right here, outside of Salem. She's a Towne, really busy this time of the year. I'm sure someone would introduce her on Sunday at the Nurse Homestead. She'll be there. Ask for Matilda Putnam. I collect her pots, started when I still worked for the family twenty years ago in Danvers." He smiled widely, now toying with Sophie. She realized her ego had given her away. He continued, "We'll have to have a group photograph for your picture book before you leave today, so you'll always remember me."

Sophie half-smiled and said, "How could I ever forget you?"

He chuckled and walked over to the DVD player and started the movie. Sophie watched him go into his glass-doored office and paw through his Rolodex. He was on his cell phone, pointing with his right finger, his expression exaggerated and almost comical, his face growing flushed. The movie was ending, credits rolling. Sophie reached over and whispered to Dylan they had been found out. Time to walk the grounds, tie the bundles, and leave. Their honoring was almost complete. She would explain the whole story later.

This was the feeling she had had all morning through breakfast: someone was watching her, breathing down her neck. She thought it was caused by perfectionist behavior, which plagued her. Had she done all she could? Had her job been successful? She had had to grandstand, showing off her knowledge to the ranger, part of the Confederacy himself. Maybe even a Tarbell, or surely one of the ten other families.

They all slipped through the door, the big man still on his cell in animated conversation. They huddled quickly when Sophie made the sign. Sophie explained what had happened, the short version—the ranger was an inside man and most probably knew who they were. They decided to cross the newly refurbished bridge and place some Sage in the lower mill room, where the energy was dense and cold. The river, now only contours hinting at its original location, just gentle marshlands left, had been blocked up and diverted for city use over a hundred years before. Sophie visually followed a lone branch hanging over what once was flowing water. It was fairly easy to get to, just down the side of a gully and up a small slope. She could do it herself. She decided that the girls, dressed in their Friday finery and fancy socks, would have a group shot, just of feet, over the wood-chute for the mill, the entry point for many bodies. She had to get the shot before her cute pink-and-white argyle socks were made an ugly shade of beige from her walking up the opposite bank of the river. Feet rule our understanding, she kept reminding herself, needing a strong dose of her own Medicine.

In short order, and off state property, Sophie tied her red Honor Bundle on the long branch, honoring the dead, honoring their sacrifice, their stories, all lost to the world and their descendants. The four walked arm in arm up the pebbled path, just expanded the previous Spring, privately funded. The ranger had told Sophie all about the facelift. Their fundraising had been very success-ful since 1992 and the three-hundredth Anniversary of the Witch Hysteria. They had a renewed patron from Salem who met all their financial needs till 2012. They were thrilled with their patron's generosity, and all the rangers were proud to be from the Massachusetts Bay Colony, Sophie was informed.

She wondered if bone fragments were still being found on the site, in the riverbed. Were they still being covered up? How long would such evidence survive? Her thoughts went to the millions of bodies incinerated in Poland and she realized she had never heard of Nazi archeological evidence, either. Maybe not a fair comparison for some, but for Sophie it was close to home.

The four were just rounding the far corner of the house, thinking they had slipped from detection, when the ranger called after them. "Let's have our photo now, shall we? I have a friend, just visiting from Danvers, who's going to take the shots, with both our cameras. I want a picture of the wom-an who knows all about Saugus and the Tarbells."

"Sure, why not? Let's have photos of each other, always good to know what your friends look like." Sophie motioned for everybody to line up in front of the main doors. An old man about eighty-five walked in front of the assembled group. His gait was measured, but his twinkling eyes told a story of vigor and passion. The ranger surrendered his camera first—snap and he was done. Without hesitation, the old man reached for Sophie's camera be-fore it was offered. She noticed his cheeky smile and asked his name. "Well,

Ms. St. Cloud, my name is Donald Putnam, good to meet you." He extended his old withered hand. Sophie accepted it with a faint smile, knowing Donald was Drake Putnam's father. They had been watched this morning. Of course they had been. It was one day from Hanging Day, one day before their work was done.

"Nice to meet you, Mr. Putnam. Obviously you knew we were coming?"

The old man, his gray eyes bright in the clearing hot haze, bowed slightly and said, "It's a very curious situation, don't you think? Of course we have investments to protect, matters and people to consider."

"This Work is my own, Mr. Putnam. I am not here to cause you financial damage. I am here to do my spiritual Work, long overdue, and then go home, never to return. Nothing has to happen between us, other than a handshake. We can part and no one will be the wiser, both of us keeping our secrets hidden. I am sure the candy store land is secured." Sophie sniffed hard, wondering why she always had to take one step over the line.

Old Man Putnam seemed to enjoy the irony and answered, "It's on a ninety-nine-year lease, caught up in probate for at least another two hundred years."

They shook hands and smiled. Everyone in the party heard the uneasy, sometimes challenging conversation but decided to follow Sophie's lead and each shook his hand, white-man style. Sophie, caught up in the enthusiasm, an enemy faced without damage, grabbed the old man in a tight embrace and whispered in his ear. "Have Drake back off. The Inner Circle won't have any work left by the time we leave."

"Indeed!" was his only response.

Sophie, frazzled but undefeated, walked into the foreman's house and made her way to the curio case and the waiting ranger, smiling a cat-ate-a-bird grin. "Thank you for holding the anvil. That will be all today." She paid for the treasure, avoided shaking the ranger's hand, and exited into the light of late morning. She began walking briskly down the pebbled path, away from the mill, away from Old Man Putnam, uneasy but full-circle. How she wished this meeting, if it had to be, would have happened after the Integration Walk. Only another distraction, that's all it was. She was not to worry.

September 21, 2007, 1:00 p.m.

THEY TRAVELED NORTH, the pressure easing by the time the border of Peabody was crossed. Sophie had embraced one of the people who frightened her the most in the world and had survived it, actually made herself feed on the chaos of the incident, clearing her head and body from the fatigue and pain caused by the vigorous work at Sawyer's Hill. Her friend Saraa used good Russian vodka to clear her mind of distractions. Sophie harnessed the waste of anxiety, the energy of chaos, other people's fear as her drug, adrenaline the most palpable fuel around, and the easiest to find, refine, and redirect. It was efficient and did the Great Mother a favor, cleaning up messes and soothing surface wounds, recycling. Transformation is the favorite tool of the Mother's, molding pearls from garbage, diamonds from hate—the Mother had her ways. It was a give-and-take experience, taught to her by her mother. A Witch needed to know all the angles to work a room effectively; people expected a good show. Sarah was a Leo and loved the spotlight, and she showed Sophie how to work it early on.

Donald Putnam had threatened her before, through other people. Sophie had received a full-sized smiling photo of him once, before he shaved his mustache, and he had fewer wrinkles. Donald was still vain. His picture proclaimed: "*Watch your step, young lady!*" The middle fifties are young for someone as grizzled as Donald, ninety-four at last count, although he didn't look a day over eighty-five. Today, he had not been intimidated by the likes of a middle-aged woman, easily dismissed, no different from Martha Corey or Sarah Good.

Sophie grabbed the marked AAA roadmap stuffed carefully between the seat and emergency brake. She reached into the Trader Joe's bag and found her special red Sharpie and marked Saugus with a red star. The 21.8-mile triangle was complete, no more side trips. Their travels would be concentrated in Salem, Danvers, and Peabody till they flew out of Logan at four on Sunday afternoon. Sophie opened her notebook and began writing shopping lists for the three others to fill. They had to find Challah before sundown and kosher grape juice for the Yom Kippur toast. They had to step on it and gather the needed supplies.

She had been looking forward to a nice lunch out with Dylan, time just for the two of them for a change. She was sure that Dylan had been looking forward to it too. But now, after the incident this morning with Old Man Putnam, she needed to calm down, restore her waning energy. She needed rest. What would be the real effect of integrating an eighty-one year old man, half-starved, in poor health after five months in the gaol, broken and battered, bludgeoned to death? How would her body change? The final outcome would buy her psychic peace, but at what price, she wondered.

And by five, she wanted to be downtown again, get her sea-legs, know where she was headed. She had to be extra-prepared tonight. Fate was a force she could not predict. The rest could be planned for.

She asked Dylan to leave her off at the hotel; they would skip their lunch. He didn't show irritation but instead he encouraged her to recoup and prepare for the Integration Walk. Pulling up to the hotel, he slid out to help with her backpack and whatever else she wanted to carry upstairs. She reached for him and hugged him gently. Three quick pats on his back and she turned and faded through the sliding glass doors.

Dylan climbed back into the SUV.

Dora and Poe stayed in the back seat and Dora called out, "To the shops, Dylan," in a fake English accent.

"That was quite a row you had with Sophie this morning, Dora," Dylan said.

"Shut up, Dylan! What are you trying to do, read minds again? You are not going to stop me from enjoying myself this afternoon. Do you understand me?" Dora flamed.

Poe looked up from her green journal. "Are we back in grammar school now? Get a grip, y'all!"

Dora took charge of the three lists, making her own figuring and mapping out the acquisitions. "Dylan, take the first left into the strip mall. There's a linen place next to the craft shop. We can buy the blanket at the linen shop and the ribbon and stationery at the craft store. Sophie wanted small roses; we might have an easier time finding them in a supermarket. That's where we'd find the Challah too. There's a market in the shopping complex next to Trader Joe's. I'm sure we'll have luck there." No one disputed her precision when it came to shopping, especially shopping with someone else's money.

Poe announced she was going to take a nap in the back seat while Dylan and Dora did the shopping. She wasn't feeling well, she said, and she did look pale, despite her freckles and tan. Regrettably that left Dylan the burden of being Dora's only pack mule. Dora remained solidly in charge, waltzing in and out of stores, sporting other's treasures. At the last store, he made her show him the list to review. It looked complete, although he had a nagging feeling they had missed something. Poe sat up when they opened the trunk. It appeared she had not slept, but her color had returned. And he knew Sophie would be pleased with their gathering, except for the miniature tea set. They had had no luck in finding one. Dylan decided to hit an import or toy shop on the wharf.

Dora climbed into the front passenger seat and let Poe stay stretched out in the back for their ride to Salem proper. She looked down at her swollen feet and said, "I want to get downtown to the dress shops and try on witchy-looking outfits for the Country Fair and the Fairy Festival. Maybe I'll find new wings and a hat to match. Sounds like what I need to win Best Costume at the Witch's Ball in Eugene on Samhain. I can taste victory! I've saved all year for this afternoon!" Dora never looked up for the others' reactions, just kept checking her lists and counting her money.

Dylan rolled his eyes and sighed loudly, even though his reaction was ignored. He wanted to grab a bite to eat, maybe a dessert, and likely Poe did too. Wanting to spend time on the wharf in the open air, Dylan and Poe separated company with Dora. She wanted shopping in Old Town.

There was one shop Dylan and Poe wanted to cruise—Laurie Cabot's shop on the wharf. Sophie had often spoken of how much she respected Laurie, despite her wild clothes, always black, always flowing. Sophie had a blind spot for modern Witches, and Dylan adopted her position. Sophie herself wore Native Regalia for dancing and praying, so what was the difference with Laurie's choir robes? Just the audience was different, no big deal. He was with her—he had made his peace with the whole Neo-Pagan sentiment. Dylan and Poe would buy something from Laurie, just as Sophie would have. Maybe Laurie was even there. Probably not, Dylan assured Poe: she was too famous to be available for the tourists on a Friday afternoon. They shared the hope that Laurie would have a big ritual planned for Mabon the next night, the Autumnal Equinox—Yom Kippur too, the perfect night for the Liberation Feast!

Their excitement grew the closer they got to the newly built shops at the refurbished wharf. You could smell the new money, crisp and green, the shops squeaky clean and glossy. Dylan and Poe said this kind of development would never happen in Santa Fe, because of historical zoning laws. Laurie's shop was new; you still could smell the carpet with its fresh formaldehyde. It burned their eyes as soon as they walked in. The shop was tidy, clean, and beige. No purple or orange or black, the stereotypical colors for Witches, no green-faced Morrigans either. Long sharp rows of books and a full curio case of crystals and gemstone jewelry greeted their eyes, few Pentacles, no skulls or cross-bones, devil-heads or flying Witches. It felt like a metaphysical store anywhere in the country, except for a small shelf with Laurie's own spell kits and potions, posters, and books. Dylan bought one postcard from the bland-looking dishwater blonde behind the counter, "Do come back again," she said as they strolled out the front door. Sophie had missed nothing here, although it would have been a treat to see the two women come together and watch what would happen, Dylan thought. Would they lamely shake hands like competitors or would they embrace each other as Sisters of Magick?

"I'm glad Laurie's shop is normal and positive. It's a departure from the ghoulish tourist displays up a couple of blocks. It's more ordinary but a welcome surprise." Dylan only half believed his words—he would have paid to see Laurie and Sophie side by side, what a show!

They ate vegetable lasagna and chocolate gelato at a family-run café with umbrellas and outside service. Finally watching the boats drift by in the warm salty breeze, they would forgo the beer. They needed to be sharp this evening.

Dora found Poe and Dylan as they were shoveling the last bite of gelato into their greedy mouths. They were happy and enjoying each other's company. Poe and Dylan were used to each other. They spent every Tuesday night together reading the Tarot Cards and Journeying. Dora limped to the table, her hands full of colorful bags, with purple and silver tissue paper. She must have spent a fortune. She said she had plans. Neither Dylan nor Poe commented on Dora's swollen and bleeding feet. She tried getting the red shoes off without bursting too many blisters. "Hey, I couldn't find a miniature tea set for Sophie. I know she wanted one in the worst way, but I just couldn't find one. I didn't look off the pedestrian walk. I wanted to spend my time close to the dress and costume shops. Oh well."

"I'm sure Sophie will figure out an alternative. We all did what we could. We have one more stop tomorrow morning at the veggie stand for the flowers and pumpkins and we're set! Oh, maybe two stops, the spiced rum has to be found too. Oh no, we didn't get the roses or the Challah or the kosher grape juice." Dylan was upset. "Let's get out of here, go to a couple of markets and buy the flowers and juice, the bread. There are no substitutions for those items!"

Dylan left a generous tip, waved farewell to their hosts, and walked to the SUV, arm in arm with Poe, Dora limping behind them.

Salem
1692

Chapter Twenty-Four

THE INTEGRATION WALK
September 21, 2007, 5:00 p.m.

DYLAN TURNED OFF THE HIGHWAY and began circling the route for the Walk, just as Sophie wanted. Turning the corner from Bridge Street to Howard Street, Sophie felt a lump in the pit of her stomach. Performance anxiety rising. She knew the waiting was over. An hour and ten minutes till the walk began. Dylan turned right on Brown Street, the loop around Howard Street three-quarters complete. Finally, he turned on St. Peter's Street, where the Walk began at the Pressing Place across the street from the Morency Complex.

The SUV was dead quiet. Dylan turned West into the municipal lot behind the Museum Place Mall and parked. Sophie slipped from her seat, feeling wan and looking wasted. She turned clockwise, trying to shake anxiety, when she noticed a sign on the mall's rear wall, "*Quan Yin Imports, Special Gifts for the Traveler.*" Sophie knew the perfect stress release: shopping for a miniature tea set. "Let's take a peek in the Quan Yin shop. Who could resist the name?" Sophie said with a faraway smile. Dora and Poe sighed heavily. Sophie had found the Salem equivalent of the Dollar Store and she was excited.

"Do we have enough time for shopping, this close to the walk?" Dylan was not in the mood for diversions. He wanted it to be six o'clock, wanted this part over. He feared the future after Integration—he didn't know if there would be room enough for him in Sophie's life after Giles had taken his spot, or maybe he would no longer make a place for Sophie in his life. He was weary of the tribulation of reincarnation memory. He wanted the future to be now, with a full belly, down the street at the Lyceum Bar and Grill,

Salem's understated fine dining, Witch restaurant, with a casual calm. No one outside Witchcraft Circles would guess it an unofficial hangout for practitioners of the cunning arts, with its white walls, wood bar and trim, French doors and beige starched napkins. It looked so normal, although the ghosts had ears and everybody was heavily connected. Dylan wanted Gallows Hill over too. He was in no mood to face Martha. What would he say to her?

Sophie looked at her watch. "We have a full hour. Let's shop and gawk for forty-five minutes or so, then make our way up the street."

"We'll meet you at the SUV in forty-five minutes, then, Sophie. Poe and I are going to have a coffee next door—you know, get juiced for the event, take a weight off," Dora said, halfway down the block.

Sophie thought of the no-caffeine rule and swallowed her disappointed words. All of her rules—and she the only one to abide by them. "Don't be late, Dora. I'll start without you if I have to." Sophie was firm, but not acerbic. Dora looked puzzled, as if she couldn't imagine Sophie actually beginning without her. Yes, things had already shifted; Sophie no longer depended on Dora. Sophie felt it like a dull ache, clearing her throat more than once; rattling her chest, thinking it would clear the feeling of dry toast crumbs caught in her throat.

"Got it, Sophie, don't want to miss this anyway." Sophie stood watching Dora hobble off, refusing to say a word about her feet or the five miles of walking ahead of them. Sophie shook her head—exorcizing black flies from an imaginary veil—and headed into the covered mall looking for her favorite House Goddess, Quan Yin.

Dylan and Sophie were warmly greeted by two lovely Chinese women, in their late sixties or early seventies. With dyed black hair, eyeglasses on chains, dressed in black silk pajamas, they looked like finely crafted dolls, masterfully brought to life with a sorcerer's wand.

"May we help you? Something special for you?" one of the life-size dolls asked.

"Yes, please!" Sophie smiled and asked if they carried miniature tea sets.

"Of course, we do! Oh yes, I order them myself, a whole shelf of them." She spoke from behind the counter, spectacles on her nose, pen in hand. "My sister will show you." The woman's mirror image appeared before Sophie, steering her by her right elbow, leading to a choice of ten beautifully crafted sets, small enough for Barbie dolls. She wished she had room to bring them all back to Oregon. She would settle on one now, but pledged right then and there that she would start a collection of miniature teacups and stemware when she got home. Sophie selected a resin set, painted shades of yellow and gold and carved to look like ears of corn. Overlaid on the ears of corn were carved parrots with painted beaks of gold. Corn for Mabon, the Second Harvest Feast, Parrot symbolizing the Spirit Realms, shades of yellow because the Sun is in the Air Sign of Libra, the Autumnal Equinox, 5:51 on Sunday morning. The set would be perfect. She would fill the cups and teapot full of kosher grape juice and toast all the Spirit Helpers and the Little People for their love and inspiration.

Sophie was delighted and placed the set on the counter, the sitting sister commenting on her choice: "My favorite! I love parrots. They talk to me, you know." The old woman smiled sweetly and Sophie was inspired to make her purchase pile larger. She added t-shirts for both Dylan and her, and brimmed hats, and a travel tote, all with the flying Witch insignia of Salem. Added to her purchases from the Historical Society on Pressing Day, she was satisfied with her travel kitsch.

The purchases were bagged, the tea set carefully boxed for travel, when she noticed the time: twenty minutes to six. "Time to make our move, Dylan. Thank you, ladies, we enjoyed your shop." The women smiled warmly and locked the shop doors behind them, closing early because of the crowd expected. There was an Old Salem family wedding scheduled for six at St. Peter's Church, the sisters informed Sophie. The lot had had perhaps ten vehicles in it when they left for the import shop. Not an extra parking space was available by the time they walked back to the SUV. They wouldn't have had a base of operations if they were not early getting downtown. Sophie rolled her eyes and felt grateful.

She took a deep breath and looked across the street at the long line of guests arriving, women dressed in silk gowns in warm Autumn hues and men in dark suits and tuxedos. It was a lavish affair. The police directed traffic, making way for the horse-drawn carriages, with women drivers in top hats, dressed in beautiful English riding clothes.

Cars had squeezed in on both sides of the SUV, giving no room to open the doors. Getting into the vehicle was almost impossible. Some of Sophie's important tools were in the front seat, blocked, with only an arm's width to reach in. How ironic, Sophie thought. What were the odds it was a Confederacy wedding. These, their cars, blocking her entrance to the tools she needed most to make the Integration possible. She didn't have the time for this drama. She opened the back hatch and implored Dylan to crawl in and get her bags from the front seat, which he did without protest, only minutes now before they had to start.

Poe and Dora, five minutes late, sauntered to the car, mesmerized by the wedding, the pomp, the clothes, the grandeur of the event unfolding, exactly on the same sidewalks they would have to walk, dodging hundreds of guests, children, horses, a calliope of excitement.

"Sophie, look at the sky, now!" Dora implored. Sophie arranged the over-shirt she was pulling on and looked up as Dora had ordered. There, one moment a sky of blue, only a hint of coming sunset. The next, deep misty yellow, behind a sharp black horizon of buildings still recognizable three hundred years after their creation. A rising three-quarter Harvest Moon, glowing orange, beaming through the rapidly growing darkness.

"What did we expect? It's seven minutes to six. Giles is ready for his constitutional." Sophie layered on her black fleece vest and purple rainbow gloves, her second pair, fastening a Maglite flashlight to her right wrist. "See? My lantern." Everybody nodded, remembering Sophie's lectures about Indian people being adaptable, using whatever materials at their disposal for their Medicine and magick. Every pocket she had, in shirts, pants, and vest, were crammed with Celtic sea salt, charms, sacred herbs, an inhaler, lozenges and hard candies, maple sugar, shiny new pennies, nickels, and dimes. Dylan would carry her pack. She wanted her arms free to swing at her sides, pacing her arms with her legs' strides. She planned on building friction, kinetic energy, as she walked. Luckily, the day had darkened and gotten gusty, cooling the air rapidly. They were all cold, standing, preparing their gear beside Sophie.

They stared at her, blazing the sight of her into their memory banks, knowing she would change after Integration. Dylan grabbed Sophie's face between his hands and looked deeply into her hazel eyes. "Dylan, I don't have time for this. I love you, but you must back off, give me room to breathe!" Dylan felt like crying—he wanted sympathy and all he received was a snippy remark. Not how he wanted to remember Sophie, in case she didn't survive the Walk.

There were rumors. At least once a decade, a supposed crazy woman, past her prime, wearing the title of High Priestess, came to Salem, usually in September, to set Giles free from his haunting. These misguided, although well-intentioned women were of the mindset that the Corey Curse was in full force and everybody needed freedom from it, Giles most of all, bless their hearts. They didn't know the curse was Corwin fiction. Giles was not responsible for such foolishness; he simply wanted to kill them for their abuses, slowly. This is where the rumors came in: at least three women in Sophie's age group had been killed trying to free Giles. Two, exactly ten years apart, had died because of hit-and-run drivers. These unfortunates died during Donald Putnam's time as Dragon's Head; the title stuck in the eighteenth century, the Big Boss, *the man.*

Dylan thought of all the traffic distractions on the Integration Walk, the enormous wedding party, the horse-driven carriages, coming and going. Many road hazards dared discovery this evening, and the road and sidewalk work being done ran one quarter of the loop of Howard Street Cemetery. Dylan saw Sophie leading the way with her tiny flashlight, walking without a sidewalk on Route 107, Bridge Street, and cringed to think of the possibilities. The traffic was frantic—and in the dark, Sophie dressed in a black vest—it was an accident waiting to happen, so many variables. Deep in thought, worrying, viewing many possibilities, Dylan sighed in Sophie's direction and realized there was nothing he could do, other than believe in her. The rest was in Spirit's hands. Sophie seemed to hear Dylan's realization—she smiled, winked, and nodded in his direction, a three-way sign of knowing. She knew his confusion, could feel it—it raced her own sense of doubt, so she had to beat it back, before it destroyed her confidence.

The route consisted of five full clockwise revolutions of Howard Street Cemetery. Giles was famous for walking a straight line, from the corner of Bridge and Howard Streets, to the corner of Howard and Brown Streets. Sophie wanted the entire long rectangular-shaped area covered, since Giles's Pressing Place, the whole of the Old Salem jailhouse property, Howard Street Cemetery, and two churches, Episcopal and Catholic, were also within the rectangular block. Lots of juice. In addition, dozens of houses, densely packed, dating from the late seventeenth and early eighteenth centuries, filled every other available nook and cranny in the area. Once the five revolutions were complete, Sophie would turn down Brown Street, follow Brown till it crossed New Liberty, crossing Essex Street to Liberty Street, till they came to Charter Street and the red line. One full revolution of Charter Street Cemetery would signal Haunting Giles's final tour, destined to walk no more. Five miles, perhaps more, by the time they wound their way back to St. Peter's Street.

Time was shifting, church bells rang, seconds before the hour, while the group passed the *"Bingo! Every Friday Night at 6 p.m."* sign. The wedding guests filed into the church, freeing up the sidewalk. Things were as they needed to be. This was Sophie's ultimate love story. She would marry two of her lifetime personalities, one female, one male, and create one working whole, aged and consolidated, balanced, one Core Being. Sophie thought of the true essence of a First-Degree Wicca Initiation, the marriage of corporeal and spiritual Selves, joined with the mortar of the Middle World, pride and the ego, the world of manifestation and magick. Higher and lower bodies joined, the white robes, the white flowers, white the color of innocence, of blending, containing all possibilities and colors, like marriage itself.

Sophie took a determined right into the parking lot, the Pressing Place, just being locked by a security guard. Before the lock was fastened, Sophie asked the guard if she could leave something in the lot—it would only take a minute. He looked confused and a bit vexed, but relented and let her slip in, as he stood looking at his watch, pretending to time her movements. She ran to the far end of the chain-link fence, closest to the jail, and tied the bundle at eye level, the best she could do. She quickly searched for Dylan's bundle, tied on Wednesday. It had been removed. But just beyond the fence, on the handle of the doorknob of the garden shed, a lone bundle on red ribbon gently swayed in the growing wind. Sophie smiled and quickly threw a handful of herbs and sugar into the sinkhole and was out of the enclosure before the guard had a chance to say a word.

Sophie tried to breathe her anxiety away. She hadn't even officially begun her Walk and the chaos and the building tension was hard to handle. She could feel her spine pump with rising blood pressure and her head throb with a tension headache. She had five miles to go and had to get started now, before her courage waned. It was beginning to leak out on the edges of her sanity. She took a deep cleansing breath, looked at her confused friends, and nodded to them with a slight smile. "Let's get started." She took a hard right on the sidewalk on St. Peter's Street and instantly felt stinging on her left side. A racing bicycle flew by the group, touching Sophie, a feather's distance separating her from the biker. The bike came to a sliding stop. The teenage biker—eighteen, muscular, and heavily tattooed—stood in front of the party. He stared at Sophie, standing with his arms crossed. The reason for the sign of intimidation was not evident to the party; they were jarred by this young man's aggressive behavior toward them, too confused to be shaken up.

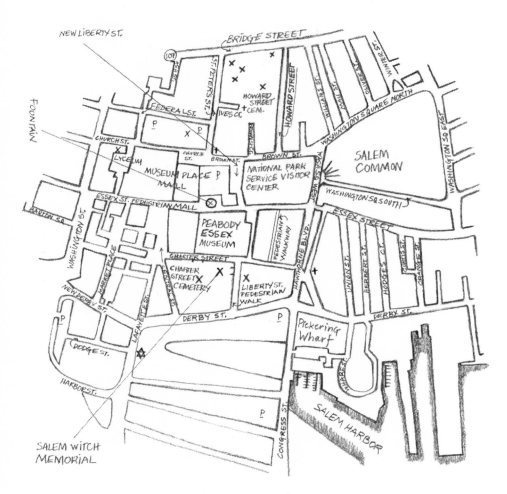

Salem Old Town & Integration Walk

Sophie, frustrated, a young thug blocking her progress, turned on the switch of her flashlight and shined it in the biker's face. She would equal the sides with her own forms of intimidation. She moved forward, adjusting her hat, intent on beginning the first lap of Giles's route. She walked directly for the biker, eyes locked, flashlight making long sweeping motions, back and forth, yards ahead of her path. Feet away, the biker looked shocked, jumped on his bike, and turned the corner. The group called the corner Pigeon Bend, because of the thousands of psycho dancing birds. The biker rode at full clip into the burial grounds, taking a sharp right and came to a halt. He stood above her—the ground elevated and held up by a stone wall—the sidewalk at least eight feet below him. He rested under a huge oak tree, filled with other teenagers dressed in similar bedraggled black, holey fashion. Sophie quickly counted thirteen. She scanned the area, seeing coolers, piles of blankets, and tins of food. This was their place. Sophie was now the intruder.

Sophie's first corner was directly in front of the Salem Victorian Jail Complex, protected from the road by yet another chain-link fence. Few people realized the decrepit brick building with its Victorian turrets, walks, and windows, boarded against vandals and the elements, was next to the actual Old Salem Jailhouse of 1692 legend, where almost two hundred people rotted, some for over a year, deep in the basement gaol. Sophie stepped onto the highway, now dark, cars whistling by on the state road under construction. Dylan held his breath, watching Sophie navigate the traffic from the distance of about half a block.

When Sophie walked directly under the huge, multitrunked tree, the kids began whistling strange catcalls, calling Sophie out, demanding attention, asking her intention. "Whatcha doin' with that flashlight? Hey, like Giles Corey's old lantern, tryin' to scare us? Good luck, you old bitch, nobody frightens us, we do the scaring round here!"

Sophie endured the harassment, pretending to be unafraid; she kept on walking, until all three of her friends were caught under the tree. Sophie stopped, and said, "Why are you pestering us? We have a job to do, one not involving you. We are not interested in keeping you from your tree, leave us to our walking, please." Sophie held her ground, until her friends were within feet of her. "What say you?" called Sophie, authority in her voice.

The older biker, the one trying to intimidate the party earlier, crossed the cement-covered top of the embankment—holding Howard Street Cemetery together—and placed his arms over his chest in a menacing fashion. Sophie stood with her legs apart, arms crossed, head up, looking far more menacing than the teenager, as adrenaline pumped furiously under her cool features. "Well?" she called. The young man gave one up-and-down shake of his head, an affirmative sign. Sophie returned the same sign and turned her back on her friends and continued around the second corner to Howard Street.

Sophie could feel Giles. What little hair she had left on her body, between stylists hell-bent on shaving her head and Indian ancestry, stood at attention. Adrenaline shot through her system, prompting her to throw up. She stopped the anxiety reflex in time and began, in all earnest, to begin her Walk afresh, unafraid of the territorial corner-pissing of the teenagers. Not surprised—birds by day, teenagers by night, chaos 24/7. Sophie felt pity for the Haunting Spirits caught in and on this ground, on the fringes of John Marston's Army of the Dead, close, but leaderless in comparison to Charter Street.

She became aware of several young men, under the direction of the tattooed biker, following her Walk from the inside the burial ground boundaries. She felt oddly comforted by their presence. There would be no solitary ambushes with kids as witnesses. What was she afraid of at this point? Were all the distractions this evening intentional roadblocks to Sophie's Work, or were they manifestations of the collective unconscious, many people feeling her anticipation and impatience? Oh, how she wanted this to be over, ended finally! She much preferred a good memory to an anxious ride.

Howard Street had an incline, not particularly noticeable in the center of the block but by the end, your calves are stretched too taut from the uphill pull. Brown Street, a sharp right, clockwise, surrounded by bricks. People dressed in their finery, walking between wedding parties, coming and going from the fashionable restaurants scattered throughout the pedestrian mall. They smiled at Sophie; she nodded back, maintaining a stern, far-away look. How many couples were out tonight instead of tomorrow, Mabon, the seventh Witches Sabbat of the year? Massachusetts, with all of its old money, had old money Witches, different from their Western counterparts all glitzed-out like Halloween in Las Vegas, always a party. Halloween in Salem was a front, a sham; the old money Witches made it so. Old money sentiment suited Sophie's temperament; the tradition was grounding and took its superior place in the pecking order.

Halfway down Brown Street, Sophie heard the hooves of horses standing in place. The carriages, bedecked with flowers, streamers, and a professionally lettered sign, "*Just Married*," awaited her at the corner of St. Peter's Street. On one side of the Episcopal church, which was built of brick and stone and old growth pine from Northern woods, finished with local oak and cherry, was a fenced area, tiny, perhaps five feet wide and thirty feet long, crammed with dozens of gravestones. The bodies must have been stacked when buried, to fit in such a congested area. She noticed bits of burnt-sienna-colored dust across the church front, where the brick of the church's basement met the reinforced cement brick-paved sidewalk. Reaching the front door, she noticed whole chunks of brick separated from the church because of extreme temperatures, she guessed. The brick lay in scattered piles, dust and debris, slowly moved by the wind. This is our Essex County clay, Sophie thought. Dylan had taken the cornerstone brick from the jailhouse, but its charge was so negative you could not wear pieces of it as amulets. It would have to be packed away in cloth, surrounded with sacred herbs and salt. But these small shards would be perfect. She hesitated by the front doors of the church until the others caught up to her. Signaling with Spirit Sign, she directed her friends to look at the ground and shined the Maglite over the piles of brick shards. The three looked confused and never did figure out the reference. Once the Walk was completed, Sophie decided she would collect several piles of brick shards for jewelry-making projects and charms. Perfect, she thought, clay from hallowed ground, just as Spirit had directed. Paired with cobalt blue beads, she could create a powerful charm for psychopomp and Oracle Work.

The long rows of yew trees, thick with orange fruit, brought the memory of their adventure on Wednesday to mind. Just a few yards after the bingo sign and Ives Court would mark one full revolution. Four more to go. She felt detached from the pain in her body. It was there but did not cloud her path. Challenge mode was her reality and it showed, no longer afraid of the Bogie Man. She began the second revolution.

Several bicycles monitored her progress but kept their distance. They became sacred witnesses, as Spirit requested. The relationship between the kids and Sophie had morphed, become beneficial. They knew the power of what she was doing and had figured out Sophie and the three were on some kind of magickal mission, a walking ritual having to do with Giles Corey. The freaky Goth kids in and around the oak tree were Giles's loyal fans; they had read everything they could find about the old sailing man turned farmer. One of the older boys had memorized the governor's witness's account of

Giles's pressing; another had acquired a replica copy of Giles's original land deed from the Peabody Essex Museum and kept it on him, folded tightly and placed in his wallet, alongside a fresh condom; he was always well stocked.

There were three sixteen-year-old girls who actually saw Giles—the reason they met in the oak tree every Friday night at sunset, weather permitting. From the ancient oak's tall branches, Giles's entire haunting walk, corner to corner, was visible. The three young women were held apart from the others in the Circle, sensitively treated and revered because of their Second Sight talents. The young women were positioned high in the tree, ready and able to signal the others if they spotted movement in or around the grounds or the roads surrounding them. Trouble from Spirit or human was easily detected. The three were defined by fashion: one with purple streaks in red hair, dressed in colorful capris and friendship bracelets matching her hair; one dressed in black from head to toe, including nail polish, lipstick, eyebrow pencil, draped with stainless steel chain; the third, a butchy Chica in cut-offs three sizes too large and a near-shaved head. Sophie could relate to each personality, saw a bright future for all three if they remained patient and stayed put, making Salem their base of operations. Would they offer future competitive balance for the Inner Circle? Surely they would feel and see Giles's departure from this place. They would miss him and try to will him back, although Sophie would reason with them in the Ethers, away from the week-to-week dramas and seasonal changes of Salem.

Sophie turned the corner from the highway onto Howard Street for the second time. She expected to feel Giles again, to feel static electricity as she had the revolution before. This time, she saw him, a faint outline, six feet tall, clean, with a regal bearing, wearing a brown felted wool hat. He was in the pink of health, in age his prime, fifty perhaps, chest swollen with pride. He carried a lantern, four-sided, with a large top handle; he swayed the lantern side to side as he walked. Sophie copied his motion, sending a solid stream of light from the Maglite on her right wrist, from one side of the narrow lane to the other, jammed with houses and graves. Sophie and Giles were dancing a slow Fire Dance—light their inspiration, Giles with company, the best kind: his own. They were in sync, Sophie and Giles, although both were challenged to keep it that way. Sophie speeded up her pace, stepping with long strides; her legs were short. Sophie was five-foot-four compared to Giles's six-foot height, but she persisted. Giles slowed and shortened his gait, as much as he could and still walk with power and command. Confidence was his secret to the walk; Haunting Giles loved his Friday night display of bravado. In the Spirit Realms, he was whole and fierce and frightened his enemies, the East-West sway of his lantern daring challenge from petrified onlookers, especially if they smelled anything of guilt. Giles loved to scare his adversaries; it would have to do as a substitute for evening the score through murder, his true desire, although since Sophie's committed partnership to help him/them heal three years before, his blood lust had waned considerably.

The kids sensed movement. None could see Giles, but all felt him. Something had changed; they could see parts of Giles's shadow, his lantern, the synchronized back and forth sway of Sophie and Giles together, but they only saw Sophie's outline and profile as she walked with a determined stride, too long for her body to keep up for long. She looked taller, stronger, her back straighter as she swung her right lighted arm.

The wedding crowd had thinned considerably on the second turn of Brown Street. Giles faded at the corner, the end of his walk, till another bend of Bridge and Howard was taken. Sophie felt relief, able to slow her pace and take her accustomed stride. Giles was hard to slow down for. His legs ruled his movement. Both Giles and Sophie walked with solid shoulders, John Wayne style, always one step ahead of a fight.

Streetlights lit the outer perimeter of the pedestrian mall, the museum, and visitor center. The sky grew blacker with each step to the West. A steady white mist moved in from the sea behind her, light at Sophie's heels. The bricks held the heat of the day, making rippling rising patterns in the mist as the cool sea air hit the warm brick paving. Sophie felt as if she were in the center of a humidifier, or a snow globe before it was shaken, the skin between her shirt and gloves ice cold and clammy.

The streets were clearing out. Only muffled sounds of pre- and post-diners, high heels tapping and clicking on bricks, were heard. Sophie rarely felt the three friends accompanying her. Occasionally she heard Dylan's cough, or Poe's sniffle, a strange heel-toe staccato from Dora's labored steps, but they were removed, secondary. She was transported between the worlds, her constant trails of Sage grounding her steps in the Middle World, ensuring her return to corporeal reality. Walking rituals encapsulated pilgrims in energetic bubbles, which grow with the friction of their intentional movement. The bubble insulates the walker from spiritual harm, although it does not muffle the senses of the physical planes. The walker maintains a space of knowing calm, separated but united with the world, breathing the same air. The horses were now gone, gone with the darkness, with the mist, the newlywed couple sheltered from the foggy cool, now warm and toasting with champagne.

For the third time, Sophie stepped off the jailhouse curb onto the buzzing highway, the mist lifted over the oak tree, the teenagers quiet in their witnessing. Young men followed at a safe and distant pace from her, in and out of the grounds, on foot and bike. They were the only people she saw now.

A tall protoplasmic cloud the shape and height of Giles waited for her at the corner. As she turned, Giles stepped with her, closer than the last lap, their strides feeling carefully choreographed. Sophie could smell pipe Tobacco. It clung to Giles's woolen coat and hat, a sweet and earthy smell, familiar and not unpleasant, but far different from Padre Pio's Tobacco bouquet.

Lights switched on and dogs were released into yards, barking at the sound of Sophie's long footsteps in the loose gravel by the side of Howard Street, dirt and rock forced from the ground by the dancing feet and wings of thousands of birds. Sophie and Giles were walking through bird footprints, the Bird Goddesses of Eastern Europe, Sophie thought, pantheon focus and code for the Dance of the Shaman, her dance of transformation. Luxuriating in the feeling of working in harmony with Giles, she regretfully parted with him at the corner of Brown Street. She longed for him to be at her side: it was difficult to go on without him.

By the fourth revolution, the teenagers had stationed a boy in each corner of the grounds, sitting on top of white five-gallon buckets. One of the kids must work at a pizza parlor, Sophie thought: a good recycling effort. Giles waited for her, but instead of walking close to Sophie, he stepped into her left leg, halfway in and halfway out of her body. She could feel her body stretch in height, finally fitting her abnormally large chest and ribcage—her head felt aligned in the right place for the first time. With Giles's right side of his body joined to Sophie's left, he no longer held a lantern. Instead, Sophie could feel the burning metal light box where her heart was, not in place of her heart, but in conjunction with it, fueling it. She felt braver, though her Maglite was alone. Sophie and Giles made a solitary shadow, distinct from the lap before. One of the girls noticed a shift and signaled to one of the corner guardians with the light of a large flashlight, the size of a small square breadbox. Sophie felt quieter; a subtle shift had begun within her, not a calming as she thought earlier, a deepening. Haunting Giles entered

Sophie's body at the approximate age of fifty, close to Sophie's real-time age. She felt relieved he took the form of a virile man in his late prime, instead of his bloodied, battered end-self. She was grateful, to say the least!

Now parallel with the front entrance of the burial grounds, in the center of the block on Howard, she noticed a light source from within the grounds, where she had created the Medicine Wheel in Captain Gardner's honor last Sunday. The light looked different, smaller, more concentrated than the flashlights of the teenagers. She felt she was being watched, felt uneasy, but with Giles filling half her body, she felt full of piss and vinegar and ready for a fight. For a change, she wasn't worried.

The last revolution began with whirling mist, circling, engulfing her, her magickal bubble discovered and outlined by the swirling whiteness. No longer alone, Giles was walking inside her, sharing her left side from head to toe. He looked down on the top of Sophie's head, trying to feel her next move. She was tired and thirsty. Warm apple cider would do the trick, she thought, followed by a smile of acknowledgment. Would apple replace dark chocolate as her favorite flavor now? Sophie would strike a bargain and agree to shared-sweet status, Giles reminding Sophie he loved coconut, especially from Putnam Pantry. She realized she was having an internal dialogue with Giles; he was no longer outside her in ghostly form—he was inside her, a piece of her—they were swapping stories and tastes already. Sophie grinned and felt like skipping when she began the fifth revolution in front of the Pressing Place. Giles reminded Sophie to not get carried away: they still had work to do and a long way to go before they completely melded.

Sophie looked up, wanting to see the three young women, the gifted Seers of the group, but saw no one sitting in the tree. Instead, they lined the rise over Route 107, looking down on Sophie's progressive line, the final revolution in progress. All three of the young Witches saw Giles sharing Sophie's stride. They knew what was happening and were joyful.

Sophie felt a jerking back into the Middle World of concrete manifestation, back from latching on to the prayers of the three young women. As she stepped around the bend onto Howard Street, she thanked the young women for their love and support and tugged the brim of her hat to let them know she was thinking about them, was grateful to them. If she hadn't been retiring, she would have taken their numbers and called them when they turned eighteen. Sophie stopped her crazy wanderings, thought of the ultimate failure of training Dora as her heir, and breathed into the now.

She felt as if toilet paper was stuck to the bottom of her left shoe. She shook it once and it seemed to grow, felt longer and heavier. She looked down and realized it was gauze, yards of it, manifesting from the Ethers, coming out the bottom of her pant leg. It was then she realized Giles wasn't there, not his left side, only the gauze of his bindings was left. She wasn't alone, so what had happened?

Sophie walked on, not noticing the tears and embraces of the three young women, now collapsed in each other's arms, taking credit for Haunting Giles's release. They had watched from above, standing on the cement ledge, as Giles stepped completely into Sophie, fused with her. They knew Giles was now a fifty-something woman, short and stout. They didn't have to know why. Later they would research. One of the boys had found a website the year before about a large three- by four-foot painting of Giles Corey, dressed in the cloth of clouds, called *The Emancipation of Giles Corey*. The girls didn't trust the source, so they didn't give it a second thought. They would now investigate and find out who this middle-aged woman was, the same age as their mothers.

Sophie could hear Giles clearing his throat. It felt odd. He was talking from inside her head. It echoed strangely, sounding tinny: "*Bend down and pull the rest of the gauze from my foot. Do it now, Sophie. You'll see why!*"

She stopped, looked around, and saw a man slowly creeping toward her. His approach was determined. He was under the illusion he had not been seen. He had a video camera and was crouched low, shooting. Sophie recognized him and would give him time to catch up to her. He was Brian-the-monk, Robert Ellis Cahill's anonymous Spirit photographer. Sophie remembered that one of his favorite places to shoot was Howard Street, from six to nine o'clock on Friday evenings, when the mist came in thick from the ocean. Of course, it was Brian.

Sophie could hear Giles say: "*Are you ready, woman? Tear the last bit of gauze from our leg now!*" Sophie complied with one hard yank. She felt faint. Giles totally merged with her. They had one system. He would whisper now, not yell, not demand. They would work together. She took a deep cleansing breath and looked directly into Brian's camera—the red flash now visible—only yards from her face. She smiled broadly at him, tipped her hat in his direction, and stood tall, ready to complete the Walk.

Behind the Catholic Church, on the South end of the burial ground, the tattooed biker whistled by, coming to a skidding halt in the last ring of bird gravel, creating a soft cloud of filth, which slowly drifted to the ground in the heavy mist. He righted himself, balancing his bike behind his knees. Defiantly, he stood before her with his arms crossed, revealing a continuous pattern of tattooed snake from one arm to the other, beautiful greens and violets coming into view, the color sparked by the shining porch lights. Sophie walked up to him as before, though not shining the Maglite in his eyes this time.

"They chose you to protect them," she said. "They will need you, sooner rather than later. Stay close and keep your eyes open!" Sophie smiled warmly at the young man, now melting, his eyes filled with tears. He nodded softly, no doubt feeling more afraid than he ever been before, knowing Sophie was right. They would need him, the three of them. Their combined power would surpass three hundred years of Inner Circle work.

Sophie walked on, noticing Brian-the-monk had followed her out to the street where he continued to shoot video footage. Sophie felt the agitation of the biker, who was about to storm in Brian's direction. She knew he was trying to stay calm, but she needed to soothe his actions, make him think before he acted. "Let him be! He filmed this Walk, Haunting Giles filling me with his Spirit. My job is not done—I have other stops to make. I need witnesses, Spirit has deemed it so. I want you to urge the photographer to follow you. You must tell the three girls they need to see what is going to happen at Charter Street in a few minutes. Go and be useful, please, and protect my friends while you are at it." Sophie encouraged him with a dictatorial edge he found familiar and comforting. She was sure he was grateful for the focus.

Sophie rounded the corner of Brown Street. The back brick wall of the Salem Visitor's Center, now dark, shed strange shadows on the street. She zipped her vest entirely closed, covering most of her mouth, the chill in her bones growing as her steps turned left on New Liberty Street. She would cut across the backs of important buildings and attractions and wind her way down to Charter Street Cemetery. On the fringe of the pedestrian mall, a narrow wooded walkway connected New Liberty Street to the grounds of the Peabody Essex Museum, where so many secrets were stored. Sophie's mind was on Charter Street, not entirely in the here and now. Without thinking of the possible physical dangers surrounding her, she walked into the dark walkway. She had stopped to adjust the herbs in her vest pocket when she realized people were standing and sitting, lined up on both sides of the walkway. She began recognizing faces and clothes, the white-and-red striped socks of one of Dorothy's Goth kids; she had friends in the strangest places. She waited until she could hear her friends' footsteps behind her, signaling all was well, before she moved on and faced Charter Street Cemetery once more.

On the Eastern point of the burial ground, across the street from Dorothy's shop, stood Walking Giles. Sophie had worked with Walking Giles planning the Walk; he was waiting for her as planned. Sophie would only come to the burial grounds if the integration of Haunting Giles had been successful. She could plainly see Giles's smirk as she crossed the street, her path lit by enormous floodlights of the museum. As Sophie stood next to Walking Giles, he reached out to her, feeling the energy of Haunting Giles in her body. He had tried to get Haunting Giles's attention to no avail for centuries. Now, here he was, close and touchable. Walking Giles reached out and softly placed his left hand on Sophie's Solar Plexus, feeling her Core change, grow, making room for him. *Excellent!* is all he said.

He urged Sophie to walk on the inside of the path for the clockwise revolution of the grounds. "It has to be so, Giles!" Sophie snapped, already taking charge of the two men, one from the inside, one from the outside.

She didn't recognize this direction. She felt a strange vertigo. Remembering the group's intense hand-to-hand counter-clockwise revolutions, she slowed her pace. Feeling fatigue and low blood sugar, she whined internally until Walking Giles softly tapped her on her left shoulder and said, *We're here and we are fine, Sophie. Please rejoice. Our work is near its end!* He tenderly squeezed Sophie's shoulder, knowing his life was changing, would never be the same, a different kind of prison, Sophie's body. Eventually it would become his hallowed Temple and a way to gain more power than he had ever dreamed. It would be fine, he thought. Feeling shy, he snatched his hand away, like a child burning himself on the stove for the first time. He was not used to showing his emotions openly. His life was destined to change completely now, knowing Sophie lived for raw, open, unedited emotion. Even if it hurt, the feeling was genuine and therefore of lasting value, according to her worldview.

When Giles and Sophie turned right on Derby Street, on the backside of the burial grounds, Sophie's heart started to race faster the closer they both got to the imprinted hand in the cement grout of the stone wall. Giles and Sophie stood touching sides, in front of the hand, and sighed in unison. Sophie placed her left hand in the imprint; Giles reached over Sophie and placed his right hand over Sophie's left. They breathed in unison. They were aware of Sophie's friends standing still at the corner, watching, wondering what was going on. The light was strange with multiple sources, Spirits and Prana, creating mini-whirlwinds and unexpected reflections. They also knew they were being watched by several bikers across the street, figuring the three girls were close to the Witch Memorial waiting for pyrotechnics. They breathed deeply. Sophie did a Cobra Breath, opening her Kundalini, connecting Root with Crown, with one deeply violent breath, transporting her into a higher level of consciousness. The Cobra Breath was accumulative in its effects, building through the years; it was second nature for Sophie now. As the last bit of breath was forced out of Sophie's lungs on her exhale, Giles downloaded his memory banks into hers, his memories blending with hers, finally sharing each other's thoughts without guesswork and special timing.

The mist cleared. One shudder of thunder and the skies opened and a fresh chill rain fell. Giles and Sophie faced each other, looking at the reflection of their joint future. Finally snapped awake by Dylan's cough, they began moving again, walking hand-in-hand, continuing the final burial-ground revolution. They walked in step, feeling like pull-apart rolls before the point of separation. They created heat, their intention blending, their need fierce to become one. Sophie had never felt so powerful a draw, not ever, in trance or sex. This need for another to complete oneself was a frighteningly new experience. Their eyes filled with tears, feeling like a floodgate ready to open, a back-up of hot mustard, inspiring a good sneeze. Close to the final corner of the revolution, they noticed the three young women across the street on the lawn of the museum, eyes glued to the Dance drawing to a close. When they passed the colonial sign of the burial grounds, they heard Miss Mary clearing her throat. They looked ahead and found her settling into a place on the opposite wall on the corner of Charter and Liberty—she was ready for the show. Their attention was pulled to the right, to the three rusted anchors, their sign of the three Coreys—yes, Giles, Martha, and Mary. But, most important, the three of them: Walking Giles, Haunting Giles, and Sophie in all her complexities just a little bit bigger, so many memories she held, both their Cores now blended. Walking Giles and Sophie—both understanding Haunting Giles was no longer an independent entity—stopped, embraced, and stepped back from each other for the last time. They looked at each other, noticing their similarities, feeling their differences, both wondering how it would feel in ten minutes, tomorrow, or next year. They were nervous, but not afraid. They each took one step forward into each other's body. Right leg into left, left into right, torsos matched, Giles's ribcage fitting perfectly into Sophie's chest, her spine feeling more stabilized than it had in years.

Sophie felt full, her hunger placated by the girth of two full-grown men over six feet tall living inside her. She headed directly for Miss Mary. Close enough to touch, Miss Mary said, "Good to see you, Giles. I wanted to tell you I am feeling better now, since the middle of last week, have been feeling pretty spry. I will be leaving this place by Halloween. I have a home to go to now. Thank you. I have hope; I no longer need abuse to feel whole—just wanted to let you know." She bowed her head, pulled her blanket tightly around her round body, and sat down on the wall, watching Sophie walk away.

Sophie wound her way back the way she had come, feeling different, light-headed, overstimulated, and prickly cold. Her nerves were frayed, her body exhausted. The walkway crowd of admiring teenagers had evaporated, their leaders now gone, the show over, their future courses set. She crossed Essex Street to her familiar turn onto Brown Street, a half a block from the church on St. Peter's Street. She chuckled, first soft little muted sounds, then whoops and cheers, Dylan, Dora, and Poe joining in the chorus.

Sophie stopped and waited for her friends to catch up to her. Being this close made no difference—separation was no longer necessary. The Integration had occurred, twice, successfully. She smiled at them and shined her flashlight, illuminating the small piles of brick shards. "Hey, y'all, didn't you see what I was showing you?" Of course they hadn't, but Sophie liked to state the obvious. "It's our clay! Usable pieces, from hallowed ground, as Spirit deemed. Dylan, you have the supplies we need for the Pressing Place?" Dylan smiled and nodded affirmatively. No one was about to talk until the Walk was complete. It didn't matter how chatty Sophie would get—they wouldn't relent. Sophie quieted and smiled, hearing them clearly in her mind. A sharp right and they stood where they had begun, seeing the red Honor Bundle hanging on the chainlink fence, lighted by the mounted posts on the Morency Complex.

Dylan took off Sophie's pack and handed it to her. All of them were transfixed, the light shifting and eerie, the Moon, now out and almost full, the floodlights, the protoplasm, and the last clinging masses of heavy mist. Sophie had divided the Challah earlier, an enormous loaf Dylan had proudly gathered on his way to pick Sophie up at the hotel. She brought out a bag containing five small pieces of the bread and a small bottle of kosher grape juice and four paper cups from the hotel. She crouched close to the ground, took out a votive candle, and lit it. She smiled, and then she cried, the prayers eluding her. She surrendered to the ground and sat on the blacktop and poured four glasses of grape juice.

"Shabbat Shalom!
May our Mother Shekinah and all the Lords of Israel
bless and keep you all the days of your life.
This is the New Jerusalem, it is so! Amen!"

Carefully, she handed out the cups of grape juice with a "Blessed Be!" When it came time to fill her glass, she raised it to the Waxing Moon over head:

"Blessed Mother mine,
sweet woman of the Moon,
fill us with your knowing and your desire."

She swallowed the juice in one long gulp, saving just a sip for the Mother, which she poured onto the pavement.

"In perfect love, in perfect trust, we drink you, Great Mother!"

Another splash of juice hit the pavement, while they all drank their cups dry. She handed out the pieces of torn Challah. "Blessed Be!" They all ate their pieces, saving a corner for the Spirits, which Dylan expertly threw over the ten-foot fence, all landing in Giles's sinkhole. Dora filled her hand with sunflower nuts and threw them through the fence. Sophie wondered what the sunflower pattern meant. Giles would have to teach her how to read the shells. Wouldn't the meanings translate to sunflower nuts?

On the way back to the SUV, in the now deserted parking lot, Sophie started going over the list of things to complete before the honoring ceremonies began in the morning. The supplies were gathered, mostly, Dylan acquiring extras of all the foodstuffs. He was good at gathering and so generous—it always worked in his favor.

Sophie melted into her seat in the car, not wanting to talk. She didn't have to worry; her friends were silent, not a word was spoken about anything, not until Sophie and Dylan were alone in their suite at the Marriott in Peabody.

Dylan looked at Sophie, the bathroom light shining into the dining area of the common room. "Wow," he sighed, his voice heavy, his energy drained but unusually awake, alive. All the hours of concentration, ceremony, ritual, focused energy now seven days strong made the ringing in his ears deafening.

They sat at the table, Sophie eating oatmeal, Dylan eating dry cereal and milk. Suppers for heroes, Sophie thought, modesty now a commodity of the past. They would look up from time to time, eyes filled with tears, looking over the items for the Liberation Feast Altar: pieces of Essex County clay from hallowed ground, just as ordered, a black metal anvil from Saugus, Giles's Maglite lantern, maple syrup from New Hampshire, candies from Putnam Pantry, spiced rum for the Witch Memorial, the pink satin sash from Graves Beach, oak leaves from Sawyer's Hill, sticks for wand-making from Charter Street and Pentucket Cemetery, beach glass from Singing Beach, the miniature tea set for a toast to the Little People, the Earth Spirits. The story faced them, their journey illustrated with objects. The white roses and red ribbon, tasks to be completed. They would take their time; their energy needed to be rationed until they got home to Oregon. They cried together until their bowls were empty. Now the real Thanksgiving Feast would follow, tomorrow night, Yom Kippur, the Day of Atonement, on the Autumnal Equinox, on the three-hundred-fifteenth anniversary of the last Witch hanging in Salem. They sat silently, in the dim room, too tired to move, too overwhelmed to speak.

Finally unable to hold her head up, Sophie kissed Dylan good night and crawled into her soft bed. She began dreaming before she was able to recite her nightly prayers…

The three young women had been little girls when they discovered Giles. One September night, the girls were having a slumber party, while their mothers and nine other women got together and partied downstairs. Caught up in the excitement of their all-night party, fueled by sugar, they wanted to share their secrets and happy times with their mothers. They could hear them talking behind closed doors. They had made a group decision to surprise the women, now chanting familiar tones behind the heavy carved oak door. All three pushed, the double door giving

way during the final Binding Prayer of the ritual. The three children were sur-
prised by the organized ritual, the older women caught in the act of performing it.
They all stood dazed until Aunt Lori asked the girls to join their mothers and finish
the ritual. Lori spoke the Spell Binder, wrapping the last bit of gauze binding over
a large beeswax figure carved in the shape of a man in Puritan dress. They would
burn the effigy later, Lori whispered, thinking the girls could not hear.

The girls loved moving with their mothers, surrounded by other strong wom-
en, bold and beautiful in their flowing robes. They knew the prayers and how to
bid farewell to the Quarters, thanking them for their favor and granting them al-
legiance and faith. They knew the Powers of Earth, Air, Fire, and Water and were
learning about the properties of the Fifth Element, Spirit, the powers of Ether,
on Saturdays, in an organized gathering for Pagan children called the Goddess
Scouts. Before the girls were settled into their sleeping bags in the upstairs loft bed-
room with the Pentacle nightlight, they were told about the Curse of Giles Corey
by Aunt Lori. She snuggled down deep in their piles of pillows and blankets and
told them the short form of the story: they were protecting the interests and health
of Salem and all the families and children of Essex County, protecting them from
the evil curse of an evil man. By the time the girls were thirteen and were feared
by their fellow students in middle school because of the Glamour Magick they all
practiced, they had learned the Inner Circle was a lie. Their mothers imprisoned
Giles for the Putnams, for the money families who bought their Samhain costumes
and Yuletide presents.

The crickets were the first thing Sophie heard. Sarah always said they
were good luck. It was still black outside—the deep night surrounded her.
Spirit had given her a gift-dream; so many blanks were now filled in. Rubbing the sleep from her eyes, she thought of the price of living an extreme
lifestyle, the inevitable backlash. Sophie had seen it a hundred times, kids
born into metaphysical families becoming born-again Christians as adults,
initially out of rebellion, then staying out of fear. It had happened in her
family and destroyed it. The three young women, as focus for their rebellion,
took the ultimate enemy of their mothers, Giles Corey, and befriended him
as their personal project. They knew Haunting Giles well, had known him
for three years, the same amount of time Sophie had been actively working
to integrate Giles. It had taken three long years of rituals, incantations, and

Soul Retrievals to make the American Camino possible. The girls had loved Giles's memory, feeding Sophie long distance, not even realizing each other's power. Sophie had inside connections, more than the Steeles, to the Inner Circle now. She knew where the source was.

Chapter Twenty-Five

THE HONORING
September 22, 2007, 6:00 a.m.

DYLAN ROSE EARLY, EXCITED BY THE PROSPECTS OF THE DAY. He wondered if they would be challenging or pleasurable. Opting for a combination, he was elated and already in a festive mood. No one would cheat him out of his revelry. Success was theirs. The rest didn't factor—Dylan more than subconsciously had moved on. Sophie was still in the shower when he left. Getting to Bagel World for his morning fix was a priority. He intended to shovel as many bagels as he could into his backpack for the trip home. He settled on salt bagels today. The sky had a heat haze to it, muting the Autumn sky to sun-bleached French blue. The wind blew hard enough to infuse air, clothes, and hair with a damp salt smell, fresh, needed in the heat. Saturday was ruled by Saturn, Karma, and fate, Dylan always wore black on Saturday. He was grateful for the haze, his black shirt half soaked already. Fortunately, he had back-up black.

There was a long line when he arrived at Corey Vegetable Stand. He held the atmosphere tight, implanting the knowing of this place, the Fall crops, the warm colors, the pumpkins, the sweet apple smell, pears and nuts and squash. If he concentrated on the blue of the sky, he saw this land through Martha's eyes, walking a rolling countryside in thigh-high grass, humming a fresh tune or a haunting hymn. His mind, if he let it, filled his body with sense-memory, body recognition of place and person.

He bought nuts, freshly roasted here, for the feasting table. The corn was tempting, but he would have to abandon the ears to Dorothy for cooking for Miss Mary on Sunday. All leftovers would go in Mary's direction. Six perfect orange pumpkins were on Sophie's list. They already had the apples cleaned and ready to go. The freshly cut sunflowers were waiting for Dylan. He flushed with recognition at their color and gigantic petals. Sunflowers. He remembered Martha loving them, his favorite flower and spiritual symbol now, still and again. The sunflower's nuts shed, ripe enough for the birds, perfect! He would plant the biggest one on Gallows Hill. He'd find the place. He needed a job today. Carefully, he loaded the organic treasures in the back of the SUV, the sunflowers wrapped in wet paper towels and plastic bags.

He had yet to find a recycling center in Essex County. Oregon seemed advanced in regard to environmental issues and organic offerings. Frustrated, he finally relented and stopped trying—it was their last full day in Peabody and he had other things to occupy him. He filled paper bags at the hotel, clearly labeled "recycle please": the water bottles, glass, and plastic bags, with a five-dollar bill paper-clipped over the lettering. He was mentally composing a letter to hotel management, urging them to recycle more. This measure would have to placate his sense of duty.

He tooled the sleek silver SUV around Peabody, picking up the last of the bits and pieces, including spiced rum. Sophie wanted extra for the memorial. He would miss this sweet ride, a brand new car. His conscience would never allow him to waste the fuel at home, but if he inherited his father's Fortieth Edition collector's red Mustang, fuel costs would become secondary. He smiled at his hypocrisy and shrugged to himself and chuckled, sardonically, barely audible. If he were at home today, he would be cruising around town, doing the weekly shopping and bank deposits, talking to his favorite store clerks, and flirting away the morning on his cell phone and with the pretty post office clerk, the busty blonde in a pony tail. Too quickly his gathering was complete. It was time to focus and begin another grueling day, although he was determined to keep his mood light, despite Gallows Hill, or maybe because of it.

He opened the suite's door to find Sophie finishing the feast invitations, prepared for hand delivery. Thirty-three white roses had been fashioned into fifteen bouquets, honoring a dozen locations and VIPs. Four single roses were kept separate for the Feast Altar. He knew she would later dry them for the copper tin of Salem Spirit Tokens, representing the group of four on the American Camino. Sophie tried to think of everything—an impossible job as everybody knew, but it didn't stop her from trying.

Poe and Dora followed Dylan into the suite, both with full mouths of bagel. Dylan had a salt-sesame bagel for Sophie; she didn't wait to thank him before shoving it into her greedy mouth. She nodded thanks, with a broad smile, stuffed mouth showing white. Boy humor, Dylan loved it. Sophie and Dylan quickly put the ceremonial offerings in boxes just the perfect size. He had found them at the liquor store. He had been the first customer at the local state-owned store. The clerk must have wondered who bought rum at 8:30 in the morning, especially someone so cheerful and in a hurry?

Sophie pulled out the long list of sites destined for rose bouquets and read it aloud, a powerful prelude for their morning ritual of cleansing, centering and grounding, and thanksgiving to the Spirit Realms. The daily planetary drama was discussed, but all negativity was dismissed. The Moon was in Aquarius, Sophie's own and favorite sign. She warned that the Moon's placement could keep people distant and aloof, and she urged Poe to keep her heart and mind open. Dylan was already on fire with expectation and Dora would be Dora, regardless what anyone said. Dora was skipping the frustrating politeness of anticipation. Sophie would guard against being the First House Sun she was, a natural dictator; Abraham Lincoln and Franklin Roosevelt had the same placement, so she felt she was in good company. They were all laughing to themselves this morning and nodding heads to silent one-way conversations, spiritual bobble-heads. Aquarius' keywords were "*I know*"—they all had their personal insights and thought they knew the secrets behind the dramas. Sophie laughed out loud, hearing everybody's inner dialogues, and declared there was only one Aquarian here and she was it!

The night before, Sophie had realized she'd forgotten to list a major contributor to the American Camino, when she was fashioning the ribbon-covered bouquets. Some bouquets had two roses, others three, and a few had single roses with closed tight buds beside them. They were less perfect than she had planned, as Great Spirit preferred. Habitually, Sophie reminded herself: "Striving for perfection is a futile venture and disrespectful to the Creator/Creatrix, denigrating the role of choice, prayers, fate, and destiny in everyday life." When people pointed out one green bead in a sky of deep blue as an obvious mistake on her Dancing Belt, she would explain to the newbie it was a Spirit Bead. A single bead, unmatched with its surroundings, standing out from the others, carefully placed, so Great Spirit would know each time she wore the belt that she would abide by a set of rules of conduct: noncompetitive, in a mind-set and spiritual place of surrender, knowing perfection is impossible for a human, even one of the People. It was a form of tempering the ego, separating pride from arrogance. It was unforgivable of her to leave out the valuable role of Dunkin' Donuts, offering direction and shelter at every town they traveled through on the American Camino. The four knew the slogan: "America runs on Dunkin": she would honor them righteously. The closest donut shop was across the highway from Dora and Poe's hotel, barely five minutes away. "Y'all need anything from your hotel? Our first stop is across the street."

"Yes, Sophie, I need an extra pair of socks for the afternoon." Dora's feet were swollen and bandaged. She wore running shoes and capris today and a plain black tunic.

"Perfect!" Sophie said as they piled into the vehicle.

Dylan parked the SUV in front of the Day's Inn. Dora walked to the back, and Sophie studied the building across the busy highway. There was a long line of cars in the drive-through, and lots of young families with strollers, and softball teams waiting for donuts. She didn't want to stand out. On the opposite side of the drive-through window, three small, radically pruned evergreen shrubs grew, surrounded by Cedar bark and colorful Winter-blooming cabbage. The tree side of the building was quiet, away from traffic. She set her course, weaving her way across the busy road, over the curb to the sidewalk, and leisurely strolled to the bark-covered patch. She crouched and tenderly placed a rose bouquet over the bark on the backside of the shrub closest to the building. "Thank you! Blessed Be!" she whispered and made her way back to the car. To overlook Dunkin' Donuts would not have been right. The three sighed before Sophie got back to the car, rolling their eyes, calling her silly. She climbed in, smiling broadly. "Never forget your obvious allies. If you do and take them for granted, they will not support you when you need them most." Reaching for her water bottle, she found everyone looking at her strangely, half-hearing. It was her turn to roll her eyes.

South of the Marriott, the Putnam Pantry candy store awaited their greeting. Dora and Poe made their lists and counted their change. They would buy chocolate while Sophie made her offering. The young women sprinted from the back of the SUV, the fastest they had moved in days. Sophie made observations now not motivated by judgment, although discernment would help her see the light eventually. The American Camino had been for her alone, all along; the others were there as her support. Their vested interest was Sophie herself, no more complicated than that. She could see benefits manifesting already for Dylan and Poe—would they? Dora was another issue. Sure, they came to see pyrotechnics too, but that was another issue.

The truth was Sophie could not have been as successful in the psychopomp work without them. They had generated an amazing amount of fuel, just as she had taught them, and kept it clean and pure, undiluted. It had afforded Sophie the strength to move unencumbered. Her prayers and actions had been swift and flowing, hard work but not laborious per se. She hadn't had to fight for it, keeping success as a constant companion, unwavering and unacceptable to settle for less. This was the great gift of the three: energy resource batteries. To undervalue their energetic presence on the American Camino would be dishonorable. Sophie wouldn't let herself be swayed by overzealous recrimination and judgment this close to going home, over candy, red shoes, yawns, and far-away looks.

Change was inevitable. To keep the status quo would be to cheat themselves, to hold evolution and reinvention at bay. She wouldn't hold anything or anyone too tight again; this lesson was clear. These two women were full-grown; they weren't young, as one uses the word commonly—they were not girls needing guidance—they were guiding themselves, affected occasionally by Sophie's beliefs and work, but not shaped by it. Sophie was the one confused. The others didn't need her—they wanted her or felt obliged. Sophie kept reminding herself that things would sort themselves out later, after they got home—the same answer, the same closing, the easiest one in painful situations. No one likes to discover how dumb she or he really is, not even Sophie, and she loved radical truth more than anyone.

There were two bouquets for Putnam Pantry, one to place under the yew bushes in the front of the shop to commemorate Giles's true burial place and one for Drake Putnam. Sophie prepared a special token for Giles: a strip of her best red trade cloth, lined with Sage and Tobacco, for cleansing and prayers, a single rose and bud laid carefully atop the strip of cloth. She had to crouch low, finally crawling on all fours to the back yew tree. Dylan blocked her actions from view—it was still early and the shop still slow—it was easy to pull off.

Dylan held the other bouquet and waited for Sophie's hand, a silent plea to help her stand. Her knees were wet and it made her legs cold. They were beginning to seize in muscle spasms. With his help, she rose and brushed her pant legs clean. Standing in the warm morning sun for a couple of moments, she warmed her body, ending the cramping. She reached for the bouquet and walked up the ramped boardwalk entrance. She wanted to make a point, but not grandstand—this was her chance for closure with the Inner Circle. Sophie asked to speak to the manager. A few minutes later, a tall woman with brittle dyed-blonde hair, wide with large hands, faced Sophie and asked if she could help. "Yes, please. I want you to give this bouquet to the owner, to give it to the Putnam family," Sophie said with quiet confidence.

Sophie couldn't get a handle on this woman. She could not figure out if she was angry or annoyed. "The Putnams no longer own the shop. It was sold a number of years ago." The woman answered a little too smugly for Sophie's taste.

"Yes, true, that is why I want you to give this to the owner, an old friend of the Putnams. I am sure he would want Drake Putnam to have it, as it was intended."

The large woman flushed a deep crimson, pulled out her phone, and before dialing said, "Wait here for a moment. I'll be right with you." She walked behind glass doors, surrounded with workers in hairnets and plastic gloves, handcrafting the masterful chocolates. Sophie watched her intently; she wanted to register all changes of emotion. After a short time, the woman was engaged in a tense conversation, her brows lined with deep furrows. Crisply, she clicked the phone shut and walked through the double glass doors. The employees left their stations and moved to watch the encounter through the glass. "Yes, fine, leave the bouquet. The owner thanks you for your gift."

"Send him my best regards, will you?" Sophie smiled, feeling Dylan behind her, shuffling his feet, obviously tense over the encounter.

"Whom shall I say called?" the towering woman asked.

"Oh, he knows who it's from. Thank you for your concern. While you are here, I would like to take this opportunity to thank you for your assistance today and your staff for their efficiency and kind service when we shopped here the other day. We had a large order to prepare for travel and it took a great effort to get it just right." Sophie looked behind her back, seeing Dora and Poe paying for their chocolate stashes. "And it looks like our party is not through shopping! Thanks again."

The woman cleared her throat, stood her measure, and said, "Have a wonderful trip back to Oregon."

Sophie looked at the horse-faced woman for the last time and asked her if they shipped chocolates directly to post office boxes. The woman gave her a wicked smile and said, "No, we have to have your physical address to ship via UPS." Sophie had figured out the catch to ordering her favorite chocolates online.

Without maps or direction, Dylan found the Corey Memorial at Crystal Lake effortlessly. Don and Angela began running from the long line of fishermen toward the silver SUV. Sophie knew this would happen; it wouldn't change what she needed to do.

They all climbed out of the car and kept Don busy with accounts of the lake and the veterans, all his charges. Angela went from person to person hugging hard, with sincere feeling from an uncomplicated place of love. Touch was her magick! Sophie, removed from the others and free to work, began moving items from the back of the SUV: two bright orange pumpkins and two freshly polished apples, bright yellow and red with splotches of chartreuse, the same color as the water reeds in the lake. She had not been able to figure out what kinds of apples these colorful, crisp, extra sweet orbs of fruit were. What were the chances these were apple descendants from one of Giles's established orchards? Three hundred acres was a lot of ground, some of it still dense and fenced, in private hands of Moultons and the Confederacy. How many secret orchards were still cared for by distant relatives or enemy campers? How many secrets were buried deep in this Peabody land? Sophie's attention didn't stray. She stayed focused on the Coreys, still having many questions that would probably go unanswered until she had a revelatory dream or vision or she skipped over them forever, finally deeming them unimportant.

She noticed many of the offerings were gone, buried elsewhere, taken by animals perhaps? Of course they would dig for nuts and candies. Edible gifts to the Spirits Realms are meant to be used. Sophie felt honored that her gifts had been accepted with fervor. In her puttering, she noticed many kernels of Indian corn were buried deep in the bark and wondered how many would sprout in the Spring. With her miniature trowel, she made indentations in the dry earth under the bark and planted several corn kernels deep in the rich lakeside soil of the mock graves. Close to Giles's memorial stone, Sophie cleared a small area about the size of a dollar bill. She worked the soil carefully, digging a shallow hole and making a neat pile to one side. The others had drifted off to talk to the fishermen, prompted by Don's excited gestures. She was grateful to have them all occupied. She needed a private moment to clean her skin with alcohol, pierce her middle right finger, the fate-giving finger, and bleed into the freshly dug hole. She covered the blood, tamping over the hole and covering the cleared area with bark. A Corey apple was placed over Sophie's bloodspot, a sweet treat for the Earth Spirits. A perfectly round miniature pumpkin was placed next to the apple, over freshly ground nutmeg. Finishing her Honoring, she placed one white rose bouquet over Martha's grave, in loving memory of a woman who gave with her entire heart. Martha was the truly stubborn one, but she bent her will consistently for the benefit of others, always a giver. Her sacred hallowed place would wear white roses for the end of feuds, marking a time of consensual peace, accented with the red of passion and commitment. Martha would remember this day as a time of peace, united with her husband in the light, set free from the ravages of the gaol, free to sail into the sky, without tether, chain, or wedding ring.

Sophie waved her hands wildly, getting the attention of the others. Angela ran to Sophie, thinking the signal was just for her. Hugs and more hugs—Angela didn't want to let go. She knew she wouldn't be seeing Sophie again, or the others. She felt their story and pain, and she knew their job was healing. Angela was an angel, simple and beautiful in all ways. She knew more secrets than any of them, but was smart enough to keep them to herself.

Sophie held Dylan's hand; he reached for Poe's and Poe reached for Dora. Expectedly, Angela reached for Dora and urged Don to take her hand. They stood at the lakeside washed in the hazy white heat glow and watched the swans glide over the glass surface of the olive-green lake. They stood there, silent, watching for minutes, although it felt like seconds, each soaking in the love of this place. Sophie was willing to share, even though she was first to break the holding line. It was time for goodbyes.

It didn't take much time to find the highway from Crystal Lake. They soon crossed the invisible line into Danvers and began the search for the old state hospital. They followed the rainbow flags—supported on tall white flag poles—to the top of one of the area's tallest hills. There, on the hilltop overlooking a beautiful valley of tall golden grasses and oak wood, the one-time residence of Ann Putnam had been leveled, and a Victorian brick building, eerily similar to the Salem Jail Complex, was built in its place. These Victorian turrets guarded a different kind of captive, the insane, a condition with no end in the Victorian era. The entire hilltop, the huge hospital with its dormitory wings and many outbuildings, had been refurbished, redone to fit the burgeoning over-inflated condominium market.

Beautiful tall clay planting pots decorated the main entrance of the original asylum. Not wanting to spend a great deal of time honoring the insanity of the accusers, especially Ann Putnam's, Sophie walked over to the planter area and placed the bouquet in the back of the most lavish pot. Done! Time to move on. No tears of forgiveness were given to the accusers, with the exception of Mary Warren. She had earned her pardon, through three hundred and fourteen years of soul-division and heartache. Different from the others, she was a pawn who suffered at the hands of the Confederacy and its agents. Sophie had not put her in the enemy classification, had always known better.

Inspired by the general creepiness of the Victorian insane asylum, Sophie walked to the edge of the development, overlooking ancient woods of oak and evergreen and beyond the wood, the valley below. She had always planned to go to the Nurse Homestead on Sunday, their last day in Essex County, and the Towne Association's last big shindig day, the family reunion part of the festivities. She now saw a different need, a need for stealth, for quiet.

Sophie joined the group. "We need to change the itinerary. We need to get to the Nurse Homestead today, end the full ritual before the Feast tonight. We are just a few minutes away, a clear shot to the homestead property. If we wait till tomorrow, true, we won't have to deal with armed men, but we would be dealing with something far more sinister, the main gathering of the Confederacy itself. At least one member from each of the ten families will be at the family reunion tomorrow. I don't know what I was thinking, us sauntering uninvited into their closed reunion, into the jaws of the lion. Let's go directly there now. I have to gather dirt from the place and bleed into the ground there too. Let's be done with confrontation today and leave tomorrow for a nice breakfast and a farewell to Miss Mary and Dorothy. Let's be kind to ourselves for a change."

What was the point of arguing? They knew Sophie was thinking out loud. It didn't matter who was listening to her dialogue, the decision had already been made. Without discussion, the group climbed into the car and drove down the hill in silence.

Passing Wadsworth Cemetery, Sophie shivered, remembering the sheriff cruiser speeding past them last Sunday, their first day of rituals. They began to fidget and sort their supplies. "No need to pack a thing. I have a plan. Dylan will drive right into the upper grounds parking lot. Today is the reenactors event; there will be hundreds of cars parked in the upper lot. We'll hope there will be a place to slide right into, next to the tree line. Did you notice a line of watered grass at the edge of the aggregate road surface? Well,

I did. I'll slip out of the car and bend down and pretend I'm tying my shoe. While I'm crouched near the ground, I'll gather a dirt sample and bleed into the ground on the same spot. I'll leave a quarter over my blood, so we won't bring any Spirit or negative programming back with us. This will work! Y'all don't even have to get out of the car—it will be over in about a minute or two. Well?"

"I like the plan, Sophie. Going to the homestead property on Sunday always made me nervous. This is a good solution. Let's agree to stay in the car while Sophie does her thing, okay?" Poe and Dora agreed with Dylan's idea. They didn't want to deal with men with guns.

Fate was on their side. Just as Sophie had suggested, Dylan slipped into the parking lot. With cars coming out and cars going in behind him, he slid into a parking place next to the narrow strip of watered grass, only two parking spots from the main gate. An easy getaway was the plan. Sophie had a plastic bag for dirt, her mini-trowel, alcohol, and penlet ready as they pulled to a stop. Without a peep, Sophie slipped out of the vehicle, went down on one knee, gathered worked soil in the snack-sized zip-lock bag and bled into the ground. She left her DNA in the land of her enemies, not forgiving their deeds or mind-set, just balancing the energy, leaving room for the place and people connected to it to heal. They would atone for their sins, as surely as snow falls in New England, in their own time, in their own way. It was not Sophie's job to make judgment calls or to pass sentence, nor was it her job to forgive her persecutors. Balance was the aim. Forgiveness of one's abusers is a Pauline Christian concept, ensuring that believers would not wage independent wars within the greater society. Its aim was to control the masses. Sophie would not wage wars of any kind—Witch Wars were not her style either—she didn't like to play games with people hell-bent on proving Karma indolent or random. Sophie knew Instant Karma too well for lazy vengeful behavior.

Dylan started the engine and heard Dora opening the back door; she had decided to take a sample of dirt for her own secret purposes before they left. Dylan didn't shut off the motor. Dora looked pleased with herself as she climbed back into the SUV, wiggling and shaking the fairly large snack bag full of dirt. Dora wanted to share her plans for the organic matter, but no one asked her. Sophie came close, but her words came out, "Oh, how handy. You'll get good use of the dirt for breaking spells of enchantment, good for undoing love spells too." Dora did not respond and Dylan didn't wait for a conversation. He slowly backed up and turned out of the crowded lot, onto the manicured lanes of the outskirts of Danvers.

They felt relief being off of Confederacy land. Putnam Pantry Candies was a safer distance, close enough to tease, not frighten. Dylan felt he knew Danvers fairly well, which did not keep him from getting lost a couple of times, before Dora, frustrated, with frayed nerves, took over the job of navigator once more. They hit Salem traffic close to noon, fitting for the Honoring of the Old Salem Jailhouse and the Pressing Place. Dylan pulled into the closest parking place to the back door of the jail and the parking lot sinkhole, the spot fortuitous. Every other space this side of the pedestrian mall was taken.

Sophie began gathering items from the back end of the SUV. Dylan asked her for the bouquet intended for the jailhouse. He was playing it safe today, too tired to climb over a barbed-wire-topped chainlink fence, especially when he knew an alternative. Sophie smiled and kissed him on his cheek, so grateful for his company. Through all the dramas of the last week, she had found Dylan to be her rock, her grounding; he actually saw some of the magick happen. She doubted the others had; or they felt too shy or judged to speak of it. She refused to let it get to her anymore. Her mantra, one of many today.

Dylan wound his way through a maze of unlocked parking lots and found the wall he had climbed Wednesday, a worn small wall with embedded glass shards in shades of green, cobalt, and beer brown. He carefully maneuvered over the glass and reached the jail grounds unscathed. Wearing a victorious smile, he walked slowly to the single basement window encased in red brick. Some sources said it was the only outside light source for the gaol.

Sophie remembered the dim, the dark, more than the light; those moments of full light from inside the gaol's perspective were too gruesome to dwell on, horrid sights of decay and disease, malnutrition, the tragedy of end-times. The light was too harsh for survival; the dank dark disguised the truth of their demise and was painful to see, then and now.

Dylan bent down, picked up a small dried hunk of Earth and rubbed it between his hands until he created loose dirt, a light brown, speckled with burnt sienna of brick. He took a snack bag out of his pocket and put the majority of the dirt in it. With what remained, Dylan washed his hands in it, covering all fingers with the dust, up to his wrists. He took the crumbs of dirt uncaught by the bag and formed an Equal Cross over the decaying windowsill and laid the perfect white rose with its bud companion over it. He saluted and thanked Spirit for protection and rubbed his dry hands together, trying to leave the remaining dirt where it came from.

Without pomp or lingering, he climbed over the short wall, zigzagged his way back to the SUV, and brought a gallon jug of spring water to the center of the parking lot, where the three women stood, soaking in the place without feeling its inherent pain and persistent decline. He handed Sophie the gallon jug and asked her to slowly pour the water over his hands, directing the extra water into the sinkhole, his way of cleaning the dirt under the black top shell. The water collected, making a shallow pool in the center of the hole. Sophie bent over and placed the bouquet of three beautifully formed roses, her symbol honoring the three days it took Giles to die, over the sitting water and straightened to watch it float. They all took hold of each other's hands around the floating roses, inhaled one deep breath, bringing their united hands over their heads, and released the long breath, directing it to the center of the sinkhole, while they brought their hands back to their individual sides. "Blessed Be!" sounded. They unlocked hands. Dora scattered a handful of sunflower nuts. They were finished.

Sophie was the first one to turn around. There, in front of her, driving a black truck with an extended cab held idling in the center of the street, a horse-faced and dour woman stared in her direction—the doppelganger of the Putnam Pantry manager, although her hair was a muted dyed red instead of fried blonde. The woman had a scowl Sophie recognized. Sophie had never seen Rose Desmond, the historian for the Inner Circle, but she had talked to her several times over the phone. Sophie had picked up a specific picture of Rose during those phone calls and she now faced the portrait in her head. She made eye contact with the woman, tugged the brim of her hat, hard, and began walking in her direction, in the same manner she employed with the tattooed biker. Rose, not frightened but alert, reached for her black cellphone camera and began shooting photos, one after the other. Sophie's intention was to reach for the truck door handle, open it, and expose the full length of the spying woman, but two short paces from the truck, Rose shifted into drive and peeled away.

The four looked at each other without fear, strangely elated. What Sophie had not yet realized was that instinctively, all four of them, Poe on her right, Dora on her left, and Dylan directly behind, walked in tandem. They were no longer a discordant band, but a working whole. Once again, transformation happened directly in front of them. This time, all were caught unaware of the process. They were victims no more. The four moved as a single assertive force and it felt good from the top of their heads to the bottom of their feet. They were empowered—and it was a rush of monumental proportion. They all roared with laughter, to the point that people rounding the corner of Route 107 crossed the street to the Morency Complex side. They howled and Sophie felt she would pee her pants. Fortunately she had not overdone the water this morning, which was all the rational thought she could summon. The outburst of laughter, the sound of release felt so good: another unexpected win.

Dylan opened the back of the SUV and all four dived in for refreshment. Dylan hissed them all out of his territory and handed everyone prepared slices of brie and apple, and, of course, bagels. Poe and Dora were groaning at yet another bagel and opted for chocolate. "Eat an orange, then, ladies," Dylan snipped, throwing each an orange, then a napkin with a wet-wipe. "Women cannot live on chocolate alone."

All three women looked at him in shock. How could he even think such a thing? Chocolate was the staple of the Gods. Dylan didn't take no for an answer. "We have to fortify our energy for Gallows Hill, so eat and drink your fill now. The walk is fairly steep, it's hot today, and we are all wearing black, not too obvious, huh? Drink as much water as you can, we'll dehydrate faster in these clothes. That reminds me, I need to share something. When I picked up the sunflowers at the Corey Vegetable Stand this morning, my Higher Self spoke and urged me to be strong, to lead the way up the hill. I held the tallest sunflower in my hand and knew I had to plant it in the center of a meadow, on the side of the hill. It's probably the hanging spot, my spot, where the gallows was set up. I need to be the one to lead the prayers."

"I thought everyone was hanged in a tree, Dylan. Sophie has never mentioned anything about the hangings; of course, Giles was in the gaol by the time Bridget Bishop was hung. She was hung in a tree, wasn't she, Sophie?" Dora asked.

"Yes, Bridget Bishop was hung in a tree, on the way to Gallows Hill, I understand. Bridget was the first hanging. They had not had the taste of blood before. It was new for them, the public cries and elation, at least. By the time July nineteenth came, they had installed a proper gallows, about three-quarters up the side of Gallows Hill. I've heard if you are parallel with the Salem city water tower, you'll find the spot. We'll soon find out." Sophie stretched, happily eating her bagel, dipping it into a blueberry yogurt every other bite, blueberries being one of Giles's favorite treats.

Dora navigated Dylan up a series of small hills, crisscrossing densely packed neighborhoods, finding their share of dead ends and one-way lanes, divided by tall hedgerows and looking more like English countryside than New England city. Sophie urged Dylan to follow the water tower. They paused at a stop sign with the windows rolled down, trying to catch a stray breeze, when they heard the sound of unbridled laughter. Dylan followed the shrieking sounds, which led to a playground at the base of a hill, in the shadow of the town's main water tower. A sign greeted them with *"Welcome to the City of Salem Parks Program,"* in small letters underneath the welcome: *Gallows Hill City Park.* Dylan parked facing the playground and the base of the hill. They watched people climb the paved walking path winding up the tall hill. Depending on who was scaling it, a small mountain would be a more accurate description.

The park grounds have a separate ecosystem from the rest of Salem; the altitude changed the colors dramatically. The gentle golds of Salem were transformed into shades of deep harvest, bright oranges and splashes of china red, legendary New England colors, not seen by the group before now. It was real, it actually existed—Gallows Hill. When you learn of a place, discuss theory and landscape, it remains abstract until you are faced with it in corporeal reality. Then, boom, it hits, this really did happen. Martha died on this mountain, with seven other innocent frightened souls on September twenty-second, three hundred and fifteen years ago today.

Some accounts say the wagon got stuck halfway up the hill in deep mud, despite the unusually hot day. Corwin's men forced the women and forlorn Samuel Wardwell out of the cart and made them push the heavy wagon the rest of the way up the hill. Think of the women, wet and slick with mud in only their muslin shifts, how vulnerable they were, working their last precious energy off before their executions, similar to the forced labor of war, always producing the same outcome: death. The stuck wagon is legend, mind you. Considering the eight were all on the brink of starvation, it's hard to imagine them having the strength to carry through, although adrenaline and the threat of death produces amazing amounts of energy.

It is said that it rained for two weeks before the last hanging, unrelenting, pelting rain, drenching the scorched countryside after a Summer of drought. It flooded in spots and settled in the marshlands. In the gaol, the

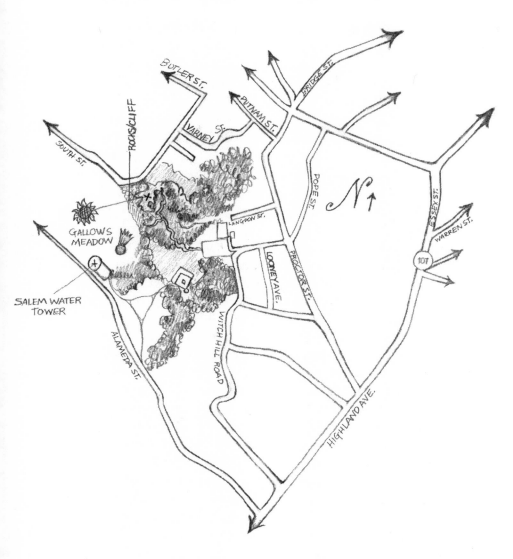

Gallows Hill, Salem

people were cold and the place was overloaded with mold, which grew wildly on the bricks and straw. They were weak and near death by the time they were forced into the bright September sunshine. Goody Corwin had traded for everything they owned in exchange for stale scraps of bread. They had nothing left, not even their dignity to carry them to the next world. Martha Corey was the lucky one: she had Giles, fresh to the light to meet her, escort her to the next dimension, her heaven: blessed relief of release.

Dylan felt suspended, hanging off a cliff, one step over the edge, taking direction from the Fool Card. He had to break his inner dialogue to take charge of the Walk; he knew it was time to make his move. He opened the driver's door swiftly and closed it too hard, jarring the women awake, pulling them from their expectations into the now. They followed his lead and waited for instruction. "Dora, please carry this sunflower with you up the hill. Be careful with it, I need its stalk in good shape. I'll carry the Trader Joe's bag. Have your eyes peeled for a good digging stick. Let's walk separately, feeling our way up, quietly, open to impressions and mental pictures as we climb. We'll come together at the top of the hill." Dylan made sure everyone had plenty of water; the temperature felt as if it had peaked, stabilizing at ninety-one, according to the instrument panel of the SUV. The wind was picking up, coming out of the East, forcing sea salt into already salty sweat. It would cool as they climbed, breezes washing over black cotton.

The woods appeared to be third- or fourth-growth deciduous, else it would be climaxing into evergreens after three hundred and fifteen years, so Sophie thought, but botanist she was not. The hill had been stripped many times, for more than one purpose. This hill, the highest in this part of the valley, represented their incorruptible New Jerusalem. The Puritan symbol of peace, living oneness with the Divine, was used to execute innocents, victims of greed. This hill would become one of the founding pillars, carrying the weight of the country's spiritual destiny, a negative charge so great it forced many unconscious people living in its shadow to disregard the importance of individuality, diversity, and change. This hill needed to be exorcized, transformed, changing the hearts and minds of millions. But this daunting job would fall to others; their job was done, except for the prayerful Honoring planned.

The greens seemed greener, the colors richer on this hill. You could feel the years of magick done on its ground. Many foolish acts and abuses performed by disenfranchised devotees wearing goat-head pendants and hand-made tattoos of Pentacles could be felt, balling and wiggling on the surface. Through the veil of illusion, deeper in the Earth and psyche, more than imprudence existed in this place. Seasoned and wise Elders had prayed here, trying to bring their charges of positivity to the Earth where so many tears were shed. Catcalling, spitting, and slinging of rotten vegetables had happened here too, and the corrupted prayers for redemption overwhelmed the Ethers, then and now. Still Reverend Mather's condemnation of the wretched and forlorn on this hill rang out in the shadows, echoing off the wall of tonal chanting meant to undo the harm said and done.

They climbed at their individual paces, enjoying the calm, trying to keep the goosebumps to a minimum by increasing their uphill pace. Dora and Poe made it to the top of the hill faster than Dylan or Sophie, their strides so long and stretched; they could not hear or feel much over the sound of their own breath. Dylan stopped before topping the hill, drifted into a meadow, trees on two sides, rock cliffs on one, parallel to the water tower painted with the city insignia of a flying Witch. Sophie met him in the center of the meadow, both knowing what he had found. Dylan knew this place, blazed on his memory as if it were yesterday. He didn't see all the pictures, didn't have to. He was seeing through Martha's eyes now, closed much of the time, her face smeared with the oil of sweat and filth and the snot of fearful tears. He had gone right there, found it before anyone—of course he did.

"This is the spot, Sophie, where I want to plant the sunflower. I found a good digging stick and rocks to support it. I want the sunflower to be here for a while, if Spirit allows, at least through our feast. It's Saturday. I imagine lots of strange people will be milling around after dark, looking for trouble. We'll say a special prayer for its survival. Being the symbol of immortality, it should be fine. Have you noticed all the abandoned fire rings? Some were thrown together without stone, dangerous in these grass meadows, here close to the top, with the wind gusting all the time." Dylan marked the spot with a red Honor Bundle.

They walked the remaining way up the hill together—eyes open—certain Dylan had found the right place. Sophie found it just after he did, but Dora and Poe climbed on without notice, or so it seemed. The women sat at the top, perched on a picnic table. Sophie started laughing, out of breath and exhausted from the climb. She roared with laughter and pointed. She couldn't stop although she knew she needed to—this was not a time for joviality. The three looked in the direction Sophie pointed and saw a parking lot and an old neighborhood, perhaps a hundred years old. The town had filled in the backside of the hill and had developed the area and made it easily accessible, even for the disabled. Sophie finally stopped laughing and sat hard on the picnic bench and wiped her eyes and nose. The irony, she thought.

Dylan led the way to the meadow, crossing yet another directly below them, off the path, filled with orange leaves, yellow swings, and red slides, the colors of the Goddess Diana, Goddess of the New Moon, of new possibilities, beginnings and adventures. A beautiful omen they all seemed to understand.

Slowly they walked to the meadow, set apart from the rest of the hillside park, yellow grass with many bald spots from overuse. Squinting in the haze, Dylan saw the gallows set, room enough for eight bodies to hang, one at a time, then together, kicking, swelling, gagging, dying. The cheering—he could hear it and it amazed him, cheering at someone's untimely death, tragic, but universal. It made him think of the execution beheading he had witnessed in Riyadh, Saudi Arabia. The charge was capital murder. The large crowd, expectant, excited, and on edge, felt frenetic; they tasted blood before it was shed. The Saudi beheading was silent, though, unlike the rowdy righteous Puritans screaming their praises of death. When the beheading was over, people faded into deserted streets and were gone behind walled compounds or in Mercedes-Benz sedans. In comparison, the do-gooder Puritans lingered on the hill, some sharing picnic feasts and gossip of Witchcraft rumors, further afield every day.

The four formed a Circle around the newly planted sunflower, surrounded by Indian corn, pumpkins, M&Ms, sunflower nuts, and two apples from Corey land—one for Martha, one for Giles, united here in the Ethers after their long painful ordeal. They slowly chanted *om* eight times, one for each person hung on the twenty-second, and without prompting began singing.

> *"The Circle is open,*
> *but unbroken,*
> *may the love of the Goddess always be in your heart!*
> *Merry meet and merry part and merry meet again!"*

They sang the song three times, the number of manifestation, of reality. This hill was real, woven into the patterns of their lives through the centuries. The only token taken from the hill was dirt from Dylan's sunflower's place, the gallows swing spot. The digging stick, stones, orange leaves, and acorns would all stay in this place of haunting and push-pull magick. Dylan was released quietly today from Martha's diabolical end, knowing she was never trapped like some of the others because of Giles, prodding and pulling, entreating her to the light. When she flew into Giles's arms, Martha didn't realize Giles was not staying with her. He had already divided—the trauma could not be undone, not then. They only had minutes together. Martha finally understood the separation was inevitable and lasting, until this week.

Dylan was now free to explore who he really was in the here and now, without threat of reprisal, and without the neediness of Martha. He was free to enjoy Martha's Core now, where she had always dwelt but never entirely felt she belonged until this very moment.

Dylan and Dora set the course for Charter Street, their last stop of the day's Honoring. They yawned incessantly, not wanting to think about the energy needed to honor the twenty dead and to invite the guests. *Don't do it if you do it half-ass,* Sophie believed. *If a job needs doing, follow through till the end. There are no prizes given solely for intention.* They all could hear Sophie's lecture begin.

Sophie had chosen forty-five guests, symbolizing closure, transformation from letting go. She listed the obvious Spirit choices but threw in a dozen living members of the Inner Circle and the Confederacy, just to ignite the energy of the event. She even included Drake Putnam and Lori Otto, Rose Desmond too, although she was probably in hiding after their encounter at the Pressing Place at noon. You never knew who you would bump into at the Lyceum Bar and Grill on Saturday night, and this night was special, the Seventh Witches Sabbat of the Natural Year, the celebration of the second harvest, Mabon. Sophie wanted to be prepared. Regardless of what manifested, she had to put her best foot forward and complete the feast with the highest level of integrity, without getting cocky. Fortunately she didn't drink alcohol, lessening the need for bravado, but the other three did, and she promised them absolute freedom to make asses out of themselves tonight. They had certainly earned the right!

Salem
1692

Chapter Twenty-Six

THE WITCH MEMORIAL

September 22, 2007, 2:00 p.m.

TROLLEY CARS, TOURIST BUSES, AND MINIVANS filled the Old Town area of Salem. The pedestrian mall was full too. Waves of tourists and locals gathered and went, t-shirts bought and pictures taken. Most did not realize today was the last Hanging Day. It was special and Sophie, more than the Spirits, wanted average people to understand its significance, not just historians trying to prove theories.

The group of four was out of juice; their energy and attention span had waned after planting the sunflower on Gallows Hill. They would manufacture protection energy, but all other expectation was finished. The SUV was filled with a palpable feeling of loss, almost defeat, far from the reality of their work—almost complete, successful. Charter Street Cemetery and the Feast were the only important elements left: the *i*'s dotted and the *t*'s crossed.

Their dragging energy inspired Spirit. Dylan, exasperated, circling Charter Street for the third time, stopped dead when a car started its engine and pulled out of the same parking place they had parked in for the Opening Ritual last Sunday. Their beginning was a world away from them now, until the parking space Spirit provided—beginning to end. This was the simple miracle needed to wake them out of their exhausted emotional coma. It was the little signs and omens that impressed magickal people the most, the instantaneous manifestations of destiny, too in-your-face to ignore, like parking spaces, black and white columns, Dunkin' Donuts, tangible signs of faith, reminders to stay awake. Nestled under the familiar golden hawthorn trees, they all took a deep breath in unison, their energy building. Five minutes before they had been half-asleep, too tired to move.

Now, energy tingled and itched, egging them on to take action, planning who would carry what.

Sophie jumped from the car with determination in her step. She had felt another stride would finish her off after Gallows Hill. Now she felt renewed, under her own spell of closure. She was driven to complete the Honoring with a sense of dignity and history at her heels. The twenty-second of September would be remembered for all time in American history; there was no way around it. People would forget October third, the official end to the Court of Oyer and Terminer. Many Essex County residents had wanted the court reinstated after October: they had not had their fill of blood lust. Eventually public efforts to continue orders of execution had been successful, although no more court-appointed killings were actually carried out. The Puritan mind-set would not learn from its mistakes; for that reason the movement died a quick death, morphing from Puritan back to their original roots in Congregationalism. Still other dates would fade, but the twenty-second of September never would, especially for people who wore the modern self-given title of Witch. If Sophie had her way, there would be a national moment of silence on the date. Her activist mentality was charging her energy, and the others were filling up on her passionate excess.

She called everyone near and laid out her plans for the Honoring. Looking up, Sophie saw into the grounds through the trees, seeing dozens of people, maybe hundreds, milling around the stones. The tourists were loud, too; for them it was a Saturday in the park, not a historical burying ground on a solemn day. An audience was in place; they would have to adjust and adapt.

Items for Charter Street Cemetery were separated from the memorial's ritual items and gifts. They would thank John Marston and his Army of the Dead first, leaving a bouquet of roses near his stone. Mary Corey had to be acknowledged next, her love of Corey land unsurpassed. A sunflower, apple, and pumpkin would be laid over her grave; in addition, a single white rose, a sign of finished business and cases closed. The relationship between Giles and Mary Corey would finally be complete—no need to revisit the friendship—all debts and allegiances between them would be released today. Sophie divided the supplies among the walkers, using the liquor store boxes. Dylan would carry the sunflowers and the rose bouquets, the apples and pumpkins, for the memorial. Dora would carry the gifts for Mary Corey and John Marston and a gallon jug of water. Poe would carry the Challah and rum. Sophie carried the stuffed Trader Joe's bag with all its special magickal tools and herbs, plus the Feast invitations and all the special Honoring cards written in calligraphy the night before.

They stood together outside the grounds and quietly reinforced the Protection Magick employed first thing this morning. They needed to maintain their focus. The reality was they were playing to an audience of Spirits and humans; they had to be prepared for anything, love as well as hate. None of them were frightened of the Confederacy any longer. The greatest threat now was to cause offense to the Spirit Realms. If any of them still feared being judged, now would be the time. The plan was to honor John Marston first, then Mary Corey, followed by the Witch Memorial Honoring Ceremony. The ceremony would be done in assembly-line fashion, each person responsible for the specific offerings Sophie gave them charge of. They would stack the boxes before moving into the memorial itself, making a better presentation. They were all given white plastic shopping bags as back-ups to the boxes, if needed. Regardless, all unused materials would be recycled. There would be no waste.

Under the tall whispering trees of Charter Street, the group gathered around John Marston's black stone for the second time. Last Sunday they had petitioned him for help; today they thanked him for his invaluable assistance throughout their journey. His stone and grave still manicured from Sophie's attention the Sunday before, she touched up the area with the rainbow glove, humming as she worked. The first time she had performed this rite, she had been nervous, worried that John and she would not see eye to eye. This time she wore a broad smile and held fondness for him, recalling Miss Mary's story of the once-sheriff of Essex County and his organized work parties of the colonial dead, always busy building. Sacred herbs were offered, and water for the Great Mother was poured on the stone, followed by a healthy swig of spiced rum. A piece of Challah was torn and offered him for the Great Father; a white rose bouquet was laid to one side of the bread with a silent *thank you*. Dora bound the Honor Spell with her usual handful of sunflower nuts. Sophie wondered if Dora had bought Putnam Pantry's entire stock of chocolate-covered nuts for this purpose. The thought pleased Sophie; Dora had absorbed some of her mentor's teachings over the past decade—some did and would continue to stick. There was no such thing as wasted time, Sophie reminded herself. Dylan sprinkled a few M&Ms over the offerings, and John's Honoring was complete.

Feeling surrounded by alien energy, they looked up and noticed people were queuing up to inspect the newly decorated grave. Some, standing close to the group but not in their way, madly looked through guidebooks, trying to figure out the historical significance of John Marston. Sophie wished them silent luck and smiled slightly in one woman's direction. The woman was distraught, almost crying because she could find no information. Sophie got the woman's attention with a hiss and signaled for her to come close. She whispered to the woman, "John Marston was a beloved sheriff of Salem, dying almost a decade before the Witch Hysteria." The uptight woman dressed in a blue-gray pantsuit looked relieved, touched Sophie's right shoulder, and, with lip-sync movement, thanked Sophie for the information. Tourists needed to take responsibility to research before traveling—it would be less frustrating for them. Sophie sighed, knowing she expected too much from everybody.

How many people admitted to remembering past lives? Tourists were attracted to Essex County for a reason that was obvious—many faithful visitors to Salem, never missing a Halloween or a Spring regatta, had lived here in other times. They were like messenger pigeons coming home to roost. Few remembered or gave room for the possibility in their minds or even their hearts, shutting down the important answers before they could decipher their meaning. She knew the numbers were low, people opting to forget or deny instead. Sophie felt more alone than she had ever felt before, under the whispering trees of Charter Street.

Her mind lost focus and wandered frantically, letting the woman's touch of her shoulder throw her. Would local historians still refer to the Corey Curse in all their books and pamphlets? Probably. She couldn't take it to heart, couldn't hold too tight, couldn't demand that others see the successes unveiling: it's right here, in front of your faces, open your eyes! Why couldn't she be mellower? Now that presented a challenge. She was weary with overwork, but she would work on her obsessions more seriously when she got home, she vowed. It sounded like another deadline brewing, working hard not to work.

Sophie looked high in the trees, searching for a sign. Her eyes told a story of recognition, light streaming through golden leaves, whispering poems in the steady breeze. She heard the hum of approval from the Earth Spirits, the squirrels, the bones beneath her feet, some wrapped in silk, others in old bed sheets, all gone now, returned to the Earth for transformation.

Single file, with a quiet band of tourists in tow, the group of four moved knowingly across the grounds, finding Mary Corey's grave close to the chainlink fence. The sunflower nuts and M&Ms were gone, eaten by the small critters living in the cracks and hollows of the old grounds, but sprinkles of maple sugar survived, not carried away by hungry sugar ants. Sophie knelt and tenderly cleaned the area of grass trimmings from the front of the stone marker. Giles could *almost* remember picking out the stone, but the real boss for a few years on Corey land was Goodwife Mary Corey. She probably arranged for her own stone, remembering her independent surly ways. Sophie signaled Dora to lay the sunflower on Mary's grave. She laid the rose bouquet herself and touched the stone and whispered, "Goodbye, Mary, be well." She quietly wondered how long it would take Dora to leave her side for good. Sophie knew it would be soon. They both needed to move on—they had been holding too tight for too long. The cycle had to be broken, was broken, was ended now.

Sophie poured water and a chug of the down-island rum over Mary's stone, saying, "Drink deep, Mary." A chunk of torn Challah was placed next to the roses with, "Eat well, Mary."

Dora picked up the pumpkin and apple and prepared to place them on the grave when Dylan reached over Dora and asked, "May I?" Dora smiled her way, a straight line across her mouth, a hint of warmth in her eyes, and nodded an okay. Dylan held Dora's open hands for a moment, eyes locked. He whispered, "Thank you for caring for Giles and the land. You did an excellent job and I am grateful." Dora's expression didn't change, although Dylan may have hoped it would. He laid the offerings on Mary's grave, just as Dora rained down sunflower nuts, ending Mary's Honoring.

One box for the roses and sunflowers would do the trick. Dora carried it. Dylan would carry the apples and pumpkins in shopping bags. Poe carried the Challah in her right hand, the rum in her left. They stacked the boxes and placed them at Miss Mary's side. They no longer needed them. Miss Mary's seat gave her the only fully unobstructed view of the memorial. She was expectant, knowing a ritual was about to happen. Surrounded by hundreds of gawking tourists made it all the more fun for Miss Mary.

The group wore the color of Saturn, planet of Karma. Dressed in jeans, yoga pants, and capris, forgoing the robes of covens, they had donned black: the color of funerals, the dead, newness, the womb—death meets life in the primordial ooze and prepares for rebirth—all in black. Sophie put down her bag and the others followed, centered in the grassy area of the memorial. People began to gather in, although staying out of the memorial proper. The group quickly grounded, moving in unison, revisiting a familiar sensation. More people gathered around the outside of the memorial, knowing real Witches were working. Sophie raised her arms in the crescent shape of the Great Mother.

> *"Great Goddess in all your faces,*
> *Maiden, Mother, and Crone,*
> *please hear my prayers!*
> *I stand over your Earth and under your Sky and I reach for you,*
> *for love, protection, for balance.*
> *Bless us in our praising of your children,*
> *in our honoring of your Sisters and Brothers,*
> *twenty in all,*
> *giving their lives prematurely to the greedy whims of others.*
> *Bless those who have gone before us gathered here,*
> *victims and criers for justice,*
> *Mothers and Fathers, Daughters and Sons.*
> *We remember your children, Great Mother,*
> *Help us remember their sacrifices!*
> *Blessed Be!"*

The onlookers placed their hands together, as to clap, but held back their enthusiasm, pretending they all knew the ways of magick. Sophie felt their awe, their excitement. She had been in similar situations, unannounced, and forced into work on some level publicly. She was always warned not to grandstand, not be a Leo temperament, making the whole world her stage. Sometimes it had been unavoidable. Sophie could see her mother, Sarah, in her mind's eye, training her to be bold, to catch other's attention. It was natural now, so many years later; Spirit would have to forgive her if she overstepped the bonds of ceremonial correctness, this time. She wasn't coming from ego today. She simply had to act, had no other choice, was so close to victory she would risk disapproval on all levels, yet again, in an attempt to finish what she had begun three years earlier. She was not going to be camera-shy today, no—leave it to the newbies to be wallflowers.

The Memorial Stones were arranged in order of death, the dates dictating name placements. Grouped together, set apart, they flowed from one to the other, in the sharp U-shape of the stone block memorial.

June 10, 1692:

Bridget Bishop

July 19, 1692:

Sarah Wildes, Elizabeth Howe, Susannah Martin, Sarah Good, Rebecca Nurse

August 19, 1692:

George Burroughs, Martha Carrier, George Jacobs, John Proctor, John Willard

September 19, 1692:

Giles Corey

September 22, 1692:

Martha Corey, Mary Easty, Alice Parker, Mary Parker, Ann Pudeator, Wilmot Redd, Margaret Scott, Samuel Wardwell

Bridget Bishop was the first one to die a public death, hanged solitarily on a lone tree, resigned to her fate, angry, alone. Where was Giles when she needed him? It was because of Giles she was being persecuted, buying his rum and Carib Tobacco, befriending him, despite his constant trouble with the Confederacy. How Bridget loathed the Putnams and their disciples, the family tentacles of blood. A loose woman by whose standards? The crazy over-starched priggish elite of the Massachusetts Bay Colony? Sophie was hearing Bridget's ranting: belligerent, fearful, chaotic—all over the place—although making sense. Sophie knew the secrets, remembered their relationship. Bridget was a pirate too, profiting from Giles's wily-gained booty.

Bridget had not accepted the blame for her own demise, had not seen sin or provocation in her relaxed dress and fishmonger mouth. She felt no harm in bright colors, purple her favorite, attracted to canary yellow and crimson too. She was a God-loving woman, not a God-fearing woman; she wore the distinction as a badge of honor. Now she needed to be courageous too. Her tormentors wanted to make a statement with Bridget's death. No woman—regardless of age or connection—had the right to parade her loose ways openly for other women to imitate. The powers that be would conjure fear in other women and men who supported independent-thinking women by killing her without mercy.

Sophie, kneeling, brushed the surface of the stone clean with her rainbow glove, careful not to displace others' charms and offerings. She thought of Bridget, thought this process would go smoothly, quickly, easy even. But seized with feelings of remorse, of guilt, the weight crushing Sophie's enthusiasm and creating plump tears, she learned her expectations were incorrect. Sophie could not separate her feelings of guilt and shame over Bridget from similar feelings in this life with Ali, her younger sister. Sophie had kept Ali's secret for a long time: Bridget was Ali, Ali was Bridget, one and the same. Sophie's tears would not stop. She placed the apple from Corey land in the center of the stone, not obstructing Bridget's name, and poured rum, floating it in the apple's top. She meant to begin the call-and-response prayer, but instead a small, choking voice came out of Sophie. "I'm sorry, Ali; I didn't mean to leave you alone. Forgive me, Baby Girl." The last word came out in a long rasp. Sophie caught herself, took a deep breath, and said,

"When Spirit drinks …"

The three responded,

"We all drink!"

Sophie wiped her eyes on the sleeve of her black t-shirt and continued to lay the sacramental Challah on the right side of the rum-filled apple. Before the call-and-response, she whispered, "Good Shabbas, sister."

"When Spirit eats …"

The three straightened and replied,

"We all eat!"

Sophie brushed her pant leg off with one solid stroke and stood up quickly. She took a rose bouquet from Dora's box and placed it over the calligraphy card she had made for each of the twenty.

"Bless you always, Bridget!"

Sophie found a rhythm by the third stone after Bridget's. The rainbow glove's movement tidied the stone surface, followed by a single apple from Corey land, used as a goblet for floating spiced rum, a hunk of torn Challah, a single carefully lettered card stating the person's name, place of origin, and death date, placed far away from the feathered drips of rum. The memorial would wear four rose bouquets, Bridget's being the first. All stones would carry Dora's chocolate sunflower nut sprinkles, Dylan's M&Ms, and Poe's touches.

There were no plans to take breaks, time taken for tears and the lament of whys. Sophie thought she would find detachment today, unlike the Sunday before, seeing the memorial for the first time. The sight of it had hit her, a punch in the gut and a blast to the tear ducts. She had cried, despite her hardened exterior. She felt as if she had been beaten by hundreds now. Were today's spectators the same people gathered for the hangings, calling obscenities and throwing their insecurities in the form of filth?

Sarah Good, her name written in stone, transported Sophie to a different time. A woman at the top of an oak stair, dressed in a sheer pink chiffon gown and satin dressing cap, cries at the landing. Sobbing, her words are heard: "What are you trying to do, kill me?" At the base of the stair, three children stand, mouths open, tears streaming from the corners of their eyes. They are stunned by the accusation of the exhausted woman.

"No, Mom, we're getting ready for school, just like we do every morning," Sophie says with an edge.

"Mom, why can't you be like other mothers? Cook for us, like *Leave It to Beaver*'s mom does?" Ali is crying hard, hiccupping, wiping her nose on the back of her right arm. "Don't you love us, Mom? Have you ever loved us, ever wanted us?" Ali is inconsolable.

Sarah stands at the head of the stair, hearing Ali's cries of neglect. "Get a grip, Ali, you know I love you all the same. The question today is do you love me enough to let me rest?" Erick says nothing, picks up his pile of books and stomps out the door, slamming it behind him, one less kid to make a racket.

Erick refuses to see his mother so vulnerable and lost; he would always run at the first sign of expressed emotion.

Sophie knew why her mom stood above them several times a week asking the same question about killing—it was the past calling—her mother caught between sleep, wake, and loss. She had lost her baby daughter, Joan. She could no longer look at the expectant faces of young children in a classroom without feeling pulled apart and shattered. She was no longer a schoolteacher at heart. Sophie's mom was empty at the top of the stair, as she was above the gallows swing spot, when the noose was fitted around her once broad neck, and she was hanged for being resourceful. Sophie missed her mother, her theatrical demeanor, her rich full voice.

Sophie collapsed on the ground, her knees hitting stone as well as grass, when she saw Sarah Good's stone. Her plans for decorum evaporated in the afternoon heat as she hit hard. "I miss you, Momma!" Sophie cried. She felt hundreds of eyes staring at her raw declaration. She must pull herself together, finish the Honoring without falling apart; she was so close to the end. Knowing the origin of pain was no longer enough! Sophie was faced with follow-through—she had to rise above empathy and find her connection through compassion, a usable form of appreciation. "See you soon, Momma, be good," Sophie whispered. Her tears would dry, she promised herself, as she laid a rose bouquet containing three roses and a bud, each rose symbolizing the three children left after Joan's death, the bud for the baby lost to the gaol, Sarah's baby, then and now.

Giles's and Martha's stones were placed next to each other, a beautiful sentiment by the architect of the memorial. When it came time for placing the sunflower on Giles's stone, Dylan insisted on doing it. His and Martha's favorite flower had to have his juice on it. He laid it close to the stone wall, away from the deep indentations of the letters of Giles's name. Giles's stone was full, as Martha's soon would be: apple, bread, card, pumpkin, sunflower, and roses, topped with the now traditional sprinkling of nuts and chocolate. Sophie placed Martha's sunflower on the cool stone and touched Martha's name gently, remembering the good times, remembering Dylan and Martha, Giles and Sophie. Remembering the long hours of work and of rest, of communion and the rest of life's sounds and feelings. Sophie's tears were dry, evaporated in the Ethers.

The stones shone with a renewed freshness, the energy of the Honor Gifts uplifting this corner of the county. The spiced rum overflowing from the apple top goblets soaked into the stones, leaving a sharp scent of clove and cinnamon, Sophie was aware of onlookers sniffing the air, some sensitive enough to smell the Spirits at work. The last stone Sophie had special gifts for was Samuel Wardwell's, a father with young children and a pregnant wife to feed, who made pennies telling fortunes and divining the weather. Samuel, like Giles, was a magick man, not entirely innocent of the crime of Witchery, although fortunes should never draw a fine so great as to take a life, regardless of worldview. So many others did much worse with no repercussions, of course: the way of nepotism and priceless connections. Sophie dug to the bottom of the Medicine bag, finally bringing forth a small cotton-lined jewelry box. Inside lay thirty-three pink-colored glass scallop shell charms, topped with rosewood beads from India. Scallop shell was the universal symbol for the European Camino, which ended in Compostela, Spain, Sophie's adopted symbol for the American Camino. Rose was the divine wood, used in medieval Europe to fashion wedding rings, symbolizing everlasting spiritual union. Only special people would be gifted the charms, ones who were deserving, ones agreeing to hold Sacred Space for the travelers. Sophie closed her eyes and reached into the box of charms, feeling for Samuel's. There, she found it, her gift for a deserving person, a magickal person overlooked and undervalued for over three hundred years. She placed it tenderly on his stone and said, "Hang in there, Samuel. Your time is coming." Sophie touched the stone lightly with her right index finger, which acted as her magic wand, energizing Samuel's memory.

Sophie stood facing East, at the end of the long line of stone shelves. She quickly saluted Spirit through the Cardinal Directions, collected the large shopping bag, and walked clockwise to the rock wall on the Western side of the hard U-shape. There, Sophie stared at the chest-high, loosely stacked rock, symbolizing the makeshift burial spots for many of the twenty dead, their lifeless bodies stuck haphazardly into the rocks, some parts exposed to the elements entirely. Legend had it that George Burroughs's right arm stuck out from his rock- and dirt-strewn grave, balled in a fist. George had reached for the miscreants who had done the terrible deeds, warning them justice would follow.

She produced a zip-lock bag full of forty-five tiny, carefully rolled white scrolls, tied closed with red thread, the Liberation Feast invitations. Sophie divided the scrolls among her friends; they would find tiny fissures in the rock to place them for safe keeping, for the Spirits to find. She was curious what would happen to the scrolls meant for the living. Her satisfied smile shone across the memorial. All could see Sophie beam the completion of the Honoring Ceremony. And so it was done.

They needed a group picture for their travel book. Dylan and Dora produced their cameras and asked a family of three, a middle-aged man with two teenagers, to take a series of group shots. The family felt honored to be chosen. Handy was more like it! The older teenager—overeager and determined—approached Sophie as soon as the pictures were taken and started blasting questions. He wanted to know the meaning of the ceremony, why Sophie spent more time with certain stones and not with others. Why, why, why, is all Sophie heard, thinking of young Jamie, one of the nine ghosts of Sawyer's Hill. Sophie raised her hand and placed an open palm over the young man's heart and told him to stop. This was not a time of explanation. He would have to do his own reading about the importance of the twenty-second of September. She motioned the boy to stand aside but not to go away. She motioned for the boy's father to come forward, which he did without hesitation.

"I know this will sound a bit odd, but perhaps you will understand I mean no offense. Your child is motivated to be here, to take part in our rites. He has followed us for over an hour—all of you have—from the first grave we visited in the main burial ground through the entire ritual. I know your kids are underage—they look it—the reason I am asking you permission for them to share in an alcohol toast to honor the twenty dead. I do not mean to offend. If alcohol is not allowed, I entirely understand. I never touch the stuff myself. What are your feelings, sir?"

The man was humbled, his head down, eyes full of tears. He slowly raised his head and found Sophie's eyes. "My son has asked to come to this place since he was a small boy. Whenever I asked him where he wanted to go on vacation, he would say, 'Salem.' I thought he was touched, frankly. I took him to Disney World instead, for a more wholesome 'American' experience." The man made air quotes and smiled before continuing, amused at his own words. "I always take him somewhere for his birthday, every September. This year, his eighteenth birthday, I surprised him with this trip. It's his birthday today. I believe he and his girlfriend would be honored to take part in your toast."

"Excellent!" Sophie said, signaling Poe for the rum, asking Dylan to dig out the shot glasses and shortbread cookies from the Trader Joe's bag. The father chose to stand outside the Circle, feeling nervous and not wanting to cramp his son's style. He seemed to know this was an important spiritual rite for his son. He likely could feel it; it made him shiver from head to toe.

Before enjoying the Sacrament, Sophie decided to move the revelry to the outside of the memorial, still on hallowed ground but away from the memorial. Many people were curious with the offerings placed on the stone shelves and had queued up to view them. They were quiet and orderly. Even whole families with small children felt honored to be in the group's presence and acted respectfully. The memorial area hummed with positive energy, Prana visible through the tree canopy of gold.

Once the party walked to the opposite side of the memorial wall, inside Charter Street Cemetery, they formed a Circle, inviting the young people to join in. Once formed, Sophie instructed the young man, never catching his name, to stand in the center of the Circle. Surrounded, the young man, unable to contain a genuine smile, beamed with excitement.

"Happy Birthday, young man. You were born on an important day, the last day of the hangings in the Witch Hysteria of 1692. It is my guess you are connected to this place in a very real way, through reincarnation. This is the reason you have always wanted to come here. There are no coincidences in the Universe. Know this to be true!"

Sophie poured the first glass of rum from the big bottle left over from Corey land and poured it onto the ground, which greedily soaked in the elixir. The second glass was for the young man. "Drink it down and leave a sip for the Spirits, as I just did."

The boy followed her directions, chugging down the rum in one fluid gulp, which brought another batch of tears to his eyes. His girlfriend used the same glass, Sophie's glass, since she did not drink anyway. The Sacrament continued around the Circle clockwise, as always, ending in an enthusiastic "Blessed Be!" The cookies were eaten, each person sharing crumbs with the ground beneath their feet. The teenagers were visibly touched, feeling flushed and emotional because of the rum.

"Thank you for joining us for our blessed Sacrament. I trust you will research your birth date, in regard to this place, and find your individual story within the complicated archives of Essex County. Blessed Be and Happy Birthday!" Sophie hugged the boy first, then the girl, and waved to the father, smiling graciously in his direction.

Miss Mary rose from her padded place perched on a low dividing wall between memorial and cemetery. She was glad to see the party and hugged each one enthusiastically but stopped short of Sophie, knowing that Sophie still refused to touch her. Miss Mary seemed to respect Sophie's choice, although it was sure to sting a bit. Sophie had her Shamanic taboos: she could not touch anything dead, she could not touch the insane, she could not ask money for spiritual work…so many do-nots that Sophie barely kept track of them. No worries, Spirit had Sophie covered. "We'll see you tomorrow morning sometime, Miss Mary. We have something for you. If we don't see you for some reason, we'll leave your goodies with Dorothy, alright?"

"Thank you, Giles. I look forward to seeing you tomorrow, even though I will not be happy about your departure, no matter what you say. I'll be here, one way or the other. May I have the boxes you left behind before your ceremony?" Miss Mary mumbled and lowered her head, knowing the encounter was over.

"Of course, Mary. That's why we left them near you. If you don't want them, Dorothy will recycle them for us. I've talked to Dorothy and she knows if you really need someone to help you in case of emergency, she'll act in my stead." Sophie wanted to cradle the women but knew it wasn't a good idea—a classic way to carry ghosts, ghouls, and negative programming home. Instead, Sophie smiled broadly at Miss Mary, bowed slightly, turned around and walked away—toward the waiting silver SUV, a cool shower, her best clothes for the Feast. Sophie was done, only Yom Kippur and Mabon toasts and prayers to be said, and food to be eaten, scraps laid for the critters.

Chapter Twenty-Seven

THE LIBERATION FEAST

September 22, 2007, 5:00 p.m.

BETWEEN THE THOUGHTS IN HER HEAD, the three's questions, the tourists, and the general urban noise, Sophie was ready for solitary time, the bliss of quiet, without deadline or stress. Dylan climbed into a cool shower and, still wrapped in a damp towel, hit his bed with a heavy thud. He would cherish the needed sleep before the evening revelry set in. Ah, she found room to breathe. The purr of the hotel air cleaner soothed deeply. Finally alone, she began to move. She needed space to pace the floor without distraction or interruption. Caught in routines of pacing, enjoying motion joined with the constant pictures in her head, Sophie relaxed, skeletal pain relieved by walking and gentle swaying. She needed to move. Sometimes in the middle of movies or in the middle of a conversation, her bones demanded movement, her head screamed for it. She prized her solitude. She was lonely only when others pointed out her lacks or interrupted her intentional movement, asking what the problem was, the reason for aimless walking. Few understood her needs.

Sophie's shower was cool too, washing away the dusty salt of the hot day. Dressed in nothing but a lavender t-shirt, her joy factor was growing by the minute. She felt oddly free, whole, a little scared. In the back of her mind, she was anxious, having second thoughts about bringing out her Prayer Shawl in front of people at the Lyceum, though this was the reason she had brought it to begin with, to wear it for the Yom Kippur prayers, part of the Feast Ceremony she planned. Sophie believed in breaking some rules, but she didn't like to be watched while she did it.

She had never had a Bat Mitzvah. She had asked for one, but her parents were too broke and too counterculture to do something so traditional.

Besides, her sister Joan was ill, almost on her deathbed when Sophie turned thirteen. Everyone had to sacrifice. This was Sophie's turn to suffer silently. She wouldn't have a First Blood Ceremony either, or a Sweet Sixteen birthday party, a prom, or a white wedding. Her parents loved her but had little time or energy to give Sophie the sense of tradition she craved.

When she asked Dylan to buy her a traditional blue-and-white Prayer Shawl a couple of years earlier, he had found an Israeli artist who hand-painted silk shawls just for women, mainly for Bat Mitzvahs, in pastel colors of pink, blues, and purples. He bought one designed to look like a desert sunrise, in shades of magenta and lavender, with a pink yarmulke to match, and presented it to her with such pomp that she shook with expectation and almost fainted. Sophie had to be gifted her spiritual tools. She had been taught that tools used for sacred missions did not work effectively if you purchased them yourself—another one of her rules, this time attributable to her mother, Sarah. She opened the gift and gasped at its beauty, touching its delicate chiffon, so soft and dangerously special. She packed it away in white tissue paper and placed it next to her precious Pendleton blankets in her magickal chest, so proud of the piece of wearable art. Sophie saw herself in her mind's eye wearing it as a scarf to a movie premiere or a fancy feast, not presided over by her. She would be a guest, dressed to impress. But for her spiritual work, she wanted a traditional Tallit. Undaunted, Sophie expanded her original request, asking for two Prayer Shawls, both blue-and-white, one with gold thread and one with silver, each worn depending on the cycles of the Moon or based on an ethereal whim. Dylan knew he was stuck and had better buy the requested shawls immediately, or else she would ask for three the next time.

Sophie took her shawl from its carrying bag, kissed its fringe, and placed it over her shoulders. Regardless of who was at the Lyceum, she would risk disapproval again and wear the blue-and-white silver-threaded Tallit for Star Nation with pride, as she chanted the Yom Kippur prayers. This was her night; she had to do it her way.

Sophie dressed in black and white, Spirit's chosen colors for the American Camino, the High Priestess's pillars leading the way. The white blouse, the same blouse worn during rituals, Holy Days, and initiations celebrating Giles's life and death for the past three years, would last for one more party before finding its way into the magickal closet. Sophie's black-hole Regalia closet had a life of its own, filled with cloaks, swords, conical hats:

the spooky stuff Witch-lovers live for. The blouse, though limp because of over-laundering, was full of Sophie's DNA. Her plans made and executed, the rites allowing Giles to claim his freedom were embedded in the fabric, lived and breathed and remembered the chants and sacrifices, her comfort zone tonight.

Minutes before Dylan and Sophie were due to pick up Dora and Poe at their hotel, they began packing the Liberation Feast atar offerings. So much had happened since they had gathered the treasures. Sophie stood transfixed above the packing box, with no time to spare, thinking of the dramas transporting her to this moment, the endless prayers and pleading, the tears, the suffering, dreams so horrid that Sophie rarely dreamed anymore. Her brain had created new pathways, avoiding dreamtime and lurking night-terrors, the main reason sleep was a dying art for her. Dylan snapped her awake, moving sharply, dressed in cobalt blue, the color of the Spirit Realms, of Medicine Ways. He moved the precious altar box, creating a diversion, and headed Sophie out of the door toward Salem for the Feast, three years in the making.

Dora looked stunning, dressed in muted shades, beige and rust, accented with red bead Moroccan earrings, her dark eyes set off by her auburn halo of hair. She carried herself with a new grace; she was a different person than last week, fully grown and separate. Her future loomed before her; she would search for a ring worthy of grabbing. Dora was remote, lending to her film-star good looks and exaggerated tango posture. She had decided against a public separation announcement or even a brief letter passed to Sophie on the plane. There was no need to sever the bonds between young and middle-aged women. The apron strings were already cut; it would be stating the obvious. Dora had felt Sophie's sharp magickal scissors at Mary Corey's grave. She finally understood what Sophie meant by goodbye. Her feet were bound tightly with bandages, disguised cleverly behind the red leather of her shoes. She strutted her way into the Lyceum, knowing all eyes were on her.

Poe stood in contrast to Dora; she chose to mute her fire, wanting to fade more than shine tonight. Her long streaked blonde hair fell down her back in lazy waves, over a mauve-colored clingy knit dress. Poe walked through the main door of the restaurant, smiled, then hesitated, looking around for familiar faces seated at the bar before going into the Lyceum proper. Her radar was engaged tonight. She didn't want to miss a thing.

The four stood in front of an oak podium, appointed with a brass plaque:

"*Please wait here. The manager will seat you.*" In a matter of two minutes, a waitress and a bartender asked them for drink orders. "Are you the special party for the back room, the people from Oregon?" asked a tall broad man with golden hair, deferring to Sophie, awaiting her reply. Now, the Lyceum was used to dealing with powerful women, Sophie thought. The handsome man thought to ask the older woman for information, instead of the man, or the two beautiful younger women. "Yes, we are. St. Cloud is the name. How did you know we were from Oregon?" The bartender did not answer, just lowered his smiling face and sashayed back behind the bar. The restaurant manager and another waitress appeared, excited to meet the party of four. They had heard through the grapevine an important magickal feast was planned tonight. They all suspected the Oregon party was where the action would be.

"Ms. St. Cloud, good to meet you. I have heard much about your work." The manager greeted the party enthusiastically. "I am a fan of the internet. I saw your name in the reservation book the other day and it sounded familiar, so Google you I did; now here you are." He continued, eyes sparkling, full of excitement: "You asked for a fairly private table, for six instead of four, because I understand you brought an altar? Well, please forgive me, but I took the liberty and set up our back room for your feast. It's set for forty-five. I assure you, you will not be bothered. However, your table is set in the center of a large pair of French doors, overlooking the main dining room, so our other guests will not be able to hear you, but they will be able to see you. I hope it's not a problem. We are booked solid, so I am unable to change the arrangements now. I hope you understand."

"I thank you for respecting our needs in such a generous fashion. We are used to audiences, especially in Massachusetts. It will feel familiar. Thank you, I am excited to get started!" Sophie smiled at the pleasant manager.

"Of course, please follow me."

The party was led, single file, Sophie leading the pack, through the main dining room. The cream-colored room, with starched beige and white linens on honey-colored oak tables, hummed with excitement, tables filled with colorful plates of food and wines in exotic bottles, pastries and cream and special little coffee cups. The fire roared in the painted brick fireplace on the Northern wall, its mantel decorated with the sacred colors of Mabon, the colors of dramatic Western sunsets, dotted with golden mums and miniature pumpkins. From Corey land? Sophie whispered to herself. Knowing

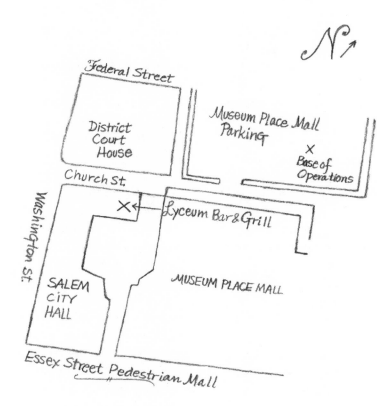

Federal Street

District Court House

Museum Place Mall Parking

× Base of Operations

Church St.

Washington St.

× Lyceum Bar & Grill

SALEM CITY HALL

MUSEUM PLACE MALL

Essex Street Pedestrian Mall

The Liberation Feast, Salem

Witches had set the mantel, that it was their Sabbat Altar, made her feel safe and warm. She turned her head, hearing someone listening to her thoughts: she sensed it like radar. An elegant woman in beige tweed and chunky gold jewelry sat stirring her cup of coffee with an extended pinkie. She was the listener. She found Sophie's eyes and said, "Welcome!"

Sophie bowed to the woman, who was a decade older and a world richer than she, and said, "Thank you."

The manager came to a stop. Sophie tried to quiet her wandering mind, wondering who the woman in tweed was. Still lost in her rambling thoughts, she almost fell into the manager as he struggled to open the glass French doors leading to the restricted dining area. The manager, finally successful with the lock, opened the door in, revealing a dangling sign: *"private party"* in red lettering. Sophie looked around the beautifully appointed, understated room, thanked the manager for his kindness, and closed the glass door behind him. There was another door, closer to the kitchen, for the staff and party members to go through. They wouldn't have to deal with the glass door and its sticking lock again. She did feel a bit imprisoned at first, after the doors closed behind the manager. Through the glass, she couldn't help but see a couple of hundred eager diners watching every move she made. The closeness came with another realization: the room was entirely windowed, back and sides, as well as front, a fishbowl. Completely surrounded by glass, everybody and anybody could view the party of four, lip-read their prayers, see their altar, know what they ate and how much they drank. The party was on display, as much to the outside world as the inner-Lyceum crowd.

Unnerved, but not surprised, Sophie put down the box containing the Feast altar offerings. She needed to mill around the room, inspect the tightly laid table settings. The glass room had one round table and many square tables. The round table was their main feasting table, with four over-padded chairs set around it in a half-circle pattern, facing the large public dining room. The woman in tweed smiled again, this time raising a brandy snifter in Sophie's direction. Sophie knew this woman, but could not place her.

She wanted to relax, but the altar needed to be set, prayers had to be made, Spirit Guests greeted. Dora wanted to help Sophie set the altar—she wanted in on the action, on the fun part. Dora had bought a South-African–made black three-legged cauldron the day before, shopping in Old Town. She insisted the cauldron be the candleholder for the Mabon burgundy candle. Sophie enthusiastically agreed. The two women were delighted with themselves, with the party taking shape. The room was beautiful; drinks were already being delivered, brought by the management, paid for by the lady in tweed. The party of four was beaming, all shapes and sizes, thrilled with the heady lightness of success. This was the Liberation Feast. Now the others knew why Sophie had named it so. They were free in the now to be exactly who they were. All could feel their newfound freedom brewing, on both sides of the glass.

Caught in the moment, drinks delivered to an adjoining table, Sophie reached for a chilled bottle of Perrier. "A toast: to us!" The three reached for their choice of alcohol: glasses of pinot noir, mojitos with down-island rum, vodka martinis. Whoever ordered the drinks knew the party. Was it Dylan who ordered? He shook his head no. He had been too preoccupied to put in a drink order when initially asked by the bartender, having been thrown by the tall man's questions. Standing, they all faced the dining room audience, raised their glasses and waited for the diners to respond, which they did in quick turn. "L'Chaim!" Sophie proclaimed, echoing into the confines of the dining room. The party of four toasted and clinked their glasses, feeling sharp, a little edgy, already having a ball. The diners smiled and continued their conversations, from time to time gazing into the fish-bowl party's direction.

The altar set-up was complete, everything but the candle. Sophie would handle it as part of her prayers. She entreated all to sit, relax, drink, and listen. The Spirit Guests had been greeted; all extra glasses and drinks delivered to the set tables, one for each. The three would exchange full glasses for empty as the night drew on; many had been delivered.

Sophie began her gratitude speech. "This was an almost impossible feat, this American Camino. We walked, rode, prayed, and cried through it and now, here we are, as the restaurant manager said. I counted while I was packing the Feast Altar offerings. One hundred and sixty-four broken Spirits traveled to the light on the American Camino—one hundred and fifty at Graves Beach, one in Haverhill, four at B'nai Brith, nine at Sawyer's Hill. Still more—George Jacobs, for one—were shown how to find the light when ready. Many are now free to move on, are no longer in pain, no longer confused or lost. It is their choice how they spend their time now. They are no longer needy. Do you realize hundreds are now free among John Marston's Army of the Dead, no longer clinging to old belief patterns? Hard lines have blurred, leaving more for interpretation. Many, over the next year and a day, will decide to reincarnate, to leave this Massachusetts Bay Colony behind for now, for good perhaps. Many still love it here, are still bonded to it. The first anniversary of tonight will be insightful; we'll know so much more in a year, we'll have hindsight on our side by then.

"Thank you for being here, for your support, for your valuable energy. I would not have been able to complete this job in one trip without you. I am honored to have worked with you. Please accept these signs of my gratitude." Sophie reached into her bag and brought out a wrapped gift for each of them. Poe and Dora both had necklaces made of silver Sun Crosses with hanging rose-colored scallop shells, suspended on Italian chain. Dylan's necklace was a silver Equal Cross with a red Swarovski crystal on a black silk cord. Just tokens, Sophie thought, small enough to travel with, special enough to say thank you. She was truly grateful, to them, to the Spirits, even to the Putnams.

She began to smile—wider than usual. She turned to the woman in tweed and gold, who was staring in her direction. The beige woman rose, followed by three men, one striking and dark in his fifties, the other two taller, sixtyish, with the same smile as old Donald Putnam. It hit her. Of course, Donald's children, his three sons and daughter. The woman in tweed noticed Sophie's huge smile; she nudged her brother and Drake smiled in Sophie's direction. See, he received his rose from the candy store. Wonderful, she thought, her heart full.

The Putnam party was met by the enthusiastic manager, planning on escorting them out. The three men and one woman in tweed—regal, lovely, and refined—turned to Sophie and her friends and waved in their direction. Sophie waved back. The other three sat bewildered. She would fill them in later.

Encouraged and excited to move ahead with the simple ritual planned, she reached the adjoining table, used now as a bar. Bringing the kosher grape juice close, she gathered wine glasses on a bar tray. She reached over her chair between Poe and Dylan and picked up the miniature tea set. The bottle of juice was offered up, blessing the fruit of the vine, and giving thanks to the Gods for bringing them to this celebratory place in time. The vessels were filled and passed out, with instructions not to drink yet. She brought out a lighter and a blue birthday candle and cleared her throat.

Out of the box she retrieved her Tallit, folded in its bag, wrapped in white cloth, white the color for Yom Kippur: an empty sheet of paper, devoid of hate or remorse, clean and face-to-face with one's Creator. Carefully she unwrapped her Prayer Shawl, making sure it never touched the ground, just as she handled Eagle Feathers, alert and respectful. She kissed the edge of the shawl close to its tassels and offered it above her head to all the Directions, beginning in the North, and placed it carefully and slowly over her shoulders, now aware all eyes were on her. She turned clockwise, energizing her Circle and faced the West: the direction of Mabon, the Door of the Dead, and the glass French doors.

"O blessed Mother Shekinah,
Sweet Mother of the desert people,
our roots are your arms reaching for us.
We are your children.
You are our beacon, our light, shining our way home.
You are our ally in a world harsh with bitter thoughts and memories.
I reach for you on this Holy Night,
asking for your ear,
hear my claims of chaos sacrificed to you,
making amends to my Creatrix Mother.
O Lords of Israel,
Masters of destiny through your Holy Words, thirty-six thousand strong,
hear our prayers!
Blessed are you,
our Master with names too great to utter,
our Creator of time and space who enriches our lives with holiness.
You have brought us here,
to this place and time,
removed from the past,
but yet of it,
prepared to go forward.
You have planted bits of us here,
in this ground.
On this night of faith,
you have commanded us to kindle the flames of destiny,
cleanse our hearts of the shame of deeds gone wrong.
This is our night,
child and parent blended in a synchronized dance of renewal,

washing away regret.
On this Yom Kippur night,
hear our praises of your light,
flaming in our hearts for all to see."

Reaching over her chair once more, she lit the blue birthday candle, the color of mental calm, and ignited the tea candle in Dora's new cauldron. It hissed awake and glowed. The restaurant followed suit, dimmers activated throughout the restaurant and candles blazing, even in their segregated space. Had the staff tiptoed in during the ritual and lit all the candles without their knowing? No re-run button on Sophie's brain tonight. She accepted the happening as ambiance of this old building, in sync with the prayers filling it, sharing sacred feasts for hundreds of years. Why would it be different now in the twenty-first century? This is precisely what makes the Lyceum special!

Sophie passed out the wine glasses filled with grape juice, clockwise, raised hers and said,

"In perfect love and in perfect trust, we drink you, Great Mother!"

They all drew long sips from the fluted glasses and sighed as the sweet dark fluid hit their taste buds. They were hungry, finally relaxed, not even noticing the ogles and stares and expectations of pyrotechnic displays from the diners in the main room.

"Blessed Mabon, Blessed Yom Kippur, Blessed Liberation Feast!"

Once again they drew long sips, keeping their sighs to themselves this time.

"Drink deeply, honored guests,
may you never thirst!
Eat well, friends beyond time,
may you never hunger!
We are gathered in peace,
under one Sun and one Moon,
may you never be lost!

Bless this Earth, your home and Mother,
may she be well enough to provide and endure.
Our everlasting Queen,
you have returned our lives to us with mercy,
We are forever grateful and full of love for your generosity!
Blessed Be!"

Sophie slowly and carefully unwrapped her shawl from around her shoulders, kissed it once again, offered it up to the Directions, and folded it, placing it gently in its bag and tightly wrapped its white cloth, tucking it like an envelope. The ceremony was complete. It was time to toast, to drink, to eat, to tell stories.

They enjoyed a feast fit for world-class gourmets. They toasted friends, old enemies, and the living who keep the illusions alive, friends who shatter it in their wake. Special toasts were made to the Putnams: for Donald, Drake, the sister in tweed, and the two distinguished fair-haired brothers. There were no more fights to be had; the Putnams were no longer rivals. They would be left with their hidden skeletons and secrets too impossible to believe. Sophie had no room for them. They would no longer haunt her; everything was exposed, not a corner left in the shadows. There was no time for wasted talent. Times were too intense to hoard brainpower and sensitivity—the world was changing each day, closer to catastrophe. Perhaps the work done on the American Camino would shift the power away from destruction. They prayed it would. They would wait and pray for another regime, another batch of leaders who demonstrated a different way to live, one with honor given to the Earth Herself. They would never stop praying. Drama would always happen regardless of what one did. They knew some of the realities facing them.

They collected the Spirit Plate, a small dish with bites of food for the Spirits, for the critters. Sophie filled an empty mineral water bottle with the remaining grape juice, pretending each gave a sip. This was the Spirit Cup. She planned to walk a few extra blocks and leave the Spirit Plate and Cup at the Pressing Place, close by, no scaling walls or climbing fences. Off to the side would do. Pour the juice on the ground of the jailhouse property, let it soak in. The Spirits would drink their fill. The treats and bites of the Feast would nourish the critters, the Spirit Helpers, the rats and the cats. All of them would have a bite, the whole food chain acknowledged and honored.

The bill was settled and tip paid, Dylan generous to a fault, treating them all. They took their time leaving the Lyceum, absorbing the atmosphere, breathing it in, perhaps for the last time. The manager saw the party out into the crisp night, shaking hands with each of them.

They walked directly to the Pressing Place and offered morsels of Feast fare to the waiting Spirits. The offering given and formality completed, they walked and joked and sang, weaving their way through the misty brick walkways and streets. They were no longer hurting or tired, simply relieved, found, home and waiting to go home, all at once. Poe entertained the group on the way back to the car. It seemed to take hours, all laughing so hard, walking off their drunk. Poe so funny, doing impressions of her grandmother, the New York vaudevillian and Broadway gypsy. How they laughed, almost crying, obnoxious. The locals looked the other way and made room for the party from Oregon, so close to the end of their stay in Essex County. Would they ever visit again? they asked out loud, some slurring more than others, the wine, rum and vodka catching up with everyone but Sophie. She had crème brulee and grape juice to make her happy. She had her fun too.

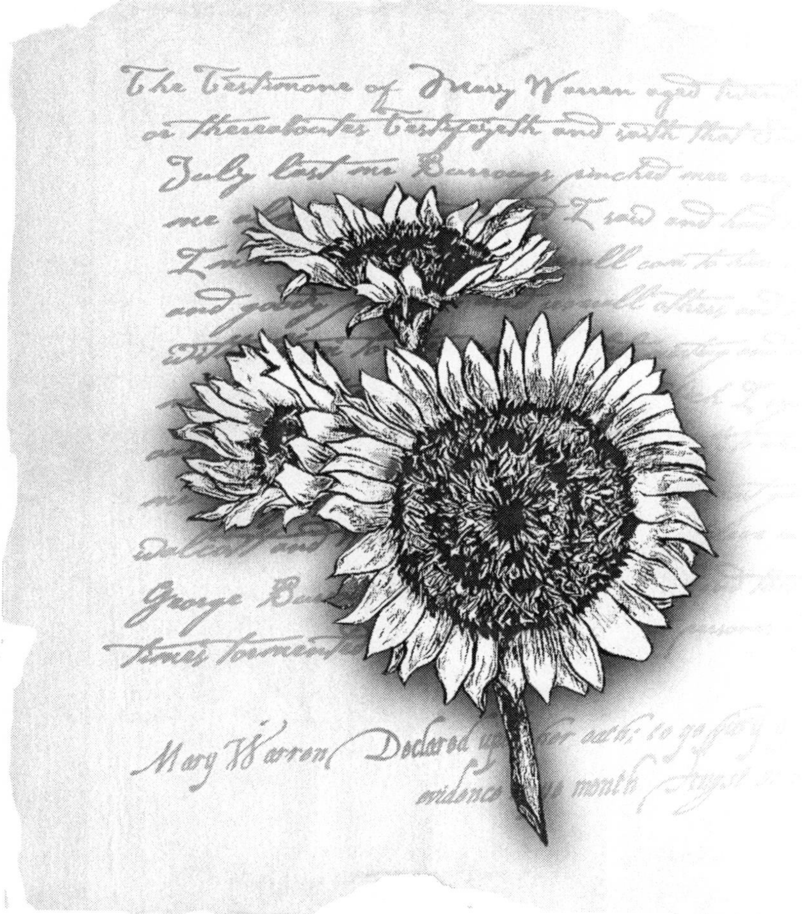
Mary Warren

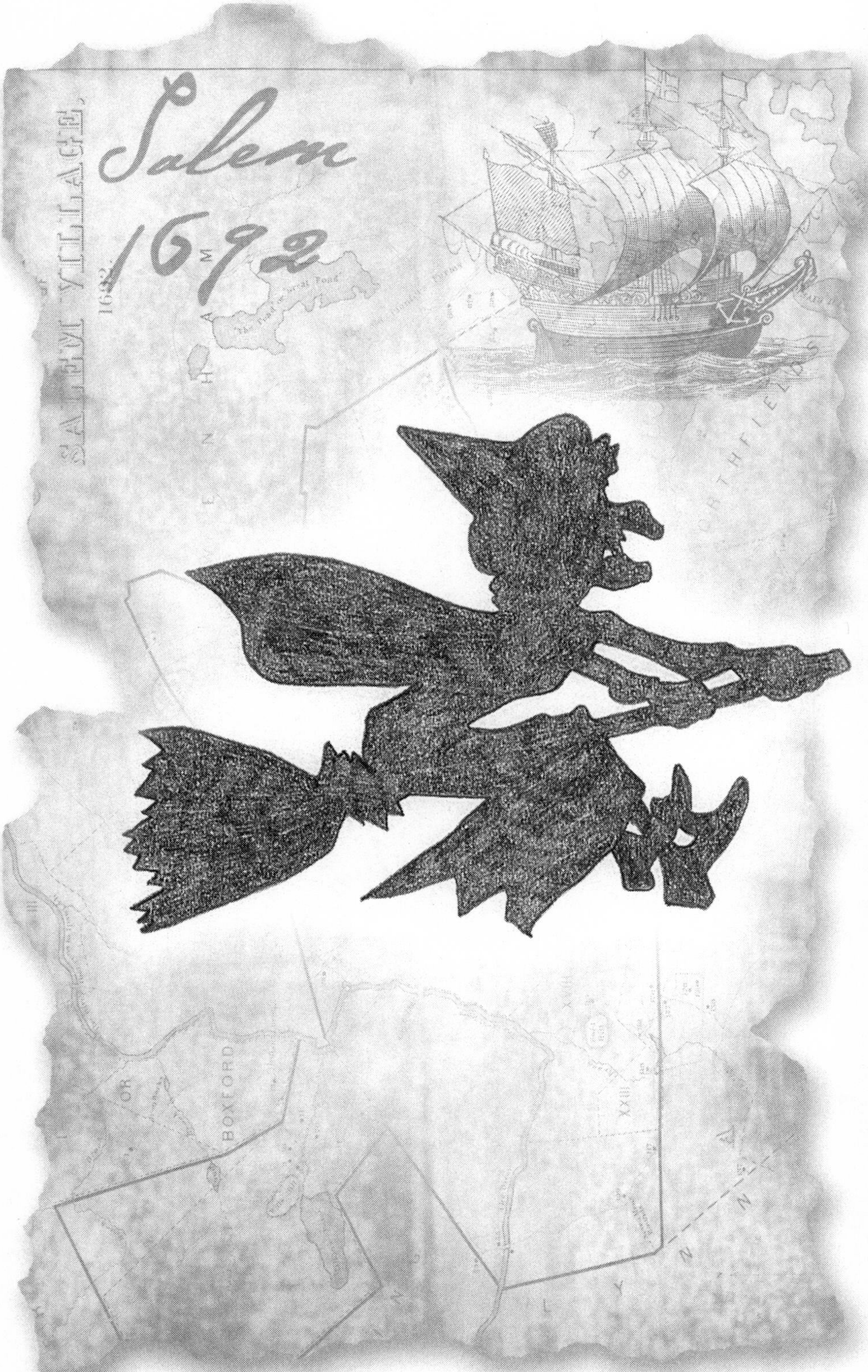
Salem
1692
SALEM VILLAGE
BOXFORD

Chapter Twenty-Eight

SUNDAY: CLOSURE

September 23, 2007, 9:00 a.m.

SORTING, PACKING, SQUEEZING, they had so much to consolidate—four full-sized wheeled cases to transport the needed equipment for the American Camino. Much was left behind in the form of offerings, but every available inch of space made was immediately filled with Spirit Tokens, gifts, books, gourmet chocolate, new maps, clay shards. Sophie didn't have to worry about keeping maps and reference books available. No art supplies were carried onto the plane. She would tote a single daypack. She was tired, no longer a Sherpa for any pay. If she wanted reading material, she'd buy neglected fiction at the airport bookstore, escapist, with happy endings.

She had decided to forgo breakfast out, since so many groceries were left from Dylan's constant gathering. The four of them could eat a several-course meal and still have groceries left over for Miss Mary. Once they were finished packing, altars included, Dylan left to pick up Poe and Dora. Sophie looked at the ingredients available and decided on breakfast burritos, Dylan's favorite, with lots of eggs, cheese, and green chiles. She felt content doing for the group; she knew there would not be many occasions like this in the future, no sleepover pajama parties. The girls were girls no more. Sophie and Dylan were not parents, never were—they'd just been confused in their roles.

The three had headaches from too much alcohol-mixing during the Feast. Sophie mixed a pitcher of screwdrivers with the last of the good Russian vodka and orange juice. It would clear their heads, bless their hearts, she thought, her silent insincere ring tarnished.

Sophie dived into her oatmeal, a feast waited for since last night. She had her set ways—her likes and dislikes, her needs—she ate cereal twice a day. Breakfast was gobbled, no leftovers, the extra tortillas rolled with cheese for emergency food. The cleanup was shared Sophie packed the rest of the groceries in a brown paper shopping bag and placed Miss Mary's beige fleece blanket on top. They were ready for Salem goodbyes.

Sophie talked Dylan out of one last cruise of Crystal Lake and Corey land. She had cried her share of tears and did not want anyone or anything to cloud her journey back home, home to Oregon. They took their time, meandering back streets and lanes to Old Salem. Old Town was deserted compared with the Sunday before, the morning of the Vernal Equinox, and half the town, tourists included, were hanging out behind locked doors, soothing their mornings after. It had been the feast of the grape, Dionysus' time to go wild.

The party of four felt wonderful, pensive but bright. Dylan pulled into a parking space around the corner from Dorothy's shop, the closest they had ever parked to the cemetery. Dylan grabbed the shopping bag and began walking toward Charter Street; they would say farewell to Dorothy on the way back. Full circle, Sunday to Sunday.

Attracted by patches of white, Sophie made her way into the memorial. The others followed. There, on top of the rock ledge, placed open and carefully weighted by small stones, were many of the tightly rolled, thread-wrapped scrolls. Why would people take the time to desecrate the memorial, open others' tokens and gifts? The closer Sophie got to the open scrolls, the creepier she felt. She noticed the invitations were no longer plain; someone had used a red marker, highlighting the individual names, living and dead. Metacomet's invitation was the only one visibly battered, other than the highlighted names. It had been crunched, walked on, scribbled on, and finally made flat again and weighted with the others. Clearly someone was not impressed with the group's Spirit allies—the defacers were not Indian lovers.

She smiled when she noticed the scroll for the party itself, proclaiming the Feast, outlining how many guests had been invited, the venue, date, and time. The Lyceum crew was not as clever as Sophie thought; they had been informed of many details. Spies were everywhere! Sophie gathered all the invitation scrolls, now just slips of paper without purpose, and balled them hard in her hands. She flattened the balls with the soles of her shoes, finally wedging them deep between the wall and the protruding rock ledges. Only tools and weather could bring the paper to the surface now, as it should be. The group had made history last night—the scrolls were proof of it. Sophie wanted them preserved, to melt and become part of the rocks themselves.

The group passed through the memorial for a final time, from start to finish, from Bridget to Samuel and everyone in between. The bread had been claimed by the critters, as had the M&Ms and sunflower nuts. The apples were still placed, smelling faintly of rum. The flowers, roses and sunflowers, remained where they had been placed lovingly. The four were pleased; the offerings were used and respected. Sophie felt confused by such honor and malice, always duality on this plane. Maybe Miss Mary was jealous—maybe she opened the scrolls looking for her name? Obviously, she had not dug deep enough, for she was invited, all three parts of her, now living in one over-sized middle-aged body. Miss Mary had looked bright and healthy yesterday. Where was she now? Miss Mary could not have been the spy. Sophie wouldn't revisit the idea.

They walked the full inside perimeter of the burial ground and all four outside corners looking for Miss Mary. She was not there. She had been informed of their visit, but she chose to be absent, instead of saying goodbye. Sophie understood Mary and had shared many revelatory experiences with her in a short time. One week and Miss Mary had changed. The magickal work of the American Camino had been successful in her regard; Sophie felt it in her bones and her bones didn't lie or exaggerate! Mary had begun to feel close to normal again; she had forgotten the feeling.

They walked to Dorothy's shop and found it deserted, except for Dorothy and a couple of skinny teens, her part-time Sunday workers. The woman's face brightened as they headed for the large counter that divided clerk from patron. Dylan slung the shopping bag onto the counter and explained it was for Miss Mary. Most of the food didn't need to be refrigerated, at least not for a while. Dorothy nodded and told the party not to worry, the goodies would find their way to Miss Mary this afternoon, if not sooner. She told a story of Miss Mary hiding behind bushes, avoiding people, particularly on Sundays. Nobody knew why she was extra freaky on Sunday; it was just the way of it.

Sophie asked Dorothy if she could speak to her in private. She agreed and walked to the back hall, on the way to a mock-dungeon, open in the afternoons for tours. Dorothy looked nervous, not knowing what Sophie wanted from her. She was determined not to agree to anything today, not before she did research to try to figure out who the good guys were, and where the bad guys lived. Sophie reached out and placed her right hand on Dorothy's left shoulder. "May I be blunt with you, Dorothy?" The woman looked stunned; she shook her head a couple of times and asked Sophie for clarification.

"I know you are looking for a new spiritual home, a new Circle. I know you are dedicated and sincere. But I'm afraid you are naïve. You've recently learned you cannot always trust other Witches. Not all Witches live by the Rule of Three and Do No Harm."

Dorothy lowered her head and shook it again, trying to clear her sense of guilt, placate her better self. Sophie reached for the slumped woman's chin, lifted it, leveling their eyes despite their height difference. "Don't be afraid of the Inner Circle, Dorothy—they are in the process of changing. No longer do they need to work covertly, covering tracks of bad deeds hundreds of years old. I believe there will be a changing of the guard, soon, within the year. You must promise me you will leave them emotionally behind, for your sake, for your psychic and emotional survival. Do you agree?"

Dorothy looked puzzled; she had sworn she would not agree to anything further with Sophie. But she couldn't say no to the short, silver-haired woman. She looked too much like her Momma, although she was dark while Sophie was light. Sophie heard Dorothy's thoughts and interjected, "I'm not as white as you think I am. My mother was Indian, through and through. Okay, a tiny bit white, but as brown as a berry and as spooky as any Elder you would ever meet!" Dorothy looked at Sophie; she finally relaxed, and let her shoulders fall and her back straighten.

"I promise I will leave Lori Otto behind—the Inner Circle frightens me anyway. I wanted to be a part of their Circle until you came to town. I had a couple of visitations from friends of Lori's last week, spooked me it did! They heard I was being supportive of your work. I never knew this town was so small—you can't have a private thought without everyone knowing the details. I'll stay clear of them. I mean it." She hesitated and added, "Really!" Dorothy's cheeks filled with air, a nervous response, sighing as the air escaped.

"Do you know the Circle of teenagers who meet on Friday evenings at Howard Street Cemetery? They have a shared leadership, three young women."

"Yes, I do know who you are talking about. Some of them are related to the Inner Circle, kids of a few women I've met, some distant relatives of the Desmonds and Ottos. They have a tattooed kid who is their bodyguard, fancies himself as a High Priest. Can you imagine, being eighteen and calling yourself a High Priest? One of the girls came here one day last Winter and asked if she could give Tarot readings in my shop. I shooed her away before I knew who her mother was. Lori Otto's niece, I think."

Sophie nodded in her direction, fascinated, seeing the Circle of kids from Dorothy's perspective. "Here's the deal, Dorothy—these kids are amazing, talented—they can help you and you can help them. I suggest you start a Circle of your own, as High Priestess, take these kids under your wing, have the girl give readings here in the off-season, as she requested. I suspect she is good and will help your business. If nothing else, her friends have expendable cash and will spend it with you. Under the surface they are respectful, good kids. I don't have to tell you to overlook the Gothiness of it all…" They both smiled, Sophie chuckling softly.

"This is your chance to get in on the bottom floor with the future leaders of this town, of this county, probably of this country. They have power; those three girls will blow everybody's mind in another decade. Be their rock, Dorothy, build a spiritual family, one you can count on for decades to come, lifetimes perhaps." Sophie ended her pleading, straightened her shirt, and turned, preparing to leave.

Dorothy's hand found its way around Sophie's shoulder, pulling her back into the hallway. The larger woman enveloped Sophie like an anaconda, although not squeezing as the huge constrictor would do. "Thank you, Miss Sophie. I told my mother about you, and she said she'd like to meet you someday. I'll sit with what you told me about the kids. I'll keep my eyes out for them, as I will continue to do for Miss Mary. Did I tell you? Mary's family found her last Monday evening; they want her to move back to Maine. The girls and I got together and bought Miss Mary a bus ticket. She leaves next week."

Sophie eyes filled with tears. The Big Work was a success. Mary was healing; she was put back together again. "Wonderful news! You've made my day, Dorothy! It's all because of you, you know, someone taking an interest in Mary, filling in the blanks for her, caring what she feels, thinks, and worrying about what she eats. You are the best friend she has ever had, know it to be true!" Sophie hugged Dorothy hard and whispered in her ear, "You have a chance to make peace now; you've got work to do with Samuel Parris. Remember, forgiveness is not yours to give, you must be strong and call him out. He wronged you and you must clear the slate. With it said and done, you'll be able to move on, claim your magickal talents for the first time in three hundred and fifteen years and make your future brighter than you ever dreamed!" Sophie pulled away from the large woman and saw plump tears falling from Dorothy's eyes.

Dorothy leaned against the door, worn out from the realizations, directions, and lecture. She sighed heavily as she waved her new friends goodbye. If they ever returned to Salem, she would make a place for them in her heart. Until then, she had work to do. After the group was out of sight, Dorothy walked to the back door of the painted black shop and opened it. There sat Miss Mary, on the large pillow-covered stump against a worn stone wall. "They're gone, Miss Mary. They really care about you. Their magick is strong, probably the reason you have a new home to go to. You can heal now. You have a family who wants to welcome you back after years of separation. You'll have to go slow, be good to yourself. Don't run away this time. We all have to give thanks."

Miss Mary, her reddened face lowered, began to cry, large rolling tears. "Giles Corey is a good man. I'll miss him, I will!"

Dorothy knew what Miss Mary meant; Mary had filled in the blanks for Dorothy earlier in the week. "Yes, I feel honored to have met her." Dorothy knelt and gently kissed Miss Mary on the cheek, "Come around the front in about a half hour. I'll have a sandwich ready for you and a bag of treats." Miss Mary nodded, still unable to talk, her tears still gently choking back her words. Mary had a second chance on life and she knew it was because of Giles and Goodwife Martha Corey, two very fine people, indeed!

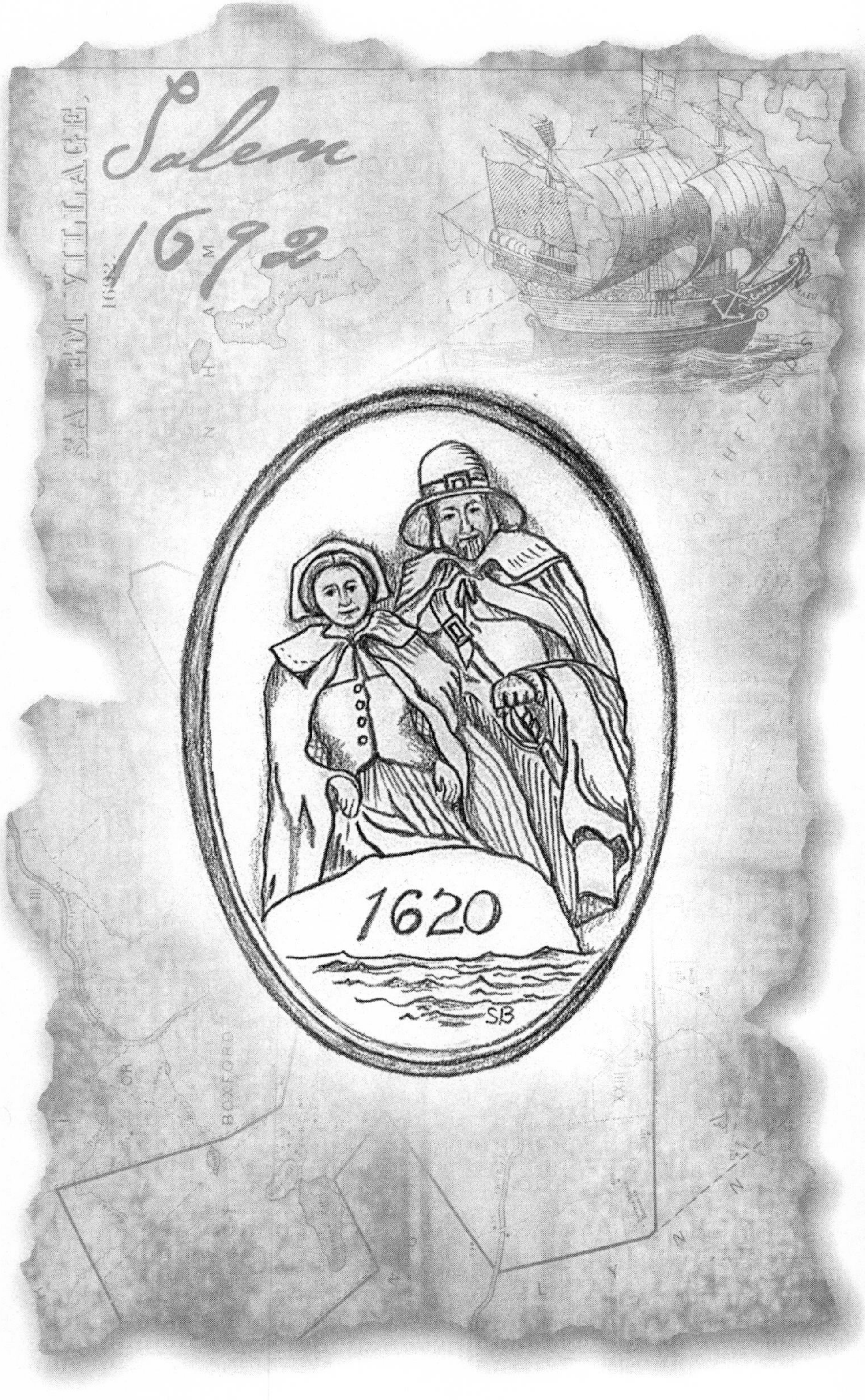
Salem
1692
SALEM VILLAGE
1620
SB
BOXFORD

Chapter Twenty-Nine

THE ANNIVERSARY

September 19, 2008, 3:30 p.m.

THE DOORBELL RANG and someone pounded on the front glass door, sounding like the Inquisition come knocking. It was Giles's Pressing Day—still unnerving. Sophie planned a day of quiet solitary reading. Despite the successful Integration, it had not changed the reality of history. She wasn't expecting anyone or anything. The knocking continued. FedEx needed a signature for a package from Lydia Dustin, insured. Lydia was too cheap for insurance or FedEx, for that matter. What in the world?

The card was a print of a painting done in the sixties: a large white bird with a goose's neck, Eagle wings, duck face, Hawk bill, Owl talons, flying East in a cloudless red sky. The flowing script, written with an old-fashioned ink pen, Sophie knew well; its swirls and dashes filled the cards serving as refrigerator art in Sophie's kitchen. Lydia always sent the coolest cards.

Dear Sophie,

I know we haven't talked much in the past year, at least not like
we used to. I miss you, but having a relationship with you is too
freaky; you keep me on edge, you lecture and give advice. I just want
an old friend's ear from time to time. I don't want you to tell me what
to do. I have other friends who know me better. I seek advice from
them. I couldn't live a lie anymore; I had to admit I have no time for
spirituality, no respect for it in any form, too much dogma, whether
Shamanism or mythology—it bores me to tears. It's a load of crap:
hypotheses, unproved theories, only other people's opinions. You obviously didn't take it well. I miss your letters and packages, but I don't
regret speaking my mind.

You asked me why I bothered writing for over thirty years, making
nice-nice, if I didn't respect and appreciate your scholarship and work.
I remained silent. You wouldn't be able to hear the simple fact that I

like you. Not your intellect, but your sense of humor—you make me laugh. It's true, I like some of your stories too, not the violent or strong ones, the gentle ones. I don't like your art, it's too intense for me. Okay, I finally said it, only took me three decades. Anyway, I was silent until now, guess I had to finish my point. I love having the last word.

I have a newfound independence; my daughter went away to college and it changed my life. I left my boyfriend—I was so over him—and got a new house with roommates. Love it! I no longer have the burden of being the only breadwinner. I feel brand new. Because of my changes, I have given lots of stuff away, purged my life of negativity, admitted lies said and bad deeds committed, almost like twelve-stepping. You know, removing the junk before the good stuff fills in the gaps. I hate to admit it, but it sounds like one of your self-improvement articles.

Okay, so there's another thing I have to get off my chest, in this new spirit of openness I am trying on. I see ghosts. Well, I used to, I should say. Ghosts I can explain as leftover electrical energy, glimpses into the past. They don't bother my agnostic sensibility. I don't care if you judge me, it's how I feel. Anyway, all the time I have known you, I've seen the ghost of my grandmother a million times removed, Hannah Dustin. I know you know her story; I read an article you wrote about her last year. Weird, isn't it? You researching my Ancestors? Well, the thing is, I haven't seen her for a year, not a shadow, not a wisp, nothing. I finally figured it out. You left my life when Hannah did, last September, and it has something to do with what you did in Massachusetts. Don't get me wrong, I'm not saying I believe in what you do. Maybe Universal powers worked simultaneously as you walked Massachusetts. I haven't figured out the specifics, don't want to know about what, why, or when. I'll get a handle on it in my own way. I just want to tell you, I am softening in regard to prayers, but that's another story... I miss both you and Hannah. I've lost you and that's fine, but still, it's different now and I'm trying to get a handle on it.

My relationship with my birth family has changed too. I've never been close to my sister, Susan, don't like her, really, or didn't. She's fat, which annoys me, and I think she's a busybody, gossips too much, and she really loved our mother, which is hard to fathom. Regardless, we got together last Spring, for a sisters' reunion, our first; it had been twenty years since we visited. This is the amazing part: we really enjoyed each other's company and plan on spending Thanksgiving together from now on. I wrote twenty pages in my journal about it. I'm still blown away. We talk at least once a week on the phone. I feel empty if I have to miss our time together.

Susan brought me a gift that freaked me out. She found it last fall in Massachusetts, the same time you were there. She traveled from Iowa to New Hampshire for the big yearly Dustin family reunion. She's up on all of the extended family. Most of them still live scattered around New England. One afternoon, one of our cousins accompanied Susan, crossing the river into Massachusetts; they wanted to go antiquing in Haverhill. They found an antique mall specializing in seventeenth-century artifacts, they couldn't resist. She found an oldish whiskey bottle—commemorative issue porcelain—of Hannah Dustin holding bloody scalps. It is so gross I can't bear to display it. I've packed it away for my daughter. Maybe she'll be able to deal with it someday. It is part of our history, I keep telling myself. The funny thing is, I can't seem to even think about parting with it. I miss Hannah's presence. My life is a bit lacking without her, emotionally, I've discovered.

I went to the flea market last weekend, the big one on the opera grounds. The Santa Fe market has really grown since our heyday, I'm sure Ali tells you the same thing. I was attracted to my usual vendors, trying to get treasures for a buck, you know me. I looked into a case and didn't believe what I found, a beautiful piece of scrimshaw: a large cabochon of ivory, with inscribed figures of a Puritan couple and a rock with the date 1620. Plymouth Rock, obviously. This gets interesting ... I was perched on the case, a crow stunned by the reflection of a shiny treasure; I was not about to move. I asked the usual woman how much the carved piece was and she said it was scrimshaw; it was dear and worth a lot. I felt defeated. She knew what it was and it had a huge price tag on it. I knew it did. I'd seen similar newer versions of cabbed Scrimshaw, the same size, going for hundreds. I was afraid to ask the price. You know how I love a bargain, love finding hidden treasures. The woman smiled up at me and said, since I was such a great customer, she'd sell it to me for twenty bucks. Well, I almost cried, peed, and threw up all at once; a deal like this could not be ignored. I told her *Sold!* before I even looked at it up close. It could have been plastic, for all I knew. But, good news, it's genuine.

I want you to have my Puritan treasure; you know how I hate all those Pilgrim figures anyway. Why I like Thanksgiving, I'll never know. It must be the pie or my warm spot for cookie dough. It's not Thanksgiving without chocolate chip cookies; my kid made it our main family tradition before she turned three. Mystery solved, must be the cookie dough.

This gift is just a gift. It's not an apology, or a bribe to get back into your good graces. I'm good as I am. I have lots of new friends, am free from past baggage, I feel reborn, that's all I need. So, let me know by email you received the treasure and we'll call our past the past. I'm okay with it. I hope you are.

If you happen to see Hannah Dustin in your travels, be sure to send her my love.

Goodbye.

Peace,
Lydia

Sophie opened the colored tissue paper wrap and saw the ivory, a portrait of Giles and Martha, arm in arm, behind a large inscribed rock and the ocean beyond. Good luck, Lydia, live your life fully, live it well. Goodbye.

Sophie walked to the Main Northern Altar, where a freshly painted Pilgrim couple stood guard over the Putnam Pantry chocolates and maple sugar drops, set aside for the Liberation Feast on the twenty-second. She laid the scrimshaw cabochon between the couple, her gift to them, a celebration of renewal, of survival. Life was complex. Sophie had few answers, which usually vexed her, but today, she smiled and continued her quiet vigil, waiting for Pressing Day to pass in peace, breathing deeply, grateful to be alive.

September 22, 2008, 7:30 p.m.

WITH THE EXCEPTION OF THE NINETEENTH, Sophie ran for a week: cleaning, cooking, freezing, crafting, preparing for the Second Annual Liberation Feast. She barely took the time to think. The pumpkin-pecan miniature cupcakes with cream cheese and sugared ginger icing took a day. The fish pies took another day, made with traditional French butter dough; the three flesh-eaters would devour the pies in short order. Tartlets, candies, roasted nuts, roasted vegetables, salads, and relishes; today was also Mabon, the Witches' Thanksgiving. Table grapes and kosher grape juice and miniature pumpkins shared cozy quarters on the seasonal altars. The scrimshaw portrait sat in the center of the Main Altar, glowing in the candlelight. Tonight promised to be special.

Poe was first to arrive, wearing her favorite moss green sweater, the one she had lived in in Salem. She hugged Sophie warmly, whispering, "Thank you for being here." She presented Sophie a package wrapped in red cotton cloth. "C'mon, open it!" Poe said, feeling festive. There, in the center of the ceremonial cloth, placed carefully on a bed of loose Tobacco, four white roses lay, wrapped with red ribbon. "One for each of us, Sophie. Blessed Be!"

Sophie carefully removed the rosebuds and placed one on top of each plate, next to the chrysanthemum place cards she had written in calligraphy. How wonderful, Sophie thought. Now each of them would have a magickal rose for the first anniversary of the successful Salem work. What a good omen!

Sophie caught the sight of Dora's beaten-up green truck pulling into a parking place across the street. Sophie wondered what Dora looked like; it had been months since she'd seen her. She caught sight of Dora, hair longer, redder, wearing the colors of sunset as the Holy Day prescribes.

Dylan opened the wine as Sophie greeted Dora, cool kisses on each check.

The evening flew by; stories of the last year filled the open room richly decorated in harvest colors. Wine was plentiful, desserts delicious. Sophie was right, the fish pies were consumed in a blink. The four were separate individuals now, not a formed group. The energy was definite, though not sharp—there was no animosity on the surface. Sophie continued to do mental battle in all matters pertaining to Dora, but there was only one cure for this kind of inner dialogue: time. She and Dora were now separate; a year's time did not mend the fissures opened in Essex County. Toasts were made and group shots taken to mark the ritual complete, now four years long.

Sophie felt different. She needed to write a guidebook outlining Shamanic dos and don'ts for Integration and Soul Retrieval. She had learned through the process what to do next time. Although she knew there would be no next time—she had truly retired from teaching and had unplugged the emergency phone. No more on-call Shamanizing 24/7/365. The change was profound, most of it positive. She had lived through it. She was changed physically, resulting in additional challenges, but her mind felt wonderful, on fire, alive! Her art sang with a fresh boldness not seen since her teenage years.

Dylan was gearing up for his second Saturn Cycle due in a year; already a sense of grief surrounded him. Both his parents were ill and the death-watch had begun. Both advanced in years, diminished in capacity, they no longer had the will to live. His ticket was already purchased for the first plane out the next day.

Dora was fully entrenched in her first Saturn Cycle, blindly grasping at losing straws, one after the other. She danced across the country, demonstrating her prowess, teaching dance, living the tango, miserable, growing older rapidly, dull around the edges, her shine tarnishing. But she had grace, a camouflage of desperation under the surface of her dancer's facade.

Poe was still afraid of ghosts, skittish and aloof emotionally. But she also carried a raw abandonment, an air of experimentation, of exploration. She was afraid but felt certain of the direction of her path. She would continue forward, with Oracle Work, with Shamanic practice, although a tamer variety than Sophie's. She also danced the Flamenco and revisited Roma Shamanism, finally awakening to her gifts of the past. Her mind was sharp and she paid attention, although to what she was never quite sure. As long as her feelings were not grounded in guilt, she felt pulled together. Poe was optimistic.

After the Feast, the guests left the mess for Sophie, her last real party of merit. Her fantasies of being waited on, entertained, and fed would become a reality, although she would be surprised how. Monday night, a work night for Dylan and Poe, an escape route given and taken by Dora, left Sophie alone in her thoughts. She closed the front door of her prairie-style house and would begin the rebuilding process, right after the dishes were washed.

Suddenly her blood began to boil, thinking to herself, "An Elder cleaning up this mess, on one of the most powerful nights of the year!" She felt like crying but laughed out loud instead, finally having to sit down before she fell down, on one of the worn dining chairs. She had always said a Shaman was a glorified garbage collector. Tonight proved her point.

She was wiping tears from her eyes when she noticed the white roses. All four were still there. One for each of them, Poe said was the intention. Poe hadn't even claimed hers. This was the sign of closure she didn't necessarily want to see but needed to see. It was the truth. The job was complete. It was time to move on, move forward, as the rest of them had.

Sitting, staring into space, lost in her thoughts, she was brought back to corporeal reality by a flash of white light. Something fell from the Ethers, manifested three feet above the red carpet of the entryway, slowly falling, finally coming to rest on the rug. Sophie walked to the white speck, bent down, picked it up, and opened her mouth wide in astonishment. There, resting in her hand, was a perfectly formed *M* with one point sharp, and one humped and rounded, Mary Warren's symbol, made of fine quality watercolor paper. The paper lining for gift baskets, Sophie reasoned, although gifts had not been given, other than four roses in red cloth on a bed of Tobacco.

White, the color of new life and beginnings. *M*, the thirteenth letter of the alphabet, the number of hard work and holy missions. Red, the color of discipline, passion through dedication. Red and white together but separate, the Muscogee colors for Peace. Truly, Sophie had come full circle tonight, with the Spirits still at her side.

Blessed Be!

*M*ichael Sortomme, writer and artist, embarked on a spiritual career that spanned more than three decades and encompassed metaphysics, the occult arts, and active indigenous Shamanic practice. Educated in archeology and modern literature, she has journeyed in pursuit of Truth that she translates into vivid paintings and equally compelling stories. Currently on hiatus from private practice and community service, Michael is focusing on her life as an author and multi-media artist.

She lives and creates under a 150-year-old Larch tree in Oregon's Pinot noir country. Her passions include *herstory*, genetic genealogy, international travel, and fine dark chocolate. Contact her through her website, www.michaelsortomme.com

Breinigsville, PA USA
09 January 2011
252965BV00001B/51/P